MISSING
DAUGHTER

BOOKS BY KIERSTEN MODGLIN

Just Married

KIERSTEN MODGLIN

MISSING
DAUGHTER

bookouture

Published by Bookouture in 2021

An imprint of Storyfire Ltd.
Carmelite House
50 Victoria Embankment
London EC4Y 0DZ

www.bookouture.com

ISBN: 978-1-80019-639-1
eBook ISBN: 978-1-80019-638-4

*This one's to the mothers and daughters.
And, of course, to my own mother and daughter—
I love you both.*

PROLOGUE

I took her because I had to.

Because I had no choice.

No one would understand it, I know that. If anyone found out what I've done, they'd hate me. Blame me. Want me to be taken away.

If the truth came out, it would be the end of everything for me. The life I've built, the happiness I'm working on, the family I envision for myself. In the blink of an eye, it would all be gone.

I can't let that happen. I won't.

I've come too far. Sacrificed too much.

This hasn't been easy, you see. It all started with a plan. A plan that shouldn't have worked, that almost didn't work, but now, with the plan fully in motion, things are finally starting to look up.

I'm grateful I took a risk.

Nothing good ever happens without risk and this, this life I'm building, is *good*.

Or, at least, it *will* be good as soon as I'm finished. There are steps that have to happen. I have to ease everyone into it or it will fall apart.

The one thing I know, the one thing I never doubted, is that no part of this plan worked without Skylar. I needed her. Trying to do it any other way—any safer way, smarter way—would've failed.

No, it had to happen just like this.

For her.

For us.

It'll be better now.

Everyone will see that in due time.

Everyone will be happier.

Safer.

Better off.

Well, almost everyone.

1 GINNY

"*You* look beautiful," Cameron's sister, Margie, said as I rounded the corner from my bedroom. I grinned, but I knew it didn't reach my eyes.

Margie was younger, blonder, with a figure not yet affected by bearing a child. I tucked a piece of the dark blonde hair I desperately needed to have trimmed behind my ear.

"Thank you."

She pulled me into a one-armed hug, her too-white teeth striking in the dimly lit hallway. "Where did you get this dress? It's to die for!"

"Target," I said plainly. "Years ago."

I shouldn't have been so self-conscious around her. Margie meant well; I knew that much. But I couldn't help the self-deprecating thoughts that filled my head. I had never been as pretty as she was, and I certainly wouldn't ever be now. Not with forty stubborn pounds still resting around my waist and too-thin hair atop my head. As much as it pained me to think about and as much as I loved my sister-in-law, since having Skylar, women like her were a reminder of what I'd never be.

I shook my head—physically shook the thoughts from it. My therapist wouldn't be pleased with my thoughts. Most days, I was doing better. Honestly, I was. But that day, when I'd been stuffed into a dress I'd worn before Skylar was born, only Spanx holding me in place, and barely at that; when my skin was blotchy and pale and I had a large, painful pimple forming on my chin; when I'd spent an hour in the shower, trying to shave every inch of my body like I hadn't in years, only to end up out of breath and miserable, today I felt the weight of it all—and I didn't just mean my own.

But today was Skylar's day. Today, I would put on a smile as I turned down the piece of cake Cameron cut. I'd sip on the bone broth I made last night and try to breathe while I pretended everything was normal.

While we all pretended everything was normal.

"Mommy!" Skylar called, as we entered the living room. She darted toward me, her arms stretched wide. I bent over carefully, hugging her back as I prayed my dress would hold up.

"Happy birthday, big girl," I said, kissing her cheek and brushing a lock of hair from her eyes.

"Can we open my presents now?"

When I stood, all eyes were on me, and it was my worst nightmare come true. There was a time—I call it BS: *Before Skylar*—when I didn't mind being the center of attention. Not that I craved it, but because at functions where both families were involved that spotlight tended to fall on either Cameron or me, it had never really bothered me. Now though, in this new body, in this new mind that seemed to constantly be ready to battle myself, it formed knots in my stomach.

My eyes darted between everyone. My parents, Cameron's, Margie and her husband, David, and Skylar at my feet, Joe and Stephen from Cameron's office, Alyssa and Norma from mine, and in the far corner, my therapist, Alex. Cameron was nowhere to be seen.

I cleared my throat. "Well, I don't know... Where's your dad?"

At the question, I heard his shoes tapping against the tile, his carefree footsteps heading our direction from the kitchen. His head entered the room first, glaring around. When he looked at me, his jaw dropped and he blinked rapidly. He stepped toward me, holding his arms out.

"Wow... You look incredible."

"Thank you. Not so bad yourself," I teased, which got a few small laughs from around the room as he pressed his lips onto my temple. When he broke away, I felt his hand slide down my back. "Are we ready then?" He looked around the room. No one seemed to have an answer.

No one except for our daughter.

"Yes!" she screamed, one hand in the air. "Present time!" This resulted in loud, uproarious laughs from all around, for which Skylar was positively pleased. "Presents!" she repeated, hoping to get even more of a reaction. "I want my presents now, Daddy."

Cameron bent down, scooping her up from in front of my legs and resting her on his hip. "You do, do you? Don't you want to eat cake first?"

She shook her head, no contemplation necessary to produce her answer. "No, presents first! Then cake."

He laughed, kissing her cheek. His lips lingered on her skin longer than they had mine. No one could deny the bond they shared, the way they seemed to speak without words and the fact that he knew everything she was talking about, everything she was trying to say, without her having to finish a sentence.

It was uncanny.

I'd asked many times during my sessions: Shouldn't I be that way with her? Shouldn't it be me that our daughter was closest to? After all, I'd grown her in my body. I'd been able to connect with her when no one else had. It was me she'd kept awake, kicking and flipping around all through the night; my bladder she'd chosen as a resting place for nine months before anyone had ever been able to hold her; my voice she'd heard every minute of every day. All the parenting books had told me I should speak to her in the womb, that it would be my voice she'd be drawn to after birth, but apparently no one had told *her* that.

No, from birth, it had always been her and Cameron. Most days, I felt like an outsider looking in. As if I'd just been the incubator facilitating their relationship, like they were ready to send me away with a tip and a pat on the shoulder.

Thanks for dropping her off, I've got it from here.

Alex, ever gracious as she was, had told me simply that children connect with their parents in different ways. That it was totally natural and fine for my daughter to seem closer to my husband for now.

But why then, I would ask, didn't I feel close to *her*? It wasn't as if it was one-sided. That I cared so deeply for her, felt so connected to her, and she'd yet to reciprocate. No, the feeling—or lack thereof—was mutual.

I loved my daughter, don't get me wrong. I would die for her in a heartbeat, protect her with my life. But most days, she felt like a tiny little stranger who'd come into the world and turned mine upside down. I felt myself waiting for the moment she went to bed until I could truly breathe.

When Cameron wasn't around and I was, by default, the parent invited to play, why did I dread it? Why would I find a million things to do around the house to avoid sitting on the floor playing with dolls? Why, whenever I went to her room to play, would I instead find things to nitpick and clean until we were both bored and frustrated? Why did I feel the distance between us as real and palpable as the smell of lasagna currently lingering in the air?

That part wasn't natural and no amount of therapy, I was sure, would convince me any differently. Still, I put on a smile and let Cameron lead me from the living room into the kitchen, where I could look over the table I'd spent the morning meticulously decorating.

Her cake had been placed in the center—bright purple with Princess Jasmine on the front, and *Happy Birthday, Skylar* written in white buttercream frosting. Next to the cake, a pile of presents sat, bigger than their recipient. I'd taped balloons to the back of

Skylar's chair and placed lollipop bouquets—only purple, white, and teal ones—in between each place setting.

Skylar darted toward her chair and, before Cameron could get there, my mom was just behind.

"Let Gramma get you in your seat," she said, lifting her carefully. "Oh, my. You certainly are three. I can barely pick you up any more." She feigned struggling to lift her as Skylar squealed with delight. I both loved and resented how easy it came to all of them—my husband, my parents, and my parents-in-law—all so easy. They could always find a way to make her laugh without trying too hard.

They found ways to connect with her that I couldn't find. I'd spent hours on Pinterest and Facebook, looking for something to do with her. When I'd find something, my version of whatever craft, game, or dessert was always underwhelming and Skylar was usually bored within minutes.

"How ya doing?" I heard the low voice behind me, jolting me from my thoughts. Alex was standing next to me, her eyes full of understanding. She waited patiently for me to answer, just like in our sessions.

I breathed in heavily and released the breath with an answer. "I'm okay, I think."

She nodded toward the table, where my mother was finally getting Skylar in her seat.

"It looks great. You must've spent hours working on all of this."

I looked away, ducking my head slightly. "Oh, it was nothing. The bakery did most of the work. I just laid out some candy and taped the balloons to the back of her chair."

She stared at me intently. "You gave her a birthday party, Ginny. A beautiful party with her family gathered around. Look at that little girl." I did as I was instructed, watching as my daughter giggled along. My mother-in-law and Margie had joined my mother in front of the birthday girl, talking to her animatedly. "You made her really happy today. Don't forget that, okay?"

Tears burned my eyes, and I fought them, blinking rapidly.

"Thank you, Alex." Some people might've thought it was strange to have my therapist at my daughter's birthday—which was why we'd told the family she was just a friend—but the truth was Alex felt like family. She was practically the only thing keeping me afloat most days.

Cameron cleared his throat, bending down near her. "Okay, sweetie, I know you want to open your presents first, but let's blow out your candles and then the adults can eat lunch while you open presents. Is that okay?"

Skylar thought for a moment. "No, presents first! Presents now!"

Cameron looked at me, seeming to wonder if it was worth the fight. He knew I would've preferred candles first, because once she'd opened her presents, she'd lose interest in everything else, but I couldn't say that. It was her day, and I knew I'd be overruled.

I gave a half-nod, my eyes closed. "Go ahead."

He grinned, as delighted as the toddler at the head of the table, and reached for the first present. I pulled out a chair and took a seat, joining the rest of the family with our phones at the ready to snap several hundred pictures of her opening her gifts.

We laughed along with her as she squealed and shrieked and held things up. She groaned and tossed the socks, underwear, and books from us aside for the baby dolls and princess ball pit from my parents. Margie and David gave her a T-ball set; Alex had chosen a ballerina bar and tutus; there was a huge set of Hot Wheels race cars from Alyssa and a race track from Norma; Joe and Stephen had gone in on a dress-up closet for her many dress-up outfits; and, when nearly all the presents were gone, my father-in-law, Kurt, disappeared. He claimed aloud that he needed to use the restroom, but I knew better.

Seconds later, I heard the whir of the motorized Jeep engine, and within moments, he appeared again, pushing a black Jeep into the room. Upon seeing it, Skylar squealed, slipping out of her seat, arms outstretched until my mother-in-law, Rita, reached for her and lifted her before setting her down, both their cheeks pink with delight.

I watched as my daughter raced across the room and leaped into the Jeep, listening as Kurt explained to her how to use it. He pulled the remote control that came with it and set her loose, watching as she steered around the cramped kitchen, nearly bumping into everything and everyone before he course-corrected for her.

The room was an echo-chamber of laughter and squeals, and I watched tensely as the space I'd meticulously cleaned the night before was destroyed in mere seconds, magnets and papers knocked from the front of the refrigerator, streamers torn from the backs of chairs and the walls.

No one else seemed to mind. I shouldn't either. This was Skylar's day. It could be cleaned. No one was judging me.

I repeated the truths over and over in my head, as Alex had often had me do, but they only helped slightly. Finally, my father-in-law helped her steer the Jeep out of the kitchen and the adults stood, following them out of the room in a pseudo-conga line with loud cheers when she'd reached the yard.

I was the last to stand, just behind Alex, who'd begun helping me clean the scattered and shredded wrapping paper that had been tossed carelessly around the room, floor, and table. I pulled a piece off the cake, cringing as I saw that it had smeared her name.

"Toothpick'll fix that right up," she said, noticing me staring at it. I inhaled deeply.

"It's okay. She won't care anyway." I wadded the paper up, forcing a smile I knew Alex could see straight through, but she didn't push it.

Once the paper had been cleaned up and placed into a now-overflowing garbage bag, Alex set to work re-hanging the magnets and drawings back on the refrigerator, and I pulled the shredded streamers from the walls, dropping the balloons into the corner of the room.

"Are you coming?" I heard Cameron ask, making me jump. I'd

been so in my head, I hadn't heard him come back inside. "She's learning how to steer it... It's hilarious!" He laughed, pointing outside, then realized what we were doing and froze. I didn't miss the muscle twitch in his jaw. "Come on, you don't have to do this right now." He rushed over, reaching for the trash in my hands. "We'll clean up after the party. Come on, I want you to enjoy yourself. She wants you to be out there with us."

What he didn't understand, what no one understood, was that I couldn't enjoy myself while there was a mess that needed attending to. I'd be outside, the whole time thinking about what I needed to be doing, while trying to pretend I was enjoying myself.

If I spent fifteen minutes cleaning it now, I'd be able to enjoy myself much more throughout the party. I weighed my options, knowing that saying that to Cameron, who just didn't understand no matter how hard he tried, would only end with him feeling angry and me feeling resentful.

I let him take the streamers from my hand and toss them into the bag before he tied it up and placed it into the corner with the balloons.

It would've taken two seconds to walk them down the hall and place them by the door to be taken out, but I ignored that. Just as I ignored the nagging, screaming voice in my head saying that I needed to finish what I'd started. That this wasn't okay.

"I'll finish cleaning up in here," Alex said, quieting the voice.

"You don't have to," I said. "It's a party. You didn't come here to work."

"It'll just take a few minutes."

I felt relief at knowing it would be done, but then Cameron spoke again. "Nonsense," he said firmly, a smile still on his face. "You're our guest, Alex. Come outside with us. Ginny and I will have this cleaned up later. For now, let's all just relax and enjoy ourselves."

Alex met my eyes once, a question in her troubled expression, and I nodded slightly.

"It's okay," I told her. "I'll be okay. It's much better than it was."

Refusing to be argued with, Cameron dragged us both from the house, holding open the door and shutting it behind us as Skylar squealed from the yard.

"Daddy, watch!" she cried, turning the wheel as the Jeep made a sharp circle. She was too close to the remnants of a tree stump we'd had chopped down a few years back, and I watched her tire hit it, the Jeep nearly turning over.

My body tensed and I let out a cry as I reached for her, but Kurt stopped her with the remote control, pulling her back in a split second. He laughed, wagging the thing in the air so everyone would know it was he who had saved the day.

"She's going to have a blast with this thing," a voice said in my ear, and I felt Cameron's arms encircling my waist, his chin resting on my shoulder from behind.

"Yeah, she is," I agreed. I was stiff and uncomfortable against him, but if he noticed, he didn't react.

"The seat lifts up, so we can put some snacks down there and let her ride into the woods whenever we go for picnics. She'll get a kick out of being the delivery person."

I gave a lopsided grin, feeling myself relax into his arms slowly. How long had it been since he'd held me like this? I felt his grip tighten, our bodies pressed together almost sensually.

Awkwardness stung me as I realized how we must look, but glancing around, I saw that no eyes were on us. In fact, everyone was watching Skylar with complete ease and contentment, telling her to go this way and that, faster and slower. They followed her as she traveled down the length of the expansive yard and toward the woods, and I felt Cameron keeping me from moving, purposefully stalling me toward the back of the line. Normally, he'd be straight up there with Skylar.

"What are you—"

I felt him nip my ear, felt his finger trail my spine. "I can't wait to get you out of this dress."

Heat flamed through my body, from the tips of my toes, lingering in my core, and spreading to my ears. I leaned my head into his, closing my eyes. He released me, swatting my butt playfully and taking my hand as the moment ended abruptly, and he pulled me to keep up with the moving crowd.

He winked at me once, his eyes following the V of my neckline with a longing gaze. For the first time in so long, I felt my insecurities melt away, and let myself be in the moment, feeling my husband's hand in mine, smelling the freshly cut lawn, and cheering for my daughter as she backed up, narrowly missing the swing set.

Everything was going to be all right, I told myself, repeating it until I believed it.

Everything is going to be all right.

Everything is going to be all right.

2 GINNY

It seemed as if the Jeep's battery would sooner die than Skylar would give up her latest gift. She'd been zipping around the yard, circling the three acres around our house, and testing her limits by reaching the tree line that surrounded us on every side.

We owned another ten acres of woods surrounding us, with just a few paths wide enough for the Jeep to fit down. Kurt had tried to send her down one at one point, but it had gotten hung up on a tree root and he'd had to pull her to safety. As the adults began to retreat closer to the house, everyone red-faced and exhausted, I stood from one of the lawn chairs I'd been sitting in between Alex and Cameron.

"I'm going to go get everyone some lemonade, I think," I said, making my way toward the long porch that ran the entire length of our home.

"Need some help?" Cameron asked, starting to stand but not pushing himself up entirely as he waited to hear my answer, almost as if he expected me to decline.

"It's okay. I'll just grab a few cups and the pitcher." He was back down chatting with Alex before I'd reached the door. I pulled it open and stepped inside, breathing easier at once. I'd never been one for entertaining, never been one for crowds and small talk, never been one to keep a smile on my face for long periods of time. It was even harder now, when it felt like every cell in my body was screaming for respite.

I'd done all I could to play the role, to make everyone believe I was fine, but the truth was, I wasn't fine. I was far from fine and everyone knew it, yet everyone pretended it wasn't the case.

I didn't want them to dote on me, of course. I much preferred that they do just as they were doing. But that didn't mean it didn't hurt.

I hurried through the foyer and into the living room on my way to the kitchen but froze when I heard hushed voices.

I turned, peering down the long hallway that led to our bedrooms. I cocked my head to the side, trying to make sense of the noise.

A soft voice.

Whispers.

Someone was in the hallway, past a point where I could see, and they were whispering, the soft, feminine voice too light for me to make out any words.

I heard a sharp inhale and froze, thinking I'd been found out. I tried to think quickly of who it would be. I'd seen everyone outside, hadn't I? Who would've had a chance to come inside when I'd stayed so close to the door? They would've had to cross in front of me and they definitely hadn't, that much I knew.

So, had someone stayed inside? It was impossible. I replayed the scenes outside in my head. Everyone had definitely been accounted for.

Surrounded by woods, we weren't prime candidates for a robbery, as someone would have to know exactly where we lived to get to us. Add that to the fact that a birthday party in the middle of the day wasn't exactly the smartest time to pull off a heist, and I knew the possibility was unlikely.

Still, though, I felt my heart begin to pick up speed. I tried to swallow down the lump that had lodged itself in my throat, looking back in the direction of the door. Should I try to make a break for it? Would I have time? Was I being paranoid?

I had no weapon and my phone was still lying on the kitchen counter.

"Hello?" I called into the silence, my voice quivering.

No one answered, but suddenly I heard footsteps headed in my direction and I watched Margie's face appear in the dimly lit hall, as if she were emerging via one of the pin art toys Skylar played with at the children's museum. David was there, too, and I found myself releasing a heavy breath of relief.

Then, embarrassment hit me. I must look terrified. Ridiculous.

Margie smiled, but it was forced and stiff. She seemed pale, her cheeks splotchy.

"Sorry, I didn't mean for you to hear all of that," she said, swiping a hand under her eyes. David put an arm around her, but she didn't lean into him.

"It's okay, *I'm* sorry. I wasn't trying to eavesdrop. I came in to get some lemonade and heard your voices. I didn't mean to interrupt." I didn't tell her that they'd frightened me or that I actually couldn't hear anything they'd said.

"No, it's okay," David added quickly. "We're embarrassed."

"Don't be," I said. "Is everything okay?"

They stared at me for an extra moment, as if they were realizing I hadn't heard enough to piece together what they'd been talking about, and then Margie put a hand to her chest. "We don't want to put a damper on Skylar's big day. I'm so sorry, Ginny, really. This is"—she put a hand to the end of her nose, tears welling in her eyes— "this isn't what I wanted to do today."

I stepped toward her, connecting with her grief in a way I'd never connected with my sister-in-law before. "Please don't apologize. I'm here for you. You aren't putting a damper on anything. What's going on?"

She fanned her eyes, staring up at the ceiling and pushing out a long, slow breath. "No, nothing. Really. It's fine. I'm fine." She smiled through the tears. "I'll be fine." She reached forward, touching my hand gently. "But thank you for asking."

I glanced at David, who was staring at her intently. When he noticed my gaze, he smiled stiffly. "We should get going."

"You're leaving already? We haven't eaten yet. Please don't rush off because I came in here... I won't say a word to anyone about this."

"No, it's not that. She's not feeling well. I should get her home."

She nodded through her tears, then launched herself forward, giving me a quick, heavy hug.

"Are you sure you're okay? I've got wine or medicine... You're more than welcome to hang out in here or take a nap until you're feeling better. Skylar was so glad you could make it down."

"We love her more than anything," she said, pushing out her bottom lip into a pout. "I couldn't have missed it. I hope she liked her gift."

"She loved it," I said, though I couldn't remember what the gift from them even was. They'd all melded together in my mind relatively quickly. "Please don't leave. You've only just gotten here." If it were up to me, I would've gladly seen them leave along with everyone else, but I knew Skylar would be devastated. Cam, too. Plus, their flight in from New York had lasted longer than their visit. I didn't want them to rush out because I'd embarrassed them.

"I know, it's just... work." She sniffled, drying the last of her tears with another forced, million-dollar smile. God, how was it possible for anyone to be so pretty, even when they were crying? "You know me. Busy, busy, busy."

"I understand," I told her, tucking a piece of hair behind my ears as I so often did when I was nervous. Whatever I'd interrupted, it seemed serious. Had they been fighting? Surely work wasn't the true cause of her tears, not when she loved her job as much as she did. "Hey, how did you get in anyway?"

They looked at each other, then back at me.

"In... the house?" David asked, a wrinkle forming on his otherwise flawless forehead as he stared at me.

"Yeah, I didn't see you come in the front door. Were you in here the whole time? I may have missed you, but I could've sworn you were out there—"

"Oh," Margie cut me off. "Yeah, we just came in a few minutes ago, through the garage."

"The garage?" Our garage door was always locked. "Oh, okay. That makes sense." Except it didn't make sense at all. "Did you happen to lock it back when you came in?" I asked with a wince.

"We didn't... It was unlocked. Do you want me to lock it?" He jutted his thumb over his shoulder in the direction of the door.

"I can get it later. We usually keep it locked because we rarely go out that way. No big deal."

"I can get it," he said, already jogging back down the hallway.

"Dad must've unlocked it when he brought the Jeep in earlier," Margie said.

"You're probably right." We stood still, staring at each other for a few painful, awkward seconds before I said, "Are you sure everything's okay?"

There were new tears in her eyes when she smiled at me. "Yeah, of course. Everything's fine."

I waited for her to say more, but when she didn't, I heard David's heavy footsteps coming back toward us, and I sighed. "I should get the lemonade, then. It's a warm one today."

"Yeah, I'll meet you out there," she said, appearing relieved to be walking away from me.

In the kitchen, I brought the pitcher of lemonade from the refrigerator and a stack of plastic cups from the cabinet, placing them carefully on a tray as I replayed what had just happened.

Why was Margie crying? Why were they inside whispering? Were they fighting? Why were they leaving? I wanted to talk to Cam about it, to see if he had any insight, but I felt bad gossiping. If whatever had happened was particularly private, I didn't feel right bringing it up.

Margie didn't trust me enough to divulge the truth, but I wanted to earn her trust. If nothing else, I could do that.

When I made it back out to the lawn, everyone was standing, hugging and kissing Margie and David as they made their way around the circle. Skylar had begun to cry, and Cameron and Margie were attempting to comfort her.

I stood back, watching it all unfold and feeling like a complete outsider.

Were they leaving because of me?

Had I managed to do something wrong? They hadn't mentioned leaving early before.

For several minutes, no one noticed me standing off to the side, but finally, Margie looked in my direction. She smiled, blowing a kiss toward me.

"Bye, Ginny. You look like you have your hands full or I'd give you a hug. We'll see you soon, okay?" David had an arm behind her back, the other held in the direction of the Tesla they'd rented.

"See you soon," I called powerlessly. Cameron moved toward me, taking the tray from my hands without a word as we all watched them leave.

Had they told everyone I'd been eavesdropping on them? That I'd embarrassed them? Somehow, the only thing heavier than the tray I'd just been relieved of, was the worry I felt festering as I watched their car pull out of the driveway, the engine's sound drowned out by my daughter's cries.

Just another thing I've managed to screw up.

3 GINNY

By the time night had fallen and the party had ended, I was exhausted. The house was mainly empty by then, as most of our remaining guests had cleared out to head home or catch their flights. My parents were the only people who'd been able to stay, as their flight wasn't for a few more hours. Cameron and my dad gathered up all the boxes, opening and installing batteries into toys, while my mother and I cleaned up the remainder of the trash, washed the dishes, and swept the floors.

I appreciated the help, I really did, especially because it meant we'd be able to get everything done and have a chance to rest before Skylar began her routine of waking up almost hourly.

Even as a baby, my daughter had never been a good sleeper. In the beginning, the doctors had said it was my fault: I wasn't producing enough milk. So, I'd power-pumped, a ridiculous routine that required me to pump every twenty minutes, on top of feeding her every two hours. I'd eaten every product sold in our grocery store that claimed it would up my supply, I'd taken fenugreek and fennel and eaten dates with every meal. I'd stayed away from anything minty, including my favorite brand of toothpaste. But it hadn't helped. Even as I saw my supply boost, Skylar still wasn't sleeping.

So, the doctors told me I didn't have her on enough of a routine. *My fault again.* I laid out our day by the minute, rigidly strict about what we should be doing when. When that didn't help, they'd said I kept the house too quiet, that I'd spoiled her by sleeping in silence. So, I'd run the vacuum cleaner, I'd leave the TV on, I'd open windows and let her hear the birds outside.

She'd sleep through it all when she was tired, but still, her sleep never lasted long.

They'd told me I'd spoiled her by rocking her. That I'd failed to sleep train her. That I wasn't holding her enough. That I wasn't doing enough to burn her energy. That I was letting her get over-stimulated. That she should sleep with the light off. That she should sleep with the light on. That she was too cold. That I should swaddle her. That she was getting too hot. That I should run a fan. That I should try a bassinet.

Every suggestion was another point at which I'd failed, everything coming down to what I wasn't doing or what I'd been doing too much.

But, as Skylar grew, the sleep issues continued. Whether or not I was to blame was no longer the biggest concern, but rather, how to get the problem addressed. As it stood, she'd never slept longer than four hours without waking up. And once she woke the first time, usually around midnight, she'd wake up nearly every hour after.

We'd taken her to see every specialist, tried every supplement, medicine, or practice under the sun, but nothing had worked. The conclusion had been simply, my daughter wasn't tired.

But her parents were.

Which was why it was so nice when, that night, after the house had been cleaned and when she'd woken up just before eleven, my mother had rushed to her side, singing to her until she was back asleep. This allowed Cameron and me to have an extra glass of wine and settle in on the couch, soaking up the day while my father snored away from the recliner.

After a few moments, my mother reappeared. "She's back

down," she said, scowling lovingly at my sleeping father. "Oh, for heaven's sake." She patted his arm. "Artie, wake up. We've got to get going."

"Thanks, Mom," I said, standing up and wrapping my arms around her neck. "Thanks for being here today and for sticking around to help clean up."

She kissed my cheek, her arms gripping me tightly. "I wouldn't have missed it for the world."

When we broke apart, she slipped her shoes on and my dad, finally awake, hugged me tightly before shaking Cameron's hand.

"Good to see you again," Cameron told them as they made their way out the door. "Have a safe flight home."

"Call me when you land," I said.

Mom blew me a kiss. "Tell that sweet baby we love her. We'll see you in a few months." She had tears in her eyes as she turned away, disappearing down the sidewalk and toward their car. It was hard on them to leave, hard for them to live across the country. When my dad's job took them out to Arizona, it was meant to be a temporary assignment, but had quickly become permanent. I knew my mother hated it, hated being away from the only home she'd ever known, away from her only grandchild, but she loved my father.

She'd asked me often about moving there, selling me on the wonders of the area where they lived, but we were happy here. We'd built a life, good careers, and now our family in Tennessee. Even if we wanted to, it just wasn't practical to leave.

I'd returned the air-blown kiss and shut the door, watching until they pulled away before shutting off the porch light. When I had, Cameron let out a loud sigh before flipping the lock and leading me into the kitchen.

"I can't believe she's three," he said, shaking his head as he lowered a bottle of whiskey from the cabinet above the refrigerator.

"I know... It doesn't seem possible, does it?"

He pulled out two glasses, pouring us each three fingers and sliding my glass across the island. We tapped them together, and I watched as he drained his quickly. I sucked in a breath, trying to calm my nerves as I did the same.

I wasn't sure why I felt nervous that night.

Why everything in my body jittered as he looked me over, refilling his glass, then mine.

"Hey, did Margie mention why they left so early?" I asked. It was the first moment I'd found to ask him about the incident without others interfering.

He rubbed his lips together thoughtfully. "They had to catch their flight, I think. Why?"

"I just expected them to stay longer. I was hoping nothing had happened to upset them."

"Don't be ridiculous," he said. "What could've happened?"

I shrugged, taking another sip of my whiskey. "Nothing, I guess. It was good to see them."

"Yeah, hey, speaking of, they actually invited us to New York in a few months."

"They did?"

"Mhm." He stared at the liquid in his glass, swirling it around in his hand. "Apparently, she's working on some indie film right now and they want us to be their guests for the premiere."

I raised my glass but didn't drink straight away. Before I wouldn't have hesitated. It wasn't as if hair and makeup artists' guests were expected to walk the red carpet in couture or anything, usually the events that Margie took us to were low-key and fun, but the idea of traveling to New York within months was terrifying. I needed six months, minimum, to lose the rest of my weight. I couldn't be introduced to people looking the way I did right then.

"Not your parents?" I asked softly.

"No, I guess not. I was thinking maybe we could have one of them come here and watch Skylar." He slid the box of cake toward him, opened the lid, and pulled out a fork, digging into a corner. He took a bite first, then offered a bite to me, but I shook my head. "What do you think?"

"Yeah, maybe."

"Maybe? I thought you'd be excited." He appeared crestfallen by my lack of delight. "We haven't gotten to do anything just the two of us in years."

"I *am* excited," I told him. "Sorry, I think I'm just tired." I finished the rest of my drink. He lifted the bite of cake toward me again, his eyes dark with desire as he stepped closer, pressing the tines of the fork to my bottom lip.

I opened my mouth instinctually, letting him put the cake into my mouth. He smiled then pressed his lips to mine, pulling back and wiping his mouth with his thumb.

"We should get you to bed, then," he whispered, bouncing his finger against my bottom lip.

He finished off the rest of his whiskey, pouring one more glass for each of us.

"I shouldn't." I tried to stop him.

"Come on, three glasses for three years. It's our tradition."

I laughed. "I think that'll start getting dangerous around year five or six."

"Best to make the most of years three and four then, hm?" He slid the glass to me, not breaking eye contact as we tapped them together and slugged the warm liquid down. Its heat spread through me as he took our glasses and placed them in the sink. Normally, I'd have asked him to rinse them and put them in the dishwasher, but I wasn't feeling normal. Besides, I didn't want to fight, and I knew that's all that would come from my nagging. Instead, I let him take my hand and pull me down the hall toward our bedroom.

Once inside, he shut the door behind us and pressed my back to the wall. Thanks to our light-blocking curtains, the room was bathed in complete darkness. I heard the click of the door being locked and then felt his body against mine. He kissed me quickly, trailing kisses from my lips, to my jaw, and then up to my ear.

"I haven't been able to take my eyes off of you all day." His mouth was back to mine. "You look... so... beautiful," he told me in between kisses. His hands stretched the neck of the dress, but I couldn't care as he ran kisses between my breasts. He stepped back, spinning me around and pressing me into the wall, unzipping the dress slowly, each inch of skin he uncovered was met with a new kiss.

When he reached the base of my spine, his hands slid the dress from my shoulders, then over my hips. I felt it pool at my feet. I started to kick my heels off, but he stopped me.

"Leave them," he instructed, taking my hand and pulling me toward the bed. He lay down across the comforter, pulling me on top of him, and I felt my insecurities begin to surface. He couldn't see my face, but I know he felt me tense up, because almost immediately he sat up, his hands cupping my breasts as his lips reached for mine. "You're so sexy, Ginny," he whispered, his hands gripping my hair. It wasn't true, but I refused to think about it.

He rolled us over, his body on top of mine, and I closed my eyes, feeling his hand slip between my legs.

Since Skylar, it wasn't as though we hadn't had sex, but it had become less frequent, of course, and more hurried. We'd had to sneak time in during snack or bath or during the few hours between eight and midnight that we weren't cleaning up the house or just trying to relax.

To be able to enjoy it like this, to savor each moment was rare, and I knew we were counting down, listening for the moment when she'd cry out and we'd have to shoot up, throw on our clothes, and try to compose ourselves.

It wasn't easy, but we'd become used to it.

It wouldn't last long, all my friends and coworkers had told me. This time in our lives would fly by, the parenting books screamed at me. I should savor every second, Facebook posts reminded me daily.

But sometimes, the moments felt like years, and the days felt like lifetimes. For now, I just wanted to enjoy what Cameron and I had, the slight reminder of who we were *B.S.* Of how we'd loved each other. Of how he'd made me feel.

He stood above me, and I heard him slipping out of his own

clothes, each button of his shirt taking an unbearably long time. The room spun, and I wasn't sure if it was from pure ecstasy or the liquor in my belly, as he slid inside of me finally, our movements slow as we melted together.

"I love you," he whispered, and I said it back, over and over again, remembering who we were and who we'd been, how much I missed this and him and myself.

I wanted it to last forever, for us to both melt into the moment, feeling that way for the rest of our lives, but I knew it couldn't and shouldn't, so I tried to savor it, to stay out of my head and be present.

Alex would be proud of me.

I forced the thought of Alex out of my head—she was the last person I needed there now—and pulled his lips to meet mine. I kissed him harder, breathing him in as if it were the last time I would feel so loved and admired and cherished. As if it were the last time he would love me this much.

For all I knew, it very well could've been.

4 GINNY

After we'd finished, we lay together, stark naked under the covers, my body still tingling from his touch. I'd meant to get up and get dressed before falling asleep, and I'd been thinking of just that as I found myself drifting off.

When I woke up again, Cameron was next to me, dressed now, and I realized, self-consciously, that I was not. I slid from the bed, careful not to disturb him, and grabbed pajamas and clean underwear from my dresser drawer. The early morning twilight illuminated the room slightly, giving everything an odd, purplish glow. I pulled my pajamas on in the dimly lit room, hoping they'd match, and tapped my phone screen.

It was just after four a.m.

My mind processed the realization slowly.

It was just after four a.m. and Skylar hadn't woken up, demanding to be let into our room.

Unless she had.

For a brief moment, I pictured her waking in the night, pounding on our door, but the two of us being in such a drunken stupor that we'd slept through it all. Perhaps that was why Cameron was dressed. Had he gone to her? Had I managed to sleep through that?

Once dressed, I turned the doorknob, unlocking the door, and glancing down. The hall was empty, Skylar wasn't sleeping on the floor, exhausted from the crying fit we'd slept through, thank goodness. I wrapped my arms around myself, feeling a chill, and walked cautiously down the hall.

Was I crazy for doing this? If I opened the door and woke her for no reason, I'd only have myself to blame.

Maybe she was finally growing out of the phase. That's what every book and doctor had told me would happen. One day, she'd just start sleeping through the night. It would happen. It always did. And she'd soon become a teenager who slept all hours of the day.

Maybe the party had just worn her out.

Either way, I couldn't shake the feeling that I just needed to check on her. When I reached her door, I put my hand on the knob, turning it slowly. I pushed it open, expecting it to squeak, but to my relief it didn't.

In the wash of light from her window, I could just make out her bed. I took a step closer, my eyes adjusting to what I was seeing, trying to make sense of it.

Skylar wasn't in her bed. I flipped the cover back, hoping to find her there, hiding somehow, but she wasn't.

She wasn't there at all.

I flipped on the light.

"Skylar?"

A shiver of panic ran through me.

I checked under the bed.

Moved her pillows.

Moved her blanket.

Moved her mattress.

"Skylar?" I called louder, fear taking hold of my organs, gripping them with spindly, ice-cold fingers.

No.

No.

No.

"Skylar?" My voice shook, choked by tears, as I darted across her room, checking the closet. *Nothing. Nothing. Nothing.* I checked her bathroom. Her bathtub. I tugged at the windows in her room, making sure they were latched.

Think. Think. Think.

She had to be there. The house was dark. Skylar was afraid of the dark. She wouldn't have just wandered off. She'd be crying. She'd be looking for us.

Suddenly, I heard footsteps.

I froze. Listening. Waiting. Praying.

They were too loud to be hers. Too heavy.

Cameron appeared in the doorway, one eye squinted closed. "What's wrong?" His eyes flicked to her bed and back to me. "Where is she?"

"She's..." I searched for an explanation that would make sense, but nothing made sense. The doors and windows were locked. The house was still, and she'd just vanished. "She's gone, Cam. She's just... gone."

Realization swept over his expression, no longer coated in sleep, and his jaw tightened. He took a quick glance around her room, but landed on me again.

His next words were an accusation. *"What did you do?"*

5 CAMERON

SIX MONTHS BEFORE KIDNAPPING

When we brought my daughter home from the hospital, a stranger accompanied us.

Not in the literal sense, I guess, but in every way that mattered. My wife—the beautiful, funny, charismatic woman I'd asked to marry me just three years earlier—had been whittled away by the long, difficult pregnancy with one complication after the next, the never-ending bedrest and hospital stays, the nearly forty-hour labor, and the eventual emergency cesarean.

By the time Skylar made her entrance into the world, we were both exhausted. Exhausted from the stress of it all, from nine months of constant worry and vulnerability, from the mounting medical debt, and from the outright weight of all we'd gone through.

I'd nearly lost her. Nearly lost them both, I suspected, though the doctors never said as much. There'd been too much blood lost, too much damage, as they worked to separate my daughter from my wife. Ginny's stats had plummeted, then at the last second rebounded, and she'd survived. It was nothing short of a miracle, they said.

We'd spent the next week in the hospital, Ginny struggling to recover while she also struggled to nurse Skylar, and Skylar constantly crying from the newness of it all. I'd expected our first few days as parents to be filled with love and warmth and pure, inexplicable joy, but this was nothing like that.

I tried to do all I could, to offer support to her, to hold the baby when she wasn't nursing, to tell her how good she was doing. I let the nurses know when Ginny was in too much pain, wiped up blood from the floor whenever she'd been able to walk to the bathroom and had left a trail behind her, and told her it would be okay if Skylar took a bottle instead.

Somehow, that had only made things worse. I seemed to have gotten extraordinarily good at making things worse since she'd become pregnant. Always saying or doing the wrong thing...

So, when we finally made it home, I took over the primary responsibilities that came with our newborn. I changed her diaper and gave her baths, dressed her and held her, and brought her to her mother whenever she needed to be fed.

I tried to involve Ginny as much as possible but found myself walking a thin line between putting too much on her and excluding her altogether. It didn't help that Ginny seemed to have no interest in our child. I tried not to feel resentment over it, but how could I not?

From the moment Skylar had appeared, my wife had begun retreating from whom she'd once been. The doctors had warned of the *baby blues* and how Ginny might be emotional for a few days after her birth, but the emotional state never met an end.

Her moods flipped like a switch—angry one moment, sad the next. Some days were good and I'd convince myself that we were finally rounding the corner, that things would be better from here on out, but then a day or two would pass and I'd find her in bed in the middle of the day, the covers pulled up over her head, tears streaming down her face.

So, I tried to do even more. I talked to her parents, invited them to stay with us for a while to help us both out, but that only seemed to annoy her. I convinced the partners to cut down my billable hour threshold at work, so I could work less without getting fired, and began to work from home so I was always around. It wasn't what I wanted—I loved my career and I'd worked hard for it—but what choice did I have? Nothing made my wife happy anymore, least of all me. I had to do what I could to protect our daughter, to make up for the failings of one parent. Everything fell squarely on my shoulders, and it was a weight I wouldn't have laid on my worst enemy.

Still, Skylar was the silver lining. She was what made it worth it for me. I knew I'd do it all over again, a thousand times, for her. I almost felt selfish for how much I loved our daughter because I knew how much pain and darkness my wife was dealing with and how much of that she blamed on our child.

At least, I thought I knew.

I called two different therapists, convinced her to try them out, but she'd decided after just a session or two each that they weren't for her.

They'd given her medicine that she took daily, but even that was a fight. She didn't want to do it. She didn't want to do anything, but I'd given her no choice. She needed to take the meds or she'd lose us both. It was that simple, and that complicated.

In the beginning, the medication seemed to help, but it felt like the bad days were somehow worse since she'd started taking it. And the good days came less and less.

I was at a loss on what to do. More than anything, I wanted my wife back, but there were days it felt like I'd been asked to choose between them both.

On those days, right or wrong, I'd always chosen Skylar.

I walked into the bedroom that morning to see my wife was already up and sitting at her vanity, applying her makeup. I kissed the top of her head and set the mug of coffee down in front of her.

"You're up early."

She nodded, setting down the tube of black liquid she'd been applying to her eyelashes and placed her hands around the mug of coffee. "You have your meeting downtown today, don't you? I set an alarm in case you needed to leave early."

"I do," I said, easing down on the edge of the bed. I was worried she'd forgotten. "What are you planning to do while I'm gone?" I thought I'd phrased it decently, trying to make it seem like I was curious, not concerned. I didn't like leaving them, not for any period of time, but certainly not for the entire day. But this meeting was too important for me to pass up. I'd tried to arrange for her parents to return for a visit, but schedules hadn't lined up.

"I'm going to take her to the park for a while," she said simply, then spun around, her eyes narrowing at me. "We're going to be fine. Today's a good day."

I tried to shove down the worry I felt clawing its way through my chest as I reached for her hand, squeezing it gently. "I'm glad to hear it. It'll be good for you both to get out of the house."

"Weather's good," she said carefully. "Sunny."

I nodded just as I heard Skylar cry out from her bedroom. She was awake and the conversation was over. For now.

We stood at the same time, and she placed a hand on my chest. "I've got her."

"Are you sure—"

"You need to get ready for work," she said firmly. "I've got her today. I can handle it." Her palm warmed my chest but departed too quickly as she hurried out of the room.

I watched her go, debating on checking in, but ultimately decided she was right. I really did need to go.

I had to trust that everything would be okay.

That she'd take care of Skylar.

That she was going to be fine and today was, in fact, a good day.

I had to trust my wife.

I just wished she hadn't given me so many reasons not to.

6 GINNY

It was sunny that day—early spring and the park was in full bloom, with beautiful white flowers cascading down from the trees with each gust of wind. I pushed the stroller slowly as Skylar pointed to everything we saw, shouting the names she knew.

"Look! A tree! Pretty, Momma! It's blue!"

"Yes, yes, it does have blue flowers, Sky. Good girl."

"Can I pick them?"

"No, we'd better not pick any flowers from the tree. It's up too high."

"Look! A flower!" She pointed to one on the ground, and I scooped it up for her.

We reached the neighborhood park within an hour of leaving the house, though normally it would've taken half the time. Typically, we'd drive the distance, but that day, I'd felt like walking. I'd walked slowly, enjoying every minute of being outside in the warming air.

I loved living in the South in the spring. There was nothing like the way everything was in bloom and sunny, everything a reminder that even after the harshest winter, filled with misery and gloom, better days would come around again.

"Look!" *Look* was her favorite word lately, and she needed me to look at *everything*. I loved seeing her face light up, her genuine excitement over the most mundane things, but sometimes I just craved the mental peace that came with silence. "Look! Slide, Momma! Can I play?"

"Yes, baby. If you want to."

"I do, I do!"

I slowed the stroller next to the small toddler play area, complete with a sandbox, a small slide that connected via a swaying bridge to several tunnels, and climbing walls no more than a few feet high. There were three other children playing in the sand, all of whom looked to be around her age. I kissed the top of her head and backed away, moving to sit on an empty bench.

If Cameron had been there, he would've sat in the sand and played with her, or pushed her on the swing. He wouldn't have cared what any of the other parents sitting and watching their children play would think of him acting silly just to get her to laugh.

I couldn't do that. I couldn't stand in front of them all, in the space where their eyes would be focused on their children, and play. I wasn't at all comfortable with my playing skills as it was, I certainly didn't need an audience for it.

As it stood, it didn't seem as though she needed me anyway. Already, she'd stood up and moved over next to a younger girl with an oversized bow in her hair. The girl had given Skylar a pail that matched her tiny yellow shovel and they were beating them on the ground with laughter.

"Do you mind if I sit here?" I heard a voice ask, startling me.

I looked over my shoulder, to where a woman stood. She had thick dark hair that matched the black pea coat she'd wrapped around herself, as if she were still cold in the sixty-five-degree weather.

"Oh, uh, sure." I scooted from the middle of the bench to one end, and she took a seat.

"Thank you. I guess I picked a popular time to come," she said with a chuckle. "I went to use the restroom and came back to every bench full."

I smiled, glancing at her briefly, but didn't reply.

"Do you live around here?" she asked.

"Not far, yeah," I said simply, not feeling the need to divulge my address to a complete stranger. Cameron would've said I was being paranoid, that she was just friendly. I tried to channel what he would've done. "What about you?" The question, though the same one had been directed toward me moments ago, felt unnatural. Why would I be asking her where she lived? It felt intrusive.

"I live on the other side of town, actually. Near The Avenue. But this is my niece's favorite park."

"Your niece?"

"That one." She pointed to a girl who looked to be a few years older than Skylar, walking slowly across the bridge, her tiny hands gripping the rails. "Raven."

"She's adorable."

"Thanks." The woman beamed with obvious pride. "I don't get to see her all that often, so when she does come to visit, we spend nearly every day doing something she loves."

I felt a pang of jealousy. Skylar's only aunt was Margie, and as doting as she was, her life in New York was way too busy to accommodate her niece staying with her for any length of time. Not that we'd ever expect her to, but it was nice to see some families made it a priority. I felt sad that Skylar would never grow up close—in proximity, at least—to our families.

"That's really sweet. It sounds like she's lucky to have you."

"Most days, I'm pretty sure it's the opposite. She keeps me sane." She laughed. "Which one's yours?"

I hesitated, but only slightly. She'd told me so much about her own life, it would be rude not to reciprocate. "The one with the pigtails." I pointed to Skylar, her curly, brown hair drawn up into tiny pigtails on either side of her head.

The woman visibly melted, clasping her hands in front of her mouth. "Oh, my goodness, what a doll baby. Look at those little cheeks. I miss Raven being that little. It goes by fast."

That's what everyone had told me. Reminders were constantly

smacking new mothers in the face that everything happens fast. That time flies by. That if you aren't soaking up every moment, because God forbid you go to the store alone, dare to take a Pilates class or allow yourself thirty minutes in the bubble bath, you might miss something you'll never get back. These moments are precious and fleeting, and you need to catch and carefully document every single one from now until forever. Eighteen years is the longest and shortest time of your life.

"You okay?" the woman asked, and I realized I'd been staring at her with a strange expression for way too long.

"Yeah," I said quickly, rubbing my eyes. "Sorry. I'm just tired. I think I zoned out a bit."

"It's hard when they're that young," she said, seeming to understand. "They're precious, no doubt, but they're also exhausting and demanding and irritable." She laughed. "I didn't know if my sister was going to survive the terrible twos... That's actually when we started these weeks with Auntie."

"It's really kind of you to have helped her out."

"I didn't mind it. I love my niece, and I love my sister. It was the least I could do. Besides, it takes a village." She shrugged one shoulder. "Do you have family around that can help you?"

"Just my husband. I mean, we do have family, but my parents are in Arizona and his parents live in Florida. He has a sister, but she's in New York working in the film industry, so she's always busy." I paused. Then, trying not to sound so incredibly pathetic, added, "But it's fine. We make it work, you know?"

She nodded slowly. "It sounds really hard."

I looked away, trying to fight back the tears I felt stinging my eyes. The truth was, it *was* hard. And no one had ever acknowledged that. Not our parents, who were constantly reminding us that it would be easier if we just moved closer to them. Not the doctors, who would tell me what a great job we were doing, dismissing my concerns. Not the therapists Cameron had insisted I visit, who'd asked me to relay my childhood for them, dissecting my relationship with my own mother, as if she were somehow to blame for my own failings. Not even Cameron, who made it all look too easy. No one had ever looked me in the eye and said those words. *It's hard.*

"I'm Alex, by the way," she said, holding out a hand to me.

I sniffled, wiggling my nose in hopes of getting the tears to disappear before I turned to her and shook her hand.

"It's really nice to meet you, Alex. I'm Ginny, and I'm sorry I'm such a mess."

If only I'd known how big of a mess my life was about to become.

7 CAMERON

Ginny seemed to be getting better. For the first time in a long time, it had been over a month since her last bad day. As time went on and the good days collected, I'd begun spending more time at the office, picking up the slack I'd let build up for too long.

That day, I'd won a big case and thought I'd surprise her by coming home early to celebrate. When I got home, I realized she wasn't there. I pulled out my phone, dialing her number, and waiting...

"Hello?" she answered on the third ring. I heard the wind blowing through the speaker. She was outside.

"Where are you?"

"I'm..." She paused. "At the park. Why? Where are you?"

Still wanting to carry on the surprise, I said, "No reason. I could hear the wind, so I knew you were outside. Anyway, I'm at work but getting ready to leave. I thought I'd pick up dinner tonight. Any special requests?"

"Whatever you're craving is fine," she said absentmindedly.

"Okay, good. How's our girl doing?"

"She's playing in the sand. She loves being out here."

"I miss you girls."

"We miss you too."

The conversation was dry and flat, as if she wanted me to let her go. I knew she'd been spending every day with clear weather at the park, and from the research I'd done, spending time in the sun was a good thing to help liven her mood. So, I tried not to pry too much. I wanted them to bond. I wanted Ginny to continue getting better.

"Okay, well, I'll see you in a bit then."

"See you in a bit."

We ended the call and I walked back toward the garage and climbed into the car. I drove down the long driveway and curvy, winding roads that led to the neighborhood park.

Her car had been in the garage, which meant she'd walked this way. I searched for her amongst the crowd of parents and children, identical strollers parked all along the grass.

Finally, I spotted Skylar, playing in the sand, just as Ginny had said. But, as I looked harder, I was positive my wife wasn't there.

Where was she?

I stepped from the car and hurried across the parking lot, toward the sandbox, checking every woman's face, searching for my wife.

No.

No.

No.

No.

They weren't her.

She wasn't here.

I stepped into the sandbox, sand filling my Allen Edmonds loafers, and scooped up my daughter. My heart thudded in my chest as I looked around, trying to locate my wife.

"Daddy?" Skylar asked. "What are you doing?"

Where had she gone? How could she have left our daughter unattended?

"Excuse me," came a shrill voice I didn't recognize. "Can I help you?"

I turned around to see a woman with thick, shoulder-length

black hair and bright, silver eyes. She was staring at me strangely, her arms held out as if she wanted me to hand Skylar over to her.

"I need you to put her down please." She was an entire head shorter than me, but the way she said it almost made me want to listen.

"Who are you?" I demanded, looking at Skylar's face to make sure I hadn't grabbed the wrong child by mistake.

"My name is Alex. Sir, I need you to put the girl down and step away before I call the police."

"I'm her father." I panted, spinning circles. "Where's my wife?"

She hesitated. "What's your wife's name? Sweetie, is this your daddy?"

"Of course, I'm her dad," I answered before she could say a word, growing angry and furrowing my brow. "And my wife's name is Ginny. What concern is it of yours? Who are you? Why are you talking to me right now?"

She let out a sigh of relief as I'd said my wife's name and clutched her chest. "Okay. Sorry, I'm Alex—"

"You've already said that."

"Right. I'm watching Skylar while your wife uses the restroom. She should be back any moment."

I stared at her dubiously. "She left her with a stranger?"

"Well, I'm not exactly a stranger. Ginny and I have been meeting here almost daily for more than a month."

Her words sent shock through me. How did I not know about this? Shouldn't Ginny have told me she was meeting this woman regularly? *Daily*, even? Was she trying to hide it? If so, why?

"You have?"

"Yes. I bring my niece to play with Skylar. That's her." She pointed to a small girl sitting in the sand, carefully setting up what looked like it was supposed to be a sandcastle. "Ginny didn't mention it to you?"

"No, she never—"

"Ah, here she comes now," she said, pointing behind me. I spun around to see my wife approaching quickly, confusion on her face.

"Cam? What are you doing here?" Her hands were out at her sides.

Relief flooded through me as I finally felt I could let my guard down. "I came to surprise you," I said, ducking away from Skylar as she stuck a finger in my ear.

"Look! Daddy's here!" she cried.

"I see that," Ginny said breathlessly.

"I panicked when I didn't see you anywhere."

"I was using the restroom—"

"Yeah, that's what your friend said." I jutted my head toward Alex.

"Right," she said, her eyes landing on Alex behind me. "Sorry, yes. Alex, this is Cameron, my husband. Cam, this is Alex."

I held out my hand to shake hers, and she reciprocated. "I'm sorry if I scared you," she said with a giggle, then grinned at Ginny. "I thought I was going to have to fight him right here and now when I saw him pick her up."

"Oh, God. I'm so sorry." Ginny put a hand over her eyes and slid it down her face, looking mortified.

"No, it's my fault, really," I said. "I panicked when I didn't see you here, and I wasn't thinking. I rushed forward and scooped her up. I guess that's what I get for trying to surprise you."

"It's sweet that you did," Ginny said. "It was an honest mistake. No harm done." She tucked her hands in the pockets of her yoga pants. "Are we ready to head home, then?"

I nodded, not letting go of Skylar. "It was nice to meet you, Alex."

"You too," she called. "Raven, tell Skylar bye."

"Bye!" came the quick response.

Skylar flapped her hand in the air at her. "Bye!"

I waited as my wife pulled Alex in for a hug. Apparently, everything Alex had said was true. My wife wasn't a hugger in general, so for her to hug anyone must have meant they were close. Why hadn't she mentioned her?

It bothered me for reasons I couldn't quite explain. Like she'd purposefully kept this from me. But why?

"It was good to see you again."

"Same time tomorrow?" Alex asked. So, they had a set time and everything?

"As long as the weather holds up." Ginny looked to the sky with worry.

"Just text me if something changes," Alex told her with a wave over her head, and Ginny turned back toward me, letting me lead her away from the park and back toward the car. They'd exchanged phone numbers? Why the hell didn't I know about any of this?

I buckled Skylar in, kissing her cheek. Even though I knew now she'd never been in danger, the adrenaline from that moment hadn't totally subsided. I was so grateful she was safe. I made my way around the car and sat down in the driver's seat, starting it up as I tried to figure out how to broach the subject without starting an argument.

Once we'd pulled out of the parking lot, I said, "Alex mentioned you've been meeting her at the park almost every day... I didn't realize you were going so much."

"I told you I have been," she said plainly. "Is it an issue?" There was a slight attitude in her voice that reminded me of the way she used to be.

"I just thought you would've mentioned it to me. I mean, I should know who our daughter is spending the day with, shouldn't I?"

"She's spending the day with me."

"Fair enough, but I would've told you if the situations were reversed. It feels like you were keeping it from me."

She stared straight ahead, her jaw locked. "I wasn't keeping anything from you, I just didn't feel like you had to know. I told you I was going to the park. Am I supposed to tell you about every single person I meet?"

"Why are you getting defensive right now?"

"Why are *you*?" she retorted.

"Look, I'm not trying to fight with you. I think it's great that you've made a friend." I reached over, taking her hand, and she seemed relieved. "I just wish you would've told me so I wouldn't have looked like such a jerk back there."

She sighed. "I'm sorry. I don't know why I didn't... I guess it just started off as a stranger I was making small talk with, and I suppose it's natural that you start getting to know them after a while. Maybe I just didn't want to jinx it? It's been so long since I felt like I had a real friend, you know? Since Skylar, all my friends from work have slowly disappeared into their own lives. It's nice to have someone else to talk to."

The anger we'd both been feeling seemed to fade away quickly, for which I was grateful. It didn't matter that she hadn't mentioned her, really. The fact was that now I knew and now I could do something about it.

"I'm happy you've found her, then. We'll have to have her come over for dinner one day. Her and her daughter... Husband, er, or wife, too. It'd be nice to have a couple new friends. If she's married, I mean."

"Raven's her niece," she reminded me, and I realized I knew that. "And she's not married. But yeah, dinner would be nice. I'd like the two of you to get to know one another. She's so much fun. In a strange way, it's like she's helped me to get better."

I slowed the car into the driveway, pushing the button on my visor to open the garage door. "I'm happy for you, babe. Truly." I put a hand behind her head, and she leaned over toward me, kissing my lips.

"I'm happy too."

Despite the genuine joy on my wife's face, I couldn't help feeling jealous that someone else had made my wife feel so happy when I'd spent the better part of three years trying and failing to do the same. However, a sense of dread was building in my stomach as I thought about Alex. It was why I'd suggested we invite her for dinner. I wanted things to work out for Ginny. I wanted her to have a friend.

But if I was going to let anyone around my daughter, I wanted to know everything there was to know about the person first.

And if I didn't like her, I'd have to find a simple way to break the news to Ginny. Skylar was my daughter, and I deserved a say in who she spent her time with. Especially when I was the one who cared for her the most.

8 GINNY

Sunshine and friendship are no cure for depression. I knew that. Honestly, I did, but it didn't stop the hope I felt at having so many good days in a row.

I'd so completely conformed to the idea that I'd managed to heal myself, that when I woke up that morning dreading getting out of bed, without the energy to even roll myself over, I began to cry immediately.

I'd been better and I'd taken *better* for granted. How had I let it happen? How had I let myself trust that I could be better? Do better?

I heard Skylar crying from her bedroom, but couldn't make myself move. I was exhausted. So utterly exhausted despite the hours of sleep I'd managed to get.

The bedroom door opened and Cameron stood in front of me. "Do you want me to—"

He must've recognized the look on my face, because his own expression fell. "Bad day?"

I shook my head, swiping my tears.

"Can I bring you something? Something to drink, maybe? I've got tea brewing, or I can whip up breakfast really quick." He checked the Apple watch on his wrist.

"No, I need to get Skylar," I said, though I made no move to get up.

He appeared to be contemplating before he sighed. "No, you should rest. I can work from home today and take care of her."

"I'm okay, Cam. I'll be okay, I swear."

He moved toward me, sitting on the edge of the bed and reaching for my hands. "I know you will," he said firmly, rubbing his thumbs over my knuckles. "But you aren't right now. How about I turn on some Netflix for you? Or I could make a quick doughnut run? What can I do to make you feel better?"

I thought about it for a moment, no real answer because I knew I'd never feel better. I'd lose myself in this despair, unable to fight my way back.

"Can you hand me my phone?" I croaked eventually, holding out my hand.

"Your phone?" he asked, lifting it from the nightstand and flipping it over. "Why?"

"I need to call Alex and let her know I'm not going to meet her today."

"Oh, you were meeting her today?" he asked.

"Not anymore."

"That's probably for the best, yeah. You need your rest. Don't want to overdo it."

I pulled my lips in, nodding. My head throbbed, my hand feeling too weak to hold the weight of the phone. The truth was, the thought of canceling on Alex made me feel worse. I worried about letting her down, about ruining the only friendship I felt I had. But, as much as I wanted to see her, I couldn't bear the thought of her seeing me this way. Over the past month, I'd told her a lot about my life and my struggles, in my marriage and in my own head, but this was a new extreme. My bad days were miserable for me and the people around me. I wouldn't subject her to that. Some days, it felt like Alex was the only thing keeping me together. I couldn't lose her.

From her room, Skylar began to scream louder and Cam ran

his hands over his legs. "Are you sure there's nothing I can do for you?" He looked ready to leave.

"I'll be fine. I just want to call her so she doesn't think I stood her up, and then I'm going to go back to sleep. Thank you for staying home." I tried to offer an appreciative smile, but in my attempt to fight back tears, I knew the expression fell flat.

He studied me for a moment before giving a surrendering nod. "No problem. I'll figure it all out. You just rest." Skylar screamed again from her bedroom, her sobs getting louder, and he stood up. "I'll go take care of her."

When he'd gone, I selected Alex's name from my contact list and pressed the phone to my ear, adjusting in bed carefully.

"Hello?" she asked, answering on the second ring.

"Hey, it's Ginny, from the park."

She chuckled. "Of course, I know who you are. What's up?"

"I need to cancel today. I'm sorry. Skylar and I won't be there."

She sucked in a deep breath. "Oh, no. Why? Because of the weather? It looks like there may just be a sprinkle midday. Nothing to worry about. Is there something else wrong?" I could hear her shuffling something around, and I tried to picture her at home. How did she live? Was she messy or neat? Did she have coffee in the mornings or a glass of wine at night? Did she keep her house warm or cold? All the windows open for natural light and fresh air or closed up for privacy?

All the information I'd collected about my friend over the past month—which, admittedly, now that I thought about it, wasn't much—had done nothing to give me a glimpse into her home life, though she knew so much about my own now.

"Ginny?" she prompted. "You still there?"

"Sorry. I, um, I spaced a bit... It's nothing. I'm just not feeling up for it."

"Oh, okay then. Is, um, is something going on?"

I forced the half-lie, though I didn't even want to do that. There was something about Alex that made me want to open up. "I'm just not feeling well."

"Oh, no. Are you ill? Do you need me to get you anything? I know this great little place that makes the best chicken noodle soup."

"No, no. Nothing like that. I just need to rest."

"Okay..." she said, dragging the word out. "If you're sure. Would you rather just meet me for coffee? I can find a sitter and we can chat. Or I could bring some to your place. Super calm and laid back. You'd be surprised how much talking through things can make you feel better. Even if you don't realize something's bothering you." She laughed. "I'm sorry if I'm pushing too much. I guess I hadn't realized how attached I'd gotten to our daily chats."

"No, it's okay. You're fine." I paused. Truth was, the idea of talking to her did make me feel better somehow. Just her voice, familiar, soothing, and warm, brought me peace that even Cameron's didn't.

I pushed myself to sit up, fighting the urge to lay back down immediately, and cleared my throat. "Actually, coffee—well, as long as they have tea—it sounds great... If you're sure it's no trouble."

"No trouble at all. One of my favorite places is near the park and, as luck would have it, they have a great tea selection. When would you like to meet?"

I glanced at the clock on the wall. Would it be too assuming to ask her to meet me now?

"Would you be able to meet in, like, half an hour? Or is this afternoon better for you?"

"Half an hour's perfect." She told me the name of the coffee shop and directions to get there, and I nodded along, trying to get my mind to focus on the instructions but knowing I'd end up just plugging the shop into my GPS.

We ended the call by saying we'd see each other soon, and I sank back onto the pillow, allowing myself a full minute to recover from the exhaustion of speaking with another person.

Then, I slid out of bed. I couldn't muster the energy to brush my hair, so I pulled it into a messy bun, ignoring the thin layer of oil on my roots. I pulled on black yoga pants and a worn and faded T-shirt I'd gotten in Destin, Florida, a few years back.

I slipped on my shoes, refusing to take one last look at the bed, as I knew if I did, I may never leave the room. Instead, I opened the door.

Cameron was heading toward me. His wide eyes trailed up and down the length of my body. "Oh, wow. You're out of bed. Are you feeling better?"

"No, not really, but, um, I'm going to meet Alex for coffee." I spit the sentence out as if it were poison, ignoring the guilt I felt for leaving him at home to take care of Skylar and the disgust with myself for choosing to spend a morning decompressing with a friend rather than doing what I should've been.

His expression changed from confused to worried. "You're what?"

Was he mad? Should I change my mind? I could go to the park if I drove. I could take Skylar and decompress there...

But that would require constant worrying and monitoring. It would mean potty breaks and juice breaks and kissing skinned knees and pushing her on the swing whenever she demanded it. It would mean mediating fights when someone took her toy or when someone knocked down her sandcastle. It would mean being a parent, but at that moment, the mere thought was completely exhausting.

I needed to lose myself in a conversation that didn't revolve around nap time or household chores. I hoped my husband could understand that.

"I just... I think I need to talk to her. She makes me feel better, Cam. Having a friend makes me feel better."

"And you can't talk to me? I'm not your friend?"

"It's different with her. She just *gets* it, you know? I swear I won't be gone long."

"And what about me? I'm just supposed to figure out how to work from home and watch our child while you gallivant around town doing God knows what?"

"I'm not *gallivanting around town*, Cam. I'm going for tea to try to help me work through this day. Can't you understand that? You were planning to stay home with her anyway. Does it really matter whether I'm here or there?"

He scoffed. "Of course, it matters, Ginny. Of course, it does. I was going to watch her because you couldn't get out of bed, not because you wanted to have tea with your friend. If you're able to keep her, I need you to. I've got so much going on right now."

"Daddy, let's play!" Skylar said, running her hands through his coiffed hair.

My shoulders dropped. He was right. No matter how much I needed a day, needed a chance to vent and let my grief out, it wasn't fair to him. None of this had been fair to him. "You're right." I shook my head. "I'm sorry. I don't know what I was think-ing." I outstretched my arms for her. "I'll take her. Just forget I said anything. You should go to work. Of course, you should." Suddenly, I felt embarrassed, angry with myself, and exhausted. I wanted to go lie down. I wanted to fall asleep and wait for this to pass.

He studied me for a moment, then kissed Skylar's forehead. "Go ahead and go potty. Daddy will be right there."

She trotted down the hall gleefully, en route to the bathroom, and he gave a sad smile with one side of his lips. "It's fine. Just go."

"No, it's not a big deal. I can stay with her."

"No, you can't. I can see that on your face. You aren't okay right now. I'd have to stay home with Skylar anyway, you may as well go and see if it helps you."

"Really?" A ray of sunshine spread in my stomach, muted by clouds of gray, but it was there.

He didn't look happy about it, but still, he said, "Yeah. It's fine. I'll... I'll figure it out. Like always." He moved past me without a word, leaving me standing in the hallway alone. I should've turned around and tried to fix it, but I didn't have time.

I needed to keep moving. The thought of seeing Alex again

was the only thing keeping me going, but I couldn't explain it to Cam because I still couldn't explain it to myself.

I had no experience with true friendship to tell me if this was what it was supposed to feel like. All I knew was that Alex made me feel listened to, understood, and accepted in a way I never had.

With that, I was off, out of the house and arriving at the coffee shop within twenty minutes. To my relief, Alex was already there. She'd chosen a small, wrought-iron table in front of the large bistro window, holding her phone with one hand while the other idly stirred the coffee in front of her.

The brilliant scent of baked goods and fresh coffee greeted me as I entered the coffee shop, my presence announced by the *ting-ting* of the metal bell above the doorway.

Alex spun around, raising her hand with a small wave in case I hadn't seen her. I held up a finger and made my way to the counter to order a chai tea.

Once I had it in hand, its warmth spreading through my fingers and up my arms before I'd had the first sip, I joined Alex at the table.

"Thank you again for meeting me," I said, trying to ease the awkwardness I felt. Did she think I was dramatic? Did she think I was an attention-seeker?

"You're more than welcome," she said softly, her eyes locking with mine in a way that said *no, I don't think any of those things. I'm glad you're here.* She held eye contact with me for an extra second or two. "You know I'm always here for you."

At her words, I felt tears welling in my eyes. I looked away, my cheeks flaming with embarrassment. Why couldn't I keep myself together? I swiped my eyes with the back of my finger. "I'm so sorry."

"What are you sorry for?" she asked, her head cocked to the side slightly.

"For falling apart." I chuckled through the tears that continued to fall. "I don't know what is wrong with me."

"What do you mean? Why would there be anything wrong

with you? We all have down days." She said it so simply, as if everyone had days where they didn't want to leave the bed or couldn't stop the free-flowing tears. But that wasn't the case, was it? In three years, I'd never seen Cam go through anything similar to what I experienced almost weekly.

"Yeah, but I have them a lot."

Something in her expression changed and her tone was serious, almost clinical. "How often, Ginny? How often are you having days like this?"

I sniffled, choosing to lie about the frequency. I'd told Alex a lot about my life, about how I'd struggled to return to work after having Skylar. About how my marriage had begun disintegrating at the introduction of our newborn. But I'd never spoken to her about my mental health struggles. I knew it was nothing to be ashamed of, but still, I felt ashamed. I couldn't shake the feeling that somehow it was a failing of my own strength. "Maybe once a month?"

Her mouth twisted in thought and she hummed thoughtfully. "Hm. Have you thought about seeing someone? Talking to someone? Professionally, I mean."

I rolled my eyes at the memories of the two bumbling psychiatrists Cameron had asked me—no, *forced me*—to see. "Cam—my husband—" She knew that. Why did I feel like I had to over-explain everything to her? I knew the truth; I was buying time. "He wanted me to. After Skylar was born... Things were really bad for a while, and he pushed me to see a therapist. I went to two different ones, but they just... It felt cold, you know? Impersonal. I'm a really private person, and having to spill my guts—the inner workings of my mind and marriage to a stranger in an unfamiliar place—it just all felt wrong." I shrugged. "I do take medicine though. Every day. I've mostly gotten it under control without therapy anyway. There are just occasional days where it's bad..." I trailed off, then shrugged, taking a sip of my still too hot beverage. "I've always thought anyone who could sit around and listen to strangers' problems all day is probably just as sick and twisted as they are anyway."

She smirked, and I watched her cheeks pinken.

"I'm sorry... Do you see a therapist? I didn't mean to suggest—"

She held a hand up, cutting me off. "It's fine, Ginny. Actually, I *am* a psychologist, and you may be right about us being sick and twisted." I felt horrified by what I'd said, but she merely looked amused. "But, underneath all of that, most of us genuinely do like to help people recover from trauma and improve their lives." She lifted her drink to her lips. If she was angry, she hadn't shown it. I would've been angry if I were her. I'd tell me to leave and never again face such a nasty, heartless, insensitive woman who'd make a mockery of my entire profession.

"Alex, I'm... God, I feel like such an idiot. I'm sorry." I put my face in my palms. "I spoke without thinking. I didn't mean... I mean, of course you do... Can you forgive me?"

"There's nothing to forgive," she said plainly. "I encourage my clients to speak freely and honestly." She reached forward, squeezing my hand. "Friends, too." Her hand withdrew from mine. "Besides, everyone's experience with therapy is different, and it's so important to find the right fit. Can I ask who you saw?"

I hesitated, trying to recall their names. So much from that time felt muddled.

"If that's too personal, just say so. I have a bit of an issue with boundaries as I'm generally paid to cross them."

"No, it's not that. I was trying to recall... I think the man's name was Graham. He had an office downtown. A brick townhome. The woman was called Jessica. Or maybe Renee... I'm sorry. It was just after Skylar was born, during that first year, and my memories are all sort of a blur."

"It's no problem," she said, waving her hand. "But, if you'd like, I can refer you to a few psychiatrists I recommend. It sounds like they could really help you. And, if they weren't a good fit, there'd be no hard feelings on my end. Therapy is something I'm really passionate about. I think everyone, no matter their situation, can benefit from it in one way or another."

"Oh, I don't know..." I said quickly, the thought of it making my stomach tense with trepidation.

"Well, just think about it, okay? The offer stands. The right therapist will make you feel like you're doing little more than," she paused, thinking, then gestured toward her cup of coffee, "meeting a friend for coffee." She giggled. "Or tea, in your case. It's just supposed to be a conversation."

"Well, that's just it though. It's not meeting a friend. It's meeting a doctor... Someone who is trying to analyze and diagnose me more than they are listening."

"It's possible to do both," she said softly. "Therapy isn't supposed to be stressful, Ginny. It may not always be a pleasant experience, but the things you learn from it, the questions you'll be forced to ask yourself, they're meant to help you. To help you look at things from a different viewpoint. And when it's done, you should leave feeling lighter. You'll understand yourself more."

"Maybe that's how it's supposed to go, but nothing about my experience made me feel light. I left feeling like there was even more wrong with me than I'd initially thought."

She was silent for a moment, and I worried I'd pushed back too hard.

"I'm sorry, Alex. It was just such a bad experience for me. I don't mean to say there's anything wrong with what you do. Of course, you'd be an excellent therapist. You make it so easy to talk to you and feel understood." Suddenly, I was realizing why I'd always felt so at ease with her, how she'd been able to crack me open and have me talking about my life every day at the park. Was I undergoing therapy with her before I'd even realized it?

"Well, thank you." She tucked a piece of stray hair behind her ear. "The truth is, I know all about bad therapy. But I also know the absolute healing that good therapy can bring. I wasn't always on the side of the room I'm on now."

"You went to therapy yourself?" I saw the answer in her eyes before the question had fully left my lips.

"I did. Actually, it saved my life. The truth is, I had a really traumatic childhood, and just before I graduated high school, I started seeing a psychologist who really helped me to turn my life around. It's the only reason I do what I do. To be frank, it's likely the only reason I'm still here today."

I felt my breath catch at her confession, blown away by the confidence with which she'd said it. How could she hold eye contact with me while splitting herself open in such a way?

"Oh, Alex..." I looked down, trying to compose myself. "I'm so sorry."

"Thank you," she said. "You can make it up to me by considering talking to someone yourself. I have so many good recommendations I could give you. People who could really help you."

"Anyone like you?" I asked, looking back up.

"Well, we all have our own methods, of course. But, yes, ideally, I'd want to find someone who could relate to you on a level similar to this. Someone you feel comfortable talking to."

"I don't know that I'd ever feel that way with a stranger."

"Well, we were strangers when we first met, and look at us now. With enough sessions, they wouldn't be a stranger either. That's the point. You go to sessions until you've built a familiarity with them, a rapport. You learn to trust them as much—more even —than you trust your husband, me, even yourself. They see things that you can't. After that, there's nothing you can't tell them."

"I just don't see how I could ever get there."

She pursed her lips, tapping a finger on the table. "Don't sell yourself short. You got there with me. You'll get there with someone new."

"Yeah, but I've told you so much about myself because we were friends. I wasn't seeing you in a professional setting. That's when the walls come up for me. Talking to a professional just feels so... formal." I shuddered, wrapping one arm around myself.

"You've been talking to a professional all along, and you didn't realize it."

"It's not the same and you know it," I said, glancing out the window at the busy street.

"Fair enough. You're right. I can't force you to do anything, just... Just consider it, okay? Will you promise me that?"

I thought about it for a moment, tossing an idea around in my mind. "Well, what if I started coming to see you?"

"Me?" She appeared bewildered by the suggestion.

"Yeah," I said. The more I talked, the better an idea it seemed. "We're already friends. I already trust you enough to tell you most things. We could skip that initial phase of feeling awkward."

"I don't know..." She tapped her finger on the back of her phone, thinking. "It's really not considered healthy for us to take on clients we know from real life—friends, family. There's meant to be a boundary there to protect us both. You're supposed to be able to tell your therapist anything without worrying about their opinion of you when they see you outside of the office. It's a really personal space."

"But I've already told you so much, and you've never judged me—"

Her brows drew down with obvious concern. "No, of course not. I wouldn't."

"So how could I ask for a better fit than that? Like you said, it's meant to be a conversation. I don't see how I could ever trust anyone enough to open up more than I trust you."

"But I'm just a psychologist. If your medication needed to be adjusted, I'd be unable to do that. Or if I thought you'd be better suited for a different prescription, it would be impossible for me to do anything about it without passing along your case to someone else... No, I'd really feel more comfortable with you seeing a psychiatrist straight from the get-go. One I can recommend. Given time, I think you'd find yourself just as comfortable with them as you are me. Maybe even more."

My expression fell, though I tried to hide it. "I'm sorry. I don't mean to push you. I don't want you to be uncomfortable. You're right. It's a silly idea. I'll take the recommendations and consider seeing someone new again. Thank you for offering to give me some names."

She pulled her purse from the floor and grabbed a pen and notepad from inside, laying the notepad flat on the table. I watched as she wrote down the first name, trying to read it from upside down. When she looked up, she frowned. "Tell me the truth."

"About what?"

"Will you call them? Honestly?"

I hesitated. She wanted me to say yes, but I wouldn't lie. "I'll consider it. That's all I can promise."

She was silent, her eyes darting back and forth between mine. Finally, she shoved the notepad back into her purse. "One session. *One*. And, if it doesn't work for either of us, we call it off. No hard feelings. When you step into the office, what we have between us here"—she moved her hand between us in the air—"doesn't exist. I'm your doctor, and you're my patient. We have to establish that boundary."

I could hardly contain my smile. "Are you sure? Like I said, I don't want to make you uncomfortable." I allowed myself to be vulnerable, admitting, "You're the first person I've considered a friend in years. I want to protect our friendship."

"I could never forgive myself if I let you suffer and didn't at least try to help. But, if I think a different medication could help you, I'll have to ask you to see someone else, even if it's in addition to the work we're doing." She smiled, but it was small, suppressed. "I'm not sure about this, Ginny, but I want to help you, so I will do everything I can to do so. You just have to swear one thing."

"What's that?"

"You can't lie to me. Not ever."

"I wouldn't," I vowed, nodding solemnly. "Thank you, Alex. Thank you so much."

"Don't thank me just yet." She took another sip of her drink, and I felt my heart flutter with newfound hope.

No more lies, starting now.

9 CAMERON

When my wife mentioned she'd decided to give therapy another try, I'd thought she'd finally seen the light. When I'd suggested it so many times in the past, she'd always claimed it wouldn't help. Even after the attempted sessions, she'd left just as bad, if not worse, than when she'd gone in.

So, for her to suggest starting back on her own, it seemed like nothing short of a miracle.

But quickly, I began to question just how much of a miracle it would be.

Since starting therapy, Ginny had become withdrawn and quiet. She did sessions three times a week and had started sleeping more than usual. Every evening after her session, she'd come home and go straight to bed. It was a lot. Everything was falling on me once again, and no matter what I said to Ginny about her behavior, I wasn't getting through.

And, when she wasn't in therapy, she was with Alex. The newest member of our marriage, apparently, though I'd still yet to meet her more than the one evening at the park. I didn't trust Alex yet. Not completely. But my wife would hear nothing of the sort. We still hadn't managed to schedule the dinner that Ginny had promised. She spent more time away from home, on play dates with Alex during the day and in her sessions in the evenings, than she did with me, never acknowledging what a burden she'd put on me and our marriage with her newfound social life.

I tried to be supportive, I really did, but my wife's new hectic schedule meant our already-slim time together had been cut more than in half.

No longer did we spend the evenings cleaning up after dinner and relaxing on the couch for an hour's worth of Netflix together, or go for hikes through the woods on Saturday mornings.

No, now she seemed almost entirely unavailable to me. She claimed the exhaustion was because they were doing such extensive work in her sessions, because she was having to deal with the trauma of her pregnancy and childbirth all over again, reliving every painful detail. But I just didn't know.

Even when my wife was at her worst, practically a shell of who she'd once been, I felt as though I'd seen her more than I was seeing her now.

It felt almost selfish to push the issue. I wanted her to do the work and heal. I wanted her to get better. I wanted her to return to the person she'd been before her pregnancy.

But at what cost?

Was this better?

Would it someday be better? I just didn't know.

So, that night, when I got home from dinner and approached my wife, I tried desperately to remember just what I'd planned to say to her. I'd spent my day at work completely distracted by the plans I was forming, structuring the sentences the perfect way so as not to offend or upset her, but merely to voice my concern.

But, as I laid eyes on her, her back to me as she scrubbed the last of the dishes in the sink, I forgot everything I had planned. The carefully constructed sentences flew out of my head, leaving me with only a discombobulated pile of concerns and wrong words.

When she heard me nearing her, she shut off the water and dried her hands.

"Hey, hon, how was work?" she asked, apparently in high spirits.

"Oh, you know, same as usual. Where's Skylar?"

"Napping," she said. "We came home when the storm rolled in this afternoon, and she was worn out."

It was the perfect time to bring it up to her. We had the house to ourselves. I had to do it, but I couldn't think of a single thing I'd wanted to say. My mind was blank. I was sure to screw this up.

I had to try anyway.

"Can we talk for a minute?"

She laid the hand towel on the counter, staring at me strangely. "Sure... What's wrong?"

"Nothing, I just... Let's sit down, okay?" I took her hand and guided her toward the table, my breathing growing erratic.

"You're scaring me," she said cautiously, sitting down across from me at the table. "Tell me what's going on."

"I wanted to talk to you about your therapy," I said in one breath.

"What about it?" I'd struck a nerve already. I watched a muscle in her jaw twitch.

Pinching the bridge of my nose, I tried to think back to what I'd planned to say. How was I planning to bring this up again?

Come on, Cameron, think. Think. Think.

"It's just, uh, well... I wanted to talk about... Well, I know you're enjoying it, and I'm glad, don't get me wrong. It's just that... You've been so tired lately and—"

"I told you why that is."

"I know you did. I just thought, is that healthy, I mean? Is that how it should be?"

"My doctor doesn't seem concerned about it." She pursed her lips.

"They'd know more than me, obviously. I'm not saying you have to give it up. I'm glad it's working and that you're enjoying it, or I mean, not enjoying it but... you know what I mean—"

"What are you trying to say, Cameron? Just spit it out."

It was never a good sign when she said my full name, nor when she was glaring at me with such a narrow gaze. "I'm just trying to make sure you're okay."

"Because I don't seem okay?"

"Because I'm worried about you."

"For once in the past two years since having Skylar, I'm finally seeing a therapist and getting my life together, unpacking all that I went through with my pregnancy and all the trauma I'm still dealing with, and now because I'm a little extra tired, that's a problem for you?"

My mouth dropped open, shocked by her bitterness. "Now, wait, I never said it was a problem. It's not. I'm happy for you. I'm just checking in, that's all."

"Well, thanks for checking in, I guess," she said, but there was no gratitude in her tone, only anger. "Sorry my trauma isn't convenient for you."

"You're not being fair," I said, feeling resentment swell in my chest. How dare she act this way? After all I'd done to help her after what she went through? After working so hard around the clock since Skylar's birth to help keep the house running, my career in check, and to take care of her on top of everything else. And never once had she heard me complain—so for her to be so angry now was ludicrous. "I'm not blaming you for what you went through. If you remember, I was the one who suggested therapy in the first place. But I'm remembering how you told me it was too hard on you and, with your exhaustion lately, I just wondered if this was doing more harm than good. You've been so tired and... listless, maybe, is the right word... I don't know. It's really hard for me to watch you go through this, and I try not to complain or let on how much I'm struggling, but I am. And, if it's all worth it, fine. But I just need to know that it is."

"What do you want me to say? How am I supposed to guarantee you anything? You see the progress I'm making."

I scoffed. "Progress is a stretch. If anything, you're regressing."

She opened her mouth as if she were going to argue, but closed it again. I watched her lip begin to tremble, her eyes fill with tears. "I'm doing all I can. I'm trying. I want to be better. You know I do. And this is the first thing that's ever made me feel better. I'm sorry that this is hard on you. It's no cakewalk for me either—"

"Of course, it's not. No, of course. You're right. I'm-I'm screwing this all up. I just miss you, that's all." I reached across the table and stroked her hand, taking it in mine. She let me do so, but her hand remained flat, stiff. She wasn't giving in.

"I miss you too, but this isn't about you, Cameron. Or Skylar. Or anyone but myself. I have to do this for me. It's helping. Even though I'm exhausted. When I'm awake, I'm feeling the best I've felt in years. It's helping. The therapy is helping. Don't you see that?"

"No, I don't. And I'm sorry for that. I'm glad to hear that you feel it's helping," I said, releasing her hand. "And, as long as you do, I won't press the issue. I just wanted to check in. I'm sorry if I upset you. I'm really proud of all you're doing for yourself. I know you're trying."

She nodded. "I just don't need a reason to feel self-conscious for the way I'm processing my grief."

"Grief?"

"Yes, grief. Therapy has made me realize I'm still processing grief over the trauma of my pregnancy and birth. Everything we'd planned was ripped away from us because of the complications, and I never fully worked through that. Alex is helping me to see where the issues were, issues I didn't even know I had."

"Alex?" I demanded, staring at her strangely.

She blanched, sitting back in her chair. When she spoke again, it was with a forced confidence, her chin stiff. "Yes, Alex. Alex is my therapist."

"By that you mean you're having tea with her and she's letting you talk?" Why was this the first I was hearing of it? Was this what she'd been calling therapy all along? Who were my checks going to each week?

"No, Alex is a licensed psychologist. She's been the one I'm seeing. I really think that's why I've been able to deal with so much. She's my friend; I trust her. It feels different with her. We have tea and chat during the sessions, so it makes me feel comfortable, but she is helping me to process my feelings and heal. If I can't confront what I went through, I'll never get better."

I struggled to process what she was telling me. "I don't understand... You're meeting in a coffee shop and talking about your personal life?"

"No, she has an office. In her home, but it's a real office where she brings other clients."

I stared at her. Was she telling me the truth? It felt wrong. Why was I paying this woman to have tea with my wife? Wasn't that what friends did? Was she taking advantage of us? "Why didn't you tell me?"

"Because I was worried you'd downplay the work I was doing by suggesting we were just meeting for tea and talking through things."

"But that's not what you're doing?"

She groaned, pounding her fist into the table. "No! It's not at all. I'm meeting her in her office. It's legitimate therapy. The best I've ever received. She's different to any of the others, Cam. She understands me in a way no one else ever has. The other therapists I saw... Alex just understands me. I don't know how else to explain it. She's different. It feels different with her. I've never felt so understood and... seen. Validated."

My stomach tightened, my body having a visceral reaction to her words. I'd never made her feel that way? After all I'd done for her? All I continued to do? It was Alex who swooped in and saved the day, all while charging us two hundred and fifty dollars an hour? I pushed the worry away, silencing it.

"I just wish you would've told me."

"I'm sorry, I felt like I couldn't."

Now my jaw tightened. It was as if she were trying to push me away. Trying to start a fight. "I'm sorry you did, too." With that, I stood from the table and made my way back down the hall, regretting the conversation almost entirely.

Still, something wasn't sitting right with me about the entire situation. I just wished I could put my finger on why. Ginny had never lied to me before, never purposefully kept something from me. So, why this time?

Why Alex?

10 GINNY

Friday evening, after Cam arrived home from work, I headed out for my last session of the week with Alex. Things at home still weren't great after the fight we'd had. If you could call it a fight.

Cam had tried to smooth things over by pretending like it never happened, but I couldn't forget. I couldn't forget the judgement in his eyes when he talked about my latest sleeping habits. After more than a year of saying he'd do anything for me to get better, that my happiness was what mattered to him most of all, now that I was actually making progress, he had a problem with it.

Now, I was getting judged for the work I was putting in emotionally and the toll it was taking on me.

As much as I tried to forget it, I couldn't put that look on his face out of my mind. It sat with me when I closed my eyes. The pity, the worry, the fear... Somehow, it was an amplified version of the expression he'd worn even on my worst days.

How was I supposed to take that? That me sleeping a few extra hours a day was worse to him than depressive episodes where I couldn't summon the strength to leave the bed or dress myself for days at a time. Was it because he wasn't the one helping me this time? Because this round of therapy had been my idea? Because he hadn't had a hand in it?

I parked the car on the street next to the two-story, yellow house where Alex ran her office, and jogged across the sidewalk, up the walk, and rapped on the white, wooden door.

Within moments, Alex's muddy shape appeared in the small, frosted window. I saw her smile grow as she pulled the door open.

"Ginny, how are you?" She stepped back, allowing me inside.

"Feeling okay today." Because I hadn't been in for a session since the fight, I hadn't yet told her about the conversation with Cam. We'd been doing well to keep our therapy-based conversations inside the office, while everything else could be discussed at the park. Still, I wasn't completely sure if I wanted to tell her what had happened or why it had upset me. We'd made such great progress, I didn't want to derail it with a detour. Progress wasn't linear, I knew. Alex constantly reminded me of that fact, but still, I felt like I could, and had, dealt with the issue in the best way possible. I'd shut down any further mention of it. I wasn't going to stop therapy no matter how much it inconvenienced my husband. I knew it wasn't fair to him, but I was and had been barely holding on for too long. I'd gone through months of trauma bringing our child into the world and two years after that dealing with post-partum depression. I deserved to take care of myself and prioritize my healing. As hard as it was to admit it, as selfish as I felt, it was true.

"I've got your favorite already on," she said, pointing to the small hall table where she had the electric kettle brewing and a stack of paper cups along with several sweeteners and stirrers next to it.

"It's stronger today," I said, lifting my nose upward and inhaling. "I smelled it before I'd made it to the door."

She was still for a moment, then shook her head. "Oh! No, that's probably the mint I've planted outside." She opened the door slightly and pointed to four potted plants sitting on the covered porch. I'd missed them coming in.

"Ahh, well that explains why it smells so amazing."

"To us, maybe, but they keep the wasps and bees at bay. I

planted some a few summers ago, but it doesn't seem to be working anymore. I'm not sure if they've grown a tolerance for the plant or if I just need to add a few more. So, here's hoping." She crossed one set of fingers as she swung the door shut, and I poured myself a cup of tea, adding a packet of stevia and stirring it.

Once I was done, she led us into her office. It was a large sitting room to the left of the entranceway, with an oversized maroon and tan rug in the center of the room, two olive green wingback chairs and a matching sofa, all gathered around a modern marble-topped coffee table.

It was obsessively tidy, not a thing out of place. Somehow, even in the old, slightly rundown house, she'd managed to look both modern and rustic all at once. She had a lamp on the far table and artwork on her walls, next to bookshelves lined with old books with faded gold lettering on their spines.

I sat down in my usual spot, the worn cushion of the olive sofa, and Alex took her place in the wingback chair on the right.

We were ready.

At our battle stations.

She picked up a notebook in front of her and clicked her pen. I liked that she still used paper. My other therapists had used iPads and styluses, something that added to the coldness of the environment.

Here, in this house, surrounded by so much warmth and comfort, I felt at home. At peace.

"So, last time we ended the session while we were talking about how Cameron's attachment to Skylar leaves you feeling left out at times. Do you care to pick it up there?"

I nodded. "Sure."

She clicked the pen twice more, folded one leg over the other, nodded at the clock on the wall, and began. "So, when you say," she read from her notes, "you feel like your husband is closer to your daughter than you, do you mean closer to her than *you are* or do you mean he's closer to her than he is to you?"

I picked at a piece of skin near my fingernail, shifting uncomfortably. "Both. Maybe."

She didn't break stride, didn't study me, just kept going. "When do you think you started to feel that way?"

"I want my husband to love my daughter, don't get me wrong. I'm so grateful to have him there to help me out and so thankful they have a good relationship. I sound selfish even thinking this way." I shook my head, pressing my fingers to my temple.

"You can be grateful to have such an amazing father for your child, while also feeling unseen in your relationship to him. It's not all that uncommon. We see the roles reversed more than not, that the mother is so devoted to her children she loses sight of her marriage, but either parent can experience something similar. Given the role that Cameron took on after Skylar's birth, while you were experiencing postpartum depression, it makes sense that the traditional roles would be reversed for you." She paused, waiting for me to say something while I tried to decide what to say. Finally, she prompted, "Tell me, what is your relationship with your own father? You've mentioned your mother quite a bit, but rarely him."

"Our relationship is okay. My parents are both excellent people—hard workers, compassionate, smart. They love me. They love Skylar."

She waited for me to go on, but I held back.

"Ginny, even now," she pressed, "when I'm asking specifically about your father, you're speaking in terms of *they*. Both your parents. I'd love to know more about your relationship with just your father." She tapped the pen on the notepad.

"My relationship with my dad is complicated. I love him, but we just..." I paused, sighing. I felt guilty even saying it. "We don't really have a relationship, I guess. Growing up, he worked long hours and would travel out of town for months at a time. It was always just me and Mom. When he was home, things were more tense. I mean, don't get me wrong... He was a great dad. He cared about us. He wasn't abusive or mean-tempered. I think sometimes it just felt like he was there, but he *wasn't* there. Even when he was home, his mind was usually on work. It was as if my mom and I formed our own secret club, and we couldn't talk about it when Dad was home. I know it was hard on her, him being away so much, but she was almost lighter when he was gone. Freer somehow. Now that I'm older, we talk less and less. Exchange texts now and again, but it's my mom I have a real relationship with. He's never shown much interest in Skylar either, aside from a hug or two. It's like he's never really known how to have a relationship with..." I paused, thinking back. "Anyone, really."

"So, do you think maybe it bothers you that Cameron is the exact opposite of what you saw modeled as fatherly behavior growing up? His priority, despite his work, has been to build a healthy relationship with his daughter. He prioritizes his relationship with her, and even his relationship with you, over everything else, from what you've described. His standing as a husband and a father comes first for him, and that's not something you're used to seeing happen."

I laced my fingers together slowly, thinking through what she'd said. Was she right? Had I been pushing Cameron away, complaining because he wasn't my father?

"I guess when I got pregnant, I pictured our life turning out like my parents' in a way. We'd already discussed how I may want to take a bit of extra time, even a year or two, off from work after Skylar was born, like my mom had. I thought I'd have this great relationship with her, like we did. But Cam has that instead."

"So, in a way, that's another thing that was ripped away from you because of the difficult pregnancy and traumatizing birth. You lost not only the expectations you had for those stages of your life, but the expectation of what your life would look like once she'd arrived as well. It seems to me like maybe you're punishing yourself for not being your mother, by punishing Cameron for not being your father."

I sat with the weight of her statement. Was she right? *Yes.* The answer was there in my gut. A resounding voice saying what I'd known all along, what it had taken *her* recognizing, for *me* to recognize myself. I was disappointed in myself for not doing better, for not having as easy a time with early motherhood as my own mother had. And seeing it all come so easily for Cameron made me hate him. It made me bitter. Resentful.

I felt the coldness of those emotions seething through me and realized they'd always been there.

How had I let this go on for so long?

She was silent as I worked through my feelings, processing the flood of them at once.

"You're right," I said finally, choking back tears. "You're absolutely right."

"Everyone has a picture in their head of who they'll be as a parent. But the truth is, we just never really know. And, when we become someone different, that can be traumatizing. It's important to remember, we are not our parents." She said the statement firmly, and I thought back to her comment about her own traumatizing childhood. "We are not. And we can't compare ourselves to them or hold ourselves to their standards. All Skylar needs from you is for you to love her. To love Cameron. To be there. Kids are resilient. They don't have expectations. You're the only mother she's ever known. She has no one to compare you to, yet. No friends' moms, no perfect TV moms. She already thinks you're the greatest thing... You just have to quit being so hard on yourself and let this idea of who you are in comparison to your mother go."

"I wish it were that easy."

She laid the notepad down in her lap, uncrossing her legs. "I know you've mentioned before that you feel uncomfortable with your ability to play and interact with her. What would you say to bringing Skylar in so I could watch the two of you interact together? We could bring in some toys and just let her play. She'd have no reason to know what we were doing, but it could be a great way for me to offer suggestions as to how to play with her effectively. Children learn and bond through play. I think breaking through that barrier could be really helpful for you, and I'm certain we can do it."

"I don't know..." I trailed off, thinking of Cameron. He already wasn't sure this was right for me, what if he thought bringing Skylar in was a bad idea too?

"I've seen you play together at the park, of course, but that's different as there are other kids around to steal her attention. Seeing how the two of you react one-on-one would be really helpful for me to help set you up for success with her. Once we break down those walls, I really think you'll find yourself feeling much more confident with her."

"No, I think it's a good idea. It's not that, it's just that..."

"What is it?" She tilted her head to the side, waiting.

I huffed out a breath. "Cameron isn't sure this is working for me."

"What? Do you mean therapy?"

"Yes. The sessions... I come home so tired afterward, like I've told you, and he thinks they may be doing more harm than good." I hung my head, as if it were my own shortcoming. "I've told him what you said, about it being part of the process and the result of all the emotional work we're doing here, but he brought up stopping the sessions with me a few days ago. I'm just not sure how he'd react to me bringing Skylar here too."

"I see... And what was the consensus about quitting the sessions? Are you considering it?"

"No," I said quickly, shaking my head. "I told him it wasn't an option. This is important to me. I am exhausted when I leave, but I do feel like I'm getting better. I feel at peace when I'm here. I've found ways to cope with the feelings I'm having and am learning so much about myself and the way I process things. Quitting would be the worst thing I could do right now."

"I'm glad you feel that way, Ginny. Truly. It means so much to me that I've helped you in any small way. And, for the record, I really do see so much progress in you since we started." She pressed her lips together. "What if I talked to Cameron? Do you think you could convince him to stop by my office? Not for a session or anything, but just as a way to air out any grievances or concerns he may have about this. Hearing it from someone else, maybe it'll help him understand how important the work is..." She shrugged one shoulder. "You know him best. What do you think?"

"It's worth a shot." I didn't know if Cameron would do it or not, but I thought, if I told him how important it was to me, he might consider it at least. Hearing her out, and then maybe letting Skylar come in as well. If he disagreed, I'd never bring her in behind his back. It wouldn't feel okay to me. "I'll ask him tonight."

"That sounds great," she said, picking the notepad up again. "Therapy is very solitary work. Sometimes the spouse can find themselves feeling excluded or worrying about what's being said here. While I'll never tell him anything you've told me in confidence, I'm hoping I can reassure him that it *is* working and hopefully help him to feel more assured in his role in your progress."

"Thank you, Alex. That sounds great. Honestly, whatever it takes for him to agree. I want to get better."

She wrinkled her nose with a sly grin. "I know you do. We all want the same thing here." Again, she clicked her pen, looking over her notes. "Now, where were we?"

11 CAMERON

I checked the address Ginny had texted me, comparing the number to the one displayed next to the door on the old, yellow Victorian-style house. She looked as if she'd been a beauty in her day, but she could use a good power wash now.

I made my way up the small walkway, then the three wide stairs that led to the wraparound porch. The air smelled of peppermint and eucalyptus, reminding me of the essential oil baths my mother had given me when I was sick as a boy.

I knocked on the door cautiously. There was no sign to tell me this was a therapist's office, so I hoped I had the right place.

To my great relief, a familiar shape came into view in the opaque glass, and Alex swung the door open. She looked different than she had at the park. She'd dressed in a deep purple dress, and her dark hair was gathered into an updo, rather than down. She seemed confused when she saw me.

"Can I help you?"

"Hey. Yeah, didn't Ginny tell you I was coming?"

Recognition flooded her expression. "*Cameron*. Of course. Sorry, you caught me off guard. Come on in." She stepped back, allowing me inside. The house was old—*wallpaper on the walls and a runner on the stairs, old*—but she'd decorated it nicely. She led me to a room on our left, with an ugly green couch and coffee table with a ring of condensation on the marble. When I turned around, she was removing her hoop earrings and placing them on a small side table. "You'll have to forgive me for being unprepared. I just got home from a meeting. Can I fix you some tea? Water? A beer?"

"Are you allowed to give out beer?" I asked, one brow raised.

"Well, you aren't a client," she said simply, "so I don't see why not."

"I'm okay, thanks. I can't stay long anyway. Ginny is expecting me home."

"Of course," she said, holding out a hand to gesture that I could take a seat. I tried to picture my wife there, sitting on the couch I was now sinking onto. It felt strange. Unreal. Was this really where she felt comfortable spilling her secrets? What truths did these walls know? "Well, we'll just get straight to it then, hm? Ginny had mentioned to me that you might have some concerns about our sessions." She smoothed her hands under legs as she sat down in the chair across from me. "I wanted to see if I could be of some help."

"Well, first of all, it's nothing to do with you, I hope she mentioned that." I hesitated, stirring uneasily, my fingers tense as I waited for her to confirm that she had. When she didn't, I cleared my throat, choosing my next words carefully. "It's just that she's been feeling so tired lately. Especially after her sessions, but really all the time. She's been taking naps almost every evening. I've never known my wife to be a napper. And, on evenings after your sessions, she'll come home and sleep straight through the night. The only time I've really seen her sleep this much was when she was going through the worst of everything after having Skylar. I just wondered... I mean, what if this is making her worse, rather than better? What if it's pushing her further toward the depression, rather than away from it?"

She was still, as if she was waiting for me to go on. "What if it is?" she asked after a moment.

"That's what I'm asking you..."

"What would it mean to you if your wife's depression worsened? If she were to regress back to, as you called it, *when she was going through the worst of everything.*"

"I don't want that," I said quickly with a firm shake of my head. "That was the worst time of my life. Hers. Ours. We barely made it through. I... I don't think we'd survive it again."

"I think Ginny senses that." She paused. "And it terrifies her."

"What do you mean?" I leaned forward.

"I think it's always in the back of your wife's mind that one bad day could cause you to leave. That she's always one fight, one day of extra exhaustion, one nap away from you deciding you've had enough—"

"That's ridiculous. It would never happen."

"That doesn't mean she doesn't believe it could." She leaned forward, matching my stance, our eyes locked on one another. "Your wife is a strong woman. She's smart. But she's hurting right now. She's gone through a lot and, for a long time, she felt like she couldn't process what was happening. The loss that came with not getting to enjoy her pregnancy, with not getting to have a birth plan, with laboring for hours only to have an emergency c-section that nearly cost both her and your daughter their lives. I know you went through it too, Cameron, but it's different. Not less traumatic, I don't mean to imply that, but different. She needs to process what happened if there's ever a chance for her to heal. So, yes, we're in the weeds right now, but there is light at the end of this tunnel if you allow her to find her way through it."

I sighed, feeling like shit for even suggesting she give it up. Feeling like shit for everything I felt. The anger, the resentment, the frustration...

"That's all I want, Alex. I do love her. I've tried for so long to get her to see someone... I don't want you to think I'm not supportive. It just scares me, you know? It scares me to see some of the old habits coming back."

"I get it, I do. And there will be a time and a place for you to talk about this with your wife, to let her know what your experience was with all of this. I know it's unfair to say that time isn't right now, but the time *isn't right now.* This is your wife's time. And she needs this time, so if you love her like you say you do, you have to give it to her." She paused, pressing her lips together. "I have to be very careful about what I tell you, but it's no exaggeration to say I don't think your wife would survive giving up on these sessions right now. I think she needs them more than you or I know."

"You don't mean..." I could hardly bear to think of the words, but I saw the truth of what she was saying in her expression. "No. She wasn't... I mean, she was sad, sure. But she wasn't... She wouldn't..."

"I don't know if she would or she wouldn't, but I know she holds back from telling you things because she fears the day when you draw the line. I know she feels suffocated by your expectations. Like she's constantly letting you down."

"Suffocated by my expectations? What? Has she said that?"

She shook her head slightly, her lips tight. "I can't tell you what she has or hasn't said. I can only tell you what I've observed."

But she was telling me, even without saying the words. Ginny had told her she felt suffocated by me. How was I supposed to take that? Knowing all that I'd done for her, all that I'd sacrificed and dealt with, how was I to accept her criticizing the way I'd handled things? When she'd left me no choice but to handle it all?

"Alex, I have no expectations for her other than that she is honest with me. We can make it through everything else, but I need her to tell me these things. Not you. Me." I huffed, then added, "No offense."

"I know you think you've given her the space to do that, but the very real truth is that she censors herself with you, not because she doesn't trust you, but because she doesn't trust that you can love her through the darkness."

"I've proven that I can—"

"You've done brilliantly, Cameron. I'm not judging you. I'm

only telling you what *she* believes. Your wife is a very private person. She keeps her thoughts and feelings to herself, not telling you or her parents or anyone... It was why she struggled to connect with her previous therapists. I think, if we have any hope of saving her, these sessions are it. For whatever reason, she's connected with me in a way that could save her life. But you need to know what we're in for. It's going to get worse before it gets better, and you have to keep whatever concerns you have to yourself. At least for now."

I swallowed, running a palm over my face as I forced away the anger I was feeling, making myself absorb Alex's words. "I had no idea it was so bad. She... I knew she'd been struggling, but she seemed better. Before she started coming here, she seemed like she was doing better."

She nodded her head side to side. "She was better... at pretending to be better. When we're finished, I hope she won't have to pretend any more. Even with medication, even once things are more under control, your wife will always struggle with depression. There will be worse days than others and better days than others. You have to know and accept that if you plan to stick with her."

"Of course, I do. She's still my wife."

She was quiet. "I understand it must be hard for you. I really do."

I swallowed, but didn't respond right away. Finally, I said, "I'll just be glad when this is all over."

"Do you think it would help if you spoke to someone as well?"

"What? You mean a therapist?"

She giggled, her laugh loud and friendly. "Are we all that bad?"

I felt the wrinkle in my brow lessening, and realized I must've made a horribly offensive face. "I didn't mean to hurt your feelings. I've just, I mean, I'm not against it, obviously. For her. But I'm fine. I don't need therapy. I just need my wife back."

"She's very lucky to have you." She smoothed her hands over her dress.

"Will you tell her that? Convince her that she can be honest with me? That, no matter what, I'm not going anywhere?"

She smiled with one side of her mouth, her eyes sad. "Why don't you tell her yourself?"

I couldn't tell her the truth, which was, because I'd given her a reason not so long ago, to never believe me again.

12 GINNY

The next week, instead of meeting Alex and Raven at the park, I brought Skylar in for a session, convincing her that we were going to play indoors because it may rain. Looking up at the dreary and overcast day, I was glad the weather had cooperated for once.

It was the first time we'd planned to have a session in the middle of the day rather than the evening, partly because it was easier on Skylar and partly because it was easier on me.

Once evening hit, Skylar's behavior was often even more unpredictable, her tantrums and fits growing more erratic.

She stopped by the porch, sniffing at a patch of flowers, and I couldn't help smiling. She'd always loved flowers. When we took her to the store, we had to stop at each of the aisles that contained them, whether they were real or fake, in order for her to inspect each one.

"Come on, Sky," I said, holding out my hand for her.

"Pretty!" she exclaimed, smiling. "Look! Smell this, Mommy!"

I did as I was told, leaning down and inhaling deeply.

"It smells good, sweetheart. I think those are azaleas."

She stared up at me, waiting to see if I'd say more. "It's a red," she said finally.

"Yes, they are red." I nodded. "You're so smart." She wrapped an arm around my leg, and I nudged her gently toward the door just as Alex opened it. She smiled brightly, bending down with her hands gripping her knees so that she was eye level with Skylar.

"Hi there, sweet girl. How are you?"

"Where's *Waven... I play wiff Waven?*"

"Raven isn't here today, sweetie. I'm sorry. She stays with a sitter while I have to do boring grown-up things like work," Alex said, making an exaggerated frown. "Bleh!"

"Bleh!" Skylar agreed, jumping up and down with glee despite her apparent displeasure. Alex was good with her. It was painfully obvious. Everyone seemed to be better with her than me. Why couldn't it come easier for me?

I guided her into the house as Alex stepped back.

"But don't you worry. We're going to have so much fun. I've got all sorts of toys. I've got dollies and some blocks and some cars... What do you like to play with, Skylar?" She held out a hand, leading a cautious Skylar into the office. On the coffee table, there lay a stack of children's books, two baby dolls, wooden blocks with letters on their faces, a stack of three puzzles, a box of toy cars, and a bucket of pretend food.

"Wow, you didn't get all of this just for today, did you?" I asked, placing a hand on my stomach. I'd expected a baby doll and a book, not the entire inventory of a toy store.

"No." She waved off my concern, though I couldn't be sure she was being entirely honest. "Don't worry about it. Most of them are toys from when Raven was younger. I keep extras around for other sessions with children anyway."

Most of it looked brand new, but I didn't press the issue further. "Well, thank you. For doing this. I'm still pretty shocked you were able to get Cameron on board with it."

"You'll find I'm pretty persuasive," she said with a sly smile. Once we'd made it into the room, Skylar went to the dolls immediately, picking one out and holding it above her head with a gleeful giggle. "Now, if you just want to sit down and play with her. Just as you normally would. Pretend I'm not here."

She sat down in her chair, pen and notepad ready, and I drew my brows down, easing onto the floor.

"Okay, sure." I picked up the second doll, staring at it with no idea what I was supposed to be doing. Was she going to judge my mothering? For the first time, I began to worry that maybe this wasn't the best idea. Would she think I was a terrible mother? That I had no idea what to do with my child?

"It's going to feel awkward at first, but just really lean into it. Play like you would if you were at home. I may ask you questions along the way or help to guide you, but for the most part, I just want to observe."

I nodded, picking up one of the baby bottles. "I think I'll feed my baby, Sky. Is your baby hungry?" My voice was an octave too high. Everything about the moment—my language, my actions— felt forced, awkward, and stiff. I waited for the moment when Alex would call me a fraud and Skylar would walk away. "I'm sorry. I'm no good at this sort of thing. I was an only child and there weren't a lot of kids around until I started school. I never know what to do or how to play—"

Alex cut me off, pointing toward Skylar as she lifted one of the bottles from the tabletop and, mimicking me, placed it near her baby's mouth. My daughter looked at me with a smile so bright it brought tears to my eyes. When was the last time she looked at me that way? When was the last time I'd tried to really play with her?

"She doesn't know, either," Alex said softly. "That's the beauty of kids. You're learning how to do it together. The important thing is that you try."

I pretended to rock the baby, thinking back to the nights I'd held Skylar in my arms that way. She was so tiny once. Looking at her now, it was hard to remember those days.

She was growing up so quickly.

My chest tightened with sudden sadness.

She watched me, waiting to see what was next as she patted her baby's bottom, folding her practically in half to do so.

"What do you think our babies want now?"

Her eyes lit up. "To play!" she cried, standing up and pretending her doll was dancing on the table. We put them together, making them move across the other toys as she laughed.

Had it really been this easy all along? Had I just built it up in my head so much that it became this terrifying, unattainable thing?

We played like that for the next hour, putting together puzzles and using the books as ramps for her cars. As the minutes passed, I began to lose the anxiety and tension I felt in my muscles, though the uncomfortable feeling of being watched never fully went away.

When the session wrapped up, Alex helped us clear away the toys.

"So, what do you think? Am I a lost cause?" Despite the question, I felt confident in what I'd shown her during the session.

She laughed under her breath. "You're doing a fine job, Ginny. It'll just take more practice to gain confidence with it, but that all comes with time. Today was good. You had fun, didn't you, Skylar?"

She laughed, then yawned, rubbing her eyes. "Almost naptime," I noted.

"How do you play with her at home?" Alex asked once the toys had been picked up. She stood, dusting off her thighs. "What sort of things do you do?"

"I try to find things for us to do, but typically I'll just take her outside or to the park. On rainy days when we're stuck inside, I'll get out markers and paper or a book, but she never wants to sit still long enough to do either. I've tried to work with her on animal sounds by playing with some animal toys, but... She just loses interest so fast, and then I get frustrated."

She nodded, her jaw locked in thought. "Do you have any sort of routine for her? Like, do you play for a specific period of time during the day? Or sing songs at a certain time? I know your afternoons are normally spent at the park with us, so what do your mornings look like? Routine is so important for kids."

I shot a guilty glance toward Skylar. "Our days all look so different. I wish I would've gotten her into more of a routine from the start, honestly, but things were so hectic in the beginning and we've just never made it a priority." I sighed. "It's bad, I know. I mean, typically we wake up and have breakfast and then she'll play while I do whatever needs done around the house. Then we'll have lunch and head to the park to meet you guys until Cam's off. When he gets home, we have dinner and then it's bath, story, and bed. But that's an ideal day, and most days there's a wrench thrown into the plan at some point."

"How so?"

"Usually tantrums." I patted Skylar's head. "Sometimes Cam's schedule or an errand I have to take care of. Evenings are the worst of it. We do try hard to keep the same schedule once he's home. We have the worst time getting her to sleep and stay asleep. She's always been a difficult sleeper, but it seems like as she's gotten older, that's only getting worse. Her doctor says routines can help with that, which is why we do try to stick to it, but—"

"Skylar, can you stay right here and play with your dolly again while I talk to Mommy?" Alex asked, interrupting me with urgency. I stared at her, befuddled by the sudden outburst.

She nodded, flopping down on the couch, and Alex led me out of the room and toward the entryway, keeping her voice low when she spoke again. "I'm sorry, it's just... I try to discourage people from talking negatively about their children in front of them. *You* become their inner voice, so when you say she's difficult, she starts to believe it. If you say she's hard to deal with, that's what she tells herself. It's so important to only say positive things in front of your children." She patted one of her hands in the other, making me feel as if I were a child being scolded myself.

"Oh. I'm-I'm sorry, I didn't think—"

"No, I'm not blaming you, I just wanted to bring it to your attention. It's not something most parents think about. They just assume their child knows they care. But if they only ever hear negative things, that's what their inner voice becomes. It can be really debilitating for children."

I felt my stomach tense with an odd combination of rage and

sadness. *How dare she tell me how to raise my child*, but also *how dare I make my child feel unloved?*

Before I could say anything, she went on, "I'm sorry. I shouldn't have snapped. It's really personal for me."

I thought back to what she'd said about her traumatic childhood, and the rage went away, leaving only a slight trace of indignation in its wake. "Your parents did that to you? Talked negatively in front of you, I mean?"

She pressed her lips together. "This is about you, Ginny. And Skylar. It's nothing to do with me."

I wasn't buying it. There was more to the sudden outburst than she was letting on. "Come on, Alex. We're friends. The session is over. Look, we've even left the room. This is just us talking. Friend to friend, not therapist to client." I cocked my head to the side, willing her to share the pain I saw shadowed in her eyes. "Everyone needs someone to talk to. If you've proven anything to me, it's that."

She bit the inside of her cheek, looking away and mumbling, "Yes, well, I have someone. And I pay him a lot of money to listen. Which is exactly what you're doing for me, and exactly why I can't bring up my personal life with you here."

I sidestepped. "What about here?"

She snorted, shaking her head. "Fine, if you must know, *friend to friend, my* mother was emotionally abusive to me, yes." She held onto her pointer finger with the opposite hand, rubbing circles on her knuckle with her thumb. "My father wasn't around, but my mother... She was... cruel and unkind. It took me years to recover from what she put my sister and me through." She released a slow and steady breath, not meeting my eyes. "I don't mean to suggest that you're anything like her. There's no question how much you love your daughter. I just want you to realize that she may not always feel that way if you speak about her flaws in front of her. Those are conversations you can have with Cam, away from her."

"Of course. You're right, Alex. I'm sorry. I just didn't think..."

"It's okay." She stared lovingly into the living room. "She

reminds me of my sister, I think. She's a wily one, too... It's why I had such a reaction to what you said back there."

"Raven's mother, you mean?"

"Yes. Her name's Brianna. She's younger than me, and so I always felt like I needed to protect her. Sometimes when I look at children, she's all I can see."

"Sounds like she is lucky to have you." I felt grateful for the change of subject from my horrible parenting.

She seemed embarrassed, meeting my eye for half a second and then looking at the floor again. "Thank you." She inhaled sharply. "Alright then, I've shattered my moral and ethical codes enough for one day, don't you think?" She patted her thighs, then checked the watch on her wrist. "I have another session in a half hour. I should let you get her home."

"I'm really glad you shared that with me, Alex," I told her, worried I'd crossed the line, pushed too hard.

A hint of discomfort touched her expression. "It's weird with us, Ginny. This is why therapists are not supposed to be friends with their clients. It's not fair to you." Her mouth upturned into a small, sad smile. "But what's done is done. From now on, we just have to keep things in the office focused on you. That was the deal when I agreed to take you on."

"Understood," I said softly.

Without another word, she brushed past me and back into the room where she bent down, talking quietly to Skylar. "Have fun with Mommy for the rest of the day, okay? It was so good to see you again."

"Maybe next time we see her, we can play with Raven again," I said.

"Oh, well, it may be a while, actually... I was trying to decide how to bring it up. I know they've become such good friends, but Raven's actually gone back to her mother's." She winced. "She picked her up late last night and I'm not totally sure when she'll be back."

My heart sank. That meant no more park dates with my friend. No friend for Skylar to play with daily. "Oh no."

"I know. I hate it. Don't worry, though. She'll be back at some point soon, I'm sure. I keep her for weeks at a time and then she'll go home for a few nights, but she's never gone too long. My sister works so much, you know, so I help out whenever I can. I love having her here, and she loves playing with Skylar now. Leaving this time was really tough on her. And on me." She smiled shyly. "I'm trying to soak up as much time as I can with her before she starts school next fall."

"Skylar will really miss her..." I said, the truer statement left unsaid between us: *I'll really miss you.* Between us, Skylar looked oblivious to what we were discussing.

"Well"—she patted Skylar's back—"I promise just as soon as she's back, you'll be the first people I call. And I can still meet you at the park once in a while to catch up. Plus, we'll still have our sessions. You aren't getting rid of Raven or me that easily." She gave a playful grin, and I tried to meet it, though I knew I was radiating only sadness.

I knew eventually it would have to come to an end. I knew Raven wasn't her daughter, and eventually, the seasons would change, bringing blistering heat before the winter, at least one of which would mean ending the daily visits I'd so looked forward to.

But it felt too soon. It was unexpected and breathtaking.

I turned away from her so she wouldn't see the heartbreak written all over my face. "You're right. Let's go, Sky. We'll see Alex and Raven again soon."

"Yes, you will," she promised, resting her head against the jamb of the door as I stepped out onto the porch with my daughter in tow and waved casually over my shoulder, as if my world—the one thing that seemed to keep me rooted to it lately—hadn't just fallen apart. "Very, very soon."

13 GINNY

I shot up as soon as I heard the front door slam. My head felt heavy, my mind muddled. I blinked the sleep from my eyes and looked around, then glanced at the clock.

What time is it?

I struggled to read the numbers on the clock with a heavy head and blurry vision. Suddenly, the silence in the house hammered into my chest.

"Skylar?" It was just after two. Cam wasn't supposed to be home for hours and the front door had just opened. Where was my daughter?

I rushed through the living room and toward the front door, searching for her as I went. "Skylar?" I called again, this time louder and shriller as I reached the entranceway. I pulled open the front door and rushed out onto the porch.

The yard was empty, the front porch bare.

Where is she?

My head pounded with fear, my heart thudding so loudly in my ears I could hear nothing else.

No.

No.

No.

Please, no.

"Skylar, where are you?" I bounded across the porch and into the yard. I'd definitely heard the front door slam shut, hadn't I? Maybe I'd just been confused. Could I have dreamed it?

I spun circles in the yard, then turned back to face the house and rushed back toward it. I imagined opening the door and finding her waiting there for me, safe and sound. My heart filled with hope at the possibility.

I couldn't lose her. I'd never forgive myself.

No longer tired, I pulled open the front door and hurried forward into the kitchen. "Skylar?"

She wasn't there, wasn't under the table, wasn't beside the window where she liked to sit and look out at the yard. She wasn't in the pantry where she often hid while she and Cam would play hide and seek.

I felt tears in my eyes as I made my way down the hall and toward her bedroom. She rarely played in there alone, so I didn't hold much hope, but I pushed it open with a final prayer.

No.

It was empty. The room was untouched from when I'd made the bed that morning.

I checked the laundry room, the hallway, the bathroom, the bathtub. She was nowhere.

She was gone.

I'd lost her.

I made my way back out to the hallway, realizing I needed to check the woods and the garage. They were the only places left. I should've called Cameron to tell him what had happened, but I feared his reaction.

He'd never forgive me if something happened to her. If I lost her, if we couldn't find her, he'd never be able to look at me again. Back in the living room, I picked up my phone from the coffee table, spotting seven missed calls from him.

Had I really managed to sleep through them all?

Not yet ready to face what seemed inevitable, I shoved the

phone into my pocket and pulled open the front door. Then, I gasped.

Cameron was standing in front of me, Skylar in his arms. I gasped, reaching for her, but he backed away, his jaw firm.

"Oh my god," I cried out, tears welling in my eyes at the sight of her. She was okay. She was alive. She was safe.

Then, I looked at my husband and realized the same could not be said for me. I was not okay.

We were not okay.

"What are you doing?" I asked. He wasn't supposed to be home yet. Why was he here? Why did he have her?

"Sky, will you go play for just a second so I can talk to Mommy?"

"I play wiff you!" she cried in protest.

"I'll be right there," he promised, kissing her cheek. He placed Skylar on the ground and—though I was sure she was going to argue—she walked off somewhat begrudgingly, moving past me and into the house. Then, Cameron nodded his head toward the front porch swing.

I sulked toward it, feeling like a child on my way to an inevitable punishment. I wanted to ask what was happening, but I was scared to admit I didn't know.

"I called you ten times," he said firmly as I sat down. He stood in front of me, his arms folded across his chest.

"I didn't have my phone on me." It had only been seven times, but I wasn't going to argue.

"You were asleep."

"I—" So, he knew. He knew everything.

"You were supposed to take her to the session today, so I called to see how it went and you didn't answer. Do you have any idea how terrified I was? I thought you'd been in an accident. I thought something terrible had happened. I ran through every possible scenario—"

"I'm sorry, I didn't even realize I'd—"

"You promised me you could handle this, Ginny. You promised me—"

"I can! I just dozed off. It must've only been minutes—"

"Minutes were all it took for me to come into our house and walk out with our child. Don't you understand that? It could've been anybody. Someone could've walked in and taken her, and you would've slept through it all." His eyes were steely and frenzied, his body squared toward mine. He was furious, practically trembling with outrage, and I couldn't blame him.

"I'm sorry. I don't know what happened. I was awake. I didn't even feel tired. You know how the sessions make me. One minute I was awake, and the next, I was gone. I didn't mean for it to happen—"

"But it did, and that's the issue. When you said you were going to have a session in the middle of the day so you could bring her for Alex to evaluate, you assured me you'd stay awake. That you'd protect her. That's your only job, Ginny, and you failed. You failed us. You failed her. Don't you realize how horribly this could've gone?"

"Of course, I do!" I was crying then, angry at myself for letting this happen, angry at him for being angry at me.

"She could've burned down the house, climbed on the counter and fallen, wandered outside and gotten taken, answered the door for a stranger, found a knife or scissors and gotten hurt, filled up a bathtub and fallen in. There are any number of ways today could've gone tragically wrong."

"I didn't mean for it to happen. I didn't plan to fall asleep. And she's fine."

"Yeah, thanks to me. It's always thanks to me. The only reason our daughter is alive anymore is thanks to me—"

"I brought her into this world—"

"Yeah, and you've made sure we all know what a suffering that was for you, trust me."

"I didn't mean to fall asleep."

"Maybe you should go stay with your parents for a while," he said, his voice calm and sure.

"What? You don't mean that!"

Nothing about his expression told me that was true. He did mean it; I could see that plain as day. "It's too much for you. This is all too much for you, I see that now. But I'm not sure I can help you anymore. I can't take care of you and Skylar and keep everything going."

"Cameron, please. Please don't do this. It was an accident. I never meant for it to happen. Please, I'll do better." I stood up, grabbing onto his shirt with my fists.

He pulled my hands down and moved back away from me. "Let me go, Ginny. Just"—he huffed out a sigh—"just let me go."

"Please—"

He was already gone, turning away from me to walk toward the house. Through the glass of the door, I saw Skylar standing there, watching the events unfold. She stared at me in horror, one finger in her mouth.

I'd failed them both in so many ways. I wanted to fix it. I wanted to make it all okay again. I just didn't know how.

———

I didn't leave, though I don't know if that makes me brave or cruel. Maybe Cam was right. Maybe it would've been easier on everyone if I'd just left. But I couldn't. I couldn't give up.

I wanted to get better.

I would get better.

I stayed in my room for the rest of the evening, dozing off and on as I tried to wait up for Cameron to come to bed. I'd planned out what I would say, the speech I would offer him as an apology for the mistake I'd made.

I knew he needed space. I knew he needed a moment to process what had happened, but I wanted him to know that I understood the gravity of it all.

I understood that he'd saved her from what could've been a fatal mistake on my part.

I'd almost lost my child, and I'd never forgive myself or forget that it had occurred, but I wouldn't lose either of them without a fight.

I tried to think back to what had happened. I remembered feeling tired, and the slight headache that had come over me, but when I sat on the couch, watching Skylar play with her blocks in the floor, I hadn't been close to falling asleep. I'd promised myself a ten-minute break to rest and then I'd get back up and finish cleaning behind the sofa.

But then, nothing. My next memory was the sound of the front door shutting.

I pictured Cam coming into the house, terrified that I wasn't answering the phone, and finding me asleep on the couch. Was Skylar still playing or had she moved on to something else? Had she tried to wake me up?

Guilt filled my stomach like a balloon, its weight heavy and uncomfortable as I pictured him scooping her up and walking out the door.

It could've been anyone, he was right.

It could've been someone who meant to harm her.

I closed my eyes, feeling the tears streaming down my cheeks as I felt the heavy weight of sleep descend on my body.

When I opened my eyes again, night had fallen. The room was dark, the house silent. I reached my hand behind me, feeling across the bed for the lump of my husband's body.

He wasn't there.

I was alone.

I brushed a tear as quickly as I felt it fall. He'd slept in the guest bedroom, perhaps. Or maybe in the living room. I needed to get up, to get to him, but I couldn't.

I couldn't make myself do anything. I was too tired. My head was too heavy. I lifted my head, and it fell back onto the pillow almost immediately.

That's when I heard it.

Or, more precisely, *her*.

A laugh. A woman's laugh from somewhere in our home.

I tried to open my eyes. Tried to find focus so I could understand what I was hearing. Had I actually heard it? My head was so heavy, my thoughts so coated with sleep, I couldn't be sure.

But then, I heard it again. Yes, I was sure this time.

At least, I thought I was. Truth be told, I couldn't be sure of anything. I tried to lift my head again, my vision blurring, temple throbbing. My head dropped to my pillow without volition, the room beginning to spin.

I squeezed my eyes shut, trying to focus. Why was I so tired? Why couldn't I make myself get out of bed? When I opened my eyes again, the room was still spinning. I was going to be sick.

I opened my mouth, trying to call to him, but found myself unable to summon my voice. Panic and exhaustion coursed through me, fighting to claim their stake.

Eventually, I felt the familiar wave of sleep washing over me. As I went down, one thought repeated on an endless loop in my head: *What was that? Who is in my house?*

14 CAMERON

The next day, I was up before Ginny. I got Skylar dressed, helped her brush her teeth after a quick breakfast, put cream in her hair, and carried her out to the car.

There had been a few times since she was born that I'd had to take her into work with me. It wasn't ideal, especially now that she was old enough I couldn't just lay her in a bassinet in the corner of my office, but I would have to make do.

I couldn't trust Ginny to keep her anymore. That was just the cold, hard truth. As much as I loved my wife, I couldn't overlook what she'd done, or forget how badly she'd hurt me. And it was for the last time.

I could put up with a lot of pain on my end, but I wouldn't place my child in harm's way, even if the harm came from her own mother.

So, we drove to work, singing songs and talking aimlessly about the birds that flew past our car and the clouds in the sky. It was easy with Skylar. We could talk for hours about a dog she'd seen in a commercial or a child who'd worn the same shoes as her in the store.

With Ginny, things weren't ever just fun and light and happy. They were complicated. Painful.

I wanted things to work between us, but I was realizing I was going to have to accept that it just wouldn't.

When we arrived at the office, I made my way inside with Skylar's hand in mine. I set her up a space in the corner of my office, blocking it off with boxes that she could play with and laying out the toys and books we'd brought from home to keep her entertained.

"Daddy's got some work to do this morning, okay? You just play right here until I'm done, and if you're a good girl, maybe we can get some ice cream in a bit."

She giggled, clapping her hands together happily as she sat down, opening a book. "Look, Daddy! Ice cream!" She pointed to a child eating a popsicle on the page, and I smiled at her encouragingly.

"That's right, sweet pea." Then, I made my way toward my desk, laying my laptop bag on top as I pulled out the computer and began sorting through the files I'd taken home with me.

It was hard to concentrate, as every time I'd find one train of thought, Skylar would say or do something to draw my attention to her, and I'd lose it. I'd become well-practiced at this when she'd first been born, but I'd found a false sense of security with Ginny seeming to do so well lately, and I seemed to have forgotten the trick to keeping focused.

After a few painful hours, my phone buzzed from inside the pocket of my suit jacket. I pulled it out, spying Ginny's name and placing it face down on my desk.

I didn't want to be cruel to her. Honestly, I didn't. But I couldn't take it anymore. It hurt too badly to constantly hope that she'd gotten better, only for her to prove me wrong again.

It felt selfish to give up on her, to leave her when she needed me, but I had to choose my child. If I didn't, what did that say about me?

She called three more times before lunch, but each time, I ignored the call. I'd asked her to go stay with her parents for a while, to give us time to think and calm down, but she'd insisted we could work it out. The truth was, I just didn't have the strength to argue about it anymore. Given time, I thought she'd realize it wasn't working, too.

"Mr. Hale?" a voice came over the speaker on my phone, startling me during a moment of true focus. It was my secretary, Brandon.

"Yes?"

"Uh, you have a visitor, sir." *A visitor?* "Your wife's here to see you," he added.

I stood up, moving around my desk and peeking through the blinds to look out into the lobby. Sure enough, Ginny was standing just outside, dressed in jeans and a sweater, her long hair thrown back in a messy ponytail. Her eyes were puffy with tears.

As much as I wanted to send her away, I couldn't make a scene at work. Instead, I pulled open the door, offering her a small, stiff smile.

When she saw Skylar in the corner, she began to cry again.

"Hi," she said, though I wasn't sure which one of us she was saying it to.

"Mommy!" Skylar exclaimed from the floor, waving her hand, though she made no effort to leave the safe space I'd created for her.

Ginny watched her playing for a moment before looking up at me. "I was hoping to talk about what happened yesterday."

"We can talk about it at home. I have work to do. You shouldn't have come here."

"I was worried if I didn't, you might not come home." I swallowed, not mentioning that the thought had crossed my mind once or twice. "You didn't tell me you were bringing her."

"I didn't think I had a choice."

Her shoulders fell, the first tear spilling over onto her cheeks. It broke my heart to see her crying. Killed me to know I was causing her pain. But didn't she see what she was doing to me? I'd given up so much to help her, but I couldn't continue to be the martyr. At some point, everyone has to draw the line.

"Cam, please... Please forgive me. I didn't mean to fall asleep. It will never happen again. I shouldn't have done the session during the day, but I didn't think anything would happen. We didn't discuss anything, delve into anything that should've made me tired. I thought it would be okay, but it was my fault. I understand how upset you must be with me, but please, please don't shut me out." Her eyes darted back and forth between mine, begging me to forgive her. "Say something, please," she said after the silence had dragged on for too long.

"I know you didn't mean to. But that doesn't make it okay."

"Of course, it doesn't."

"I just need time," I said. "I'm trying to do the right thing here, but I can't keep doing this, Ginny. Not if it means I'm putting our child in danger."

"I would never hurt Skylar."

"I know you don't think you would, but your behavior can be so unpredictable sometimes. Especially lately. You're hot and cold; one moment you love us, the next minute you feel suffocated by our expectations."

"Suffocated by your expectations?" Her eyes were wide. "What does that mean?"

"You know what it means."

"Cam, I don't feel suffocated by you. I love you. I love Skylar."

"That's not what you said!" I raised my voice, then lowered it back down. I couldn't allow her to get me worked up. I needed to maintain my composure, especially with Skylar watching.

"What do you mean? When did I say that?"

"You don't even remember?" I scoffed.

Her brow furrowed, outright confusion on her expression. Had she really forgotten? Had she said it so many times she'd lost count? Or had she said so many terrible things about me that particular one had gotten lost in the shuffle?

"I have no idea what you're talking about," she said finally.

I scoffed just as my phone began to ring. "I don't have time for this, Ginny. I have to take that. I'm late for a conference call."

"Are you leaving me?" she asked, as I started to walk away.

"I think we need time apart, yes. You should leave."

"We need time apart because of what I did? Or because of her?"

"Leave Skylar out of this," I demanded, infuriated by the sneer with which she said the word *her*.

"I'm not talking about Skylar," she said firmly. My phone had stopped ringing, and I could focus on my wife again, though my heart was pounding in my ears as I realized how late I was for the call. "I'm talking about the woman you're cheating on me with?"

My head jerked backward. "Cheating on you? What on earth are you talking about?"

"I know about her," she said firmly. "If you're leaving me for her, you could at least be honest. Don't make me feel like it is all my fault if you've fallen for someone else."

I gave a dry laugh. "Are you kidding me? You think I have time to carry on an affair in between running a house, keeping a career, raising a child, and managing everything going on with you? Hell, I *wish* I had the time for an affair."

She scowled. "Don't pretend like I'm crazy. I know you've been seeing someone."

"Don't put words in my mouth. I never called you crazy, but hey, *if the shoe fits*." I regretted the words the instant they left my mouth, but they were already out. She sucked in a sharp breath, her eyes widening even further, and she stared at me, her shoulders rising and falling with heavy, uneven breaths. "I'm sorry, Gin. I didn't mean that." I reached for her arm, but she jerked it away.

"I am *not* crazy," she said, her nostrils flaring wildly.

"I know you aren't. I'm just—" My phone began ringing again, cutting me off. "Look, I know you aren't crazy. That was a"—I looked at Skylar to be sure she wasn't listening, then spelled my next word anyway—"s-t-u-p-i-d thing to say. I would never purposefully hurt you. I'm just hurt right now."

"I know you are," she said, shaking her head, "but I don't want to lose you. I can't lose you, Cam. I love you."

She fell into my arms, and I let her, stroking her back gently. "I don't want to lose you either." It was the truth. I loved her. Despite all she'd put me through, I loved her. "Look, we're going to be okay, okay?"

"Are you sure?"

"Mr. Hale?" Brandon was on the intercom again.

"Daddy, look!"

"I-Brandon, give us just a minute, okay?"

"Neil's on line one."

"Can you tell him I'll call him back?"

Ginny pulled away from me, brushing a finger under both eyes. "No, I'll go. I'll take her, and we can go."

"No," I said, too quickly. "No, she's okay."

She was crushed by my words. I saw that plainly on her expression. "Cam, I can do it. I swear to you I can."

"I know you can, but I promised I'd take her to get ice cream," I said, trying to come up with a lame excuse. Did I trust my wife? *No.* It was the sad, heartbreaking truth. I hadn't trusted her for a long time, and yesterday cemented that.

She didn't buy the reasoning, but she didn't argue. Instead, she turned away from me. I didn't miss the sight of new tears in her eyes, though she tried to hide them. "I'll see you at home?"

I nodded. "Yeah, you'll see us at home."

She shut the door with a blown kiss to Skylar, and I huffed out a heavy breath. "Okay, Brandon, send the call through." The phone rang in an instant, and I got back to work, too busy to process everything that had happened.

Was I planning to leave my wife?

The truth was, I still hadn't made up my mind. The option had always been there in the back of my mind. My plan if things ever got to be too bad. But, at least for now, she didn't need to know that.

15 GINNY

When Cam got home that night, I'd showered, gotten dressed, applied makeup, and curled my hair. I'd put in effort I hadn't in years, trying hard to make him see how serious I was about what I'd said.

I was going to be better. I was going to prove to him he could trust me.

As much as I tried to ignore it, I still had the faint memory of the woman's laughter in my head. She'd been in my house last night. I was sure of it.

A woman Cameron had invited over. Was he having an affair? Was it a woman from work? Was it someone I knew? I ran over the endless possibilities in my mind, each one more excruciating a thought than the last.

I couldn't blame him for wanting to leave me, really. Not after everything I'd put him through, but now I needed to make it right. As much as it hurt me, I was prepared to ignore the pain, push through, and convince him that I could be what he wanted. That I could be the woman he fell in love with.

I heard the two of them in the kitchen as I made my way down the hall. When I appeared, Cam hardly looked twice at me, still lost in conversation with Skylar.

When he finally did look up, his eyes were wide. He cocked his head to the side slightly, then looked around the room. When his gaze fell back on me with an expression that seemed like he thought he might be being pranked, he grinned.

"Special occasion?"

"No, not really. I just wanted to dress up."

He nodded, tucking a hand into his pocket as he focused every ounce of attention on me finally. "You look really pretty, Ginny."

"Pretty dress, Mommy!" Skylar cried in agreement.

"Thank you, sweet girl." I bent down awkwardly, trying to keep my clothes and hair from getting rumpled as I held out my arms. She watched me, taking a step in my direction, then another. After that, she launched forward, nearly knocking me backward with her hug.

I laughed, patting down her hair as she hugged me tighter. "How was your day with Daddy?"

"Look!" she cried, pointing behind her. "I drawed a picture!" She stepped back, pulling a piece of paper from Cameron's hand and passing it to me.

I stared down at the scribbles made from pens and highlighters and grinned. "I really like how you did this." I pointed to a specific scribble, something I'd seen Cameron do over and over again.

She grinned up at me with pride, and I felt my heart swell. I was doing it right. Could Cameron see that? When I looked up at him, he was scrutinizing me, his expression unreadable.

"Are you both hungry?" I asked. "I made baked chicken and mashed potatoes."

"We stopped on the way home," he said simply. "She wanted ice cream, and I didn't expect you to cook."

"She had ice cream for dinner?"

"For dessert. I told you I was taking her."

My stomach tightened. "Where did you go?" The silent question weighed on my mind: *Whom did you go with?*

"We just stopped through the drive-thru. I brought your meal home." He moved his jacket from the table, revealing a bag of take-out. "I'm sorry, Gin. I really didn't think you'd go to all this trouble."

"It's okay." I refused to let my smile fall. "This will all keep until tomorrow anyway. Thank you for ordering for me."

He passed the bag to me, but I didn't look inside. "I'll just get this all put away, and then maybe we can go for a walk together. What do you say?"

He shook his head just as Skylar yawned. "Actually, I need to get her in the bath. She skipped her nap today, so if I don't get her down soon, she'll be cranky."

"Oh."

"I'm sorry," he said, touching my hand gently. "If I'd known you had all this planned..."

"No," I said, cutting of the end of an unfinished sentence. "I understand. Maybe tomorrow."

His smile was small, and he nodded. "Alright, kiddo. What do you say? Quick bath and then we can watch a movie with Mommy?"

"Can I go underwater?" she asked, already running down the hall as Cameron jogged after her.

I stood alone in the kitchen, the food I'd been cooking all afternoon cooling on the stove while the bag of fast food rested in my hand. I made my way to the table slowly, sinking into a chair and resting my face in my hands.

What exactly was I expecting?

Whatever it was, it hadn't been this.

———

A few hours later, I'd put dinner away and I was sitting on the loveseat alone, watching the end of a cartoon Cam had turned on for Skylar. The two of them were resting together on the couch, Cam's feet up on the coffee table.

As the cartoon ended, I looked over at them, surprised to find Skylar had already fallen asleep.

They were both dressed in their pajamas, while I was still dressed up, waiting for Cameron to lead the way for the conversation I knew we needed to have.

He yawned and looked down, smiling when he saw Skylar's closed eyes. He reached for the remote, checking the time and scrolling through to find something else to watch.

"I guess I'm going to go change," I said, standing from the sofa and heading for the hallway. "Do you need anything while I'm up?"

He was quiet for a moment, so much so that I almost thought he was ignoring me, but finally, he grabbed my arm as I moved past him. I stopped, frozen as I waited for him to say something.

He slid out from under Skylar's head, laying her back down gently as he moved to stand in front of me.

"I'm really sorry."

I didn't know what he was apologizing for—the missed meal, the disappointing evening, the fight, the affair. But, in all reality, I couldn't bring myself to care. "I am too," I told him, my eyes already lining with tears. "I never meant to scare you or to put Skylar in any danger."

He pressed a finger to my lips, then lowered his mouth and replaced his finger with his lips. "I know you didn't. It was my fault, too. I knew how your sessions wear you out. I should've made a point to be home afterward to help you."

"This isn't your fault. You've done so much for me—"

"Because I love you, Ginny. I do. And I'd do it all over again. The way I've been treating you isn't fair. You didn't ask for any of this. No one did."

"I just want you to see that I'm trying. That's all this has been." I fell into his arms, and he wrapped me up, holding me against his chest. I wanted to talk about it all—the woman, the fight, the sessions—but none of it mattered.

Just my chest against his, our hearts beating as one. For a moment, we stood still, just breathing and existing together. When his arms finally dropped from my back, he pulled away slowly, looking down at me.

"Can we just forget this happened?" he asked. "And move forward from here."

I wanted to. I really, really wanted to, but I also needed to know that we could move forward—just us.

"Will you stop seeing her?" I asked the question with my eyes closed, unable to meet his gaze.

He was silent so long that I had to open my eyes to be sure I hadn't dreamed the entire encounter. When I opened my eyes, he was staring at me strangely. "I'm not cheating on you, Ginny."

"But... who was the woman?"

His brows drew down. "What woman?"

"The woman who was here last night."

He stepped back, looking around the room. "Here? At the house?"

"Yes." Why was he staring at me like this was coming out of the blue? I'd mentioned it to him just this morning. "Last night."

"There was no woman here, Ginny." He said the sentence slowly and with the same weight with which one might say *there are no ghosts in the house*.

But she wasn't a ghost. I heard the woman. It wasn't a dream. I knew what I was talking about... Didn't I?

"I heard her."

"When?"

The walls were closing in around me, my vision suddenly tunneling. I tried to remember the exact sound of her laughter, but suddenly it seemed far away and untouchable. The edges of the memory had begun to blur. "I... last night I heard her laughing."

"Laughing? When? In the middle of the night?" He seemed genuinely concerned now as he looked around again. "Why didn't you wake me?"

"You hadn't come to bed yet," I said. I'd checked, hadn't I? I'd checked to make sure he wasn't in bed... I couldn't remember. The memory seemed to be growing vaguer by the minute. Suddenly, what had been crisp and clear a moment ago was now a foggy mess. Maybe it *had* been a dream, after all.

He took hold of my shoulders, meeting my eye. "Sweetheart, it must've been a dream. There was no one in the house last night, okay? Just me, you, and Skylar."

I stared at him, wanting to believe him, but how could I? Worse, how could I believe myself? What was true anymore? Had I really just imagined it all? Had it been nothing more than a dream?

The edges of reality had begun to blur even more in my mind.

"I'd never cheat on you," he said, then pulled me into another hug. The conversation was over, I knew, because what else was there to talk about? "It was only a dream."

I nodded into his chest, my own memories feeling foreign and misguided. It's a strange thing, not even trusting your mind to tell you the truth, but as I breathed in his earthy scent, my head feeling heavy and full, the memory of the laughter was all but gone and I'd almost convinced myself he was telling the truth.

Almost.

16 CAMERON

"Do you want anything while I'm up?" I called from the kitchen.

"A glass of wine would be nice," came the reply.

I opened the cabinet and pulled down two glasses, an orange bottle near the windowsill catching my eye as I placed them down. I picked up the bottle, shaking it as I realized it was still full.

I picked the medicine back up and walked toward the living room, standing in the doorway.

"When was the last time we refilled these?" I could see the date on the label, so if she tried to lie, I'd know.

She stared at me, then at the bottle of pills, squinting her eyes as if trying to make out what they were. She was playing dumb.

"Oh, I don't know. A while ago, I guess."

"More than a month ago," I said, pointing out the date. "And it's almost completely full."

"I've cut back." She focused her attention on the TV again, as if the conversation was over.

"On whose advice? Alex's?"

"No. My own," she said, matter-of-factly. "I've been feeling better. You said it yourself last week, I haven't had a bad day in nearly two months. We're coming up on four months of therapy, and I've made real progress. Alex thinks so too. I'm ready to be back to normal."

"But you can't just cut out your medication. That stuff has to be done with a doctor's guidance. A real doctor. You could throw off all your progress if you don't do this right. Did Alex tell you to do this?" I demanded.

"No, I said she didn't. Of course not. And she *is* a real doctor, but I am capable of making my own decisions."

"But this affects us all."

She whipped her head around to look at me, white-hot fury seething in her eyes. "Do you think I don't know that? I don't want to be dependent on the meds. You knew that when I agreed to take them in the first place. Now that I'm in a better place, I want to slow down on them."

"Slow down, sure. But not stop entirely. And not without any heads-up to the people in your life. This is something we should be talking about."

"We are talking about it right now," she said simply, adjusting on the couch and pulling one leg up underneath her. "Look, I wouldn't have done this if I didn't think it was the right thing to do. The medicine makes me feel foggy and out of sorts. I've felt so much clearer since I've been off of it."

"What does Alex think about it? Or Dr. Gates?" The prescribing physician. Surely, he'd have a few thoughts.

"They don't know yet and, listen..." She patted the couch, and I moved forward, sitting next to her. Despite my fears, I had to admit, she *did* seem better lately. She'd been in a better mood. I'd seen her playing with Skylar more often. Maybe she was right. "I'm thinking about quitting therapy, too."

"What?" I felt as if I'd stepped into an alternate reality. "What are you talking about? After you made such a big deal about me suggesting it? Why would you quit?"

"Because I don't know if there's anything else she can do for me. I'm feeling much better. She's helped me develop a stronger bond with Skylar. And with Gary leaving your firm, I know you're needing to pick up some of the slack. Your bosses have been so great, but we can't keep inconveniencing them because of me. Not if we don't need to anymore."

"Don't worry about my job. I'm taking care of it."

"I just don't want to add any extra stress to our situation. I've taken this time for me and it's been amazing, but now that I'm feeling better, I want to step back and help out more. You've done so much for us over these past few years. I'm feeling ready to help. That's what you want, isn't it?"

I put a hand on the side of her face. "I want your help, yes. Of course, I do. But I want you to be healthy. I don't want you to do something spontaneous that could derail all the progress you've made."

"I wouldn't do that. I've thought this through."

"How much have you thought this through? Where is this even coming from? Why haven't you told me?" There was something in her eyes I was struggling to read. What wasn't she telling me?

"I told you before that I want to take some of the stress away from you. I'm trying to be better, to do better. I can't do that if I'm constantly sleeping my evenings away and feeling foggy. I want to take the progress I've made and go the rest of the journey without crutches."

"They aren't crutches—"

"They feel like it to me," she said, her voice catching. "I didn't need them before Skylar. So, why can't I be okay without them now? I've dealt with my feelings until I'm blue in the face. I've talked through and processed every bit of trauma. At this point, therapy is just a catch-up of what's going on. I don't feel like I'm making any new progress. I think I'm done. She's done her job. And, as much as I love seeing Alex, it doesn't feel like it's necessary to pay her to hang out anymore."

I studied her. It was all I wanted. To have her back. But was it too good to be true? I'd seen the false highs before. The weeks or months of good only to be followed by a crash of bad. Alex's previous warnings about how badly Ginny needed therapy flashed through my mind.

"I think you should see what Alex and Dr. Gates think before you make any rash decisions. I respect what you're saying, but I just want to make sure you're doing it the right way."

"It's my choice," she said firmly.

"And it affects us all."

"What, because you're going to make me leave if I don't stay on them? That was what you threatened before, isn't it? I have to take the pills, or you'll leave? Except that when I take the pills and do the therapy, suddenly you're all too concerned about how much I sleep. There's no winning with you, is there?"

"Where is all of this coming from?" I demanded, feeling like I'd stumbled into the middle of an argument rather than the beginning.

She pulled away from me, her hands up near either side of her face. "I'm just so sick of feeling like I'm walking on eggshells with you, Cam. You tell me that you want me to take it easy with therapy, that you're concerned about how it's affecting me, and then when I decide to back off because I want to be with you more, you suddenly decide that I'm moving too fast. You told me I should stop months ago!"

"And you didn't want to, so I agreed we'd make it work. I'm not saying you should stay or go. I'm only saying you should talk to Alex and your doctor before you make any big decisions."

"And if I don't?"

I swallowed, trying to understand what she wasn't saying. "If you don't, what?"

"Are you going to leave me?"

"I... Where is this coming from?"

"Answer the question, Cam."

"I just want you to be healthy. I want you to take care of yourself. I'm not trying to threaten you or fight with you, but I do expect a heads-up with this sort of thing."

"Well"—she shrugged one shoulder—"here's your heads-up.

I'm back, Cam. I'm back, and I'm staying. I'm fighting for who I used to be. Who *we* used to be." She poked my chest, a sly look in her eye. "Do you remember those people?"

I grinned halfheartedly. "Vaguely, yes."

"Well, I think it's about time they returned, don't you? I miss who we used to be. We were better then. Younger. Happier."

I poked my expanding gut. "Thinner." She shrunk away from me at the comment, but I pulled her closer. "I liked those people. But I love who we are now. I love our family."

"Are you sure?" she asked, her voice trembling. I realized then, despite what I'd believed, she hadn't forgotten about the woman she'd heard in the house. She hadn't put the incident out of her mind, and this must've been some sort of plot to convince me that she was all I needed.

She didn't realize that she'd already lost the battle. She'd lose every battle for the rest of time.

I loved my wife, but I needed our daughter.

Whether or not Ginny could ever accept being second best, I still wasn't sure. But, if she was willing to try, so was I.

"Yes," I promised, hoping she bought the lie. "What we have is perfect."

After all, I had my backup plan in place if things went south.

17 GINNY

At the next session, I'd finally worked up the nerve to tell Alex how I was feeling.

"I've decided I want to go off my medication," I told her, staring at a speck of mud on the carpet.

I watched her nod slowly in my peripheral vision. "Okay... And why have you decided that? Have you been having side effects?"

"They just make me feel sort of foggy," I said. "I'm not as sad as I used to be, even on the bad days, but I don't feel like I laugh as much either. The good days used to be really good, but now every day just feels kind of... dull... is maybe the way I'd describe it."

She blinked slowly, her hand clutching the base of her neck. When she spoke, her tone was cautious, filled with concern. "How long has this been going on?"

"Always," I said with a shrug. "Since I was prescribed them."

She twisted her mouth in thought, dropping her hand from her neck. "You never mentioned it before."

"I just thought that was how I was supposed to feel on them... That was what Dr. Gates told me. That it was normal."

She let out a steely breath, looking away and nodding thoughtfully. "Okay, I'm glad you told me. It could be normal, but we definitely would want to try a different medicine to see if it made you feel less foggy." Her eyes met mine again. "Have you discussed wanting to try a different medication with your doctor since you told him about those symptoms?"

I chewed my bottom lip, looking down. "Not yet. I just made the decision that I want to stop altogether a while ago. I told Cam last night, but he wanted me to tell you and see what you think."

She moved her hand toward me, leaning forward and weighing it in the air between us. "I appreciate you telling me, but I'd just note that it's generally not a good idea to quit any kind of medication on your own." She withdrew her hand. "I'd recommend sticking with your medication until you can get in to see your doctor. He may be able to adjust your dose some, or, like I mentioned, try a different kind, rather than just having you cut it out entirely. We need to find a balance for you."

I picked at the skin near my thumbnail, not entirely listening. I'd already made up my mind, and there was nothing that anyone could do to change it. "I'll talk to him," I said flatly.

"Good. How are things with Cameron? I know we said last time you were going to carve out time in your schedule for just the two of you... Have you been able to initiate that?"

An easy smile played on my lips without warning. "Yes, actually. Last night, after we left the park, I gave Skylar her bath early and let her lay in bed and watch TV until she fell asleep, so Cam and I had an extra hour to spend together."

"And how did it go?"

I felt heat rush to my cheeks. "It was nice. You know, we're still in kind of a weird place. Between Skylar and work and the house and life in general, we stay so busy. He still hasn't completely forgiven me for..." I trailed off, hoping she'd understand.

To my relief, she did. "You've apologized for what happened with Skylar. Cameron knows you didn't mean to fall asleep. You still believe he hasn't forgiven you?"

"Not entirely, no. I mean, he doesn't bring it up as much

anymore. He's not using it against me like he was. But he's still been cold and distant. I can't say that I blame him, it's just—"

"Cameron's allowed to feel anger—fear, even—over what happened. It's completely natural. But it happened two months ago, Ginny. If he hasn't forgiven you, have you forgiven yourself?"

I looked down, tucking my hands in my lap. "I don't think I ever will."

"You have to." Her tone was firm. "You two will never move past it—you'll never give him permission to forgive you—if you can't forgive yourself. If you keep feeling guilt over it, you're handing that power to him. Is it doing either of you any good to bounce around the subject, sheltering each other from your feelings?"

"I feel like I will seem callous if I allow myself to move on before he has."

"What you did wasn't deliberate. You both know that. But if you continue on this way, I'm afraid the divide between you two will only grow. It will always be the unspoken truth between you. If you want his forgiveness, and you feel like you've earned it, it's time to make that clear to him."

I adjusted in my seat, meeting her eyes finally. "I'm starting to think I'm ready to do that."

A smile formed on her lips. "You are?"

"If not for last night, maybe I wouldn't be, but just those few hours reminded me of who we used to be. How he used to look at me. It showed me how far we've come, how hard we've both worked to get here. It made me remember why I don't want to lose him." I shifted. My knee had been bouncing nervously, seemingly of its own accord, and I stopped it. The room fell silent as I waited for Alex to respond. Had I sounded ridiculous?

"Did you tell him that?" she asked, her tone steady and calm.

"Not yet," I said, "but I will. I want him to know how much it meant to me that we were able to spend a little extra time together just the two of us."

"I think it could be really helpful to try and do that once a week. Without sitters, it can be even more tough, but what you did was brilliant. Spending time with your spouse alone is crucial for a happy marriage. That would be the perfect time for you to be able to talk everything out. Lay it all on the table and move on from there."

I inhaled sharply. "Speaking of spending time..." *Here goes nothing.* "I'm thinking about cutting back on therapy."

"How far back?" she asked without missing a beat.

"Cutting it out altogether, too." I winced. She was silent. Waiting. "It's just that our time together is so limited between his work schedule and taking care of Skylar. And now that I am feeling better, and you've helped me so much, I just think maybe it's time for me to step back and move on."

"I see..." She glanced down at her notes, reading something.

"I just want my life to go back to the way it was, and thanks to you, I finally feel like it can. I finally feel strong enough, healthy enough... You've given me such a gift, Alex. And, if it wasn't for you pushing me to do this, I know I'd still be struggling."

"I'm really happy for you. Truly, I am. You've made such progress with me over these past few months. I see that in the way you mother your daughter, the way you love your husband, and the way you talk about yourself. You should be really proud of all you've accomplished."

I met her eyes finally, shocked at her kindness, though I didn't know why. Alex was my friend first and foremost. Why would I choose to insult her by believing she'd be more worried about the loss of income than my happiness?

"Thank you. I've been so worried about how to tell you." My shoulders slouched with genuine relief.

"I'm glad you did. I don't blame you at all for wanting to get back to how things used to be. My only suggestion would be that we could taper off the sessions... Go to just once a week for a while, then every other week, then once a month. Maybe it would be an easier transition for both you and Cameron."

I didn't want to tell her that another reason I was considering quitting was because I suspected Cameron of having an affair. It was the one thing I hadn't brought up with Alex. As vulnerable as I'd allowed myself to be with her, admitting that I'd failed in my marriage enough for him to seek what he needed somewhere else, felt like the lowest low.

"I'd really just like to have more time with him, I think. It feels important right now."

She was slow to nod. "Okay. It's up to you, of course. I won't twist your arm about it." Was it my imagination, or had there been a bit of an extra bite to her tone?

"It's just that, between the tension about the day I fell asleep and everything else... I feel like the window is closing on my chance to save us."

She was silent, coaxing me to go on as she waited.

"I mean, not for me. I still feel the same way I've always felt about Cameron. It's him that I'm worried about. What if he decides he can do better? What if he wants to?"

She folded one leg over the other, staring at me intently. "Why would you ask that? Has he said something to make you think he's considering leaving you?"

"Not necessarily. It's just"—I fiddled with my hands in my lap —"a few months ago, I could've sworn I heard another woman in our house."

She leaned forward, a small line forming between her brows. "In your house? What do you mean?"

"I was half asleep—it was the middle of the night—but I could've sworn I heard a woman in our house talking to Cam." I looked away from her, knowing my eyes must be haunted by the recollection. "They were laughing about something."

"And you didn't go check to see what was going on?"

Had there been a hint of accusation in her tone then? "I, um, well, I wanted to. It's just that I was so tired. When I tried to sit up, it was like my head was too heavy. I couldn't make myself get out of bed."

"I see." She scratched her pencil across the paper in her hands, taking note of something. "When did this happen? Why didn't you mention it to me?"

"It was months ago and it hasn't happened since. I guess I've been embarrassed by it all. And confused, really. I was so tired, I can't be sure of what I heard."

"And what did Cameron say? Did you ask him? Maybe there's a reasonable explanation. Maybe a neighbor stopped by or—"

"I did ask Cam," I told her. "But he denied that it happened."

"Are you sure that it did?" she asked, pencil at the ready.

"I don't know..." I told her honestly. The truth was, the more time that had passed since that night, the less sure I became.

18 GINNY

I cleared my throat, realizing she was still waiting for me to elaborate.

"I *think* it did. But the memory is fuzzy. I was so tired, I guess it's possible I heard the TV going, or that I dreamed it entirely." I shook my head. "Maybe it was my subconscious warning me how close I am to seeing my deepest fear come true."

"Losing Cameron?"

I nodded. "More than losing him, watching him give up on me. Watching him decide he's had enough."

"Do you think that he has?"

"I'm terrified of it. That's why I need to focus on my marriage. Now that I'm feeling well enough to handle things on my own, now that I've processed all I can, I need to spend more time at home with my family. I need to make them a priority again."

She let out a small sigh through her nose. "I just want you to promise me you're not blaming yourself. What you've done here with me—what you've done for yourself—it's incredible, Ginny. You've clawed your way back from the darkness, and I don't ever want you to forget it. If Cameron can't see the work you've put in, that's on him. Not you."

"I'm so proud of myself," I told her. "Really, I am. And grateful to you for all you've done. This isn't about blaming myself. It just feels like it's time to move on."

She was still for a moment, but eventually, she nodded. "Alright then. I can't argue with that. I do want you to swear to me that you'll talk to your doctor about the medication. And remember there's no shame in attending therapy regularly and taking medication every day. I do it. So many people do. You have to do what's best for you and your situation, but please don't feel like you're failing because you're actively trying to keep yourself on track. If you ask me, the healthiest people are the ones who seek help when they need it."

"Thank you. I really appreciate that. I know I can always come back if I need to. And, it's not like I'm going to let you be rid of me completely. We can still take the girls on play dates and meet for coffee whenever you're free."

She tapped her pen on the notebook in her hands. "I'd like that a lot. So, are you officially firing me, or would you like to cut it down just a bit? Taper it off?"

"Could we try canceling the sessions for a while and see how it goes? Then, if that doesn't work, maybe we could try once a month or something less intense?"

"Of course. Whatever you want. You'll still reach out if you need anything, right? This is your friend asking, not your therapist."

"Yes, of course." I suddenly felt choked up by the prospect of not seeing her again soon. "Sometimes it feels like you're the only person I can talk to honestly about things."

"I hope we have done the work to build your confidence in your relationship back up enough that you can talk to Cameron, too."

"We have," I said, feeling tears in my eyes. I brushed them away. Why was I doing this? Why was I breaking down right now?

"What's going on?" she asked, sitting back in her chair. "You've already paid me for this hour, may as well use it. Talk to me."

"No, it's nothing. I don't know why I'm crying."

"Do you feel like you can talk to Cameron more now? From what I've seen, you guys have been laying the building blocks to re-establish trust and a solid foundation once again."

"Yeah, I can. I could always trust him. Cam's perfect, it's just—"

"No one's perfect," she corrected me.

"Well, he's extremely close. He's put up with so much."

"But he also made you feel guilty for taking care of yourself for coming to sessions."

"He's just got so much on his shoulders."

She nodded. "What about your mother? We've talked a lot about how close the two of you were when you were growing up. I know she lives far away, but I would think she, of all people, could understand what you're going through..."

I sniffled, feeling fresh tears. It was the one thing I'd managed to avoid talking about with her. The one thing I avoided talking about with anyone.

"No. She can't understand this."

"I think you'd be surprised—"

"My mom thinks I'm selfish for not appreciating Skylar more."

"Surely you don't believe that," she said breathlessly.

"She told me. Shortly after Skylar was born, Cameron asked my parents to come down and help. My mom was disappointed that I hadn't bonded with my daughter. She actually told me she thought I was being selfish." I swiped a tear away quickly. "She didn't mean it, of course. We had no idea what was going on at the time—that I had postpartum depression—and she's apologized for it so many times since then, but... It took away that trust, you know? I don't feel like I can be honest with her about certain things and, when we do talk, I feel like I'm walking on eggshells. I know she's sorry, but I can't get it out of my head. I can't make myself forget those words, the... the way she looked at me."

"I'm so sorry, Ginny. I can't imagine how that must've made you feel. I'm glad you've been able to talk it through with your mother and discuss things, but I can certainly understand why it would stick with you."

"It's just one of those things, I guess. She's never gone through it, so she didn't understand."

"She had an easier time of things? With her pregnancy?" She nodded slowly, her head cocked to the side with genuine interest.

"Oh, she..." I sniffled, pulling a tissue from the box on the table and dabbing my nose. "She couldn't get pregnant. I'm adopted."

"Oh! I didn't realize..."

"Yeah, they, um, they tried everything to have me, spent most of their life savings on IVF and a surrogate that lost their baby. In the end, they adopted me, and I was their little miracle."

She stared at me, almost as if waiting for me to go on, her body rigid, lips tight. When she realized I wasn't going to say any more, her shoulders loosened and she blinked rapidly, as if batting back tears. "That's such a heartbreaking journey for them. But a happy ending for you all."

"Yeah, so, you can understand why she has very little patience for anyone who doesn't live, eat, and breathe their children every moment of the day. I think I'm partly to blame for the issues my parents had. After I was born, my mom's mission in life, it seemed, was to take care of me. Their marriage became priority number two. I'm not blaming her. Or myself, for that matter. It is what it is, and they'd deny it if I ever brought it up, but that's what it seems like to me. She wanted me so badly she started to forget about my dad, and I think that was when he started working more. It was the one thing that couldn't break his heart."

"So you think he felt like he was being pushed away, rather than creating the distance on his own? Based on what you'd said before, I was under the impression he chose to be less involved."

"I'm not really sure how he saw it, honestly. But that's how it seemed to me. Like they could never really find common ground. Mom had me and he had his work."

She scribbled something down on her notepad. "Do you think that's why there's such a rift between you and your dad? Do you think he blames you for causing him to lose your mother... figuratively, of course?"

"I guess maybe I've always believed that somewhat. I know he loves me, but I think maybe I represent a time when his life got worse."

"And do you think Skylar does the same for you?"

The question caught me off guard, taking my breath away, and I shook my head. "I've never really thought about it." Had I, though? In a way, Skylar did represent one of the darkest periods of my life. When I thought of my daughter, was there an ache, deep down, a reminder of the pain and suffering I'd endured from the moment we found out she existed?

But how could I ever tell anyone that? Even Alex. How could anyone understand that I loved her despite all of the pain, but that didn't make the pain any less real.

"I notice a lot of patterns repeated from the way you've described your parents' marriage, to the way you describe your own. It seems to me that you play your father's role throughout some of your marriage, while Cameron has taken on more of the role that your mother played. The good news there is that you can take what you saw not working for them and put it to use. Build the relationship with your daughter and your spouse that your father never did. And, as you know, I'm proud that you've already started to do just that."

"I'm really trying," I said, letting new tears fall. Was I hurting Skylar inadvertently? Did she sense the wall I kept between us, even as I worked so hard to tear it down? Was her own wall a result of mine? Did she think Cam loved her more than I did? *Did he?* "I don't want to fail her. I don't want her to even question whether I love her."

A lump formed in my throat at the thought. What must Alex think of me? It was no wonder my mother had been so upset with me. What kind of a mother blames her child for the shortcomings of her own body? It wasn't Skylar's fault. Rationally, I knew that. I knew, somewhere deep down, that it wasn't mine, either. But that didn't stop the ache.

"You aren't failing her," she said firmly. "She's enormously lucky to have a mother who's committed to her mental health. You're a shining example to her, Ginny. And I know you're going to have a beautiful relationship, even more beautiful than you already have. She's a very, very lucky little girl."

I didn't feel like a shining example. And I didn't feel like Skylar was lucky. I felt like I was ruining any chance she had for a normal childhood. I felt like I'd failed her in every way. Suddenly, I could feel myself slipping backward. The self-deprecating thoughts were ones I'd believed I was finally rid of. But there they were, like old friends.

"Do you really think so? I'm not trying to beg for a compliment here, but I mean, you see a lot here and in your own life... Do you think I'm doing okay? Do you think all that I've gone through will damage her in some way?"

She paused, one side of her mouth drawn in. "I think all mothers damage their children in one way or another. Just like yours did when she reprimanded you for the way you behaved after Skylar's birth, just like mine did so many times... What separates the good mothers from the bad is the simple act of trying to do better. The mothers who care, who love their children, who worry about whether they're doing enough, those are the good ones. Trust me, my mother never once worried about whether she'd damaged me. You're a good mom, Ginny. You're doing just fine."

I smiled, my chest swelling with pride as I forced the last of the dark thoughts away. She was right. I'd done all I could do. And I'd continue to fight to keep my health in check so I could be there for Skylar. For Cameron. They deserved me at my best, and I couldn't let the anger and pain hold me hostage any longer. "Thank you. Honestly. For everything."

"You're more than welcome." She glanced at the clock and then at the watch on her wrist. "Oh, my. Where did the time go? It looks like our session is over. Is your mind still made up about canceling the next few sessions?"

"Yes, if that's okay," I said, patting my knees.

"Of course, it is." She jotted something down in her notebook. "But I'll do my best to leave our usual time slots open in case you change your mind. I'm always one phone call away."

"I appreciate that. Thank you. And we should make a plan to meet for coffee at some point."

"I'd love that." She stood, leading me from the room, and I swallowed down the lump in my throat. It wasn't as if I was leaving her for good. We were still friends. We'd still be in contact. Why was I feeling so upset?

"When you break the news to Cameron, will you tell him I've given the approval?"

"Yeah, I will. Why?"

She hesitated, chewing her bottom lip thoughtfully.

"Alex, what is it?"

"I don't want to say anything to cause problems. It's just that..."

"Tell me," I begged, my heart thudding in my chest as I waited for her to go on.

"I wasn't going to say anything, but after what you told me about worrying that Cameron will give up on you... Well, I just feel like you should know this. The day Cameron came to see me," she said, drawing out a long, steady breath. "Well, it's just, he sort of hinted that this was kind of the final straw for him. I told him that progress isn't linear and that you need to feel like you have a safe space to heal, and he wants to give you all of that, but I want to make sure he understands this is a good thing for you. For both of you. I know you've told me before that he insisted that you take your medication. I just don't want this to cause any problems for your marriage. I don't want this decision to cause either of you any stress. I know you want this to help, and I want that too, so I just think mentioning to him that I've given my approval might help lessen the blow."

I paused, not wanting to jump to conclusions. It sounded like she was saying this was some sort of ultimatum, though he'd never told me as much. Was he really so ready to give up on me if things hadn't worked out? Was I right to worry he was ready to give up? "You're saying he told you this was my last chance?"

"Not in so many words," she said carefully, then winced. "I shouldn't have said anything. This isn't my business. I was only trying to protect you and, after what you said earlier, I felt like I had to say something."

"No," I said, putting a hand on hers. "I'm glad you told me."

"Okay." Her expression softened with relief. "Just let him know it's a good thing. And, if you have any problems, or need me to talk to him, let me know."

I nodded, pulling her in for a hug, though my mind was racing with a million questions.

"I'll see you soon," I told her as she pulled open the door and let me walk out onto the porch. I waved a hand over my head, thinking of Cam and all that he was keeping from me. He'd told me he wanted me to quit the sessions, but he'd told her they were our final chance.

Had he really been so ready to give up on me?

Was that when the affair started? Was he planning to leave me? Had I saved us by a tiny margin? Had I saved us at all? Perhaps he was already falling for someone else. Someone healthy. Someone happy. Maybe I'd let him slip through my fingers without even realizing it.

Like every session, I was leaving with a pounding, throbbing sensation deep in my skull. Before I'd made it off Alex's street, I was already contemplating going back. I wanted to talk to her again, to tell her my new fears and worries.

In a way, I felt as if I'd forgotten how to exist without Alex's guidance. For months now, she'd been the one steering me through life, helping me to make every decision, both major and minor. She'd been the one to make me feel heard, safe, and understood.

More than anyone in my life, she believed in me. She saw the good through the bad. Unlike Cameron, she wouldn't give up on me. I knew I could trust her. Even more than I could trust him. Even more than I could trust myself most days. Moments ago, I'd been sure of my decision to cut out my sessions, but as I drew farther and farther from her house—my sanctuary—I was beginning to wonder if I'd made a terrible decision.

Then again, the only person who could tell me that was Alex.

How had I ever survived without her? How would I learn to survive again?

19 CAMERON

I'd just gotten Skylar down for bed when I heard the knock on the door. Ginny had been asleep for hours, so I darted down the hall, trying to halt the knocking I was afraid might wake either of them.

When I reached the door, flipped on the porch light, and moved the curtain aside, I saw a familiar face. I swung open the door with a bright smile. Seeing her lately just made me feel better. I didn't know whether I should feel guilty about that.

"Alex, hi! Sorry, I was just getting Skylar down. Come on in."

She stood in front of me, sunglasses holding back her hair despite the late hour, and held two paper cups in her hand. I resisted the urge to hug her.

"You're fine. I'm a bit earlier than usual. I had an errand to run after my last session, so I thought I'd just come straight over. I hope that's okay?"

"Yeah, of course," I said, resting against the door. "Come on in."

"How's Ginny?" she asked as she made her way past me and handed over the mug of tea. As she moved, I caught a hint of her perfume, a light scent I'd become familiar with during our sessions, one that made me feel instantly at ease.

"She's fine. Already out for the night, like usual. Thanks for this." I took a sip as I shut the door and led her through the foyer and then the living room.

"Always." She lifted the cup in her hand. "I guess you've had a chance to talk about what happened in our session today?"

"She mentioned that she's going to be cutting back on therapy for a while, yeah."

"Okay, good." She seemed relieved that I knew.

"And you don't think that's a good idea, based on the look on your face." I led the way into the kitchen.

"Well, it's not that I think it's a *bad* idea, I just want to make sure it's a *good* idea."

Once we'd made it to the dining-room table, I gestured toward her usual seat and waited for her take it. "Can I get you something to drink or..."

She chuckled, nodding toward the tea in her hands just as I realized my mistake.

"Sorry, habit."

She shook her head. "It's fine. Blame those charming Southern manners. We always think we have to give our guests something, don't we?"

"Yes, we do." I took a seat across from her, grinning. "Well, about the sessions, she said that she feels like she's dealt with most of the issues she needed to. And between actually coming to the sessions and being so exhausted afterward, it's taking three entire evenings out of our week. She really does seem better than she was."

"I'm glad to hear that." She paused. "She also mentioned cutting back on her medication."

"Yeah, she said it makes her feel foggy." What was the strange expression on her face? It was one I hadn't seen on those features before. Usually, she was light and carefree, but tonight, she looked troubled.

"Cutting out depression medication can be tricky, and it should be monitored by her doctor. I may be overstepping here—

and I told Ginny all of this too—but you know how she can be..."
She twisted her lips in thought.

"Stubborn," I agreed with a scoff. So, Ginny was stressing her
out, too. That particular club was beginning to get crowded.

"Exactly. I just worry that if she doesn't do this slowly and
correctly, she could really begin to backtrack after all the work
we've put in. I know neither of you want that, and I know she's
feeling really great lately, but bad days come out of nowhere.
Things resurface. Just today, we had a bit of a breakthrough on
something we'd yet to cover in our sessions."

The teasing of her statement formed a lump in my throat.
What sort of breakthrough? Was it about me? Had Ginny said
something negative about me? It pained me to think that Alex
might see me in any light other than the one I'd meticulously
painted for her myself. I shouldn't care, but I wanted Alex to like
me. Being with her, I felt like I was seventeen years old again,
trying to get a girl's attention. This time, I knew nothing could ever
come of it, but that didn't stop the desire for her approval from
filling me every time I saw her.

I glanced toward the hallway, in the direction where my wife
was sleeping. Had she acted strangely when she arrived home?
Colder, maybe? Was she angry with me for a resurfaced memory?
And, if so, what could it be? I fought against the urge to ask Alex to
tell me more.

"I shouldn't even be talking to you about this. I know that. And
I know we're keeping our sessions between us in order to protect
her, but I'd be remiss if I didn't tell you my concern."

She was trusting me with something she shouldn't. For some
reason, that made this session feel even more intimate than usual.
She'd broken a rule for me. I shook my head, trying to focus on the
conversation. "Which is that she's cutting everything out too fast?"

"Yes. I'd feel much better if I knew she was going to consult
with her doctor about lowering the dosage to wean herself off of the
medicine. I'd even suggest changing prescriptions to see if that
could help with some of the side effects she's been experiencing

before cutting it out entirely. I'm not as worried about the therapy, as it can be picked up at any time. Some people see it as a temporary thing while others use it as more of a maintenance. I know you were worried—"

"Let me cut you off," I said, a palm lifted in the air. "You don't have to convince me. I agree with you."

"You do?" Her relief was palpable.

"I do. I told her as much. If you're looking for where the idea came from, you're looking in the wrong direction."

She tucked a piece of hair behind her ear, giving me a better view of her long, slender neck. I looked down at the table when she spoke. "I'm sorry. I didn't mean to imply that you were pressuring her. I know you'd had your doubts about it in the beginning. I just wanted to make sure you understand the risks and that we're on the same page."

"We are," I told her, nodding slowly as I looked up. "Trust me, we are. Like I've told you, she really does seem to be getting better. I mean, we had the one day when she fell asleep while watching Skylar—"

"Which was more a mistake on my part than anything," she reminded me. We'd talked about the incident over and over as she helped me to process my anger with my wife. "I never should've suggested a daytime session."

"What I don't understand, is why her sessions make her so tired when mine never do." Was I just stronger than my wife? Did I handle therapy sessions so much better than the average person?

"Well, for one thing, your sessions aren't true sessions. We're talking over how you're feeling, how you're handling everything you've been dealing with, but we aren't doing it in a clinical setting. I'm here as a friend, because I care about Ginny and, by default, I care about you. We're only going skin deep with our discussions, talking about your marriage and your family, but we aren't digging into your childhood and your trauma, like I've had to do with Ginny. It's very different."

Oh. "So, you don't talk about our marriage in your sessions with her?" I asked.

She pressed her lips together giving me a sly, knowing grin. "You know I can't tell you that."

I sighed. I did know. She'd told me over and over again from the beginning. After the first time I went to Alex's office, she'd reached out to me and offered to come over after each of Ginny's sessions so we could discuss how I was handling everything I was dealing with. It seemed unnecessary, but she was persistent.

Now, months into our agreement, I wasn't sure how I'd ever survived without my evening chats with Alex. She was the only person I didn't have to hide our struggles from. The only person I could be completely honest with and not have to worry about judgement.

We'd only kept the sessions from Ginny because we were worried about Ginny feeling judged by us. In truth, the sessions weren't really about Ginny at all. We focused on my headspace, my struggles, my concerns. Three hours a week. It was the only chance I got to focus on my own problems, and though I'd been hesitant to dig in at first, I now found great comfort in being able to vent to Alex.

In truth, the idea of Ginny giving up her sessions, forcing me to give up mine, terrified me in a way I couldn't explain. I felt strangely dependent on Alex, in a way that was separate from my undeniable attraction to her. I wanted to ask her opinion on everything now. I wanted her to weigh in on every choice I made.

She was easy to talk to. *Easier to look at.* And I found myself drawn to her in a way I found confusing and endearing all at once. I'd never felt listened to like Alex listened to me. I'd never felt so understood and cared for. I knew it was her job. I knew I was nothing more to her than her client's husband, but with each session, I could feel us growing closer.

I just wondered if she could feel it, too.

"So, you mentioned getting back on her medication. Does that mean she's been off of it?" Alex asked, bringing me back to reality.

"She didn't tell you that?"

"She only said that she was considering quitting, not that she already had. That's incredibly dangerous. When did she stop?"

"This month, as far as I know." I stood and walked across the room toward the sink, picking up the bottle and carrying it back to the table. I twisted off the lid and poured the contents onto the table, counting them carefully while Alex examined the label. "There are seventeen left, so she's been taking them a little less than half the time, I think."

She nodded slowly and handed the bottle back to me so I could brush the pills into it. It was a moment or two before either of us spoke.

"How has she been doing? Really? Taking the pills half the time... Is she acting differently? More moody? Less moody?"

I thought back over the past few weeks, trying to recall any strange behaviors. "She's seemed normal to me." I let out a dry laugh. "More normal than she has in a long time. It feels like I have the old Ginny back, as strange as that is to say. Sometimes, over the months, I've caught glimpses of her, you know? Days or moments where I saw who she used to be, but lately, they seem to occur more than ever." It was true. Whatever Alex's magic was, she'd worked it on my wife as much as she had me. I'd never seen Ginny so happy. Never felt so happy myself. Was this what therapy did for people?

When she responded, her tone was cautious. "She's never going to be who she used to be, Cameron. She's a different person now. Her life has changed. Your life has changed. If you always compare her to the woman you met years ago, you're going to be disappointed every time."

Feeling as if I'd been scolded, I tried to recover. "I'm not trying to compare her to who she used to be, that's not what I mean. I just know she's gone through such a hard time, and it's nice to see her coming out of it and feeling good again. I missed seeing her smile."

Her eyes danced between mine. "I just think it's really impor-tant to control expectations here. She needs to know that you love her as much on a bad day as a good, and not that you're always waiting for the bad days to end."

"You expect me to enjoy the bad days?" I asked, feeling indignation forming a lump in my belly. "Honestly, it's all I can do to get through them. I don't show it. I put on a brave face and do everything I can to make it easier for her, but who's making it easier for me?" I pounded my fist on the table, overwhelmed with sudden bitterness. "I know you're trying to help her, but who's helping me through all of this?" I thought that was her, but now I was realizing I was wrong. She'd always be on Ginny's side, not mine. I'd misread everything.

"Isn't that what I've been trying to do?" she asked defensively.

I groaned, my fingers drawing into a fist again. "Sure, but it's not like there's some guidebook to tell any of us how we're supposed to be handling this. And every time I see you, you're telling me what I'm doing wrong, how I could support her more, but what about what I'm doing right?"

"I'm sorry—"

"No," I cut her off. It had been building up for so long that I needed to release it. Just moments ago, I'd wanted her to like me, so I'd kept my darkest thoughts hidden away, but in that moment, I couldn't bring myself to care. Someone needed to hear the things I'd never said aloud. "No. I'm not saying I need some pat on the back every time I'm a good husband, but it's really hard to be on this side of things, too. I have so much on my shoulders all the time. Trying to be a good dad, a good husband, keep my job, run the house... There's no space in this world we've created for me to take a day off or even just vent about how hard it is."

She was silent, watching me.

"So, excuse me for being excited to see her happy again. Because her being happy might mean that I can be who I used to be. Not the man who hasn't sat down for a football game on a Sunday afternoon in two years, not the man who mixes up clients' names at work because he has so much going on in his head all the time, not the man who hasn't been able to stop going, stop pushing, stop trying for even a second in the almost three years since we had Skylar." I stopped, heaving a heavy breath.

I was tired. God, I was tired, and no one seemed to notice or care. I didn't expect my needs to come before Ginny's, but I couldn't be expected to be selfless forever, either.

I could leave her. The thought was always there. The backup plan I'd formulated. My way out. I could leave my wife, take my daughter, and start fresh somewhere else. Skylar was young enough not to resent me, and my wife was ill enough not to be able to fight me properly. I had few doubts I'd be awarded full custody.

But was that what I wanted? Most days, the answer was no. I loved my wife. I wanted her to get better. To truly come back to me.

But on the hard days, the days where I felt like I could do nothing right, the days when I had no time to breathe, those were the days the plan came back to me. The reminder that I could free myself from this prison easily, if I wanted to.

It was always there.

It was always an option.

20 CAMERON

To my surprise, Alex touched my arm gently, bringing me out of my thoughts. When I looked up at her, there was a hint of understanding in her eyes.

"You're right. It is exhausting. And terrifying. I know all too well the toll it takes on a person."

She took another sip of her tea, and I did the same. When she spoke again, her voice cracked. "No one takes care of the caretaker. You've been strong for her for so long. I thought I was helping you to feel understood through all of that. I apologize if that isn't the case."

"No, it is, it's just... It's hard. It's all so damn hard." I shook my head, looking away as embarrassment over my outburst filled my chest. Alex was the one person who did seem to care about how I was dealing with everything. Why was I trying to push her away?

I looked back up at her, realizing maybe for the first time that she seemed to relate to me in a way no one else ever had. She'd been where I was. I could see that in the way she was looking at me, hear it in her voice. "You've had to take care of someone, too, haven't you? I mean, besides your clients." I huffed out a laugh. "And their husbands."

"Yes," she said with a nod and a small smile. "I was just a child, but I did everything I could to help her. In the end, it didn't matter."

"I'm so sorry." I suddenly felt as if I'd snapped on her for no reason.

"You have no need to apologize. You deserve to advocate for yourself. You deserve to have your needs met, too."

Something about her last sentence had my cheeks flaming with heat again. She drew her hand back from my arm, looking embarrassed.

"How, um"—she cleared her throat—"how are you dealing with everything today? How are you coping since we last spoke?"

"To be honest, I'm not really sure how I'm feeling. When she told me she wanted to quit therapy, I felt worried, of course. But hopeful, too. Like maybe it was the first step back to who we used to be. But it's never that easy, is it? I worry about seeing her slip back into the thick of things. I worry that we'll hit a point where I just can't do it anymore, you know?"

I paused. "I try not to think that way, but how can I help it? I've tried to forgive her for all she's done. I know it's not her fault, but after everything we've been through, I still harbor resentment for it. Maybe that makes me selfish, I don't know, but it kind of feels like my life is in this tunnel of just waking up, taking care of things, going to bed, and starting all over. We used to take vacations, go out to visit our folks. We used to take picnics in the woods and go down to the river. Now it's just like, how did we ever have time for that? Everything revolves around Ginny now. Her wants, her needs, her health. Is it a good day or a bad day? Is she happy? Is she struggling? No one can steal the focus from her, not even for a second."

I sighed. "And, God, that makes me sound like an ass, I'm well aware—"

"It makes you sound human," she said firmly. "And there's nothing wrong with that. What have you done lately that's just for you? Ginny has her sessions, she has days at the park with me—

even though Skylar's there, the visit is fun for us both. What do you ever do that's just for you?"

I raised a brow, thinking. "You mean that's allowed?" I asked with a laugh under my breath. The truth was, I couldn't think of a single thing. *Besides these sessions.*

"Adults are allowed to have fun, too. Especially ones who deal with as much as you've been dealing with."

"I'm not trying to seem weird when I say my favorite thing to do is play with Skylar. I really do enjoy it. Growing up, I was so close with my little sister, Margie. I'd always wanted to go into teaching as a kid. I loved being around children, but... once I got to be old enough, I realized parents don't trust men with their babies like they do women." I scowled. It was one of the most disappointing moments of my life, when I'd told someone I wanted to work with young children and they'd told me it would never happen.

"Well, I like to think times are changing," Alex said. "Men can do everything women can do, and all that jazz."

"Yeah, well... after that, I'd spent my whole life looking forward to the day I could be a dad. I wanted a whole litter of kids," I joked. "Enough to make a baseball team. I used to imagine the games of tag and kickball we could play. It probably seems silly." I looked down, rubbing my temple.

"It doesn't sound silly at all. It sounds really sweet, actually. So many dads don't want to be part of their family's lives, or want minimal involvement, so it's really special that you've made it such a priority."

"Thanks."

She tapped the table with her fingers, studying me. "Do you and Ginny plan to have any more children? Obviously, you want more, but have you talked to her about it?"

I shook my head, running a hand over my hair casually. "No. After all that's happened, it feels selfish to bring it up. Ginny's done having children. As much as I want more, after everything she went through for Skylar, I could never ask her to do it again."

She lifted her cup in the air, finishing off what was left. My head was beginning to spin with exhaustion as I looked at the clock. It was nearly ten—the time I'd usually head for bed—but like all of our previous sessions, I was in no hurry to see her leave. I liked talking to Alex. Not just because she talked for a living, which made her easy to converse with but because she really did seem to understand everything. There was no hiding with her. She knew all that I was dealing with, and she didn't judge me for it. Or Ginny, for that matter.

"Want some coffee?" I offered, standing from the table.

"Please." She passed the empty cup to me, and I grabbed mine, walking across the room and filling the coffee maker with water.

"Well, there's always adoption," she said finally, as I poured the grounds into the filter and pressed the button for it to begin brewing.

"Yes, there is." I spun back around to face her, resting my back against the counter as I waited.

"With Ginny being adopted, I would think that would be especially appealing to her."

"It is, I think. We've never talked about it in detail, but she has mentioned how much she'd love to foster or adopt."

"Was she in foster care, too?" she asked, curiosity piqued.

I shook my head, surprised she didn't know the answer to that question. "Not really. She was placed with her foster family when she was three, but that family ended up being Joselyn and Artie, the family that adopted her. So, she doesn't remember being in foster care, even though she technically was for... about a year and a half, I think it was."

"It sounds like she was very lucky. She might benefit quite a bit from taking in a child in need."

I nodded. "Maybe. I've always wanted my own kids, you know? But, if it's what I can have, I can't be picky."

She was still.

"That was a stupid thing to say. I'm sorry. I don't mean, I mean, of course, I'm so thankful my wife was taken in by a good family.

And I know it would be some sort of full circle thing if we could do that, too, but it's—"

"It's a big decision." She filled in the blank for me, nodding her head. "You don't have to justify it to me. It's not for everyone, and I know that. That's a really personal decision that would be between you and your wife."

"Yeah," I said with a nod, wanting to change the subject entirely. "What about you? Do you have any kids? The little girl at the park was your..."

"Niece, yes, that's Raven, whom I adore. But, no, I don't have any of my own. Kids were never in the cards for me."

"Why do you say that?" I turned around, refilling both of our cups before returning to my seat across from her. I passed her the cup, our fingers brushing slightly, making me hold my breath.

"Oh, we really shouldn't be talking about me. This is about you. And Ginny."

"Yeah, but I feel like I'm telling you so much, and I don't know anything about you."

"That's how it's supposed to be," she said firmly, though I caught a glimmer of playfulness in her eyes. "There are boundaries that shouldn't be crossed, even in pseudo-therapy-at-a-dining-room-table situations."

I snorted, leaning back as I teased her. "Now it's pseudo-therapy? I thought you said it wasn't therapy at all earlier. You said you were here as a friend."

She was tight-lipped, her eyes narrowing at me. "There are still boundaries we shouldn't cross." Again, she was teasing me. Playing along. We both knew we were playing with the boundaries, real or imaginary, and I was beginning to think she liked it as much as I did.

"One question." I held up a finger. "Just one. And I promise I won't ask you another. Besides, this is probably our last session, at least for a while anyway. Can't we break just the one rule?"

She didn't seem convinced as she folded her arms across her

chest. "Why do you care about whether I want to have kids so badly?"

"I just want to get to know you better."

Her brows raised and she uncrossed her arms, staring at me with an unreadable expression. "Why's that?"

"I find you interesting, Alex," I told her, probably too honestly. We held eye contact for a moment longer, the silence between us weighing heavily in the room before she spoke again.

"Okay, well, for starters, I don't see myself ever getting married. And, if I were to have kids, I'd want to be married too. I'd want to build a stable life for them, with two parents who love them."

"Why don't you think you'll get married? You're still young and attractive. I'm sure guys are lining up to be with you..." I ended the sentence slowly, dragging the words out in utter disbelief at what I'd just said. Why the hell had I said that?

"That's two questions," she said. Her skin turned a deep shade of scarlet as she broke eye contact with me, fighting back a smile. "And, thank you."

"For what it's worth, I'm sure you'll find someone. And you'll have a bunch of kids."

"I don't know about that."

"Come on, you've been so great with Ginny. And Skylar. That day we met, you were ready to go momma-bear on me in the park." I chuckled, and to my relief, she joined in.

"I thought you were trying to kidnap her," she said, laughing harder with a hand on her chest.

"You would've stopped me?" I asked, a sly grin on my lips.

"I would've done everything I could," she confirmed. "This is probably crossing a boundary too, but I care about Skylar as if she were my own daughter. I would've gone down swinging to save her."

I watched her, detecting no hint of a lie in her words. "See. You're just like me. You wouldn't feel whole without kids. I can see that. We're a lot alike. Without Skylar, life for me... it just wouldn't be worth it. She's everything to me. Even before she was born."

"We're not that alike, Cameron," she said sadly, shaking her head. "As much as I care about Skylar, and Raven, I'm not sure that I'm wife or mother material. I'm much better at fixing other people's lives than ever creating a life for myself. Always have been."

"Well, that's a shame," I told her. "Why do you say that?"

"That's three questions," she said firmly.

"Fine. Fine." My hands flew up in defeat. "But I can't say I'm not grateful you're so good at what you do."

Her grin was half-hearted. "Let's hope so." She sighed.

"Seriously, we're very lucky Ginny met you that day in the park."

"She's one of my closest friends," she said, tucking a piece of hair behind her ear. "Those don't come easily to me. I consider myself the lucky one, if anything. Being able to help her has been such a treat for me."

"How do you mean?"

She cocked her head to the side and, for a moment, I was worried she was going to add to the number of questions I'd asked her past my limit, but to my relief, she stared into space, nodding slowly as if agreeing with herself before she answered. "Well, I've already told you too much, I guess it doesn't hurt to say this. To be honest, she came into my life at kind of a rough time. I needed her as much as she needed me. To be even more honest, I'm worried that part of my concern over her stopping the sessions is entirely selfish."

"What do you mean? Because you won't see her as much?"

She leaned forward, as if we were two girlfriends gossiping over brunch. "Yes, which is crazy, right? I mean, of course I will still see her. But you deserve to see her more." She paused, then looked up at me from behind dark lashes. "Is it wrong for me to say I'll miss seeing you, too?"

I swallowed. Despite the distance between us, it was as if I could feel the heat radiating off our skin. Was she flirting with me?

Was I reading too much into the comment? My heart thundered in my chest, my thoughts suddenly jumbled.

"I'm sorry. That was inappropriate to say." She broke eye contact, giving me a much-needed reprieve.

"*No,*" I said. "If I'm being honest, I feel the same way."

Her eyes lit up. "Yeah?"

"Yeah. I've begun to look forward to these evening chats as well," I said, finally settling on an innocent enough way to phrase what was in my head. "You've been helpful to me, Alex." I swallowed, my eyes darting back and forth between hers as I tried to get a read on how she was feeling. Then, clearing my throat, I added quickly, "To both of us."

"I'm glad. Ginny has been a very good friend to me. Our coffee and playdates have gotten me out of the house more in the last few months than I have been in years, probably. I hate to admit it, but I'm a bit of a homebody. When Raven's not around, there are weeks and months that slip past without me having a true conversation with another person, outside of my clients. It's been really great for my own mental health to have someone who gives me a break from the monotony of the day. I didn't realize how much I missed having friends of my own."

"It's been good for her, too," I admitted, sobered by the swift change of direction the conversation had taken. It was safer for both of us if we kept Ginny front and center in our talks. I needed to remember that. "It's probably for the best, too, that we cut these off. She's been talking about going back to work recently, so our time will be limited as it is, and it just seems like the smart thing to do. Before anyone gets too attached."

"Really? She's planning to go back to work?"

"Mhm."

"She hadn't mentioned going back to work to me."

"Well, I'm not sure when or if she'll do it, but she's been talking about it more. She misses her coworkers and getting out of the house. I think that's why meeting you at the park was so good for her—like you were saying earlier about yourself, but now that fall is almost here, it'll be cooling off and I think she's worried about what being cooped up in the house could do to her."

"You don't think returning to work could be too much?"

I eyed her. It felt wrong to be talking about Ginny with Alex. As much as I felt like it was the right thing to do, the only thing that seemed to be keeping us completely professional, I still worried what we were doing wasn't right. If the situation were reversed, I would feel violated. In fact, any time I thought about what Ginny talked about in her sessions—what Alex might know about me—it made me feel that way. Uncomfortable. Bare. But, then again, Ginny was talking about me in her sessions, wasn't she? So, what difference did it make if I did the same? Why should I hold myself to a higher standard than she was? Ginny would never know anyway. "What do *you* think?"

"I... I don't know, really. I think the stress of going back to work could cause her to withdraw again, and the failure she'd feel could be damaging to her. But, I just don't know. If anything, I'd recommend she take it slow." She sighed heavily, shaking her head. "But she's not really my client anymore, remember? Now it's up to you two to decide what's best."

I nodded, taken aback by what felt like a cold comment. "We aren't jumping into anything. I won't let her."

"It seems to me no one *lets* Ginny do anything. You were right earlier, she's very stubborn."

Her comment had me feeling protective over Ginny. It felt bitter, almost, and I tamped down the urge to defend her. I'd probably read it wrong. Alex cared about Ginny. And Ginny *was* stubborn. She was right, I'd been the one to say it first. "You're not wrong about tha—" A yawn escaped me, cutting off the end of the sentence.

She glanced at the clock and shook her head. "Is it that time already? I'm so sorry for keeping you awake. You look like you're ready to fall asleep. Should I go?"

"There's no need to rush off," I said, stifling another yawn.

"Coffee will help." I took a drink of the hot beverage as if to prove a point.

"Are you sure?"

I nodded, though I wasn't sure. Not at all. Was it just the late hour that was making me so nervous around her? So desperate to continue talking to her? She was my wife's best friend, but I couldn't help finding myself attracted to her. She was beautiful, after all, but it was something more than that. Alex made me feel different than anyone ever had. It settled in my stomach with a nauseous feeling. I loved my wife. I truly did. I didn't want to hurt her. I didn't want to leave her; it was why I never had, no matter how many times it had crossed my mind. But, as much as I knew it would hurt her, knowing how I felt about Alex, I couldn't pull myself away from her.

This would be the last time I saw her alone, I reminded myself. This would be it. After tonight, what I felt for her—the silly schoolboy crush—would dissipate with time. I would realize this had all just been the result of me feeling so deprived of my wife's attention for entirely too long.

But, for now, I might as well enjoy the high I got from her presence while I had the chance.

"Yeah, it's still early. As long as you don't have anywhere to be?"

She watched me for a second before deciding on an answer, a clever smile forming on her lips. "Nowhere but here."

21 CAMERON

"Are you ever going to tell Ginny about this? Us?" Alex asked, seemingly out of nowhere a few moments later. I felt heat spreading throughout my core at her question. *Us?* She clarified, "Our sessions, I mean. Maybe it would help the two of you connect somehow. Now that they're over."

"I don't know..." In the beginning, I hadn't liked the idea of keeping something so big from my wife, but as time went on, I felt myself becoming more comfortable with it. Now, the idea of telling my wife, of letting her see me as vulnerable, needing help—it was terrifying. "I don't want to take away from the progress she's made."

"I understand that."

"Do you think it's wrong to keep it a secret from her?"

"Does it feel wrong?" she pressed.

"It didn't," I said. "I'd never lied to her about this. I didn't tell her we were meeting, but I didn't lie, so I could reason that it was okay. But then—I never told you about this—but she heard you in here one night. And she, well, she accused me of cheating on her." I forced a laugh, but Alex did not look amused.

"And what did you tell her?"

"I told her she must've dreamed it."

She exhaled deeply. "I see."

"Maybe that was the wrong thing to do. I just panicked, because I didn't want her to find out about this that way and get the wrong idea about what we were doing."

"You were afraid she would think you were cheating on her with me?"

I nodded, my mouth instantly going dry.

"Because you've cheated before?"

Her words ran through me. I wasn't sure if it was a question or a confirmation, so I remained still, waiting for her to say something else.

"Why would you say that?" I asked, when she didn't elaborate.

"I didn't say anything. I'm asking."

"Ginny told you." It was the ultimate betrayal. We'd moved past the affair years ago. It was a mistake, and she'd agreed we'd never bring it up again.

Still, she didn't confirm or deny that Ginny had told her, but I knew.

"It was a mistake," I said firmly, pressing my finger into the table. "I've apologized numerous times. I never thought she'd bring it up with you." I thought we'd moved on. I never expected her to bring it up with Alex. What could she possibly have to work through when we'd worked through it all when it happened? No, she wanted me to look bad. She wanted to make sure Alex knew I was flawed. Human. That I was capable of making mistakes.

The affair was one of the darkest moments of my life, an embarrassment I hoped to never think about again, and I'd hoped Ginny would respect that.

But I should've known better.

"Why didn't *you* tell me? We've talked so much about your marriage, but you've never mentioned that when it was such a crucial thing that shaped your relationship with Ginny."

I hung my head. "I was embarrassed. I'm no saint, don't get me wrong, but I've tried to do right by my wife. And, for the most part, I have."

"So, you still feel guilt over it?"

"Of course, I do, but I try not to think about it. It was years ago, before Skylar was even born. There was a dark point in our marriage, when the stress of her pregnancy was pushing us apart. There was a woman from work that I had an affair with. It was strictly emotional at first, but then it turned into something physical. We took it too far—just once—and I immediately called it off. She left the office shortly afterward, and I haven't seen or talked to her since. It was the biggest mistake of my life."

"Did you tell Ginny after it happened?"

I eyed her. "I think you already know the answer to that question."

"Tell me anyway," she pressed on, and I nodded.

"I didn't get the chance to. She found a text," I said. "And I told her everything then. It happened, it was a mistake, but we've moved on."

"I'm not condoning what you did, but affairs are very common. Usually, they occur when one partner isn't getting something they need from the other."

"It wasn't her fault—"

"I never meant to suggest it was. I'm only trying to understand what happened."

"After we found out she was pregnant, we started fighting over little things. Everything made her mad, everything was my fault. I felt like she was pushing me away, like I could never do anything right. Look, nothing I say right now justifies what I did—"

"Of course not."

"I regret it. I have regretted it. I would never hurt her like that again." I was saying it to myself as much as I was to her. I could never cross that line again.

"Before, you admitted to me that you'd thought about leaving her. That there were times when you went so far as to pack a bag and make travel plans to take Skylar out of state until things calmed down. When you had the affair, was that something that crossed your mind? Were you planning to leave her for that woman?"

I felt sick at her comments, felt sick that I'd ever admitted them to her. Considering and formulating a plan to leave my wife was hard enough, but admitting those thoughts to someone else made me feel disgusted with myself. I hated that I even needed to think such things in the first place. "I wasn't actively planning to leave her, no. Not then. I didn't consider leaving her until after Skylar was born. When I wasn't sure if I could ever fix her. It seemed like that might be the only solution. The only way out for Sky and me. I didn't know if I could commit to the rest of my life looking like it did right then."

Just as I prepared myself for her to judge me, her eyes softened and there was only understanding in her gaze. "It's hard when someone else's mental state determines the way your life goes."

"It's a horrible thing to admit. Feeling this way."

"It only feels horrible because you're a good person. You love her. You want to do the right thing. But you also want to protect yourself and your daughter. It's completely understandable."

"Is it?" I raised a skeptical brow.

"A lesser man might've left by now, Cameron. You've stood by Ginny's side through something most people wouldn't."

"I do love her."

She hesitated before saying anything. "Just... promise me, you will look out for yourself and Skylar first. You can love Ginny, and you should, but it's not selfish to put yourself and your daughter first. When someone is struggling as much as Ginny is—even on a good day—it's easy to let her monopolize your life. But you have to ask yourself, if the roles were reversed, would she do the same for you?"

I thought about the question. My wife had never been a selfish person, no, but she had, especially recently, put her own healing before all else. My work, Skylar, our marriage, our families... everything fell by the wayside when Ginny needed something.

I kept telling myself that her healing was important, but was it more important than all the rest? I didn't know.

"I guess I never thought of it like that."

"Well, I would expect nothing less. It's my job to make you think like that. As much as I love Ginny, I have to see to it that you're taken care of, too. You've both been my clients, for all intents and purposes, so I want to give you the advice I'd give anyone if I didn't know both sides of the story. Sometimes the people we love aren't the healthiest people for us to be around. You have to be okay admitting that to yourself and realizing it doesn't make you selfish or evil to accept the love you deserve, from yourself and others."

She was still, letting the advice, the weight of what she'd said, sit between us.

Finally, I broke the silence the only way I could think of. "Thanks. I'll keep that in mind." I glanced at the clock on the stove. "We should probably wrap this up. It's getting late, and Skylar will be back awake soon."

"I hope I haven't overstepped. I care about you, Cameron. Ginny too. I want you both to be happy, whatever that looks like for each of you. You deserve to be fulfilled, too." She drew the words out slowly, almost sensually, as she stood from the table.

As she did, I slid out of my seat, holding eye contact with her for an extra moment. "You haven't overstepped. I appreciate you being so honest with me."

She leaned forward, pulling me into an unexpected hug. I felt her skin against mine, and breathed in her warm, floral scent. Suddenly, all the thoughts I'd cast away, the promises I'd made to myself to ignore my attraction to Alex, none of it seemed to matter so much. My pulse began to race, my ears fiery hot. "You remind me so much of myself, of everything I went through with my mother. It's hard not to feel protective over you."

I felt the sudden urge to protect *her* at the vulnerable statement, wrapping my arms around her tighter.

She pulled back, but I didn't drop my arms straight away, so we stood still, connected at the waist, our faces just inches apart.

"I should go," she whispered, and I agreed wholeheartedly, but I couldn't make my hands release her.

"You should," I said. Her hands were still on my shoulders, her body heat radiating onto me. Could she hear my heartbeat from where she stood? It seemed impossible to miss. Her steady gaze bore into me with silent expectation.

"You should," I repeated.

"Yes." She wasn't going though, not as she leaned forward slowly, her lips grazing mine. I should've stopped it. I should've backed away, dropped my arms, and bid her goodnight.

I should've done something—anything—to get her out the door and out of my life. But I didn't. Instead, I felt myself leaning into her kiss, felt my hands sliding up her back in an attempt to pull her closer to me.

I loved my wife. I didn't want to hurt her.

It wasn't worth it.

But I couldn't stop.

I couldn't.

Physically, emotionally... I needed Alex in a way I couldn't explain, even to myself.

With a gasp of panicked breath, she pushed back against my chest. "I'm so sorry," she said. "I shouldn't have—"

"No, it's my fault," I cut her off. "I think I'm just confused."

"It's normal to develop feelings for a therapist," she assured me. "You did nothing wrong. This was all me. I know the lines not to cross, and I—"

She pulled away, moving out of the kitchen and toward the foyer.

"Alex, wait!" I called after her. She stopped, spinning around to see what I wanted. "Look, we can just pretend this never happened, if that's okay with you?"

My breath seemed to have solidified in my throat as I waited for her slow response. "Are you sure you can do that?"

I nodded, an outright lie. How could I ever forget? How could I ever look at her again without remembering— *No.*

I could.

I would.

I had to prove it. "Of course. If you can."

"Yes, I can. We have to. For Ginny's sake."

"Friends, then?" I asked, still trying to catch my breath.

"Friends." She reached out a hand, an olive branch, and I took it.

"Hey, you should come to the birthday party in a few weeks," I said, trying to ease the tension and fill the silence.

"What birthday party?" She hadn't let go of my hand.

"Skylar turns three. We're just having something small here. Family, mostly. I know Ginny would love that." At the mention of my wife's name, she dropped my hand, and we both shuffled a bit further apart.

"I wouldn't want to impose."

"You wouldn't be."

"Are you sure?"

"Of course, I'm sure. She'd be thrilled to have you. And, of course, your niece is more than welcome to come, too. I want things to stay the same between us. Like you said, for Ginny's sake."

"Okay. If you're not just asking because you feel weird."

I was, but I lied. "Definitely not."

"Well, alright then. I'm not sure if Raven will be in town, but I'd love to come."

I wasn't sure why I'd brought it up other than to change the subject back to something normal, but to my surprise, the tension remained. The kiss moments ago was still lingering on my lips, her smell on my skin.

"Great, I'll have Ginny invite you tomorrow so she doesn't know I've already done it."

"Thanks, Cam," she said, using the nickname my wife had always preferred. She patted my arm once more, my skin burning from her touch, and leaned forward, pressing her lips to my cheek. I sucked in a ragged breath.

She shouldn't have done that. I knew it the instant our skin touched.

The burning sensation passing through my body made my head feel heavy.

"Is it okay to call you that? Or do you prefer Cameron?" She leaned backward, batting her eyelashes at me. Once again, we'd found ourselves just inches apart, her breath hitting my lips.

"Cam's fine," I said, swallowing.

She nodded, her dark eyes darting back and forth between mine. "Cam."

"Alex," I replied, filling the silence momentarily. Something in my chest exploded as her eyes closed, and suddenly, nothing else mattered. I needed to kiss her again.

My vision blurred, my brain suddenly unable to form the words I wanted to say. I leaned forward, pressing my lips to hers. She responded instantly, her hands around my neck.

I felt dizzy, lightheaded at her touch, her smell, the feel of her hands on my chest. My heart thudded under her palm, every nerve ending on fire as I pulled her closer to me, moving back away from the door.

"We shouldn't—" she protested just once more, our lips barely parting, but it didn't even justify a response.

We shouldn't. She was right.

That was what I wanted to say. I wanted to assure her that we could stop. That we wouldn't cross the line. That we could go back to the way things were before. That Ginny would never know.

Instead, I closed my eyes, breathing in her perfect scent, as her tongue explored my mouth. I wanted her in a way that didn't seem possible and, as I felt her own heart pounding against my skin, racing just as fast as mine, I knew she wanted me too.

It was just going to be this once. We'd deal with it and we'd move on. I pulled her into the guest bedroom, already peeling off our clothes.

There were no further protests, only the sound of her whispering my name over and over again.

"Cam... Cam..."

I sank into her in every way, knowing I'd have to deal with the consequences later. That was Future Cam's problem. Tonight, I was going to enjoy every moment.

And that's what I did.

At least, as far as I could remember. When I awoke, I was alone and naked in the guest bedroom bed, and everything that had happened felt like a bad dream.

22 GINNY
PRESENT DAY

When the police arrived, we were still in a state of panic that matched with the storm raging outside, lightning brightening the sky every few minutes with loud crashes of thunder accompanying it. We'd searched every nook and cranny of our house for a sign of what may have happened to Skylar but found nothing.

It didn't feel real, and yet, it all felt *too* real.

My body was ice cold, yet my organs were on fire.

I couldn't breathe and yet I felt as if I were breathing too much.

I felt like I was doing too much and not enough.

Everything was a contradiction.

A juxtaposition, emotions and reactions colliding with each other in a strange sort of bubble-wrapped existence. As if everything was happening inside a container of Jell-o. Slow motion and stilted, no matter what I did, nothing seemed to be enough.

As we watched the officers moving through the house, I wondered if I'd searched too many places and disrupted the crime scene, or if I'd not searched enough and would, in turn, look guilty.

I just wanted my baby back. I just wanted her home. I wanted to know she was safe.

They'd separated us, wanted to question Cameron and me alone. I couldn't see him, and that scared me. I knew he must be freaking out, but what he'd said, what he'd accused me of was hurtful.

What did you do?

The question repeated in my head, the haunted look in his eyes a searing accusation.

I didn't do anything.

He couldn't have meant it, really. He was panicking. Scared. I knew that, but it didn't make it hurt any less.

He had to know I would never... Didn't he?

What was he telling the police now?

When the detective left our bedroom and made his way down the hall toward me, Cameron was left inside.

It was my turn.

"Mrs. Hale," he said, his kind but serious eyes studying me closely. I knew they all were, and I knew it was just part of their job, but it was hurtful. Our child was missing, we were in a state of pure panic, and they were interrogating us as if we were criminals.

"Yes." I stood, but he waved me back down in an instant. I could hear the footsteps and voices of the other investigators moving through the house, sorting through our things. I tried not to focus on it, my mind too full of worry as it was.

He took a seat on the edge of the coffee table in front of me, opening the notepad in his hands. "Thank you for your patience. Just as a reminder, I'm Detective Chapman. I'm just going to ask you to recount the events for me as they happened. I may interrupt you to clarify a few things, but if I don't, just keep going."

"Why... why do we need to be separated, again? I'd like to be with my husband if that's alright."

"I understand." The timbre of his voice would've been soothing under different circumstances. "It's standard protocol to separate you. Not because we think you did anything wrong, but because in high-stress times like these, sometimes stories can get muddled. It's best just to get everyone's side of things before you spend too much time talking to each other. One of you might've seen or heard or noticed something that could be crucial to finding your daughter."

Behind him, an officer walked past with Skylar's bedding in a large, clear bag.

"Where is he taking those?" I asked, my stomach clenching.

"Everything we take today will be brought to the lab for testing."

"What kind of testing?" I shivered as another man brought out her favorite stuffed elephant.

"DNA. If someone was in your daughter's bedroom who didn't belong in this house, we want to know. We're going to take a lot, okay? But it's important to do so and do it quickly."

"But... I don't understand. Shouldn't you be out there? Looking for her?" I gestured toward the door.

"We are," he said plainly, urging me to sit back down. "We have officers searching the woods and surrounding area for anything that could point us in the right direction—"

"The woods?" I felt as if I were going to be sick. My head was fuzzy with fear and confusion.

"What's important right now," he said, speaking with a firmness that told me I was testing his patience, "is that we get your side of the story. From there, we'll work any leads we have, okay? I want to find your daughter, but in order to do that, we need for you to tell us everything you know. No detail is too small."

"O-okay, um, well, we had her birthday party yesterday."

"And who all was in attendance?"

I recounted the guest list for him. "My parents." *Shoot.* I'd have to call my parents. My stomach lurched as I imagined the panic in my mother's voice, the thinly veiled judgement that I knew would silently tell me I wasn't good enough, that she'd never have made a mistake so huge. "Arthur and Joselyn Stockdale. And Cam's parents, Kurt and Rita Hale. Plus Cam's sister, Margie, and her husband, David. David Cooke. Cam's coworkers, Joe and Stephen... I'm sorry, I can't remember their last names."

"It's okay, keep going," he encouraged me, writing down every name as I said it. His voice was back to being gentle, but affirmative.

"Okay, then Alyssa Steward and Norma Andrews, my old coworkers. And Alex Kane, one of my friends."

"And who was the last person to leave?" His dark eyes searched mine, his hard expression unreadable.

"My parents. They left around midnight."

"Everyone else was gone by then?"

"Yes, that's right. They'd all left throughout the evening. My parents only stayed that late because they needed to catch a late flight."

He nodded, jotting something else down. "So, did you go to sleep before or after they left?"

"After," I told him. "We stayed up to see them out and then locked up and headed for bed."

"And who locked the door?"

"Cameron did..." I began to second-guess myself. I'd seen him do it, hadn't I? He always locked the door. Yes, I was sure I'd watched him. "Yes, he did."

"What about windows? You're out here on your own, with several acres around you. It would be understandable if you left windows unlocked occasionally..."

"No, never. I'm too much of a worrier. The windows are always locked."

"So, the windows were locked, the doors were locked... There are no signs of forced entry. Who else has a key to your home?"

"N-no one." I knew the answer, so why was I questioning myself? Perhaps because he was staring at me in such a strange, incredulous way.

The wrinkle in his tanned forehead deepened as his brows drew down. "What about spare keys? Do you keep one under the mat that someone may have known about?"

"No, definitely not. Cam and I have keys and we have one spare key, but we keep it inside. It's just in case we lose one."

That seemed to intrigue him. He leaned forward just a bit. "And have you? Lost one recently?"

"No, I haven't. Cam hasn't mentioned losing his. Hang on—" I recalled something. "I forgot we actually have two spare keys. We made an extra spare key last year for Cam's sister Margie. She and David came down to house-sit for us when we visited my parents for two weeks. But..." I tapped a finger on my lip as I tried to think. "I'm nearly positive they gave it back to us."

"Okay." He nodded with encouragement, willing me to continue. "Where would it be? Where do you keep your spare keys?"

"By the door." I pointed toward the entryway.

"Show me." He stood quickly, his body rigid as he waited for me to lead the way. I walked into the entryway, pointing toward the keyring. They were neatly labeled, the result of a day when I'd felt especially productive.

Cam

Ginny

Spare Front Door

Spare Car (Cam)

Spare Car (Ginny)

Spare Shed

He studied them, and I felt relieved to see that they were, in fact, all still there. Including the extra spare key we'd made for Margie. It meant I hadn't let anything get past me. But, if that were the case, where did that leave us? Who else could've come in our house?

"Hey, can we have someone get a picture of this and dust it for prints?" he called over his shoulder. I jolted at the sudden noise.

"Sure thing." A female officer walked into the room with a camera in hand, and the first officer led me back into the living room.

"Okay, so those are the only two spare keys? You're sure? And no one could've taken either of them without your knowledge?"

"Not that I know of. I'm sure we would've noticed them missing."

He rapped his pen on the paper rhythmically. "Could Margie have made a copy when they house-sat?"

"I can't imagine why she would've. They rarely visit, and the key's always there if she were to need it."

He nodded, writing something down, then looked up at me. "Okay, so tell me more about the party. Was anyone acting suspiciously? Were there any arguments or disagreements?"

"No, everything went great. Everyone was in a good mood. Skylar was—" My voice cracked, preventing me from going on, and I reached for the tissues on the table. "I'm sorry."

He waited patiently as I dabbed my eyes, drying the tears. "It's perfectly okay. Take your time."

But Skylar didn't have time for me to take any. She needed me to tell the story so they could put their efforts into finding her and bringing her home. Though I didn't know them exactly, I knew there were statistics about how long we had to find her before the chances were almost impossible. And I knew the longer I sat and talked, I was only taking minutes away from that incredibly small window of time.

I drew a long breath, trying to compose myself. "Skylar was so happy to have everyone here. They all love her so much."

"Your family all live out of town, is that correct?"

"Yes. Across the country. Arizona, New York, and Florida."

"How often do they see Skylar?"

"Once or twice a year generally, but it really just depends. After we had her, my parents came to stay for a while to help out."

"And how did that go?"

"Fine," I said.

He waited, his intense stare weighing on me, stubble-lined jaw tight. He had the silent, patient stare down to an art, a look that forced you to keep talking, even when you didn't know what else to say. A look that could make you spill all your secrets.

But what secrets did I have? All that mattered was what had happened last night, and for me, that was still all a bit of a blur. I struggled to piece the events together in my head, wishing I could go back and turn down every single drink. If Skylar would just come home, I'd never drink again.

He was still staring at me, waiting. Obviously, my answer wasn't good enough.

"It was a little tense, I guess. They were excited to meet her, but I was struggling with postpartum depression, so I wasn't really in the mood for company. I'm sure Cameron already told you that."

He didn't confirm or deny it. "Tell me more about it."

"It was rough at first." More tears welled in my eyes. "It's something I'm still struggling with, but I'm getting better. And I'm so grateful for my parents' help now, looking back."

"How are you coping with your postpartum depression? Do you take medication? Are you seeing a doctor regularly?"

With the way he was framing his questions, my guess was that he already knew. "I do take medication, yes. Prescribed by a doctor. And I've been going to see a therapist. My friend, Alex, she's also a therapist and she's helped me work through so much."

"Just to confirm, you're *still* taking your medication?"

I guessed he knew the answer to that, too. "Not recently, no. I've been trying to slow down on them."

"Under the supervision of a doctor?"

I felt the weight of his scrutiny then. What exactly had Cam told him about me? Had he made me out to be some sort of villain? Had he made him believe I could harm my daughter? Did Cam believe that? I thought back to the accusation he'd hurled at me when we discovered Skylar was missing.

What did you do?

"No," I said finally, realizing he was still waiting for an answer. I wanted to tell him that there was no way I could be capable of hurting my child. That whatever Cam had told him was wrong. I wanted to make him believe it. Tell him that I'd never paid a parking ticket late, never ran a red light, that I always entered through the "Enter" doors in supermarkets. I was a rule follower. Obsessively. I couldn't do anything criminal.

In order to make him believe it, I had to convince myself first.

I shook the thought away.

Cam was getting in my head.

I needed to focus.

Why was my memory of the previous night so foggy?

"I see... And you mentioned your therapist is also your friend?"

"She is, yeah. I know that's not usually a good idea, but she's who I feel comfortable seeing. As I mentioned, she's really helped me."

He moved on. "How much had you had to drink at the party last night, Mrs. Hale?"

He was reading off the paper in his hand as he asked me, and I was thankful because I knew the shock was registered on my face.

"Um, a few glasses of wine, I guess."

"How many is a few?" he pressed, his lips forming a hard line, eyes narrowing.

I tried to remember, but I couldn't. Had Cameron given him a figure? If I guessed wrong, would it make me seem like a liar?

"I... um, I'm not sure. Not many. Just a few throughout the day."

"Three? Five? Ten?"

"Um..." I chewed my bottom lip, a wave of anxiety washing over me. I wanted to get the answer right, but how could I? Who counts their glasses of wine? "Maybe four or five within the span of several hours. Definitely not ten. And they weren't even full glasses." I felt like a teenager who'd been caught drinking behind her parents back, trying to explain away my offenses.

He looked down, and I pictured him comparing my answer to Cam's. "Okay, so, you just drank the wine, then? Nothing else?"

"Well, my husband and I have this tradition of..." I grimaced as I said it, realizing how terrible it made us sound. "Glasses of whiskey for each year. Whiskey was what we drank on our first date and our wedding night. It's kind of the celebratory drink in our household. So, we each had three small glasses for the three years she's been alive."

There was no shock on his face, so I knew that was another thing Cameron had told him.

"Three glasses... That's no small amount, especially after already having wine, wouldn't you say? With a young child in the house?"

"Well, they were very small glasses and it had been a few hours since I'd had a glass of wine. But, yes, in hindsight, I guess it wasn't very smart."

"On a scale of one to ten, how intoxicated do you think you were?"

The blood drained from my face. I thought back to the night before, an array of memories coming back to me at once—the drinks, the kissing, moving to the bedroom. How drunk had I been? I remembered feeling the rushes when I'd stood or moved too quickly. After all, I hadn't eaten all that much, but I wasn't *drunk-drunk*. Was I? "Oh, I wouldn't call it intoxicated. I think I might've been a bit tipsy, but nothing too bad."

"And where was Skylar during all of this?"

"She was already in bed," I told him. "She'd been down for a while."

"Are you sure?"

"I—" I was, but his question had me questioning myself. "Yes. Yes, of course. My mother had gotten her down before they left."

"How sure are you that she didn't wake up? Would you have been drunk enough not to notice if she'd woken up and come looking for you? Or if someone else was in the house... potentially in Skylar's room? Did you check on her at all before you went to bed?"

The questions were coming too fast now. My body tingled with ice-cold pulses of electricity, my hands trembling. I clasped my hands together, trying to stop the shaking.

"No, I—I wasn't drunk. She didn't come looking for us. We would've heard her." I struggled to catch my breath, my chest suddenly tight, my throat too dry. "She was fine. She was asleep."

"And you checked on her to confirm that? You are one hundred percent sure that she was still in her bedroom, alone, when you went to bed?"

I squeezed my eyes shut, covering them with my fingers as I tried to think. I lowered my face into my lap, forcing out a breath. "I don't—I can't remember."

"You have to remember, Ginny," he said firmly, clicking his pen. I felt the urge to scream, my head spinning with the questions and the noise. I just wanted it to stop. For just a moment, I wanted it to all stop. "Ginny?" he prompted again.

I forced the panic away, uncovering my eyes and sitting up straight. I shook my head. Skylar needed me to be strong. I had to get through this for her sake.

"I'm sorry. This is all just..." I trailed off, no idea what I was trying to say. "No, I don't think we checked on her. We normally don't. She's a light sleeper."

"So, someone could've been in your home then? Someone could've potentially been in her room? Maybe they could've already taken her without your knowledge?"

"No," I said urgently. "No. There was no one else here. Everyone had left."

"Unless you checked the room, we can't be sure of that. It could affect the timeline some. The last time you actually laid eyes on your daughter was when?"

I thought back, my eyes darting side to side in panic as I tried to recall. "Around eight. We changed her into her pajamas, helped her brush her teeth and hair, and then Cam and I put her down with a story. She didn't wake again until eleven, which was when my mom went to check on her."

"Okay, so eight o'clock was the last time you or Cameron saw her?"

The thought was heartbreaking. I put a hand to my chest, trying to keep the tears at bay. "Around that, yes. But we heard her cry at eleven, when my mom went to check on her. So, I know she was still here then."

"Thank you. That's really helpful," he said, writing down a long note. I desperately wanted to see what he was writing, but I didn't dare move. When he looked up, he asked, "Do you drink often, then?"

A lump formed in my throat under the judgement of the question. "No, rarely, in fact. With the medication, I couldn't."

"And how long had you been on the medication?"

"Since Skylar was around seven months old. So, over two years." He nodded, writing something else down, but not saying anything. "And obviously, I didn't drink during my pregnancy, so I've been mostly sober for the better part of four years now. I wouldn't have had anything to drink if I thought I was putting Skylar in danger. I was just trying to relax at the end of a stressful day."

"I understand. Tell me, would you say that Mr. Hale had been drinking more or less than you had?"

I tried to recall how many times I'd seen him with wine or beer at the party. Almost the whole time, but did I know that they were new bottles? He'd never been a heavy drinker, but in solidarity with me, had given up drinking almost entirely when I'd had to because of the pregnancy and then the medication. "Probably about the same. Maybe less." He'd gotten dressed after we'd slept together, so he had to have been more coherent than I'd felt.

"Okay, so, your parents left, you had the drinks, and then what?"

"We went to bed," I said. There was no way I was reliving the more private parts of the evening with him.

"And who discovered your daughter was missing first? And when?"

"It was a little after four a.m. I woke up and realized she'd slept longer than she usually does. Most nights, she's up and down every hour or so—"

"That must get tiring."

"It is, yes, but we're used to it at this point. Anyway, I noticed she hadn't woken up, and I went to check and make sure everything was okay. When I got in there, she wasn't in her bed. I tore her room apart looking for her, which woke Cam up, and after we realized she really wasn't in the house, he called 911."

"How long had you been awake before Mr. Hale came to find you?"

"Minutes, maybe. Not long at all." It all ran together, panic-stricken moments of disbelief and outright fear.

"Were you up and out of bed at any point before that time?" he asked, his gaze drilling into me.

"No," I said, feeling uncomfortable. What had Cameron told him? Why was he looking at me that way? "I fell asleep before Cameron did. And I woke up just a few minutes before him. Other than that, I'd slept the whole night."

He cocked his head to the side slightly, brows knitted together. "How could you know you fell asleep before him?"

"Well"—my face burned with an embarrassed heat—"when we went to sleep, neither of us were wearing clothes. And when I woke up, he was dressed. But I don't remember him getting dressed."

He nodded. "You had sex, then? After you went to bed?"

"Mhm," I squeaked out.

"So, it's possible that if someone were to have either broken in or escaped with Skylar, that could've happened then? When you were distracted?"

The thought was debilitating. The idea that I'd been distracted enough not to hear my daughter cry out for me. Or hear an intruder in the house. I hated how guilty he was making me feel for normal things.

Drinking.

Having sex.

Sleeping.

These weren't crimes, but the way he was looking at me as he asked them, you'd think they were.

I scowled at him. "I guess it's possible, but I don't know how we wouldn't have heard. We have a toddler in our house. We're not exactly loud in bed."

"But you'd had a lot to drink. You don't think you might've let your inhibitions go just for the night?"

Why was he continuing to insist I'd had a lot to drink? It wasn't a lot, not spread throughout the day. I fought against the urge to argue. "I didn't. If someone had broken in, if she'd cried, I would've heard."

"You're sure of that?"

"Yes."

"Well, maybe the liquor got the best of you during the evening? Maybe the two of you snuck upstairs for a little prelude while you still had guests? It would make sense. You had people to watch Skylar, you could actually get some much-needed privacy." He raised his brows. "It would be understandable."

What was he talking about? Where were these questions coming from? "Of course, we didn't. I'm not some kind of animal who can't control her urges. We didn't sneak off to have sex while our parents were just a few rooms away." I curled my upper lip in disgust. "We slept together at night before bed. Just once. And then we fell asleep. End of story."

Without missing a beat, he went on. "You were sleeping hard then, hm? Do you think you'd blacked out, maybe?"

I scowled, clasping my hands together in front of me. "*No.* No. I didn't black out. I was just sleeping. Maybe heavily, but I've always been a heavy sleeper."

"Heavy enough to have slept through your daughter coming into your room when she woke up?"

"The door was locked..."

"Knocking at your door, then?" His eyes bore into me, laden with judgement and frustration.

"Maybe, but even if I had slept through it, Cam would've woken..." I paused, running a finger over my lip as something occurred to me. "Wait, *did* she come to our door? Was that why he was dressed?" The more I thought about it, the more it made sense. Only, why hadn't Cam told me about that? The morning was panicked, but surely that was something that would've come up. Had Skylar come to our room and Cam had comforted her? I searched my brain for the foggy memory, nearly willing it into existence.

"That's what I'm asking you. I'm just trying to get a timeline of the entire night put together. If she didn't wake up and she normally does, either she was already gone by that time, or she did wake up and one of you tended to her." His gaze narrowed.

"If she woke up, I never heard her," I swore. "But Cam didn't mention it, either."

"Okay," he said with a sigh, closing his notepad. "Just one last question: Who typically takes care of Skylar? When she needs something, which of you would she go to first?"

"If we were both here, probably Cameron," I said. "They're very close."

"And you're not?"

"We are, but she's a daddy's girl. She's with me so much that she'll choose him when she has the choice."

"Okay, good to know."

"We didn't do this," I blurted out, standing as he did and meeting his suspicious gaze. "We love our daughter very much. We just want her home. I just... I know they always look at the parents first, but... It wasn't us. We would never hurt her."

"Thank you, Mrs. Hale." He placed a hand on my shoulder gently, then turned to walk away.

"Do you believe me?" I called after him, almost positive he didn't, but hoping he could ease my fears.

The detective turned around with a sigh. "All I know is that there are no signs anyone else was in this house last night, which means whoever took your daughter—" He cleared his throat before correcting himself. "*Whatever happened to her*, there's a very good chance that someone either had a key or had access inside some other way. Now, that either means you or your husband let them in, or..." He paused, apparently deciding whether to finish his sentence.

"Or what, Detective?"

"Well, I guess that's what we'll be trying to figure out."

The weight of his accusation slammed into my chest. "You can't honestly believe we would've let them inside? There has to be something else. Someone had to have found a way in or... Or she found a way out."

He was hesitant to respond, one side of his mouth drawn up in quiet contemplation. He released a slow breath of air from his nose. "It's not about what I believe, Mrs. Hale, it's about the truth of what happened here. What happened to your daughter." He scrutinized me for a moment, then glanced over my shoulder toward the window on the far wall. "Science will help us narrow it down. If someone was in here last night who shouldn't have been, we'll find evidence. DNA, fingerprints... We're running your house through the gamut right now, so if there's something to find, we'll find it. For now, I suggest you all just stay put and contact me if you recall anything else about last night that could be of use in our investigation."

"Or if we get a ransom call?" Wasn't that what always happened in the movies?

He raised an eyebrow skeptically, before nodding slowly as he replied. I thought I saw a hint of a smirk on his lips. "Yeah, or if you get a ransom call." With that, he tipped his head toward me. "Once they finish up here, we'll have police patrolling the area for the next few days. You two just stay put and try to let them do their jobs. We'll be in touch with any news."

With that, he was out of the room and I was alone, left with more questions than answers. I felt my knees giving out underneath me as I sank back onto the couch, replaying the previous day's events and all of the moments that led us here.

I didn't do this.

Cam didn't do this.

Someone else had to...

But who?

23 CAMERON

The woods and street had been searched, but nothing—no one—was found. Our daughter had not been found.

I missed her so much it hurt.

My chest physically ached from the pain of not having her with us.

Of wondering if she was okay.

If she was scared.

What was happening.

I ached with the pain and regret of knowing nothing.

I was her father. I was meant to protect her. I had no idea how to protect her from something I couldn't control.

The officer had asked me so many questions, and I'd answered him honestly, maybe too honestly. I'd told him about Ginny's heavy drinking the night before, about her depression, and about her sudden decision to stop medication and therapy. Almost instantly after I'd said it, I found myself regretting it. I didn't want to pit myself against Ginny in all of this. We both wanted the same thing: for Skylar to be safe. But my emotions had gotten the best of me, and I'd blurted it out, casting further suspicion on my wife. It was true though. Nothing I'd told the detective was false. And besides, if Ginny wanted us to find Skylar, surely she'd want me to be brutally honest with the detective about everything. It was the only way they'd be able to find her.

All the cards needed to be on the table.

I had to believe Ginny would understand that.

He'd asked me a question that haunted me near the end: Did I think my wife was capable of doing something to harm our daughter?

I hesitated because the question had already been flowing through my mind all night. Maybe because I just needed someone to blame, but maybe because deep down, I'd always worried about it. Her detachment from Skylar had always concerned me, but I knew she loved our daughter, didn't she?

At least, I wanted to believe that. The brief hesitation was enough to cast doubt over her character in the detective's eyes. I could see that as soon as it happened. He'd begun forming an opinion of her before they'd even spoken.

I quickly tried to cover for her, telling him that I didn't believe so. That she wasn't capable of harming anyone, but now that Skylar was missing, I'd begun to question everything. Ginny wouldn't have hurt her, would she? I was so tired of wondering.

I just wanted her home with me. I just wanted her to be safe. I wanted to hold her again...

If anyone ever hurt her, I'd kill them.

I knew that in my bones. I would destroy them. If they hurt my child, if they—

I couldn't bear to think about it anymore. The officer had left me in the bedroom to collect myself, and I'd overstayed my time. It had been hours, me sitting in the dimly lit room, staring into space with anger radiating through me.

I'd wanted to go out and search, to drive the streets, to visit the park, but they'd kept us here. They'd asked us to let them do their jobs.

But that was just it. This was a job to them.

To us, to me—it was the only thing that mattered. I wouldn't clock out and go home for dinner. Hell, I may never eat another meal. Not as long as I knew my little girl was out there somewhere. As long as I couldn't hold her and protect her.

I heard the door shut; it'd been opening and shutting all morning with new officers and investigators. But this time, it seemed to snap me into awareness. I needed to get up. I needed to get out of the bedroom and find out what they'd discovered.

Had they discovered anything?

Did I want to know?

I pulled open the bedroom door, surprised to see my wife sitting alone down the hall, on the edge of the couch cushion. It was as if she were preparing to leave, but hadn't. She looked exhausted—no, that wasn't the right word. She looked... *lifeless*. It was the only way I knew to describe her appearance. Her skin was practically translucent, as if the blood had been drained from her body. Her expression was empty, her eyes hollow. I'd seen her in dark places before, days that I thought she might shrivel up into a shell of herself and never return, but those days were nothing compared to this. I wasn't sure how she was managing to keep herself upright.

I inched toward her cautiously, the reality of what I'd done sinking in.

As I entered the living room, she turned her head to look at me, her eyes wide with confusion, then relief. Even as she met my gaze, she wasn't fully there. Maybe neither of us were anymore.

"They're all gone," she said, her voice soft and gentle as a leaf landing on a pond.

I glanced around the room, confirming what I already knew. "Are they coming back?"

She swallowed, blinking slowly. "I don't know."

"What did they say?" I stormed past her and toward the entry-way, looking out the door and toward the drive. "Why are they gone? Aren't they supposed to stay? In the movies, they always stay. They're supposed to be here until she's found." I felt new tears in my eyes as I realized we were going to be alone, tearing away every bit of composure I'd managed to build. I had to face my wife, to deal with this alongside her, while I wasn't sure if I could even trust her.

She didn't answer, and I turned back around, hurrying into the living room once more. "Did you hear me? Why aren't they staying? They're supposed to stay and help us find her. What? We're just supposed to sit here? Just wait?"

She kept her chin down, her eyes locked on her hands placed in her lap.

"Why aren't you saying anything?" I demanded, overwhelmed by the sudden urge to shake an answer out of her. Why was she so quiet? Didn't she care at all that our daughter was missing?

When she finally looked up, she had tears in her soft, blue eyes. "Because this isn't a movie, Cam. This is real. She's... she's just gone." She collapsed, her shoulders caving inward as her body began to shake with sobs. It caught me off guard, and I barely moved in time to catch her before she fell to the floor. I sank down in front of her, holding her weight as we eased onto the floor together, both of us sobbing with outright hopelessness.

Neither of us said anything for a long time, and when we finally broke apart, our faces marred with sweat and snot and tears, she swiped her hand across her lips, then scooted away from me.

"Did they at least say if they'll be back today?" I asked, needing to get a straight answer from her.

"They didn't say anything," she said firmly. "They didn't tell me a thing."

"That can't be right."

"Do you think I'm lying? Like you think I'm lying about taking Skylar?"

Her words slammed into my chest, and I opened my mouth but closed it again. "What are you talking about?" Ignorance could work, couldn't it?

She stood up, sauntering away from me with a sigh. "I don't have time for this."

We walked past Skylar's bedroom, and I tried to avoid looking in as I had the first time, but I couldn't. I glanced, and my heart fell.

Her bed had been cleared, half her toys missing. The bottle of water I kept by her bed was gone.

"What happened?" I asked breathlessly. "They took everything."

"They are looking for evidence."

"Do they think they'll find it?"

She was already gone, disappearing into our bedroom. I hurried behind her, opening the door.

"What are you doing?"

"*I don't know!*" she screamed, the outburst catching me by surprise. "I don't know what I'm doing. I need to call my mom and tell her what happened. I need to call Alex. We need to call your parents and Margie. I need to go look for her... I can't just sit here and do nothing."

I nodded, trying to think. "Was that what they said? That we should call our parents?"

"What aren't you understanding? They didn't tell me anything except to stay here and wait."

"I know you said that, but—"

"But *nothing,* Cam. We're suspects. They think we did this. They certainly aren't going to tell us anything they don't have to."

I sucked in a sharp breath at the accusation. "Th-they what? Why would you say that? Of course, they don't—"

"Oh, don't even play innocent. You're the reason they're suspicious of us in the first place. You just had to tell them I've stopped taking my meds. It's not a crime, you know. Do you honestly think I could've done anything to hurt our child?" Out of breath, she stopped pacing and stared at me, waiting for my answer.

I tried to come up with one on the spot. Something that would excuse what I'd done. "I didn't say that I thought you'd done anything to hurt her. They asked, and I told them the truth. What did you want me to do? Lie to the police?"

"They asked you specifically if I'd stopped taking my medicine and been drinking that night?" She raised a brow skeptically, not buying a second of it.

"They asked me about the night, which was when I brought up both of our drinking. And they asked if anything else had been going on. I had to tell them, Ginny. Don't you see that? If they talk to Alex and find out, then they'd think we were trying to hide something."

"Or that our daughter had just gone missing and we were a bit preoccupied. Stopping taking my medication doesn't stop me from caring about our daughter. It doesn't make me a murderer."

I froze at her words, ice sliding down my spine. "She's not... She's alive. Don't say that." I bit the inside of my cheek, trying not to break down. How could she toss that word out so casually?

"I didn't mean that," she said coolly, looking away from me with one arm wrapped around herself. "I'm just... I need a minute, okay? I need time to think. I need to call my parents." She jutted her chin toward me. "You should call yours, too."

"What do we tell them?"

"We tell them the truth," she said, her eyes haunted. "That she's m—" The word caught in her throat, and she shook her head, tears welling up. "They should all come. Just in case."

I nodded, both dreading the conversation and wanting my parents to make it better somehow. They always seemed able to do that, but I knew this would be more complicated.

"Do you want me to wait with you? We can do it together."

"No," she said, her tone clipped. She hadn't forgiven me for placing us in the line of fire, and I didn't blame her. "I'll do it myself."

I took a step back, turning to leave the room before stopping myself. I wanted to tell her I knew she didn't have anything to do with Skylar's disappearance, that I knew she wasn't capable of any such thing, but I couldn't bring myself to form the words.

"We were always going to be suspects, Gin. With stuff like this, they always look at the parents first." My words were choked and muffled with tears, but I needed her to know the truth. That I never meant to hurt her. That I loved her. That I wished things had been different. "I'm sorry—"

Her hands went up to either side of her face, fingers splayed. "I can't do this right now, Cam. I just... I can't."

I gave a sullen nod and turned toward the door again, but her voice stopped me.

"How do I know you didn't have something to do with this?"

I spun around. *"What?"*

"I'm serious." She stood from the bed. "You seemed all too eager to point the finger at me, but what about you? You're the one who handed me half the drinks I had last night. You're the one who insisted we drink the whiskey. Then when I went to sleep, you're the one who was up and dressed before I woke again. How do I know what you were doing while I was sleeping?"

My heart pounded in my ears, my body suddenly ice cold. "You can't be serious. You know I would never hurt her." She stared at me, the silence heavy between us, and I sighed. "I got dressed after you'd fallen asleep in case she cried out for one of us. I never left the bedroom. You're being ridiculous."

"Are you having an affair?" she asked, the words slicing through the room, so ludicrous and out of the blue it took me at least a minute to process them and respond. "Are you planning to get rid of me and Skylar so you can start a new life?"

It took everything I had not to laugh at the outlandish theory. "Am I *what?*"

"Having an affair," she said the words through gritted teeth, but her eyes were soft. Pained. "Don't lie to me, Cam. Not now. I need to know the truth. You've avoided it all this time and I was prepared to let it go, but you need to tell me the truth—"

"I haven't been avoiding anything. I've told you the truth. I'm not having an affair. I'm certainly not planning to *get rid of you.* How can you even ask me that? Who do you think I am, Ginny?"

Fresh tears fell down her cheeks. "I know these past few years have been difficult. I couldn't blame you, really. But I've worked so hard to get better. I got off the medicine because I wanted to prove to you I could be better. I stopped the therapy. I've done the work, and I thought we were okay again—"

"We've never *not* been okay. What are you talking about? Where is this coming from?" I took a step toward her, but she moved back.

"I heard her. Here. At the house. I know you said I didn't, that I was just dreaming, but I don't think that's true. I know you're seeing someone else. Or maybe you were—that I don't know—but I kept that from the police to protect you. Because I love you. Can you even still say the same?" She was sobbing at that point, her face wrinkled with despair.

"I've never stopped loving you. Never. I don't know what you heard that night. If it wasn't a dream, maybe it was the TV. But I'm not having an affair. End of story." I couldn't bring up what had happened with Alex now, even if I wanted to. All it would do is make me look guilty.

"Why don't I believe that?" she asked through her tears.

My hand went out to my side, palm up in a half shrug. "I have no idea what you do or don't believe, or why. Quite frankly, none of that matters right now. What matters is finding our daughter."

"Why are you avoiding this?"

"Because our child is missing, Ginny, and I, for one, would like to find her." With that, I stormed from the room, angry both with my wife and myself.

I heard the door open after me, and she cried out. "How can you say I don't care? I love her just as much as you do!"

"Well, you've had a funny way of showing it for the last three years!" I told her, spinning back around in the dark hall. I was trembling with rage by that point, no longer in control of my body or my words.

"How dare you use that against me? How dare you act like any of this is my fault? I've done the best I could. It doesn't mean I don't love her! You have no idea what I've been through, no idea how badly I've suffered. You don't know what it's like to watch your body fail at the one thing it's supposed to be able to do, then have it cut apart to bring your child into the world, only for that child to always choose the other parent over you. For your body to fail you in every way, all the way up to birth, and then for your mind to jump on board with the failing, too. For your entire world to fall apart, even though no one else can see it. To feel like you are trapped in an existence, in a darkness only you can see. To feel like you're failing at being a parent in every sense of the word, and then to feel like everyone blames you for not being better at what should come naturally..." She sucked in a ragged, exhausted breath, her palm covering her mouth as tears glinted in her eyes.

The statements had rolled out of her so easily, it was obvious they'd been building for quite some time. Was that really how she felt? That I blamed her? "You know none of that's true, Ginny. And, no, I don't know how you felt going through all you did, but you don't know how it feels to be helpless watching the person you love, the person you plan to spend your life with, go through it all either. Watching you slip into the darkness, becoming practically a stranger, and feeling like I had no control over it. Feeling helpless and wrong no matter what I did... No one wins right now, okay? We could both argue our case over who had it the worst, but there's no prize for it, is there? Right now, I just want to find Skylar."

"Fine," she said simply, shaking her head. Did she believe me? It was doubtful, but none of that mattered. Nothing mattered except Skylar.

"We're in this together, like it or not, which means we have to put everything aside and move forward."

"I said fine, Cam."

"And, for the record, I don't blame you. Not for that and not for this. I never should've said—"

"I think we've both made our share of accusations today," she said, cutting me off. "Let's just call our parents and get this over with."

I took a half step back, preparing to walk away, but froze.

"Are you sure you don't want me to stay? We can make the calls together."

"No. It'll be easier alone. I just want to get them out of the way so we can start figuring out what to do next."

"Okay, agreed," I said, wagging my phone in the air as I pulled it from my pocket. "I'm going to call them now."

She started to turn back for the bedroom, but I stopped her, though I don't know why. Maybe I just needed to hear the words said aloud. "Hey."

"Yeah?"

"We will find her, you know?"

She pressed her lips together with soft, quiet worry, but she neither confirmed nor denied her belief in what I'd said. I turned from her and departed from the room, repeating the words to myself.

If she was going to give up hope, I had to hold out for the both of us.

We will find her.
We will find her.
We will find her.

24 GINNY

Cam knocked on the bedroom door a half hour later. The phone call to my parents had lasted just under ten minutes, as I'd basically spit out what I had to say and gotten off the call. Since then, as I processed all that had happened, time seemed to be moving at a glacial pace. It was all very jarring—the extreme stress of our situation seemed to make time behave rather erratically, some stretches zipping past wildly out of control and others moving so slowly it was painful.

I didn't want to talk about it. It was too hard. Just saying the words to my folks, choking them out through my sobs, was excruciating. After the initial shock, my mother had cried on the phone with me as they plotted their next move. She didn't ask many questions, didn't say anything really, just cried and listened—as if she had been silenced by the shock of it all—then told me they'd be here as soon as they could. They were going to book the next flight out.

I felt guilty for making them return when they'd only just left, especially when there was nothing they could do by coming back, but she'd insisted she wanted to be there.

Obviously.

That's what a good mother would do. And my mother was a

good mother. She would never have allowed this to happen. She'd never have lost her child.

Once again, I'd failed.

When the door opened, I'd just shed my pajamas onto the floor and was pulling on clean clothes.

"Did you get ahold of them?"

"Yeah, my parents are trying to find a flight," I told him. "Yours?"

"Mom and Dad are, too. Margie's on a flight to Vancouver for the new movie. David's going to try and reach her once she lands. He said to keep them posted."

"He's not coming?"

Cam hesitated. "He didn't say, and I didn't push it. He said he'll try to reach her to let her know what's happening. Margie was telling me this movie is one of the biggest she's worked on. I'm sure it won't be easy for her to walk away from it. And David's got work, too."

"Their niece is missing!" I whined, pulling my hair into a loose, low ponytail.

"I get that," he said. "But it's not like they're going to be much help here right now anyway. Our parents are coming; that's enough. I'm sure Margie and David will come if we need them, but hopefully this will all be over in a few days and she'll be back home with us."

I swallowed, putting a hand to my chest. The idea of going a few days without her was brutal. It hurt me, maybe even more than Cam, because of the strain between Sky and me. Having such a tenuous relationship with my daughter had always been difficult, but today—now—not knowing when I'd see her again, the grief that came with missing her was unbearable. And, with the grief, came the worry that I'd be blamed. Not just by the police, but by my husband, my parents, the rest of our family. Even if they didn't blame me for this happening, would they believe I didn't miss her enough? Would they think this served me right?

I hadn't thought about that reality yet. Somehow, none of it seemed real. It felt as if she should be walking in the door at any moment.

"Where are you going?" he asked, when I didn't say anything.

"I want to check the woods." The sentence felt bitter on my tongue, unnatural to be saying. Why should I have to check the woods for my child? It wasn't right. How was this our reality?

But denying it wouldn't make it go away.

Like it or not, this *was* our reality.

"The police already checked it, didn't they?"

"Yeah, they did, but they don't know the places she likes to hide and the areas where we've gone for picnics. I want to check them again, now that it's a bit lighter out. If she heard strange voices, she might not come out, but if she hears us, she would. She may think she's in trouble. I just want her to know it's safe to come out. To come home—" I stopped again, trying to keep myself from sobbing. Frantically, I ran through the events of the party, trying to dislodge any memory that may have been suppressed. "Where is she, Cam?" I asked him. "Where could she be? How could this have happened?"

He seemed to have no answer as he moved toward his dresser slowly and pulled out clean clothes for himself. "I don't know," he said finally. "I've been replaying it in my head. Everything that happened yesterday, everything that was said, everyone at the party... None of it makes sense. I trust everyone here. They wouldn't want to harm her..." When he turned to look at me, he shook his head, his eyes distant and haunting.

"I know. I keep doing the same thing. There has to be something we're forgetting. If not, then what else could it be? She didn't just... v-vanish..." I trailed off, beginning to cry again.

"We're going to figure this out," he said, tugging his shirt over his head.

I dried my eyes, trying to slow my breathing. "Speaking of everyone that was here, I need to call Alex, too," I said, "but I want to wait until we've searched the woods. I don't want to worry her."

He was still, studying me.

"Are you going to call anyone else? I thought maybe we should call everyone from the party—"

"I don't really think we should be calling anyone just yet," he cut me off.

"Why not?"

"Because this is a family matter. We should let the police do their jobs—"

"No. No way. What are you even talking about? We need to be making posters, contacting the local news, making social media posts. We need Amber Alerts and interviews. People need to know she's missing!"

"I agree with you," he said, "about all of that, but in the first instance we need to be cooperating with the police. We need to follow their guidance."

"We aren't just sitting here." I grabbed my rain boots from the corner of the closet and tugged them on my feet. "We're going to look for her and then we're going to make a game plan."

I was out the door without waiting for him, already making my way down the hall as I tried to think of what areas I should search first. There were parts of our woods so overgrown with trees and vegetation, we rarely ever went into them, while others were lined with easy-to-manage paths. In the center, there was a small clearing where we'd often have picnics or set up fireworks on the Fourth of July.

As I passed her room, I couldn't stop myself from looking in, despite how much pain it caused me. The covers were gone, her toys thrown about. The room was practically bare, absent of everything, including its occupant.

In a fit of rage, I hurried forward, picking up the toys they'd left behind, the ones scattered across the floor. I picked up a doll that belonged on her bookshelf and pushed a few of her books back into place, closing her drawers and putting a pillow back onto the bed.

Why they'd chosen to take some things and leave others remained unclear.

As I bent down to tug at the ear of a bunny that had fallen under her bed, the white fluff barely visible, I froze.

What the—

In the shadows under her bed, I spied a doll with orange, yarn-like hair. I pulled her out into the light, staring down at the unfamiliar, plastic face. The green eyes were faded and chipped, her hair faded and browning.

The clothes she wore over her soft body were tattered, and she smelled musty. I ran a finger across her button nose and dimples.

Where did you come from?

I was positive the doll hadn't belonged to Skylar. In fact, I hadn't seen a doll like this in years. As a child, I'd never been much on dolls, but I remembered some of my friends playing with them even up through most of elementary school. I didn't think they even made them like this anymore.

At the sound of footsteps approaching the door and stopping, I held up the toy.

"Have you seen this doll before?"

Cam's face gathered into a wrinkled expression of confusion. "I don't think so. Where did she get it?"

"That's my question."

"Was it a birthday gift?" He stepped forward, holding out a hand and waiting for me to pass him the doll. "It looks really old."

"It *is* old, but I don't remember anyone ever giving it to her."

"Well, where did you find it?"

"It was under the bed."

He studied the doll once more. "It must've been something from one of our parents, then. Was it yours when you were little? Maybe your mom gave it to her and she doesn't ever play with it?"

"I've never seen that doll in my life. Do you think I'd be asking you this if I knew it was mine?"

He ignored the bite in my question, scratching his still-furrowed brow. "Well, maybe it was Margie's. My parents could've given it to Skylar, same as yours."

"But you don't recognize it?"

"It doesn't look familiar to me, no. But, if it was Margie's, I don't know if I'd recognize it. My parents could've just given it to her yesterday, I guess, but they didn't mention it." He tossed it back onto the bed. "We're wasting time. We can worry about that later. Are you ready to go?"

"Don't you think it's strange though? A toy that we've never seen before just shows up in her room?"

"Not really, no. She usually has the place so stuffed with toys I can't tell you what she has in here anymore. And I can't tell you the last time I cleaned under her bed. It's probably been here forever. We just don't recognize it because she never plays with it. Maybe it came with Margie's old kitchen set Mom brought a few years ago, or the hand-me-downs from your parents."

"Maybe," I said, but there was a nagging feeling in my gut that I couldn't deny. Something felt wrong about the doll and about why it had been left here, almost as if we were meant to find it.

"Anyway, the police didn't take it, so obviously they didn't think it was too important. Can we go?" He took a half step toward the door cautiously, and I stood, unable to shake the worry from my bones.

"You don't think we should tell the police?"

"Tell them what? That we found a doll we don't recognize?" he asked skeptically, staring at it again. When his eyes found me, I knew he recognized the answer in my worried gaze. "They searched her room. I don't see what telling about this will do."

"They could test it for DNA."

"What exactly do you think happened, Ginny?" He was frustrated now, bordering on irritated. "You think someone came in and stole her and left behind a souvenir? Like this is some cartoon and we're supposed to put together the clues? This isn't a freaking *Scooby-Doo* episode. We didn't find glowing footprints. We found a doll that has probably been under the bed for two years. If you want to call the police, call the police, I guess, but I'm going to look for her. This is pointless."

He waved a hand in my direction as if I were a lost cause and then turned to leave the room.

Had I been overreacting? It didn't feel like it, but maybe he was right. Maybe I was so desperate to have any sort of clue that I latched onto the toy as a source of hope.

But he was right. It was ridiculous to think someone had left it behind as a clue or sign or... whatever it was I'd thought, though I still wasn't clear on that, even to myself.

Without another word on the subject, Cam and I headed into the woods. The storm was continuing to rage, heavy rain pattering down on our heads, the sky gray and overcast. Our boots squished in the mud as we made our way around the house and toward the backyard. We could've split up. I could've taken the front while he took the back and we could've met somewhere in the middle, but I had no desire to be alone, even in the middle of a fight.

I couldn't lose anyone else.

There was a squad car parked near the end of our drive, far enough away that I couldn't see anyone in it, but I knew from the officer's warning that someone was there. Watching us. Waiting to see our next move.

I swallowed, looking away. If they thought we were going to reveal some terrible secret, they were wrong.

Instead, we walked toward the edge of the woods in the back-yard apprehensively, shielding our eyes from the cool rain. They were dark, both from the gray sky and the shadows of trees as far as the eye could see.

"She wouldn't have gone in here," Cam proclaimed loudly, shaking his head. I could hardly hear him over the wind and pattering of the rain. "She's scared of the woods, even when we're with her. She wouldn't have wandered off alone. Especially not in a storm like this."

He was right, of course. There was no way Skylar would've gone there alone, but the weight of what he wasn't saying, what he couldn't say, sat between us. *What if she wasn't alone?*

25 GINNY

We stepped into the woods almost as if stepping into an alternate realm. What had once been a place of solace and family picnics now had the possibility of unleashing the most devastating moment of our lives.

We walked slowly and cautiously, listening for bumps or cracks of twigs over the rain, for tiny footsteps or soft cries. When we rounded corners, I pictured spying her, her tiny arms outstretched for us, as if she'd just gotten lost playing a game of hide and seek.

I knew Cam was right. She wouldn't have wandered here alone, which meant it was very likely that if we found anything here, it wouldn't be positive news.

But any news was better than no news, right?

Or was it that no news was good news?

I couldn't decide.

We made our way through the muck and the mud of the cool woods, neither of us speaking as we checked in bushes and near the stream. The storm seemed to rage harder the longer we searched, as if the earth was fighting back against us.

We made it to the edge of our woods, marked off by a large ditch and posts spray-painted orange. She knew she could never go further than the posts. The ditch was dangerous—home to snakes and poison ivy and other things she knew would cause her harm.

She knew the rules, but would she have listened? If it was dark, would she have even seen the posts? She was only three. Still a baby. *My baby.* She shouldn't have been out here alone.

I pictured her running through the woods, lost and afraid, frightened as lightning flashed overhead, sending her tumbling down into the ditch. My breathing caught in my throat, fresh, helpless tears stinging my eyes. Hopelessness washed over me, my body suddenly numb as we approached the edge, searching for any sign of her, or of footsteps in the mud. To my equal relief and disappointment, we found nothing.

"Skylar!" I cried out, cupping my hands around my mouth. "Skylar, it's Mommy! Are you out here?"

Soon, Cam joined in, his hands around his own mouth, his voice carrying farther than mine had. "Skyyyylar! Skyyyylar! Are you here? Skyyylar?"

When my throat felt raw from screaming and we'd heard no response, we continued to follow the ditch until it ended, then made our way around the expanse of our property, a complete circle around our house until we'd landed back where we started, staring at the back of our home.

We left no stone unturned, searching until my body was sore and cold, my teeth chattering in the wind. As much as I hated to admit it, it now seemed certain we weren't going to uncover something the police had missed. Wherever she was, it wasn't here.

Though we didn't have our phones on us to check the time, I knew it had to be around midday. We'd been searching for hours.

With every minute that passed, I was reminded that we had even less time to find her. Every hour we hadn't found her, our chance of ever doing so decreased. We'd just wasted too many hours wading through the mud. I needed to come up with a new plan. A next step. I couldn't wait around for further instruction from the police like Cam wanted to do.

I wouldn't.

Skylar didn't have time for us to delay.

By the time we'd started the trek back toward the house, we were drenched and exhausted, our tears mixing with the rain so there was no telling them apart. My throat felt raw from yelling and from the many sobs I'd been quieting. Cameron's eyes were haunted and lost.

"The police already searched here," he shouted over the storm, though I wasn't sure if he was talking to me or himself. "The fact that we didn't find anything isn't surprising. They had... I mean, they had dogs and trained people. They would've found anything if there was anything to find."

I nodded, but he wasn't looking at me. None of that mattered. We should've been able to find her. I felt sure we would, but we hadn't. We'd failed her. We'd failed our daughter in the worst way.

"We should go back and check our phones... Just in case."

"Yeah."

When we reached the edge of the woods, our home finally in view, I felt his hand slip into mine. My earlier anger toward Cameron had dissipated. He was all I had. This tragedy was ours and ours alone. No one else would ever understand this pain.

I squeezed our palms together, holding onto him for dear life. Our movements were slow, because I knew for both of us, leaving the woods felt a little bit like giving up.

"I feel so useless," he said, his voice cracking.

"I know."

"I... I keep thinking, is she lost? Is she hurt? Is she scared? She must be looking for us and we aren't there..." He stopped speaking, expelling a silent cry, his eyes closed. I spun around, and it was my turn to gather him in my arms, letting him cry onto my shoulder as new tears blurred my vision. The rain coated our skin, but we didn't notice or care. Overhead, lightning shot across the sky and we both flinched.

"We're going to find her," I whispered, pressing my lips to his ear. It was a vow. We had to. He gripped my back, the pads of his fingers digging into my skin as he cried. His body trembled against mine, and in that moment, I couldn't help thinking of the officer stationed at the end of the driveway.

From where he was, I knew he could see us, though I refused to look his way. I knew he'd be scrutinizing our every move, deciding whether we were guilty.

I couldn't think about that. I didn't care what anyone thought anymore. I just wanted to find our daughter. I just wanted to bring her home. I had to do something. This couldn't be the end of our search.

I pulled away from him suddenly, walking back toward the house.

"Where are you going?" Cam jogged after me, wiping his face with the back of his arm.

"I don't know."

"What do you mean you don't know?"

"I mean, I don't know where I'm going, but I have to go somewhere. Do something. I can't just keep sitting here while she's out there." I held my arm out, gesturing toward the world that existed outside our little corner.

"The police said we should stay put, didn't they?"

"I don't honestly care what they said, Cam." We walked into the house, him following close behind me, and I grabbed the car keys from the rack. "I can't sit still anymore. I have to drive. I have to do something."

"I'm coming with you," he said.

I shook my head, stopping in my tracks. "No. You have to stay here."

"What are you talking about? No way am I—"

"You have to, Cam. In case she comes back. Or in case the police return. One of us has to stay."

"I don't want you to be alone right now. It's storming. You're soaking wet. I need to go with you."

"Because you don't trust me?"

"No, because I don't trust the rest of the world," he said firmly. "If she's... If something happened to her..." He inhaled sharply through his nose, unable to go on. "I can't let anything happen to you."

"I'll be fine." I placed a hand on his chest. "I swear to you. I'll be safe. I just need to feel like I'm being productive."

He nodded hesitantly. "How long will you be gone?"

"Not long," I said, because in truth, I had no idea. Maybe I'd never come back. "I just want to drive through the neighborhood."

He squeezed my hand, kissing my knuckles. "Come back to me. Call if you find anything out."

"You too."

With that, I was out the door and in the car. I drove past the officer's car without a second glance, though I felt his gaze on me. I wondered if they'd have someone follow me.

Let them.

I had nothing to hide, no matter what anyone thought.

The rain had let up a bit, so I drove the neighborhood slowly, looking in backyards and down each road, hoping that each one would be the one where I'd find her. At one point, I pulled over on the shoulder of the road, resting my head on the steering wheel as I cried. I closed my eyes, willing myself to find her. Mothers were supposed to know this sort of thing, weren't they? Intuition, natural instinct; like a GPS pinging me to her location. We were made of the same stuff, our bodies, our blood, one and the same. If anyone knew where she was, why wouldn't it be me?

She was out there somewhere, maybe feet away, maybe miles. She could still be in town or states away. Perhaps someone had taken her across the border or somehow boarded a plane. Would I ever see her again? Ever get to feel her tiny hands touch my face, get another sticky kiss, or struggle while she cried over her hair being brushed?

What I wouldn't do for one more car ride while Cam and I urged her to be quiet so we could hear the music. Or one night when we'd begged her to just go to sleep.

I'd taken so much for granted. So many moments.

So many evenings where I'd chosen to sleep rather than

playing with her. Or days where I'd wished the night would come quicker.

A truck blew past me, blaring its horn and splashing gray, murky water onto my car, and I looked up, wiping my eyes. I needed to go back home. Being out wasn't doing any good when I didn't have the first clue where to look.

The rain had stopped completely at that point, so on the way home, I stopped by the park, almost as if drawn to it.

It was our special place.

The one place on earth where Skylar and I could spend hours without tiring of each other, without her asking for her dad even once.

I pulled into the parking lot and got out, walking across the pavement and onto the grass. I was a mess, still in soaking wet clothes, and my face was blotchy from crying.

I hadn't expected anyone to be out so soon after the storm, but, to my surprise, I saw a few parents watching me wearily as I drew near. I tried my best to ignore them, wanting to scream out that they didn't know how lucky they were.

I searched every piece of equipment, glazing over a half dozen tiny blonde, red, black, and brunette heads, but none were hers.

When I noticed a familiar face, I took a deep breath, shaking my head.

How was it possible?

I moved closer, confirming, *yes,* it was definitely Raven. She was swinging on one of the lowest swings, moving her legs back and forth forcefully, though it was moving her mere inches. The knees of her pants were muddy and her hair was damp.

I searched the sea of parents for Alex's face.

Where are you?

Where are you?

Where are you?

I wiped my eyes again, pulling out my phone and dialing her number. It rang twice and went to voicemail. Where was she?

Without volition, I found myself walking toward Raven, and when I reached her, I smiled, hoping she'd recognize me.

"Hey, sweetie. Remember me? I'm"—I sniffled—"I'm Ginny. I'm Skylar's mommy." A flood of tears fell at the mention of her name, and I began crying again, fighting to speak through the tears. "Where's your auntie? Where's Alex?"

The girl stared up at me with fear and began crying.

"No, no. Please don't cry." I bent down, looking around and hoping to see Alex coming from the restroom. Instead, a rail-thin woman with dark roots and yellow-blonde hair was lumbering toward us, her gaze narrowed on me.

"Excuse me, can I help you?" She was irritated. I looked at Raven again. Did I have the wrong child? I knew it was her... Wasn't it?

I stood up, embarrassed heat radiating through me, and wiped my eyes. "I'm sorry. I didn't mean to bother her. My little girl plays here with her sometimes. I was looking for Alex."

"Alex?" One brow shot up, and she reached for Raven. "What are you talking about?"

"I'm sorry, this is embarrassing. That's Raven, right?" I didn't have time to be shy or polite.

The woman moved the girl behind her, but I saw the confirmation in her eyes. I didn't have the wrong child, so what was going on?

"*Who are you?*" she demanded. "How do you know my girl?"

"Your girl?" Realization hit me, and I heaved a sigh of relief. "Oh my god, you must be Alex's sister. I didn't realize you were in town." I put a palm to my face. "I'm so sorry. I'm Ginny, Alex's friend. Raven and my daughter, Skylar, play here together. I was just looking for Alex. I'm sorry if I scared you."

The woman leaned back, as if I were speaking gibberish. "Alex who? I have no idea what you're talking about."

"A-Alex... Kane. Your sister?" She stared at me as if I'd sprouted an extra head. What was going on? "Black, shoulder-length hair. She's... she's a therapist. In her late thirties." I cocked my head to the side, speaking slowly as it began to dawn on me that she must not be Alex's sister after all. Unless she had hundreds of sisters, how could she possibly have forgotten one to this extent? "She brings Raven here all the time."

The woman stared at me, then her hard expression vanished. "Oh. *That* Alex. Shit. Yeah, I always forget her name. Rae just calls her 'Auntie.'" She seemed to relax, letting go of Raven. "She's not my sister, though. She just keeps Raven for me sometimes."

"Oh, I must've... I must've misunderstood, then. I'm sorry."

"No prob," she said, waving me off. "Anyway, she's not with us."

"Do you know where she is? She isn't answering my calls."

The woman stared at me. She opened her mouth, then closed it again. "Why are you crying? Did something happen?"

"It's..." I couldn't tell her. I just couldn't. "It's just been a rough morning."

There was a sense of understanding in her eyes. She adjusted the strap of her tank top. "I'm not sure where she is." Her response was stiff, cold. "Sorry I can't help you. Go play, Rae." She nudged the girl forward and turned away from me, walking back toward a table where two men and another woman were waiting impatiently for her to return. One of the men appeared intoxicated, his skin pale, dazed eyes empty and out of sorts. I watched him extend his hand toward the girl that wasn't Raven's mom and saw the clumsy exchange of cash for a tiny, white packet.

Drugs.

I looked away quickly, hoping they hadn't seen me watching, though they didn't seem to care. I shivered, instantly feeling guilty about leaving Raven with them, but what right did I have to say anything? I could call the police, but selfishly, Skylar was my only priority. I wanted the police focused on her.

Besides, I couldn't shake the worry about why Alex had lied about her relationship to Raven.

What else had she lied about?

And why hadn't she answered my call?

26 ALEX

The rapping at my door came in quick succession. I placed the mug of tea down and walked down the hall from the kitchen, trying to get an idea of who could be at my door. I had no sessions scheduled.

My heart thudded as I worried it could be the police. Maybe it was a neighbor. Maybe a client. Maybe a burglar.

As the door came into view, I spied a familiar shape beyond the glass. My heart dropped as I pulled it open, trying to calm my racing heart.

"Ginny? What is it? What are you doing here? What's wrong?" Her cheeks were raw with tears.

"You lied to me."

My throat was suddenly dry. I could hear my heartbeat echoing in my ears. "Lied? About what?" Which lie was she referring to?

"About Raven," she said, sending relief through me. So, not the biggest lie. Not yet. "You said she was your niece, but you lied. What else have you lied about, Alex?"

I let out a steady breath. "Would you like to come inside? I can explain."

She held her ground, both hands on either side of the door frame. "Alex!" she cried.

I huffed. "You're right. I did lie to you about that, and I'm sorry. The truth is that Ella Rae, Raven's mother, lives across the street." I gestured toward the rotting two-story home, but Ginny didn't bother looking. "She's... she *was* a client of mine as a teenager. She had Raven really young, and she's had a rough time. She's stable, for now, but it never lasts long. I keep Raven for her when she's in a tough spot. The truth is, the girl is safer here than anywhere else her mother would leave her." I paused, letting what I'd said sink in. "I'm sorry I lied to you. It was just easier to call her my niece than try to explain all of that."

"She was your client and you keep her child? Really? Because she didn't even remember your name," she said firmly, her eyes searching mine for a glimmer of the truth. "What is going on here?"

I shook my head, trying not to sound too annoyed as I answered. Ella Rae never ceased to amaze me with her lack of regard for her child. "Look, Ella Rae isn't the most responsible parent. Half the time, she doesn't remember where she lives or that she even has a daughter. She's..." I sighed. There was too much to explain. "I've told her my name over and over, but she doesn't care to remember it."

She nodded, her jaw locked as she stared at the door, processing everything I'd said. "That's terrible..."

"It is," I said, relieved to see the anger and suspicion fading from her eyes. "Is that all? You've been crying. Is something else going on?"

Tears welled in her eyes as she met mine again. "It's Skylar."

My body tensed. *No.* "What's wrong with her?"

"She's... She's gone. Someone took her."

"What do you mean?" I stepped out onto the porch, shutting the door behind me and gathering her into my arms. She leaned her weight onto me, her tears soaking through my shirt. "What's going on? Talk to me. What happened?"

It seemed like forever before she found her voice, but when she did, she said, "We woke up after the party, early this morning, and she was gone."

"Gone?" I pulled back, studying her.

"Gone," she confirmed. "She's not in her bedroom. I have no idea where she is."

"Well, she can't be *gone*. Did you check every room? The woods? The yard?"

Her hand formed a fist, her eyes wide. "Of course. Do you honestly think I'd be here telling you she was missing if we hadn't checked everywhere? We've called the police, Alex. This isn't just me being dramatic!"

A lump of worry formed in my stomach, the blood draining from my face. "Police? You've already called the police?"

"Yes!" she said quickly. "Our daughter is missing. Skylar is really, really missing."

"Oh my god." Maybe for the first time, the reality of what had happened was setting in for me. I pulled her into a hug again, tears stinging my own eyes. "I'm so sorry, Ginny. I never thought you were being dramatic, I just... I didn't want to believe it. I don't even know what to say. What do the police think? What are they saying? You guys must be worried sick."

She nodded, looking as if that went without saying because it did. "They're not telling us much, honestly. I don't think they believe us."

"What do you mean?"

"I think they believe we had something to do with it. They told us to stay put, and they've got a detective watching us."

I looked around, searching the street for the mysterious cop car that might be following her. "Well, I wouldn't jump to any conclusions. It's fairly standard for them to have a detective watching the parents in the case of a missing child. It's not necessarily because they think you're guilty of anything nefarious, they just have to cover all their bases. I can't imagine they think you and Cam could've done anything wrong."

"Well, I might've believed that if not for Cam telling them about me cutting back on my medication. And that I've stopped coming to therapy. I'm terrified they're going to try and pin this on me, but I swear to you, Alex, I had nothing to do with this. I love her so much." She was crying again, and I shook my head, shushing her as I brushed her hair from her eyes.

"Of course, you didn't. Oh, of course you didn't. I know you love her, sweetheart. I know. Listen to me. Listen, I don't want you to worry. There's nothing to pin on you because we're going to find her, okay?"

"I tried to call you," she whined, her face red and scrunched from crying.

I glanced back into the house. "I woke up late and had a session first thing. I haven't even checked my phone yet. I'm so sorry."

"I really need you today, Alex. Can you come home with me? Please? I... I can't do this alone."

I swallowed, trying to think. "You know I'll be here for you however I can. I have one session this afternoon that I can't cancel. I can move the rest around a bit, though. As soon as I'm done, I can head straight over."

She nodded but didn't look relieved. "I love her, Alex. You know I love her."

"Of course, you do," I assured her, smoothing my hands over her arms. "It's going to be okay." There were new tears in my eyes. "I'm so sorry, Ginny."

"We're going to find her," she said, a question in her words. "We have to."

I nodded, squeezing her hands quickly. "We will. I promise we will."

"I'm sorry I yelled at you," she said softly.

"You don't have to apologize to me. I'm the one who lied."

"I was just upset over Sky—" New sobs interrupted her, and I hugged her a final time.

"You don't have to explain. Just go home and be with Cameron, okay? Go home and wait. It's all going to be okay. I'm going to call my clients and rearrange my afternoon. I'll be over to your house in a few hours. I promise."

She sniffled. "My parents are coming, too. This is another thing for my mom to tell me I failed at." Her shoulders shook with heavy sobs. "She never lost me."

"We're going to find her," I said again firmly. I looked inside. "Do you want to come in? I have a little bit before my first session."

She shook her head, much to my relief. "I should get home." She dragged her hand under her nose. "I promised Cam I wouldn't be gone long. I left in the middle of the storm, so I know he'll be worried if I don't get back home soon."

I nodded, watching her descend the stairs with a sinking feeling in my stomach. "Be careful."

27 CAMERON

The phone went off in my hand, interrupting my pacing by the front door, and I looked down at the screen. It was a number I didn't recognize. Had Ginny had a wreck? Had the police found Skylar?

A million questions swam through my mind.

"Ginny?"

"Wrong girl," came Alex's soft, easy-going voice.

"Oh." We hadn't spoken, except for briefly and awkwardly at the birthday party, since the night we'd slept together. As time went on, I'd begun to piece together the hazy memory, and I felt sure that it had happened, though I desperately wished it hadn't.

I'd been an ass. I'd hurt my wife in a way I swore I never would again. It was killing me in a way I wouldn't wish on my worst enemy. I was surprised when she'd shown up at the party, truth be told, but she didn't mention what had happened once, so I hoped we could move past it.

I'd been nervous when I'd caught Alex and Ginny together—like when I'd come inside to find them cleaning up the wrapping paper while everyone else was watching Skylar with her Jeep—and I'd panicked. I knew Alex would have a million chances to tell Ginny what we did, and thought it was illogical that I could keep them apart forever, I wanted time to process all that had happened and I still hadn't gotten that chance.

Now, hearing her voice on my phone, my insides recoiled, a lump forming in my throat that I couldn't swallow down. My body tightened, muscles contracting. I could hardly catch my breath. Everything hurt.

Before I could say anything, she added, "I'm so sorry about Skylar."

It hurt to hear her name.

"We're going to find her," I said, forcing her to believe it. Forcing myself.

"Is there anything I can do?"

"Just... give us some space."

She was quiet for a moment. "I want to help, Cam."

"I know you do, but this is between Ginny and me. Our family."

"You know how much I care about both of you. I thought you'd want my help. Ginny needs me right now. I've already told her I could come over."

"Please just, Alex, please... If you care about me at all, you'll stay out of this."

"I care about Skylar, too," she said softly. "What happened between us, it doesn't matter. Ginny doesn't have to know. It was a mistake. I haven't told her—I won't tell her."

Suddenly, I felt as if she was tricking me. Like she had me on speakerphone with Ginny standing next to her.

"What the hell are you even talking about?" I asked too aggressively.

"I-the night... When we, I mean when we slept together."

I forced a cold laugh. "I have no idea what you're talking about. I have to go."

"Cam, wait!"

"It's Cameron. And don't call me again," I said firmly, and with that—though it meant nothing to anyone at all—I ended the call, my chest rising and falling with heavy breaths.

"What was that about?"

I spun around, shocked to see my wife standing there. How long had she been there? What had she heard?

"I, um"—I tried to slow my breathing—"Wrong number. They were looking for someone else."

She nodded, though I wasn't sure she believed me, so I quickly changed the subject.

"Did you find anything? Hear anything?"

She shook her head. "Nothing. Here?"

"Nothing."

She shut the door and pulled off her jacket, tossing it onto the chair next to the coat rack. It was one we'd found in an antique store that Ginny just *had to have*, but it mostly gathered dust now, when it wasn't a catch-all for whatever we brought in the house. Next came her muddy boots, which she placed next to mine. Ordinarily, she'd have made sure we cleaned them immediately, but this wasn't the time for that.

Nothing mattered except Skylar.

"Where did you go?"

"I drove through the neighborhood first, around town. Then I stopped by the park. And I ended up at Alex's house because she wasn't answering her phone and I really wanted to talk to her."

I thought back to the phone call, wondering again what she may have overheard. "Did you get to see her?"

"Yeah, for just a minute. She's planning on coming over when she finishes up with her client."

I nodded, thinking. "Do you think that's a good idea?"

"Why wouldn't it be?"

"I mean, tensions are kind of high right now. The police could come back. Do you think it's a good idea to have so many people here?"

I couldn't explain why I thought it was such a bad idea for Alex to be there, even to myself. Perhaps because of what had happened with us that night, but she was right. She'd been nothing but normal at the party. It was me who was struggling to act like nothing had changed.

Because everything had changed.

Even if I forgot about the sex, Alex had seen me vulnerable in a way not many others had. I didn't want her clouding up the space with all of her feelings-talk and questions. I didn't want Ginny to know we'd been meeting.

It just felt too dangerous to have her here any more than necessary.

"It's just one more person," she said simply. "I need her here, Cam. I need someone to help keep me calm. She knows how to make me better, and I just need her, okay?"

"Yeah, fine," I said finally. There was no sense in arguing.

"I think we should talk about last night. About everything that happened. Run through the events and all that. Was there anyone acting weird at the party?"

I paused, trying to make sense of her question. "Wait... You aren't actually suggesting anyone in our family had something to do with this, are you?"

"I'm suggesting we walk through everything that happened. We should actually go back the entire week before the party. From the moment they started arriving. Maybe it'll help jog something in our memory." She walked past me into the living room and sank onto the couch, pulling her legs up in front of her.

I followed suit, sitting down at the opposite end of the couch. "Okay, well, my parents arrived on Monday."

"Right. And mine came on Wednesday."

"Everything seemed normal to me," I said with a shrug.

"When your parents arrived, you were in the basement with your dad for a while. What were you doing down there?"

I tried to recall. "Oh, I was showing him the renovations and helping to bring the Jeep in from the back of their truck and get it hidden so Skylar wouldn't accidentally find it."

"Hey, speaking of, did he lock the door back?"

"The garage door? I don't remember, but I'm sure we did. Why?"

"Well, at the party, Margie and David had come in through that door, but I told them we keep it locked. I remembered giving them a key when they house-sat for us before, but they said the door was unlocked. I'm wondering if maybe they didn't lock it back and that was how someone could've gotten in."

I tried to think back. I hadn't checked the garage door that night, I was sure of it. It was always locked, so I hardly ever checked it. "Did you mention that to the police?"

"I mentioned that Margie and David had a spare key once, but I didn't think about the door until just now."

"Margie gave us back the spare key after they house-sat. They just had it for that short time."

She nodded, but there was something she wasn't saying. "Do you think they might've made a copy?"

"Why would they do that?" I scoffed, and then it hit me. What she was saying. What she was accusing my sister of. "Margie wouldn't have kidnapped Skylar."

"I'm not saying she did, but it would mean there's another key out there somewhere. Unaccounted for."

She was right, I realized, but that didn't make it any easier to swallow. "She wouldn't have made a key and not told me."

"Have you heard back from her? From David? Weren't they supposed to call?"

The storm had begun to pick back up outside, and I heard the spattering of rain on our windows. "Not yet. I don't know what time her flight was supposed to land. David wasn't sure, either. I can ask about the key, but I don't think they would've had a reason to make a key, and they certainly wouldn't have misplaced it. Margie isn't irresponsible."

She twisted her lips with a look I'd seen all too often. There was something she wanted to say, but she wanted me to drag it out of her. I was in no mood to play games.

"What is it, Ginny? What aren't you saying?"

She looked relieved to get it out. "It's probably nothing, but... when I came in to get lemonade, that was when I found them inside. They said they'd come in the back door, through the garage, and they must've because I never saw them come in through the front, but it was strange, you know? Why would they come in through the garage? They would've had to go out of their way to walk around the house and go in through the garage. Why not just go through the front door? Unless they were trying to hide something."

With those words, I knew where the conversation was going, but I had to pretend I didn't. I needed to steer her away from this dangerous territory.

"Hide something? What on earth would they be trying to hide?"

"I don't know, but they were whispering in the hallway, and when I found them, they were acting really strange and they left immediately after that. Are you sure she didn't mention anything to you?"

"No, not at all," I said. "She'd already told me she couldn't stay long because they had to get home in order for her to catch her flight for the shoot."

She deliberated silently and I waited, wondering what she was going to say. Finally, I added, "Margie had nothing to do with this. You know that, right? She would never have hurt Skylar. She was back in New York before we even had her down for the night."

She gave an exaggerated frown, closing her eyes. "I know. I know you're right, but, if not her, then who? Who could've done this? You have to at least admit they were acting strangely."

I felt defensive for Margie and angry with Ginny for suggesting she could've had anything to do with it. I knew my sister. I knew what she was capable of, and it wasn't this.

"Well, what about your parents, then? Your mom seemed kind of quiet, don't you think? She didn't really talk to me as much as usual."

To my surprise, she didn't look taken aback by my comment.

Was she honestly considering the idea that our families might have taken our child? I knew we were looking for someone to blame, but we were looking in the wrong place. She had to see that.

"No, she was the same as usual. She was fighting off a bit of a cold, I think, so maybe that was why she seemed different."

"Maybe..." I trailed off.

"Okay, so everything was fine then. Margie and David came in Saturday morning, but I was in the shower. I'm guessing they didn't seem any different than normal?"

"No. I mean, David was really busy." We both gave a look like *what else is new*. "So, he was on the phone quite a bit while you were getting ready, but that's not unusual."

"And when did Alex arrive?"

"Just before the party started. Maybe one-ish?"

"Same as Alyssa and Norma?"

"Yeah, they came together. Joe was here about then too, but Stephen came later. He'd just gotten here when the party started."

"Okay. And everyone seemed in good spirits, from what I remember... No one acted out of character?"

"They're our friends, Gin. None of them acted like they wanted to steal our child, if that's what you mean."

She pressed her lips together, her eyes darting back and forth in thought. "I'm not trying to accuse them of anything, but someone took her. We have to be diligent about this. We can't rely on who we trust right now."

She was right, of course. But that didn't make it any easier. "Okay, well, did we see everyone leave? I mean, actually see them?"

Her eyes narrowed as she chewed the inside of her lip. "I don't remember. Joe didn't stay long after we went outside, did he? I don't think he stayed for dinner."

"Yeah, something about his aunt's anniversary. He'd already told me he couldn't stay long. What about Norma or Alyssa? They rode together. Anyone else would've left a car."

"No, I walked them to Norma's car when we finished dinner. I really hadn't expected them to get to come, and I'd felt guilty for not getting to talk to them all night. They definitely left."

"And then Alex left and we both saw her off, then..."

"Stephen?" she filled in.

"Yeah, that's right. Stephen was next. He helped clean up and stayed for cake. Then it was my parents and yours last."

"And you locked the door, right? Definitely? The front door at least?"

"Yeah," I confirmed, thinking back. I always triple-checked it. There was no way, even with a few drinks in my system, I would've left the door unlocked. "Yeah, it was locked."

"And no one would've known about the garage door except Margie, David, and maybe your parents."

I didn't like that suddenly all the blame was falling on my family. "They wouldn't have known we didn't lock it."

"I asked David to lock it, and he said he would. I told him we rarely check it." She wasn't looking at me anymore, her eyes distant.

"Either way, they were on a plane," I reminded her, bringing her back to me.

"Right." She didn't believe me, but it didn't matter. Margie and David hadn't taken Skylar. I knew they were dealing with a lot, things I couldn't even tell Ginny, but they would've never taken my child.

"So, everyone left..."

"Except us."

I swallowed, the truth sitting heavy in the air. Everyone had left the house that night except for us. The doors and windows should've all been locked. The spare keys were accounted for. We went to bed and then... What?

What happened in the hours between us going to bed and waking up in the early hours of the morning?

It was as if our daughter had simply vanished.

28 GINNY

The next few hours moved slowly and without updates. We waited by our phones, jumping every time one went off, but it was typically just our parents or friends checking in.

No one seemed to know what to say, us included.

We spent a lot of time wandering into Skylar's bedroom—the air there seemed dense with grief somehow, but I kept hoping foolishly that being inside the walls would help me unlock the secrets they held. This had been the last place we saw her, the place we'd put her to bed and kissed her goodnight.

I'd kissed her goodnight, hadn't I?

I remembered taking off her birthday dress and pulling the Peppa Pig pajamas over her head. Had we made sure she brushed her teeth?

Cam had read her the story that night.

We switched back and forth most nights—excluding the nights recently when I'd been especially tired or in the past when I'd been struggling with my depression—and last night was his turn. I'd snuck out in the middle of the last story to get some water, as the room had felt unusually hot, probably from the alcohol sloshing in my belly.

If I'd known then that those moments might've been my last with her, you couldn't have prised me away.

But I couldn't think that way. I knew I couldn't—I had to have hope—but it didn't stop my mind from traveling there, diving deeper into the darkness with horrifying thoughts of never seeing her again and what might've happened to her.

I swore to myself I'd never watch another true crime documentary.

Never read another murder mystery.

Never again would I take pleasure in someone else's pain if, by some miracle, she would just come home.

The police let us know that they'd been in contact with everyone who'd attended Skylar's party except for Margie, confirming their alibis for after the party and asking them questions about the events they'd witnessed before they left.

I'd tried to text Alex and check in, but had yet to receive a response. Was she angry with me? I wouldn't blame her if she was, the way I'd charged at her after the Raven revelation.

It wasn't like the lie had affected me in the slightest really, but the events of the day had built up, and I'd snapped.

I could only imagine what the police must've asked her about me and what she may have revealed. Would she have told them about my struggles? About how distant I felt from Skylar? About how I worried I wasn't a good enough mother?

What sort of picture would she paint about me?

I knew Alex would protect me the best she could, but confidentiality only went so far. Alex had explained that at the beginning of our sessions—she would not protect information if it was at the potential harm of another human being. In this case, my daughter. Alex couldn't lie for me. I'd never expect her to.

Still, I wished she would call. I wished Margie would call, too, though it did little good to press Cameron on the issue. We'd heard from David once more, just to let us know that he'd spoken to the police and tried to contact Margie, but that there was still no news from her.

It was suspicious. She was acting strangely, and I knew something had to be going on, but Cameron wouldn't hear of it.

As the sky began to darken with evening setting in, I wasn't sure who to worry about more, Alex, who still hadn't shown up or Margie, who seemed determined not to answer our calls.

On top of that, our parents had both scheduled flights that were set to arrive the next day, so I needed to begin working out arrangements, making beds, and cleaning up. But I had no energy to do it. Any of it. I just wanted to sit. To exist. To worry about my child.

She'd never spent a full night away from me. The realization wasn't one I was ready for. She was spending a night away from me for the first time, and I had no idea if she was safe or scared or—the worst didn't bear thinking about.

My phone buzzed, and I looked down, hoping to see good news.

Any updates?

My mom's text sat on my screen. Likely the tenth one of the day. We'd spoken on the phone a few times, too, but texts were easier as she was packing and sorting everything out there before their flight.

I could feel the judgement in her text. Though she'd been kind on the phone, heartbroken and sorrowful, but incredibly considerate of my feelings, I felt the weight of what she must be thinking. How could I have lost my daughter?

Nothing yet... Still waiting.

Her reply was almost instant.

She's out there. Don't give up. Be there soon. XO.

I put the phone down, resting my head on the back of the couch. My cheeks were raw from crying, my eyes dry and sore. I felt unable to cry anymore. My body felt like I'd gone through an extreme workout, every muscle tense and tender.

"We should organize a search party," Cameron said from across the room. My eyes shot open. "We could put up posters, announce it on social media... People would come out to help."

"And search where, Cam? The woods have already been searched. Where else is there?"

"We could search the woods again," he suggested. "Go even farther than we did before. With a large group of people, we could cover a lot of ground."

I stared into space as I mulled over the idea, unable to move. I didn't want to think anymore. I didn't want to plan or organize. I just wanted her home. The idea of gathering in a large group of our friends, families, and nosey strangers, having to recount the events that led us here... It was all too much.

"Do whatever. We'd have to wait until morning. It's going to be dark out soon."

He glanced toward the window and stood. "I'm going to reach out to the detective on our case and ask him if they would help. Police normally get involved in that sort of thing, don't they?"

I shrugged one shoulder, wrapping my arms around myself. I was starting to give up already, I could feel it. Deep down, I felt the pit of despair coming back, the darkness clouding my vision. My body was exhausted, sore. I was having trouble focusing on anything.

I knew the signs and what they meant, the symptoms I'd finally gotten away from for a while.

I needed to speak to Alex.

Or take my medication.

But I had no will to do either.

Instead, I closed my eyes as I heard Cameron pacing in the kitchen. He was saying something, I thought, but I couldn't pay attention to it. It didn't matter.

Nothing mattered at all anymore.

29 CAMERON

After Ginny had fallen asleep, I made my way into the bedroom, reading over the string of texts from Alex. They'd been coming in throughout the day, since I'd hung up on her, but I hadn't responded to a single one. Now, though, I needed to address what she was saying.

> The police came by while I was with a client. I called them back and told them everything I know... We should talk soon.

> I know you don't want to talk about what happened between us, and that's fine, but I'm worried. About Skylar. About Ginny. Please call me when you get a chance.

> I don't want to think it and I know you don't either, but she wanted life back to the way it was before Skylar. No

medicine, no therapy, no child? Please call me. I don't want to jump to conclusions, but we need to figure this out together. I care about you all.

I'm probably just being dramatic, but I'm scared, Cameron. I'm really scared. Just tell me I'm overreacting and I'll believe you.

Did you tell the police she's off her meds?

Have you heard anything?

I'm respecting your wishes by not coming over, but you need to tell me what's going on.

Please. Please just let me know if you find her.

Cam? Are you getting these?

I clicked on her number at the top of the messages and placed the phone to my ear, letting it ring.

"Oh, thank god. I was starting to get worried," she said, all in one breath.

"You need to stop texting me, Alex."

"I'm not trying to bother you. I stayed away like you asked, and I didn't call anymore because I'm assuming she's home, but I have an obligation to report it if I think my client is a danger to herself or anyone else."

"What are you saying?"

"If you've been reading my texts, you know exactly what I'm saying. Don't tell me you haven't thought about it."

I'd thought about it more than I was willing to admit, but that didn't mean I was ready to throw my wife under the bus with Alex. "Ginny was home in bed. She had nothing to do with this."

"At least, that's what she wants you to believe."

"You don't know her—"

"I know her better than you realize. I know how her brain works. I know how she processes emotions. I know yesterday was very hard for her." She spoke slowly, letting each sentence linger in the air through the line. "Look, I don't think Ginny was ready to be off her medication. I told you when she stopped taking it that I thought it was a bad idea to stop at the same time she stopped seeing me."

"And I agreed with you—"

"I'm not blaming you. Or her, for that matter. I'm simply saying..." She huffed. "Cameron, the police asked me if I thought she was capable of harming Skylar."

The same question they'd asked me.

"And what did you tell them?"

"I told them Ginny loves Skylar and that I didn't believe she was dangerous."

I breathed a sigh of relief. "Thank y—"

"But I did tell them that changes in medication can affect different people in different ways. It affects the chemistry of our brains. I couldn't leave that out. As of now, I don't think they suspect she had anything to do with this, but I need to make sure

I'm not lying to them. I could get into trouble, myself. More importantly, I could be putting Skylar in danger."

"Alex, you know she didn't do this."

"Do I? Do *you*? The truth is, none of us know. If she hurt Skylar, Cameron, I have to report it. I could lose my license. I could go to prison. So could you. We can't protect her from this if she's guilty."

"Skylar's fine. She's not hurt. She can't be." I felt cool tears stinging my eyes.

"I hope you're right. For all of our sakes, I hope you are, but you need to keep an eye on her. A close one. And, if you start to suspect something's off, you need to tell me. Or the police. Can you promise me you'll do that? We love her, so we have to protect her, even if that means protecting her from herself. Promise me."

"I promise," I swore. I didn't know if it was a lie. At the moment, it didn't matter. I could hardly breathe, trying to quiet my sobs. "I should go."

"Take care of yourself, Cam. Take care of her. Keep me updated, please."

With that, I ended the call, new questions swirling in my mind. When the day had started, I'd accused Ginny of being responsible for this, but as the day progressed, I saw the genuine panic and fear in her eyes. I didn't still believe she could ever harm Skylar, or anyone else, did I? Things had been better lately. She'd been better. That was because she'd cut back from the therapy and gotten off the medicine that hadn't worked for her, wasn't it?

It had nothing to do with what happened to Skylar...

Did it?

30 GINNY

When I awoke the next morning, I still had no desire to do anything, which meant I had to do something.

I was exhausted, despite having slept the full night. I found Cameron at the kitchen table, a mug of coffee in his hand. When I walked into the room, his eyes widened, almost as if he'd been asleep sitting up, and he shook his head, groaning.

"You okay?"

He took a sip of coffee, nodding.

"No updates?"

"My parents' flight was delayed. Nothing from the police."

I inhaled and began filling the kettle with water. Suddenly, it hit me. "Alex never came by, did she?"

"She must've gotten caught up. Have you heard from your folks?"

"Just here and there. They're supposed to let me know when they board the flight." I put the kettle down, half-filled, and walked back into the living room, digging in the couch cushions until I'd located my phone. The battery was low and I had two texts from my mom, checking in again.

Nothing from Alex.

I went to my recent calls and selected her name, a strange

feeling in the pit of my stomach. Why wasn't she answering? Why hadn't she reached out to explain why she wasn't here yet? It wasn't like her to ignore me. It definitely wasn't like her to stand me up.

As her voice came over the speaker, prompting me to leave a detailed message, I ended the call and made my way into the entry-way, grabbing my jacket and keys.

"I'm going to therapy," I called. "I'll be back."

"Wait! You're wh—"

I was already out the door before he could finish his question, shoving my phone into my jacket pocket and hurrying toward the garage. As I pulled out of the driveway, wipers going full speed, Cam was standing on the porch watching me go.

I couldn't read his expression from there, but I knew it would radiate disappointment. I'd let him down, maybe past the point of no return, but I needed to check in with Alex, if not to save our friendship, then to save myself.

———

Half an hour later, I parked in front of Alex's house. It hadn't stopped storming, as if the sky was grieving too. I glanced at the clock on the dashboard, noticing it was just after seven a.m. I'd always had evening sessions with Alex and, truth be told, I had no idea if she was an early riser.

I tried to call her phone once more from the car, but she didn't answer, so I threw my jacket over my head and dashed up the walk and onto the porch. The glass on the door had dark curtains behind it for the first time, and I felt a lump form in my stomach. What was going on?

I rapped my knuckles against the wood, waiting patiently.

What if something was wrong?

She'd told me her last session for the day yesterday was urgent. What if the patient had gotten angry if she'd tried to move it around? What if she'd been hurt? Attacked?

I knocked harder, louder, my heart suddenly pounding in my ears. No. Please, no. I couldn't take any more heartbreak.

"Hello? *Alex?* It's me!"

Seconds later, I heard heavy footsteps headed in my direction and the curtains parted slightly. She swung the door open, dressed down in sweats with her hair in the tiniest ponytail. She folded her arms across her chest, staring around the porch as if she'd expected me not to be alone.

"Ginny? What is it? Is everything okay? Did they find her?"

The question was painful. I wanted to say yes. I wanted it more than I wanted anything. I forced the thought away. I couldn't do it... Couldn't think about it. If I did, I was going to break down.

"Not yet. Cam is organizing a search party on social media. I knew you wouldn't see it, so I wanted to invite you."

"Oh, sure. Of course." She nodded solemnly. "You didn't have to come all the way over here for that."

"Well, you aren't answering your phone, and I was worried after you didn't show up yesterday."

"Right," she said, as if she'd only just remembered she was supposed to be coming by. "Look, I'm sorry I couldn't make it yesterday. I had a few things come up with clients, and I just... I couldn't."

"I understand," I told her, though it was a lie. I was hurt by the casual way she'd abandoned me when I needed her the most. What could be more important than my missing daughter? "Is... this a bad time?"

She glanced behind her into the house. "I've got a session this morning... When do you need me for the search party? Today or...?"

"Um, I don't know yet." Tears stung my eyes as I realized I hadn't even asked. That should've been my first priority, but instead, I'd been so focused on forcing the thought out entirely, trying not to go down the dark path again. I didn't want to think about the fact that she was missing. It all just hurt too much. "I think it'll be today. Once the storm subsides. Maybe even if it doesn't. Cam's trying to coordinate it with the police." I paused. "I'm assuming they came by yesterday to talk to you."

"They did, yeah, but I was in with a client, so I had to call them after." Her eyes softened slightly. "How are you holding up?"

"Oh, um..." I was caught off guard by her question, and I felt the floodgates beginning to break. I looked down, brushing away a tear as it fell. "Scared, you know. Sad. But mostly scared."

She nodded, and I noticed her hands were trembling as she reached up to pull me into a hug. "I know you must be."

I sucked in a breath as I fell into her arms. "I miss her so much."

"I know," she said softly, saying nothing else as she rubbed her palm over my back. There was nothing else to say, I supposed, but it felt like a snub, like she couldn't care less. Why did I feel so abrasive toward her? Toward Margie and our parents, too? Lately, I felt angry about so much.

"I was worried you didn't come because you were mad at me about yesterday."

She seemed genuinely confused as she pulled back away from me, her brows drawn down. "Yesterday?"

"You know. The whole... Raven thing."

"Ahh," she said in a breath. "No, no, no, no, no. I'm not mad at you. Don't you worry another second about that. Honestly, consider it forgotten."

I nodded, but I wasn't so sure. She swiped away another of my tears but didn't pull me back in for a hug. Instead, she gripped onto the door again as if she were planning to shut it.

I lifted a hand. "Listen, I know we aren't on the books for today, but do you have time for a quick session?"

"Oh, I—" Her mouth formed the perfect 'O'.

"I wouldn't ask if it wasn't important. I'm having a really tough time, Alex. My head isn't where it should be, and... I just keep feeling like I did before. Before I met you. Before the therapy. I'm worried that going through all of this will make me regress."

She seemed to contemplate what I was saying, holding me in

an uncomfortable moment of vulnerability and suspense as I tried to decipher her unreadable expression.

Finally, she looked back into the house again. "Sure, of course. Just let me run upstairs and change into something a little more professional." She stepped back, allowing me inside.

"Oh, you don't have to change clothes for me. I'm still in what I wore yesterday."

She waved off the suggestion as she shut the door. "It'll make me feel better. Putting on work clothes reminds me that it's time to work. It's sort of ritualistic, I guess, but I can hardly make it through a session if I don't do it. Anyway," she cut herself off, "just go on in and have a seat, and I'll be right back down."

I did as she'd said and sank down on the couch, feeling an almost immediate uplifting of my spirit. My soul felt at peace there. I knew what I'd accomplished in this room, and I knew I could do it again.

I could hear Alex moving around upstairs, but I froze, cocking my head to the side when I heard a second, softer set of footsteps. Did she have a guest?

Suddenly, I realized I might've been intruding on something very private. Was this why Alex hadn't come to my aid yesterday? Was she seeing someone? Why hadn't she told me?

She knew so much about my life, both from therapy and not, but I knew so little about hers. She wasn't married, of course, but did she have a boyfriend? A girlfriend?

She'd never come across as the type to have a one-night stand, but then again, how would I know for sure?

I didn't want to interrupt whatever she had going on—

I froze as I heard a high-pitched squeal. Lightning shot through my body, the hairs on my arms standing on end.

What was that?

I stood and moved toward the doorway, concerned about what was going on up there but also not wanting to intrude or overstep.

I heard the shuffling of feet again and then a light giggle.

Alex was... *giggling?* Was she giggling or crying? I couldn't tell.

I made my way toward the stairs quietly, trying not to make a sound. The bottom step groaned under my weight, and I heard Alex say, *"Stop,"* through what sounded like gritted teeth and tight lips.

What was going on up there?

I heard a thud upstairs and took two more stairs, my body trembling. Immediately, I began worrying that something terrible was happening. Was she being held hostage? Was someone robbing her?

I reached for my phone in my pocket as I stepped onto the third stair, but before I could place the call, a door on the floor above me opened and closed quickly, and I heard footsteps headed in my direction. I froze, trying to decide whether to stay the course or turn around.

Before I'd made up my mind, Alex rounded the corner, her eyes wide. "Ginny?" She looked bewildered to see me standing on her stairs. "What are you doing?"

"Are you okay? I was worried, I thought I heard something..." I pointed up the stairs, the question breathy and powerless. I was torn between conflicting thoughts. *Please let me have heard it and not be losing my mind, and please tell me Alex doesn't have someone over while my child is missing.*

"Sorry, you heard what?" She laughed, but it was cool, her body tense as she jogged down the stairs to meet me. She put a hand on my bicep, trying to turn me around.

"I heard a noise."

"What are you talking about? What noise?"

"It sounded like..." I was trying to speak softly, hoping to hear it again, a confirmation that I hadn't imagined it. "Someone screamed."

She jutted her head forward, as if she hadn't heard the whispered phrase. "Sounded like *what*?"

"It sounded like someone screamed?" It was a question now. I was questioning everything. Had I imagined it? Was I so exhausted and worried that I'd let myself hear what I needed to?

She shook her head, her expression wrinkling with concern. "Oh, sweetie... I'm sorry. You must've heard me laughing." She patted my back, nudging me forward again and, with one last look back up the stairs, I let her lead me back down.

"I don't understand... It sounded like a scream."

She drew in one side of her mouth with flushed-pink mortification. "My *friend* stayed over last night. He was trying to get me back into bed. I'm embarrassed you heard us."

The betrayal hurt. The pain of knowing that she'd chosen sex over my missing child, even though there was nothing she could've done. I'd needed her the night before, and she'd abandoned me.

"I don't understand... What friend?" She'd never once mentioned a man to me. Not a boyfriend, or even a platonic friend. I wasn't selfish enough to think I was all she had—like she was all I had—but it stung to know there was such a huge part of her life that I knew nothing about.

"He's... Well, I don't really know how to explain it. We've been friends since high school, but he's not my boyfriend, really." The smile faded from her face when she saw my dreary expression. "It was unexpected. He travels for work, so he's gone for months at a time. He got back into town after Skylar's birthday party, and he's staying with me for a few days... I'm sorry. I just got caught up in the moment." She winced. "I'm being a shitty friend."

I was stunned, trapped between worry and anger and still coming down from the adrenaline rush I'd experienced hearing the scream.

I studied her silently, trying to decide whether to be mad, but realistically, I didn't have the bandwidth for it. My heart couldn't hold any more pain.

"Please don't hate me," she said, once we'd reached the bottom step.

"I could never hate you." I drilled my eyes into hers, searching for my best friend, but she was suddenly a stranger to me. How had I missed it? "Alex, you know you can tell me anything. You know that, right? I will understand. I don't expect you to give up your entire life to take care of me. I'm just confused about why you didn't tell me."

She ran her finger along the banister, paying special attention to a place where the grain ran a bit darker than the rest. "I didn't want you to think less of me. You and Cam have this perfect life, and here I am, older than you and still messing around with a man who only comes into town five or six times a year."

"Cam and I are far from perfect. You know that." I shook my head. I was angry with her, despite my best efforts not to be, but I couldn't bring myself to say it. I couldn't confront her when I needed her so badly. "You could've just told me. I'm not going to judge you."

She nodded apprehensively. "Well, now you know. So, are you ready to start the session? I don't have long before my next one."

With the last of my adrenaline leaving my body, I'd begun to feel drained. I glanced up at the ceiling above my head, feeling self-conscious that whatever I said might be overheard by her unnamed guest.

"I... You know, I should probably get back home."

"What? Why?"

"I don't want to interrupt whatever you've got going on any more than I have." I was being judgemental and rude, but I was frustrated with her. I felt betrayed in the worst way. She was supposed to be my friend, she was supposed to understand what I was going through, but she'd chosen to ignore my problems, choosing instead to sleep with a man who wasn't even her boyfriend.

It all just seemed so unlikely.

I felt like I'd learned more about Alex during the past few minutes than I had the past few months, and the more I learned, it seemed, the less I liked.

"Ginny, wait!" she called after me, reaching for my arm. I jerked it out of her grasp, turning to face her as I reached the door.

"It's fine, Alex. I'll let you know about the search party once we've set it up." My gaze traveled up the length of the wall. "If you have time."

"Of course, I'll have the time. Don't be crazy."

I jerked backward at the harsh words, as if I'd been slapped. If there was one thing I'd learned from Alex's sessions, it was that thoughts become things. Negative self-talk or negative thoughts affect us more than we know. She'd instructed me to never let myself think of anything as *crazy, stupid, ridiculous, insane,* etc.

So why had she just broken the rule?

"That came out wrong." She put her hands up, palms facing me as she tried to calm the situation. "Look, I know you're scared. I shouldn't have said that. I'm just... you've caught me at kind of a bad time, and I'm a little frazzled."

My gaze flicked up to the floor above, listening carefully. Was the man up there listening now? Would she go back upstairs and complain about what a crazy client I was? I felt new tears pricking my eyes, indignation welling inside of me.

"Oh, excuse me. I'm sorry if my daughter's kidnapping hasn't been convenient for you," I taunted her, pursing my lips.

"You know that's not what I mean. Don't deflect your stress— as warranted as it is—toward me. That isn't healthy."

I shook my head. I didn't have time for this. "I should go," I told her firmly, turning around and pulling open the door.

"Don't do this, Ginny. Stay so we can talk things through." Her words were smooth and slow, no urgency to her tone. She was being patient with me, but I didn't need her patience. I needed her to care that my child was missing and, when I met her eyes once more, I didn't see what I was looking for.

Tears blurred my vision as I stepped out onto the porch. My body trembled with rage that I hadn't been expecting. I didn't have time for this betrayal. I needed to find Skylar. I'd counted on her to help me find Skylar. It seemed I could only count on Cameron, but how much I could trust him—how much he trusted me—was also in question.

I jogged down the porch, hurt that she didn't call out to me, not even once. I was furious with her and ashamed at myself for believing she cared, my body trembling so hard I could barely reach for the car door handle. I pulled it open, refusing to look over my shoulder as I jumped inside to save myself from getting pelted by the rain.

I pulled out of the parking space and sped off, already beginning to question if I'd overreacted. Nothing made sense anymore, not my emotions, not my reactions, not my family, not my friends. It all just hurt.

I slammed my hand into the steering wheel.

Where are you, Sky?

I had no idea what had happened back at Alex's, no idea where I was going, no idea if I'd ever feel okay again. No idea if Cam would be on my side or hers. He'd probably tell me Alex had no obligation to help, that this was a family matter like he'd said in the first place.

But Alex had felt like family to me. That was what hurt the most, and I knew no one would understand it.

I would've crawled over broken glass to be there for her when she needed me, but I should never have expected the same.

Either way, it was done and over with. I needed to focus on my child.

The entire way back to my house, I kept replaying the noise I'd heard in Alex's house in my head. Each time I heard it, the more and more it sounded less like a laugh and more like a scream.

Like she was scared.

Had I overreacted?

Had I left her in danger?

My thoughts were beginning to jumble, as blurry as my vision, currently filled with tears and the windshield speckled with rain.

Maybe she was right. Maybe I really was going crazy...

31 CAMERON

"Okay, well, we'll see you guys in a few hours then."

"Okay," my dad's voice said across the speaker as I heard the front door open and close. I stood. "Talk to you soon. Love you."

"I love you too." I ended the call and slid the phone into my pocket as I made my way into the living room, then the foyer, as my wife slipped off her jacket and boots and hung up her keys.

"Who was that?"

"My parents. They're driving up instead of flying. The flight was delayed again because of the storm, but they don't want to wait any longer."

She nodded, but I could tell she wasn't really listening. Something was wrong. She'd been crying, her cheeks red and raw with tears, her eyes bloodshot.

"What's wrong? Did something happen?"

"I... um—" She steadied herself with a deep inhale, her clasped hands shaking in front of her waist. "I think I had a fight with Alex." Her words slammed into me with such force that I had to take a step back. What had they fought about?

"You what? What do you mean? A fight about what?"

"About Skylar. Er, well, I don't know. She was supposed to

come here, and she was ignoring my calls, but it turns out she's been with some guy this entire time."

My stomach flipped. "What guy?"

She spoke quickly, the words tumbling out of her mouth at lightning speed as she stared at me, begging me to understand. "I went by her house today because I needed a session, but there was someone there." Her eyes were wild and angry, but underneath it all, I saw the pain she must be feeling. If it were even possible, she appeared frailer than before, as if a gust of wind might knock her down. "A guy she's been sleeping with. It's why she hasn't been answering our calls. Can you believe that? It's like she doesn't care at all." Her voice cracked with the final sentence and, at piecing it all together, I felt anger bubbling in my core.

It was as if time had slowed down, everything moving in slow motion. Fury radiated through me. It wasn't brought on by jealousy, honestly—I didn't care what Alex did, but the pain in my wife's eyes was palpable. I was angry for her. She'd trusted Alex. We both had. And she'd betrayed that trust. "I'm so sorry," I said with a long, drawn-out breath. Suddenly, I felt guilty for ever considering leaving my wife. For formulating a plan that would be an even bigger betrayal than this was. She needed someone to care about her. For a while, I thought Alex would be that—if I ever decided I couldn't—but now I saw I was wrong. Ginny needed me. Skylar needed me. I felt so torn between them both. All I wanted was for my family to be together again. Healthy. Happy. Normal.

"It doesn't matter," she said with a sniffle. "She was my therapist, and I don't need her anymore. I'm overreacting."

I pulled her into a hug, kissing her temple. I felt sick over the relief inside my chest. If she was really done with Alex, my secret was safe. "We're all dealing with a lot."

She sniffled, rubbing her face on my shirt. "Distract me. Are there any updates? Have you heard from the police this morning?"

"No, but I did hear from Margie, finally."

She pulled away, obviously intrigued. "You did?"

.h, she said to keep her updated. She's booking a flight and
.ing back to us as soon as she can."

"What about her movie?"

"She's trying to get production to hire another makeup artist to
fill in. I don't know what it will mean for her as far as contracts and
pay, but she told me not to worry about that. She wants to be here,"
I told her, feeling proud to be able to deliver the news. I knew
Ginny had her doubts about Margie, doubts I knew were
unfounded, but being able to have her return would give Ginny
peace of mind. "Skylar's the most important thing. To all of us."

Ginny began crying again, without warning, and I rubbed a
hand over her hair, trying to soothe her. "Are we still doing a search
party?" she asked through her sobs. "Can we do it today?"

I sighed, rubbing a hand over my face as she pulled away,
drying her tears. "I tried, but the police don't want us out there in
this storm. The detective checked in earlier—"

"What did they say?" she asked expectantly. The hope in her
eyes killed me.

"There's no news. He just wanted to let me know they were
still working on leads and touching base with everyone at the party.
He asked if we'd heard anything and I said no, but I asked him if
there was anything we could do. I mentioned a search party in the
woods, and he said we can organize a search of the neighborhood,
but they asked that we keep people out of the woods until the
storm passes. Apparently, they plan to come back again and search
when the storm has ended, in case they missed anything the first
time. We're not supposed to go into the woods until they come
back."

Her mouth formed a thin line. "Did you tell them we already
had?"

"Yeah, they weren't too surprised by that, so I think the word
had already gotten passed around." I shook my head, feeling
incredibly useless. "I've started an event online, invited everyone to
help us with the search first thing tomorrow. We have to plot it out,
divide people up. I don't know if you saw the notification..."

Ginny shook her head, then her expression grew even more serious. "Had the police already talked to Margie?"

"Yeah, they did. Why?"

"Just making sure."

"I know you're worried Margie has some terrible secret, but I promise you, she doesn't."

"Everyone has secrets, Cam," she said, dusting tears from her cheeks again. "I love Margie too, and I'm not saying she was involved, but she is hiding something from us. I can feel it in my gut, and I'm worried it has something to do with Skylar. I'm sorry, but I am. It has to be someone who was here... It has to."

"Why does it have to?"

"Because"—she fumbled for the words—"because it just does. That's how it works."

"Well, it wasn't Margie. She was on a flight home."

"Fine. I told you I'm not trying to accuse her. I'm just talking to you about what feels off. I feel like something's going on with her, and it's strange timing, at least. We have to be objective about everyone. Can you at least admit she acted strangely when she left?"

I clenched my jaw, changing the subject. "Was that why you went to Alex's? Were you going to tell her you suspected Margie?"

She didn't answer straight away, but she didn't need to. "I was going to ask her to help me sort through my feelings. But it didn't matter, because I didn't get to tell her anything."

"You can't just go around telling people you think my sister kidnapped our child. Or anyone, for that matter. Not without proof. You know Alex would have to report that sort of information to the police. You need to be smart here, Ginny."

"Oh, so now we have to be careful what we say to the police? You had no problem telling me you thought I was involved," she said with a huff.

"Can we not go there right now? I've already apologized. Emotions were running high, and I was scared. I'm still scared."

Thunder rumbled overhead at my words, as if to remind us danger was still lurking.

Without warning, the lights flickered, and then went off. The house was silent, without the usual whirring of electricity and air conditioning.

"Not now," Ginny whined, dropping her hands and shoulders with exasperation.

"I'll find some candles." I moved out of the room and into the kitchen, digging through the junk drawer to pull out the long-handled lighter and praying it still had enough fluid to light them.

Ginny was behind me when I turned around, causing me to jump back with a start. I hadn't heard her coming.

"Did you find it?" she trailed off as she saw it in my hands. "There should be a few candles on top of the fridge."

I reached up, pulling two new ones down and walking them to the table. I set them down and pressed the button on the lighter, connecting the flame to the wick.

"Well," I said, looking around the darkness. The two tiny, dancing flames were nothing compared to the shadows that had set in. "It's something, I guess."

Ginny pulled the front of her shirt away from her chest in an attempt to fan herself. "I just hope they fix it soon. We'll melt in here."

"Maybe we should move to the porch," I agreed. I could feel cool, slick sweat sliding down my back already, and I knew it would get worse before it got better.

With the new plan in mind, I blew out the candles and we made our way outside. I felt the cool breeze instantly as we stepped outside, my damp skin chilling in a matter of seconds. The storm was raging, lightning lighting up the sky every few minutes, the water pouring over the gutters of our covered porch like a waterfall.

Ginny sat down on the porch swing, pulling her legs up in front of her as she stared out into the yard.

I sat beside her, not saying anything at first. I wasn't sure what to say. Or where to go from there.

"Do you think she's okay?" she whispered, the question catching me off guard. When I looked over, there were no tears in her eyes. Instead, she looked utterly exhausted, broken, and empty.

I couldn't bring myself to look away from her as I said, "I hope so."

She closed her eyes then, inhaling deeply. "I'm sorry I haven't been there enough for you. And for her. I'm sorry I couldn't be who you needed me to be."

I stared at her, stunned by the apology. "You did all you could," I said finally. We weren't touching, our bodies inches apart, but in every way that mattered we were connected. She opened her eyes again.

"I didn't do enough. I know that. I know how hard it's been on you. I can't imagine why you stayed for so long, but I'm so grateful you did."

"You're my wife, Ginny." The sentence was a knife to my core, a white-hot poker to my gut, reminding me of my failings. "I love you."

"I'm broken, Cam. I'm so broken. You deserve better than me."

I lifted a finger to her chin, forcing her to look at me when she glanced away. "You're everything to me. You and Skylar. You're all I want. All I care about."

She blinked slowly, then took a deep, weighted breath. I had no idea what was coming next, but I knew it would be huge. "What are you not telling me?"

I swallowed, the answer there on the tip of my tongue: *So much.*

32 CAMERON

I didn't say that, of course. Instead, I said, "What do you mean?"

"Yesterday, when I got home, you told me the person you were on the phone with had called the wrong number, but you were lying. I heard you say 'Alex.'"

My stomach dropped, my body suddenly ice cold even in the humid Tennessee air. "I—"

"You lied to me. Just like you lied to me about the woman I heard in the house. Just like you're lying about Margie. I want to know what's going on. I want to know what's going on with you and with Skylar and... if you're leaving me, if that's what this is, if you've met someone else, or if you know where Skylar is, please just tell me. Please, Cam. I'm begging you. I can't do this anymore. The secrets are killing me."

I had no idea where to begin. No idea how to begin unravelling everything she was asking about, but I had to. She deserved to know the truth, no matter how much it killed me.

"You're right. I was talking to Alex when you came in that day."

"Why did you lie?"

"Because I'm a coward," I said simply, forcing myself to look away from her. I stood from the swing and moved to stand at the edge of the porch, looking out at the yard. "I need to tell you the truth. About everything. But when I do, you'll realize you were wrong."

"Wrong about—"

"It's not me who deserves better, Ginny. It's you. It's always been you." I felt the burn of her stare, but I couldn't look at her. I couldn't make myself watch the pain I was going to cause her. "I messed up. It was an accident, a terrible, terrible accident, and I'm so sorry. I never meant to hurt you or lie to you or—"

"What did you do, Cam?"

"Remember when you asked me to go to Alex's office that day to talk about your therapy?"

"Yeah..."

"Well, she started coming to the house after that. After your sessions, when you were sleeping." I heard her gasp, but I pressed on. "She was here as a therapist for me, but I wasn't paying her. She just... I thought she wanted to help. She would listen to me, let me complain and vent and get upset if I needed to. It was stuff I didn't feel like I could do with you. That's not your fault, I know that, but I was finally able to voice the feelings I'd had for so long that I'd kept pent up to protect you."

I glanced back at her, just once, to make sure she was still there, still listening, and went on, "Anyway, when you heard someone laugh, that's who it was. You were right. I didn't want to lie to you, but it also felt like a betrayal in a way. Alex was your friend. I never wanted to take away from the work you were doing or make you feel like I was gossiping or complaining about you. I just needed someone to talk to, too, and Alex made me feel listened to in a way I hadn't in a long time."

I heard her sniffle. "But it wasn't an affair." Finally, I spun around to look at her, forcing her to meet my eyes as I said it. "It wasn't. I love you. When I cheated on you before, I told you I'd never do it again, and I meant it. I never wanted to hurt you, Ginny. I tried so hard to keep it professional between Alex and me, and I know that's a lame thing to say, but it's true." I hung my head. "We slept together. Once. About a month before Skylar's party."

She was crying then. I didn't need to look up to know. I couldn't look up, not if I wanted to continue. "I don't know how it happened, to be honest. We were talking. It had gotten late, and I was exhausted... It just happened. It was like I blacked out. I couldn't control myself. It was a mistake. I've told her it was a mistake, and she hasn't come by anymore. We don't talk anymore. I know that doesn't make it right, I do. And I completely understand if that makes you want to leave me—you'd have every right to."

"Is that what you want? For me to leave you?" she asked through muffled sobs.

"No," I told her quickly. "No. If anything, this has made me realize how lost I'd be without you. I'm sorry I couldn't see that before." I moved forward, on my knees in front of the swing as I wrapped my arms around her waist. She was stiff against me, not leaning into the hug but not pushing me away.

"I can't believe you did this again," she uttered finally, her words coming through gritted teeth.

"I never meant to hurt you."

"That doesn't matter. It doesn't matter whether you meant to. It still hurts all the same."

"Ginny, I—" I froze as my phone began to buzz in my pocket. I pulled it out swiftly, staring down at the screen. "Hang on." I put the phone to my ear. "Hello?"

"Who is it?" Ginny asked, her voice breathless.

"Mr. Hale?"

"Yes." I stood, a finger to my ear to drown out the noise of the rain.

"It's Detective Chapman. Are you at home?"

My heart leaped. "Yes. Yes, I am." I met my wife's eyes. She'd stood with me, trying to understand what was happening.

"Great. I'm going to need you to stay put. I'm going to drop by in about an hour to speak to you and your wife."

"Did you find something? Did you find Skylar?" I asked, and

Ginny moved closer to me, her eyes widening as she brushed her tears away.

"No," he said firmly, and I felt my hope deflate. Ginny recognized it in my expression, and I saw hers disappear, too. "No, nothing yet. I just wanted to check back in and ask a few additional questions that've come up. I'll see you both soon, okay?"

"O-okay." The call ended, and I stared at her, lowering it from my ear.

"What did he say?"

"He's coming to talk to us."

"About what?" she asked, her brows drawn down.

"He just said there were some additional questions that had come up." I shook my head. "I'm just... It's just... Why didn't he already ask them? I spoke to him earlier today."

"What kind of additional questions could there be?" she asked, her shoulders slumped. "They've either found her or they haven't. You should've pushed him on when they're going to search again. Either that, or we're going plan our own search without their permission. It's our land. We can't keep waiting, bad weather or not. We're losing time. This is all so ridiculous." She groaned, stepping away from me as her expression darkened again. It was obvious the momentary reprieve from our fight was officially over as she moved toward the house with haste.

"Where are you going?"

"Away from you."

She slammed the door, and I followed her back into the house. "I know you're mad—"

She gave a sarcastic, throaty laugh. "Mad doesn't begin to cover what I am."

"You don't have to talk to me about this, you don't have to forgive me, but at least I told you the truth."

She stopped in her tracks, spun around, and gave me a forced slow clap. "Well, look at you go. I guess I should be grateful. You didn't lie to me *today*, at least."

I felt two feet tall, the shame over everything I'd done weighing heavily on me. "I was hurting. Can't you see that?"

"You were? I guess I missed it because my life was all butter-flies and rainbows." She turned toward the hallway, and I jogged to catch up with her.

"I know it was wrong."

"A fourth grader would know it was wrong."

"I'm apologizing. Can't you just stop and listen to me?" I grabbed for her arm, trying to stop her.

To my surprise, she did stop, her face lined with sharp and jarring shadows. "You slept with the person I thought was my best friend. You lied about it. You invited her here, and the two of you talked about me. You lied about that, too. When I asked you about it, you made me feel like I was going crazy. You've done nothing but lie and betray me. Why should I listen to you now?"

"Because I'm ready to tell you the truth. I think that should count for something. I'm not saying you have to forgive me or stay with me or—hell—

even believe me, but I'm telling you the truth because that's what you asked for. I'm sorry if it's not a truth you wanted to hear. I'm sorry that I did it. But I won't be sorry for being honest with you. I want to fix it. I want to fix everything—"

"Do you know where Skylar is?" she demanded.

I jerked back, caught off guard by the question. "Of course not."

"Then you can't fix anything."

She jerked her arm from my grasp and walked into the bedroom, shutting the door. I heard a click that let me know she'd locked it behind her, washing the hallway in darkness.

33 GINNY

If I would've let it, the pain of Cam's confession would've destroyed me. I walked into the bedroom with the stark knowledge that I could lay in bed, fall asleep, and be okay with never waking up again.

If I'd chosen to, I could've let my depression take over, let the numbness fill me.

But I couldn't. If only for Skylar's sake, I couldn't do that. I needed to understand all that was happening. All the secrets that surrounded me. It was the only way I'd ever find out what happened to my daughter.

I was alone, that was incredibly obvious, now more than ever before, and it was up to me to find her. In order to do that, I needed to trust only what I could prove.

I needed to know more about Alex.

About my husband.

My family.

All the lies that had led us here.

I pulled out my laptop and logged into Cameron's email. It was the same passcode he used for all of his accounts.

I searched Alex's name as I heard him walk away from the bedroom door finally. Would he come back?

With the end of a hanger or a bobby pin, it was incredibly easy to unlock the door from the outside. We'd learned that the hard way just as soon as Skylar had become tall enough to reach the doorknobs and discovered the buttons that locked our doors.

Truth be told, I didn't care. I should've been snooping long ago, especially after the first affair, but I'd chosen to trust him. I'd needed to trust him, or it would've driven me wild.

His inbox was clear of messages from Alex, to my relief. Next, I pulled up his social media. There were no messages there, either, but I hadn't expected there to be. Alex wasn't on social media; she'd told me that when we first met.

She'd said it was to protect her, especially in her line of work, but I didn't think it would hurt to try and find her. I clicked the search bar, my stomach tightening as I saw Cameron's last search had been for her.

Alex Kane

He'd been looking for her... Why? I clicked the search, pulling up a few Alex Kanes, but none that were the right one.

Next, with curiosity filling me, I went to Google. There, several results for Alex Kane popped up: a journalist, a pediatric surgeon, a professor at a university in Texas. None of them were our Alex.

I cleared out and began a new search:

Alex Kane, Nolensville, TN, therapist

Listings for therapists in our area came up, but none of them belonged to Alex.

She was nowhere to be found on social media or the internet.

Nowhere to be found at all.

I heard new footsteps coming down the hall and, within seconds, he was knocking. My heart raced, my body hot with adrenaline. I couldn't let him stop me. "Gin, please let me in. You don't have to talk to me, I just want to know you're okay."

"Of course, I'm not okay, you asshole. You just told me you cheated on me! I don't want to talk to you." I bit my lip, fighting back as red-hot tears filled my eyes.

I couldn't believe he'd cheated on me.

Not again.

The pain resurfaced, and I forced it down again, another reminder that it was there, just waiting to take over, waiting to consume me. Even as devastated as I was, that devastation was nothing compared to the hole in my core over missing Skylar.

I had so much to be angry and worried about that I was having trouble focusing on any one thing. I would deal with it all when I had time, but right now, I just needed to find my daughter. I brushed the tears away, then gritted my teeth as I heard him speak again.

"What are you doing in there?"

I ignored the question, searching various combinations of her name and location, but to no avail. As a last resort, I searched the address of Alex's house, one I had memorized at that point, and clicked on a website that revealed the owner of the home we believed belonged to Alex was named *A. Smith.*

"Oh, great." I groaned and went back to Google, searching for *Alex Smith.* There were 431 million search results, the most notable the name of a famous athlete. "This is useless."

"Hello? Who are you talking to?" he asked through the door. I'd almost forgotten he was still there.

"Myself."

"What are you doing? Will you please let me in?"

Again, I tried searching for Alex Smiths in our city, Alex Smiths at that address, Alex Smith therapists, but nothing came up. The further and further down the rabbit hole I went, the further and further I seemed to be getting from anything useful. I didn't have time for this.

"Why would she have lied about her last name?" I asked skeptically.

"Who?" His voice came through the door again.

I closed the laptop. "Go away, Cameron."

"I'm not going away until you talk to me."

"Suit yourself." Sliding the laptop off my lap, I climbed off the bed and opened my drawer. I pulled on clean clothes, took my hair from its messy ponytail and tied it back again, neater this time. Then, I stalked across the room and pulled open the door.

He was standing in the doorway, one arm resting on the frame as he took in the sight of me, confused for a moment, then spoke. "What did you do?"

"I'm going to Alex's."

"What? Why?" he asked, following me when I moved past him. "You can't leave now. The detective is on his way."

"Well, you'll be here, won't you? We don't have time to sit around and chat while our child is missing!"

He grabbed my arm, forcing me to stand still in the dimly lit hall. "You need to stop this, Ginny. You can't leave. I told him we'd be here. He's expecting us both. Leaving now will only make you look guilty."

"Oh, you took care of that already, didn't you?" I narrowed my eyes at him.

He pinched his lips together, running a hand over the back of his neck. "Will you just listen to me? Please? I'm trying to help you right now. Going to Alex's won't solve anything and will likely make you look even worse to the police. Let's just take a minute. I know you're mad, and rightfully so, but—"

"Are you trying to protect her? Or me?" I asked, my chest tight and hip cocked to the side as I stared at him.

"I don't care about Alex, okay? I care about you." He ran his hands down the length of my arms. "I don't want you to put yourself through this. Nothing you can say to her, nothing she can say to you, will make you feel any better."

I scrunched my face, then relaxed it again, trying not to earn the crazed look he was giving me. "I tried to look her up, Cam. I can't find anything about her. What if she lied about everything?"

"Lied about what?" His expression went slack.

"Everything," I repeated. "Who she is. What she wants from us. Why she was here. Why she slept with you." Sweat gathered on the back of my neck at the thought.

He winced. "What are you saying?"

"I think she lied to me today, about the scream I heard. I've thought it since I heard it, but I couldn't decide why. Maybe she really did have a friend over, but why would she try to hide that? Well, now I know. I can't trust her. Whether she lied because she's in danger or because we are, I'm not sure, but I need to go talk to her."

"No, you don't. You can stay here. Tell the detective everything you've just told me. Let him handle it. Let them do their jobs. If Alex has lied to us, they'll want to know about it."

"So, tell them," I said. "But I can't just wait. I don't care how guilty I look. I only want her home safe. I don't have the time to even have this conversation." My vision began spotting as new panic set in, the truth of my words heavy in the air between us. "We're running out of time, Cameron. Skylar is running out of time."

He stared at me dubiously, and I scowled. "I'm not asking you to come with me. And I'm not asking for permission."

"I know you think you're doing the right thing, but you don't know what you're getting yourself involved in. She could be dangerous. You don't want to make her mad."

I reeled back angrily. "You mean *you* don't want to make her mad?"

"No." He groaned, pinching the bridge of his nose with frustration. "I couldn't care less how she feels. It's you I'm protecting. Look, I wasn't going to say anything because I didn't want to upset you, but when she called, she told me she thought you might've had something to do with Skylar's disappearance. You said you had a fight with her today. I'm worried if you upset her more, she might tell the police that. We need to be careful about how we approach this. Her. The police could help us."

My knees began to buckle, but I caught myself. "She said *what*? When?"

"We talked last night. I was telling her to stop contacting me, but she mentioned that she was concerned about your impulse control now that you're off your meds. She said she had an obligation to report it if she believed you could harm yourself or... anyone else."

I was suddenly lightheaded. "Sh-she told you she thought I kidnapped my own child?"

"She had concerns, yes," he said again carefully.

My vision blurred with spots of light, the room spinning. "And what did you tell her?"

"I told her she was ridiculous. That you would never hurt Skylar."

I nodded, blinking rapidly to clear my eyes, not sure whether to believe him. "Good. Okay, then."

"I know you want to go talk to her. You're angry, I get it. I'm just trying to be logical—"

"This has nothing to do with how I feel about her. What if she knows something about Skylar? What if she lied all this time to get close to us? To take her? I'd gone to that park before, what if she'd watched her? What if this was her plan, and we just brought her into our house?"

His hands were up, trying to calm me down, but I was already on a rampage. "Whoa, hold on. Now you think Alex did this?"

"Why else would she have lied? Why else would she be ghosting me right now? Why else would she have accused me of taking Skylar? She has to be involved. Don't you see that?"

He scoffed. "No, I'm sorry, I don't. Two hours ago you were certain Margie had done it, and now you're sure it was Alex. I can't keep up."

"I have to follow one lead, and Alex is the easiest one. I still don't know that Margie didn't do it. I know you think she's inno-cent, and maybe she is, but—"

"Margie had nothing to do with this!" he interrupted, his nostrils flaring.

"How can you be sure of that? How can you be sure of anything?"

"Because Margie had a miscarriage," he spat out, looking relieved and mortified all at once. He squeezed his eyes shut.

"She..." My breathing caught as I placed a hand to my stom-ach. "She what?"

"She had a miscarriage. It's why she was in the hall talking to David at Skylar's party. She's having a tough time with it, but she didn't want you to know. She didn't want to put a damper on the party, so she left. David doesn't even want her to be working on the movie right now, she needs time to heal, but she won't listen to anyone."

I blinked rapidly, trying to understand. "Why wouldn't she have told me that? I'd never have made her feel guilty—"

"Because she didn't want *you* to feel guilty. She didn't want you to have to tiptoe around what had happened or feel sorry for her. And she would've ended up feeling guilty herself anyway. The day was supposed to be about Skylar. She knew if she told you, everyone would fuss over her."

"But... Why didn't *you* tell me? All this time, I've been suspi-cious of what they were talking about, and you could've cleared it up with a single sentence."

He ran a finger over his mouth, shaking his head. "It wasn't my secret to tell. She asked me not to, and I wanted to respect that. Please don't tell her I said anything."

"I won't," I said, trying to make sense of what he was telling me. Poor Margie... "I hate that for her... I had no idea they were even trying."

"They have been for a while. It was the first time the embryo took, and she didn't make it very far. She didn't tell me the specifics, but they're really having a hard time with it all. I think being around Skylar made it worse, truth be told."

I tucked my chin to my chest, taking a long breath, then looked back up at him. "But if that's true, if Margie left because of that, and I *do* believe you... If I believe she didn't have anything to do with Skylar, who does that leave? Alex has to know something."

"Why though? It doesn't make sense to me. Alex had no reason to have taken Skylar. She had no way of getting into the house or knowing the door was unlocked. She may have lied about a lot of stuff—I don't know—but logically, there's no reason for her to have taken Skylar, either."

I waved my hands in the air wildly. "None of this is logical, Cam. What aren't you getting? Someone has taken our child, and we need to find her!" I lifted my hands to my cheeks, shaking my head. "You know what? I'm done talking about this. I need to go. I need to go now." I spun back around, racing down the hall and toward the door, surer that I was on the right track than ever before.

"Ginny, please wait! Let me call the detective! Let me see if he can meet us there."

"You'll go with me?" I met his eyes with such relief I found myself wanting to cry. I'd nearly lost faith in him. He'd destroyed me, broken my heart in so many ways, that I was sure he'd let me down again.

"Of course, I'm going with you," he said firmly, lifting a palm to my cheek. "We're in this together... as long as you'll have me."

I swallowed down the lump in my throat, the thoughts swirling through my head as I pictured his hand cradling Alex's face the same way. My body grew cold, and I turned away from him.

"We need to leave, then. Now."

With that, I was out the door and heading for the garage, my husband—the man who'd broken my heart one too many times —in tow.

34 GINNY

A few minutes later, we walked up the porch steps toward Alex's house. I hadn't called her to tell her we were coming, but that was by design. I wanted to catch her off guard, unprepared. She wasn't expecting me to stop back by just a few hours after my last visit. I wanted to ambush her with the news that I knew what she'd done. To hear what she had to say for herself.

I glanced over my shoulder, expecting to see the cop car that had been waiting outside our home, but if he'd followed us, he was doing a great job of keeping hidden. Cameron had called the detective and left him a voicemail on our way there, but we hadn't heard back.

He was probably right. Leaving when we'd been told to stay there would likely make us look guilty, but what choice did we have? They weren't working quickly enough for us.

Cameron held my hand, his thumbs grazing my knuckles with care. The curtains over the door were still pulled closed, so I couldn't see inside. What would she say? Was I right? Would she tell me she'd fallen for my husband? Did he feel the same? Was I being set up? Did she really believe I was capable of hurting Skylar?

As I was flailing internally, shooing away questions as quickly as my mind could toss them at me, my husband reached for the door, his fist at the ready.

Seconds before his knuckles made contact with the wood, I heard a sound that made my skin line with chills.

Eeeeeeeeeeeeee.

A scream identical to the one I'd heard earlier, only this time, I was absolutely positive it wasn't a scream. More so, I was nearly positive it wasn't Alex. It sounded like a young girl.

Skylar.

"Did you—"

"Hear that," he confirmed with a nod, banging his fist against the door heatedly.

"It sounded like her, didn't it?"

A muscle twitched in his jaw, but he didn't answer. What was he thinking? Where was his head? It had sounded like Skylar, hadn't it? Did Alex have our daughter?

Without waiting more than seconds, his fist slammed into the door again, this time with so much force I had to look over my shoulder to be sure the neighbors hadn't come out to their porches to see what was causing the commotion.

The door swung open and Alex was standing there, breathless. She leaned down over her knees and spoke through heavy breaths.

"Ginny... Cameron... You... scared me. What's... going on?"

Seeing her again made my stomach churn. I was angry and bitter, torn between prying information from her and attacking her. I didn't miss the way her gaze lingered on Cameron a while longer than usual. "Is she here?"

She straightened, squaring her shoulders to us while still trying to catch her breath. "Is... who here?"

"We heard the scream, Alex. It was Skylar, wasn't it? That was who I heard this morning too... Is she here?"

She furrowed her brow, looking between us. "Skylar? Of course not. Why would she be here?"

We didn't answer. Instead, I said, "We just heard a little girl scream. It sounded the same as it did this morning, and I'm positive it wasn't you. I know it was Skylar. I don't know what you want from us, if it's money... or, or... I don't know. What do you want? Why have you taken her? What will it take for you to give her back?"

There were no tears left in me, only rage. I no longer wanted pity. I wanted answers. Alex had betrayed me in the worst possible way, and I wanted my daughter safe and then nothing else to do with the woman I'd considered a friend.

"You heard a little girl scream this morning?" She looked confused. "I'm sorry, I'm not trying to be rude, it's just that I don't understand what you think you heard. It's a big house. Sound carries oddly sometimes. I'm so sorry. Believe me, I *wish* I had her. I wish I could help you, Ginny. I take it that means you haven't gotten any news yet?" She glanced over our shoulders. "Hard to have a search party in this storm, I'd imagine. It's awful out there."

"Stop avoiding the question. We heard a girl scream just now. Through the door. If it wasn't you this time, who was it?"

Her eyes widened and she placed a hand to her stomach, and for half a second, I was sure she was going to tell us we were both crazy or slam the door in our faces. Instead, she nodded. "Oh, sure! Oh, of course. Yes. That was Raven."

My head jerked backward almost involuntarily. "Raven?"

"Yes, she's here. We were upstairs playing, so if you heard a girl, it was her."

I looked into the house, trying to see what I could through the sliver of open space. "Where is she?"

"Upstairs, in her room. The guest room," she corrected herself, "but, as far as she's concerned, it's hers."

"Can we see her?" Cameron asked, his voice shaking. I couldn't tell if he was stymieing his anger or fear.

"See her?" The words came out slowly, as if he'd spoken in a foreign language. "Seriously?"

"If she's really here, you should have no problem showing her to us," he said, and I nodded along for support.

"*Skylar?*" I shouted into the house, trying to lean past her when she didn't respond.

"Shh!" she quieted me, putting her hands up. "There's no need to alert the whole neighborhood that something's going on." She groaned. "Fine. Fine. Whatever. Come in." She stepped back, and we followed her into the house. "I know you're both hurting, but this is really low. I'm trying not to be offended, but I thought we were friends. I would never accuse either of you of doing anything like this."

I had so much I could've said to her, so much I could've told her I knew, but I couldn't focus on anything else. I just needed to keep moving. I needed to find the source of the noise.

She went on, "I know I haven't been the best through this, but I am your friend and I'm supporting you the only way I know how. The least you could do is trust me."

"Trust you?" I scoffed, then bit my tongue, still climbing the stairs. I didn't want to discuss the affair. Not right then. I was almost to the top floor. "This is the only way you know how to support a person? Really? Ghosting them? Avoiding their calls? You're a therapist, Alex. Or at least you claim to be."

"What's that supposed to mean?" she demanded, stopping short and grabbing my arm.

I jerked back, looking down at her, just as Cameron said, "Let her go."

"We looked you up online and couldn't find anything about you," I told her.

"And?" She blinked, as if the insinuation wasn't clear.

"And what the hell am I supposed to make of that?"

She cocked a hip to one side, clearly pissed off. "Probably exactly what I told you about that. I told you I'm not online because of everything with my clients and because of everything that happened in my past. I have no desire for my mother's family to find me, and you know that. How dare you? After everything I've done for you. I've worked so hard, put aside everything in my life to try and help you, and this is how you treat me?" Tears glimmered in her eyes, and if I didn't know the truth of what she'd done, I might've felt sorry for her, but there was no room for regret in my chest. "It's no wonder you don't have any friends, Ginny. No wonder you have no one close to you at all—"

"Hey," Cam tried to warn her off, but I was already moving away from her. On the top floor, Cam nodded toward the first door and headed toward it, while I took the second door. I couldn't remember which one I'd seen her coming out of that morning.

"You can't just barge into people's houses," Alex cried, but we were already doing it, consequences be damned. I shoved open the second door, my heart in my throat, and gasped when I saw Raven on the floor, a pile of markers and a coloring book in front of her. She looked up and smiled at me with faint recognition.

"Raven? Hey, sweetheart," I said, fighting back tears. I looked back over my shoulder, where Alex was standing, her lips pressed together in a way that said I *told you so.*

"Hi," came a quiet, cautious voice from inside the room.

I looked back. The girl was watching us closely, her expression beginning to grow worried when Alex stepped up, knocking my hand from the doorknob.

"I'll just be a sec, Rae," she said, shutting the door and lowering her voice. "There. Are you happy?"

"Alex, I..." I trailed off, no idea where to even begin.

"Ginny!" Cameron called, and my heart lurched. Together, we both looked at the room just down the hall where Cameron still stood in the doorway.

The room was mostly bare, a small bed up against the wall and an old armoire across from it. The hardwoods were covered with various, unmatching rugs, and there was a rocking chair piled high with clothes in the corner.

"There's nothing in here," Alex said matter-of-factly, but I knew the look on Cameron's face. He'd found something.

I followed his gaze to where he was staring at the small side table by the bed. "What is it?" I almost didn't want to understand.

Chills had lined my arms, my hair standing on end, terrified of what I'd find.

"Is that you?" He extended a finger toward the picture frame.

"No," I said quickly. It was a child. An old photo of two girls... I moved forward, trying to get a better look. "Alex, what is this?"

Alex was quiet, standing in the doorway with a pained expression. I picked up the dusty frame, swiping my finger across the glass. The photo had the vague red tint of old Polaroids and showed two young girls sitting on the floor of a living room I didn't recognize.

The carpet was red and black shag, a small dollhouse between them. Ice filled my veins as I stared at the girls' faces, grinning up at the camera with toothless smiles and stained clothing.

I focused on the younger girl, bringing the picture closer to my face. He was right, but he couldn't be. It was impossible, and yet, it was true.

It was me.

Looking closer, I recognized the doll in the photograph as the one I'd found in Skylar's bedroom. How was this possible? What did it mean?

"Why do you have this?" I asked, looking up from the picture at her.

She stared between the three of us—me, Cameron, and the photograph—before reaching out to take it from my hand.

"It's not you, Ginny." The statement was powerless, as if she wasn't even trying to convince me.

"Of course, it is." I didn't have many pictures of me before my parents adopted me, but I knew what I looked like as a child from the ones I did. We had two photos of ourselves as children next to our wedding photo in our bedroom. I'd recognize myself anywhere, and Cam had, too. "It's me. And that doll... I found it in Skylar's room. Why did she have it? What is going on?" I felt as if the room had shifted, everything I thought I'd known suddenly falling away.

Nothing was real.

I was walking through a fun house mirror, the lines between truth and lie, fiction and reality blurring swiftly.

There were new tears in her eyes, and she shook her head, walking away from me and pulling open the bedroom door. "I don't have time for this. I need to get back to Raven. You need to go."

I placed two fingers to my temple, unbudging as I tried to sort through it all in my head. "I'm not going anywhere until you tell me what's going on. Why do you have a picture of me in your bedroom? Did you take that from my house? Have you been stalking me?"

She shook her head slowly, her forehead crinkled in despair. "No, I didn't steal this from you. It's mine."

"It can't be."

"It is—"

"*No!* It's not. I know that it's mine—"

"It's not your picture!" she said angrily. "It's mine. This is me." She pointed to the girl that wasn't me.

"I don't understand." That was Cam, filling in the blank when I couldn't summon the energy to do so.

"I know that the girl is me, Alex. If you stole it, I won't be mad, I just want it back. I only have so many pictures of myself as a kid—"

"Why aren't you listening to me? Why aren't you getting it?" Her eyes widened, and she shut the door, collapsing to a squatting position with her face in her hands.

"Getting what?" I watched it happening but couldn't move to comfort her.

She sobbed into her hands, shaking her head as she did.

"Alex, please talk to me." I moved to bend down, snapping out of my trance just as she started to stand up.

"Don't you understand? It was all for you, and now you hate me. All I've *ever* done is love you, and still you're blaming me when I've done nothing wrong."

"What was all for her?" Cameron asked, his voice solemn.

To that, Alex sniffled, wiping her eyes. "You wouldn't understand. You'll think I'm lying, like always."

"Try me," I pushed, giving Cam a sideways glance.

She stared at me for a moment, her lips pressed together, then turned the lock and pointed into the office. "Sit down. Both of you."

I started to go, but Cameron held his place.

"Why?" he asked.

"Because what I'm about to tell you... You're going to want to be sitting down for it."

She stood and pushed the clothes off the chair and onto the floor, then gestured toward the bed. "Either or, I don't care."

"We should go downstairs," Cameron said slowly, not moving.

"Whatever," Alex said, opening the door again. Within minutes, we'd made it back down the stairs, Alex still clutching the picture frame. She led us into the office and, in unison, we sat. She sat in the chair across from us, where she'd sat for so many sessions before and, like always, she crossed one leg over the other.

Then, in one heavy breath, she said the sentence that sent my entire world in a tailspin:

"Ginny, I'm your biological sister."

35 GINNY

Biological sister? What was she talking about? That wasn't possible. I stared at her blankly, as if expecting the room to dim and someone to yell "End scene."

"Did you hear m—"

"I-I heard you," I said. "But I don't understand."

"My sister that I told you about before? Brianna? The one Skylar reminds me of? That was you. Your name was Brianna Wallace. Before. And I was Alexandria Wallace. We were five years apart, so... You don't remember me."

I knew the name, though. At least *my* name. Brianna Wallace. I recognized it from the adoption papers I'd found in my baby book. My parents had never kept the adoption from me. I'd known about it my whole life. But they hadn't told me much about my family or that I had anyone more than a mother.

"This photograph"—she clutched it to her chest—"is one of the only things I have left of our childhood. It's one of the only pieces of you I still have."

"I don't... I'm sorry... I don't understand." I'd said that already, I thought. But I couldn't seem to form any other words. The room spun out of control, my vision tunneling, my heartbeat loud in my ears. Cameron reached over, clutching my hand, and thanks to the shock, I didn't have the energy to push him away.

"You were three when we were taken from Momma the final time. I was eight. We were placed together a few times before, but that last time, the family that could take you, they couldn't take me. I was getting older. Harder to place." She dusted a tear from her eye. "I hated being away from you, even for just a short time. I'd always protected you. At home, first. With Momma and whatever guy she was dating at the time, but then with our foster families, too. I'd show you the ropes, help you get to sleep at night. There was this song..." She started singing a familiar lullaby, badly, then laughed. "You probably don't remember it."

I shook my head, not because I didn't remember it but because I was sure this was all a dream, and she went on.

"Anyway, I thought we'd be separated for just a little while, but then, that was it. When I found out you were getting adopted, it destroyed me. I didn't know how either of us could ever build a home without the other. My social worker was supposed to arrange visits for us but"—she shrugged and sniffled, looking away—"it never happened."

"So, we were Wallace? Are you Kane now? Or Smith?"

Her head drew back quickly. "How did you know about the name Smith?" she asked.

I shrugged. "I found property records for the house... I didn't know if it was true."

After a moment, her chin tilted down with a half-nod. A confirmation. "It is. After I aged out of the system, I changed my name to the plainest name I could think of, so no one would ever be able to find me. I didn't want anyone connecting me to her." She curled her upper lip in apparent disgust.

"Where did Kane come from, then?"

To my surprise, she clamped her lips together with a suppressed smile. "I made it up on the spot, actually. At the park, the day we met. There was a man there with a... a cane. It just came out."

I nodded. "You lied about... everything..."

To my left, Cam pulled his phone out and glanced at the screen, before shoving it back into his pocket. His face had blanched, but Alex went on without noticing, and my attention was called back to her.

"No. Not everything. Not about how much I care about you. Both of you. And Skylar, too. I never thought I'd get to know my niece." She stood and walked toward the window, looking out of it. I could feel Cameron's gaze burning into me, but I couldn't look his way. "This house belonged to our mother. Our mother's mother before that, I guess. It was where we grew up, off and on. We shared the bedroom where Raven is staying now. Do you... I'm sure you don't remember."

I shook my head, this time honestly. Nothing about this house felt familiar on the surface, but I couldn't deny the odd sense of comfort I'd had when coming here. I'd always believed it was because of Alex, but could it go deeper than that?

"No, you wouldn't... You were so young. Anyway, I kept an eye on you, even though I wasn't allowed to see you. Your parents moved you away, to a different school, but I'd call your house occasionally, listen to your little voice on the answering machine. Sometimes your mom would answer and she'd say you'd call me back, but... you never did."

"I didn't know..." Why had my mother kept it from me? My own sister. How could this be true? *Could* it be true?

Reading my mind, Cameron said, "How do we know you're not lying? You could've gotten that photo from our house."

Her eyes narrowed at him. "I didn't exactly come with proof, if that's what you mean. If you don't trust the photograph, you can at least see the doll you're holding is the one I gave to Skylar." She glanced at me. "It was yours, when you were a kid, Ginny. Actually, it was mine first, but I always gave you whatever you wanted." Her bitterness faded away as she smiled wistfully through her tears, turning back toward the window. "Anything to make you happy. I'd kept it all these years, but I wanted your daughter to have it. I gave it to Skylar at her party."

"What if I would've recognized it? What if I would've recognized the house? Were you ever going to tell me?"

"I was trying to figure out how. I just couldn't work up the courage." She hung her head, her shoulders slumped.

"There are probably thousands of these dolls out there," Cam said with an unfocused gaze, obviously thinking as he spoke. "That still doesn't prove anything. If you'd found the picture, you could've found one just to make us believe your story." He gripped my thigh protectively. He was right, I knew.

She looked over her shoulder at us once, unbothered. "Well, that's all I can give you. If you don't believe me, you don't have to, I guess. Like I said, aside from this, I don't have any old family photos or anything. Momma wasn't the type of parent to keep memorabilia. And the neighbors here, they think I bought the house from a bank. They don't know it was handed down. They don't know who I am, or who you were. I guess you could ask your mom about it, but... if she hasn't told you about me yet, I don't know why any of this would change her mind." Finally, she spun back around, resting her back against the window with her arms folded against her chest.

"But why are you here now? How did you find me?" I pressed.

She drew in one side of her mouth, her expression soft. "I've always kept a close eye on you. I started sending you letters in high school, after the phone number I'd been calling finally got disconnected. But you never returned the letters either, so I took the hint and tried to give you space." She paused, dropping her arms from her chest and sighing as she began to pace the room. We followed her with our gazes. "I could never leave you completely alone, though, not really. You were my baby sister." She gave a sympathetic frown. "The only person who'd ever needed me. I couldn't move on just because you had someone else taking care of you now. Although, in truth, the day we met, it was actually an accident. I'd taken Raven to the park when I saw you sitting there. Alone. And I

just thought... Now's my chance." Her eyes widened, obvious pleasure in the memory. "So, I approached you, and you didn't recognize me." She shrugged. "I don't know, Ginny. I didn't have a plan,
honestly. I just wanted to talk to you. I just wanted to be close to
you again."

"So, you lied to me?" My jaw went slack, and I felt Cameron
grip my thigh tighter, his thumb running circles along the seam of
my pants.

She scoffed. "What was I supposed to do? For all I knew, you
didn't want anything to do with me. If I told you the truth, there
was a good chance you'd run away and I'd never get another
chance to get to know the woman you've grown into." Her expression wrinkled, brows drawing together. "I'm... I'm so proud of you,
sister. You have this beautiful life. A beautiful baby girl. An
amazing husband." Her gaze lingered on Cameron a moment too
long. He broke eye contact with her, clearing his throat and looking
down. I couldn't help the jealousy that seethed in my stomach.
This wasn't the time to bring up the affair, but I hadn't forgotten
that despite all of what she was saying, she'd betrayed me.

I'd never forgive her for that.

Unless Cameron had lied about it?

Suddenly, I wasn't sure whom I should trust.

"So, what?" Cameron asked, changing the subject. "You
became a therapist because of what you went through? And you
tried to help Ginny deal with some of the repressed memories?"

She winced, sucking in a deep breath through bared teeth.
"Actually, no. See, I'm not really a therapist." She drew out the
sentence, pausing in between each word, the pauses growing
longer as she neared the end of it.

"*You aren't?*" I asked.

At the same time, Cameron said, "*What?*"

It felt as if the floor had dropped out from underneath me. If I
hadn't been sitting down, there was no doubt I would've collapsed.
I'd told her so much about my life. So many personal things. I felt
violated. Angry. Betrayed.

I clutched my chest, trying to catch my breath.

"I know, I know. Don't hate me, okay? I wasn't trying to take advantage of you. In truth, I can only afford this house because it's been in our family for generations. When our grandma died, she willed it to me. You weren't born yet, and I think she knew, even then, even before Mom got too bad, that she was only going to get worse. I do okay for myself cleaning most of the houses on the street. It gives me a flexible schedule, and I like it. I've always found comfort in working with my hands and, after living in filth for most of my life, I enjoy cleaning. I need my space to be tidy, so it makes me happy to do it for others too. For once in my life, I actually feel useful."

I scratched my temple, trying to make sense of what she was saying. "But why would you tell me you were a therapist? I was already your friend. You didn't need to lie to me."

She stared at me as if the answer were obvious. "Because you needed one. I could feel you slipping away from me. The day you called to cancel our play date, I worried you'd stop wanting to see me. I needed a reason to keep you coming. And, honestly, I've been to enough therapy in my life, most of what I told you was really good stuff." She leaned back against the windowsill, looking sheepish.

Cameron leaned forward with his elbows resting on his thighs, his hands clasped together. He tempered his anger as he spoke, but I could tell he was doing everything he could to hold it together. "Alex, that was really dangerous. Ginny needed your help, and you took advantage of her. We paid you to help her!"

"I know." She winced. "It was wrong, but I was desperate. I just wanted to get to know you more." She held out a hand, gesturing toward me. "And I did want to help you. I thought this was a way I could do both. And, of course, I'm happy to give you the money back if—"

"This isn't about the money!" he said angrily, losing his resolve. "What if you'd made her worse?"

"Cam," I shushed him. "I don't want to do this right now. I can't."

"Wait—" Alex moved toward me as I stood, but I put a hand up, stopping her in her tracks.

"I just want to find my daughter. I hear what you're saying, and... and I get it, okay? And there will be a day I do want to work through all of this, but today is not that day. My daughter is missing and this is the least of my concerns." I met her eye, still unsure what—if anything—I'd ever feel for this woman and all of her secrets. "I'm sorry. We need to go."

She nodded. "I really am sorry, Ginny. I'm sorry for everything I've put you through—"

"Alex, I can't." I moved past her, my head frazzled, spinning with questions as I felt Cameron's hand on my back. I didn't know who to be more angry with, or whether I should just feel ashamed of myself for trusting them both. What I did know was that staying in this house wasn't going to put me any closer to finding my daughter.

We were nearly to the door when I spotted the kettle on the sofa table in the hall, the one she used to refill my tea throughout the sessions. Suddenly, something Cameron had said earlier rang out through my mind, giving me pause.

"Do you mind if I take a tea with us? I'm feeling tired, and I could use the caffeine."

She looked shocked. "Um, sure?" It was a question, and I was sure she was questioning my sanity more than anything. "Do you both want one?"

"No," Cam said.

But at the same time, I said, "Please."

"We don't have time for that," Cameron added, but I widened my eyes slightly, letting him know to shut up. Alex was already out of the room and in the kitchen.

I stood between Cameron and the door, ignoring his attempts to get me out of it and, within minutes, she'd reappeared, two cups of tea in her hand, the tags hanging over the edges of the cups. I took them from her, noticing the lingering eye contact she held with me.

"Thank you," I said.

"Take care of yourself, okay?" she asked.

Cam opened the door, and we ducked out of it without another word.

He didn't ask why I'd made a big deal about the tea, or why I was being silent about everything else, and I couldn't tell him, even if he had.

I had so much to process. So much I needed to think about. And, on top of that, I had a theory I desperately wanted to test out.

36 CAMERON

I had three missed calls from the detective when we left Alex's house. He'd left a single voicemail, instructing me to call him back.

We'd missed our appointment with him, and I knew how that would make us look, but how were we ever going to explain all that we'd learned?

We had to tell him, didn't we? We should let them know about Alex, but would that only muddy the waters of the investigation? I wanted them focused.

I had a headache forming—I assumed a result of the whirlwind of questions in my mind, not the least of which was what was going on in my wife's head. But she was giving me nothing to work with.

Ginny didn't speak most of the way home. She just sat in the passenger's seat, gripping those cups of tea with the most haunting look in her eyes. I wanted to ask her what she was thinking, what was going on in her head. I wanted to help her unpack the revelations we'd just uncovered, but I couldn't.

I couldn't ask her anything.

I didn't deserve to.

In all honesty, I was surprised she hadn't kicked me out of the car and made me walk home. It would've been what I deserved.

I needed to wait for her to speak. Wait to see how she wanted to approach what had happened. All that had happened.

If she needed to process alone, needed to focus on Skylar, that was what we'd do. We could deal with everything else when she was ready. I'd wait forever if that was what it took.

It was nearly evening already. Her parents' flight was supposed to land around midnight, and mine would be there the next morning, and though we were still waiting to hear an ETA from Margie, we were officially in countdown mode until we had more feelings and personalities than our own to deal with.

I hoped she wouldn't tell our families about what I'd done, but I couldn't ask her not to. I couldn't ask her anything yet.

I wanted to gauge where she was, how she wanted to handle everything, but I was getting nothing from her.

When we pulled into the driveway, I spied the cop car that had been there all day. So, he either hadn't followed us, or he had beat us back. I shut off the car and we sat in silence. I waited for her to make a move.

"I'm going to see if the detective can come by in the morning," I said finally. "I'll just tell him you needed to see Alex today. I'm hoping he understands."

She nodded but didn't look at me.

"Do you think he came by here anyway? Would the other officer have let him know we left?"

She shrugged one shoulder.

"Well, I don't want you to worry about it, okay? I'll handle it." I pulled out my phone, staring at the reminder about the missed calls as I tried to rehearse what I was going to say in my head.

The lights of the officer's car came on in the distance, and for a moment, I thought he was going to move forward, drive down the driveway and confront us, but to my surprise, he began retreating, the lights getting further away.

"Shift change?" I wondered aloud, more to myself than anyone. I wasn't even sure Ginny was still listening to me.

As if summoned by the mere thought of him, my phone began to ring again, the detective's number on my screen, and I cleared my throat. "It's the detective. I'm going to answer it."

Again, there was no response from my wife.

"Hello?"

"Mr. Hale, you're a very busy man," came the dry greeting.

"I'm sorry we missed you. I tried to call. Something came up and we had to visit my wife's therapist. It's kind of a long story. We're back home now."

He didn't say whether he knew that or not. "Are you planning to stay put?"

"Yes. We're in for the night. Is there any news?"

"Nothing yet, but the storm's clearing up. We'll be back tomorrow to do a thorough search of your property. That's when you've planned the search party for, isn't it?"

"Yeah, it is," I said, glad he remembered. He hadn't responded when I'd texted him the details earlier.

"Well, good. I'll come early, then. Before we start, I was hoping you and I could go over your finances. I've found an account that concerns me. I'm sure you know what I'm talking about."

Fear washed over me, and I glanced at my wife. She was listening, even if she wasn't looking at me. I knew what he was talking about immediately. The emergency fund I'd begun building when I'd charted out my escape route. A couple hundred transferred over here and there, nothing Ginny would ever notice, but enough that, if I ever decided to leave, I could do so without a worry.

I swallowed. "I'd assume you're talking about the emergency fund I set up. Skylar's beneficiary. It has a couple thousand in it."

"That would be the one," he said. "Why didn't you tell me about it when I had you turn over your financial information?"

"Didn't I?" I chuckled nervously.

"No. You didn't."

"I, um, well, it must've slipped my mind. I don't use it for anything."

He was silent. "You'd better not be lying to me, Mr. Hale. If you are, I'll find out about it."

"I'm not lying," I said, swiping a hand across the back of my neck as cool sweat began to gather there.

"Well," he said, not confirming whether he believed me or not, "I'll be digging around to make sure of it. Lots of digging tomorrow, in fact." There was something callous about the way he said it. "If you or your wife have any skeletons in your closets, now's the time to come clean."

"We've told you everything," I choked out, answering for us both.

"You had a chance to talk to me today, one on one. Tomorrow won't be so easy. Now, stay put. I'll see you both first thing in the morning."

"Oka—"

The line clicked before the call had ended, and I looked at my wife. I knew we shouldn't have left the house when we did, but this was hardly the time to bring it up.

"It was just an emergency fund," I lied, praying she'd believe me.

She gave a small nod, wringing her hands together in her lap.

"We'll get it all sorted. They'll search the woods again. Our families will all be here…"

It felt as if the moment went on forever, her staring blankly ahead, before I added, "We've got several people going to participate in the search tomorrow, too. Lots of RSVPs…"

"Are you sure you don't want to be with Alex?" She blinked slowly, then turned her head to look at me.

"What?" I scoffed. "No, of course not. Why would you ask that?"

She placed the cups of tea into the holders between us, rubbing her lips together. "The way she looked at you today, it wasn't just lust in her eyes. She cares about you, Cameron. Do you feel the same way? I need you to be honest with me, for once in your life."

I bit back a response to the last part of the sentence and instead chose to take the high road. "I don't care about Alex. And, I don't think she cares about me, either. Not really. I think, more than anything, she's jealous," I told her. "But not because she has true feelings for me. Because you have a beautiful life and she is alone."

"A beautiful life?" She tossed her hands down in her lap angrily. "My daughter is missing and my husband just cheated on me. *Again.* Forgive me, but I'm failing to see the beauty in it at the moment."

I fought against the urge to reach over and take her hand. What had I been thinking sleeping with Alex? I hated myself for it. Hated myself for letting it happen. For falling into Alex's trap. How could I have been so naïve? So weak? I wanted to tell Ginny all of that, wanted to tell her that she deserved better, that I was guilty of a lot of things, but falling out of love with her wasn't one of them.

As much as I'd tried to tell myself I could leave, I knew now it was all a front. I could never have left her. I loved her too much. Despite all my failings, Ginny was the love of my life. As messy, complicated, and flawed as our story was, I never wanted to be without her.

Perhaps this is what it took for me to realize it, but I had.

I'd glue our marriage back together at the seams if that's what it took.

I cleared my throat, trying to decide what to say. "I know. And I'm sorry. God, Ginny, I'm just so sorry. I know that doesn't fix it. I don't know if you'll ever trust me again, but I want you to know, I'm here for you no matter what. You're not going to deal with any of this alone. I know you must be furious with me. Hurt by what I did. And rightfully so. But it didn't mean anything, I swear to you it didn't. I love you. You're the one—"

"Cam, please—" She cut me off, a hand in the air. "I can't do this right—"

"Just listen to me, okay? *Please.* I know what I did was wrong. I know what you're dealing with, what I've put you through on top of everything else. Skylar, Alex... I know there are going to be a lot of feelings today, and going forward, and I'm going to try my best not to overstep or do the wrong thing, but if you need to talk or... or cry or... Whatever you need. I'm here. I'm here forever unless you ask me not to be."

"I need to find our daughter," she said simply, lifting the mugs of tea from the cupholder and handing one to me. "I need you to drink this, and then we need to find our daughter."

I nodded, unable to speak about how badly I wanted to find Skylar. It just hurt too much. It hurt too much to even think about how much it hurt. I took a drink of the tea, feeling instantly soothed.

"It's good, isn't it?" she asked, lifting her own cup to her lips.

"It is."

"I just thought maybe it would calm my nerves. It was the least she could do."

I nodded, taking another drink. She opened the car door, and we made our way through the garage and into the house. She led me into the bedroom where we changed into new, clean and comfy clothes, and she sank down on the edge of the bed. I took another drink of my tea and she did the same.

"Can I ask you something?" she said after a minute.

"Anything."

"The night that you and Alex—"

"I've already told you what happened," I told her, taking another drink of my tea and leaning back on the pillow. There really was something so soothing about the warm drink. "I'll answer any of your questions, but really, there wasn't much else to tell."

"No." She smiled, not meeting my eye. "It's not that."

"Then what is it?" I asked with a yawn.

"I just wondered... Why didn't you tell me about it? Why didn't you tell me that she'd been coming over in the first place? I get that you didn't want to make me feel weird, but why wouldn't you have at least asked me? I wouldn't have minded if you would've told me about it from the start."

I sighed, thinking back. Truth be told, when Alex had explained it, it made sense not to tell her, but now, looking back on it, it was a mistake from the start. I had no idea why I hadn't just told her what was going on. "She said she didn't want you to be bothered that she'd come to check on you. She asked me not to say anything. I didn't see the harm at the time."

"And, that night, the night you slept together, how long did she stay?"

"Not long. Under an hour. We sat at the table and talked for a while and then... well, you know. And she left right after. Actually, I fell asleep and when I woke up, she was gone."

She raised a brow. "You said it was like you blacked out, right?"

"Well, it was the middle of the night. I was tired and I had a headache, I think." She was silent for a while. "It doesn't excuse what I did. I know that. It was a mistake that I'll regret for the rest of my life."

"Did she bring tea with her that night? This tea?" She tapped her finger on the cup.

The question caught me off guard. I thought back, the memory of the night muddled a bit in my memory. I remembered meeting her at the door. The sharp taste of spearmint. "Yeah. She did, actually. Why do you ask?"

Her expression grew weary, and she nodded. "No real reason. Just curious."

"That was all you wanted to know?"

"Mhm," she said casually, looking away. "I was just trying to get a better understanding, I guess."

"I'm sorry, Ginny. I've said it a thousand times, and I'll say it a thousand more. I feel like an ass. I was an ass."

"I don't want to talk about it anymore. Honestly, I can't." I drained the last of my drink and she stood, taking another drink of hers. "I'm going to brush my teeth and throw these away. I want to get a nap in before my parents' flight gets here. Do you need anything?"

"No," I said with a long, drawn-out yawn. "I'm not going to

sleep, but I want to rest for a second. Can you set an alarm just in case?"

She nodded. At least, I think she did. What I remember clearly was at that moment, the world dimmed, and then grew dark.

I slept with a dreamlike stupor.

37 GINNY

After my husband had fallen asleep, my suspicions about the drugged tea confirmed, I poured my full cup down the drain. I'd suspected it slightly for a while, when the sleepiness hadn't subsided, even after the easier sessions, but I'd never wanted to believe it. It was ridiculous. Why would she be drugging me?

I'd wanted to trust Alex then, to believe she was only trying to help me, but now I knew I never could.

It was no wonder I'd slept through her visits with my husband. Maybe that was her plan all along.

As I'd thought through a plan of my own, I knew I needed to confront Alex about the rest of what she'd done alone, and in order to do that, I needed Cam to sleep. He'd never let me leave the house alone, not after what I'd just found out. It was why I'd insisted on the tea. I could test my theory and get Cam out of my hair all at once. Two birds, one stone.

Once I was back in the car, my mind swirling with everything I'd just learned, I pulled out of the garage and the driveway and retreated in the direction I'd just come from.

I wasn't done talking to my newfound sister, not when I was sure she was still lying to me.

Once I'd arrived at her house, I decided to sit across the street, far enough away that it would be harder for her to notice me, but still close enough that I could see her standing on the porch talking to a young girl. Was that Raven's mother? She didn't look like her, but I couldn't be certain.

I now knew it couldn't be a client.

So, if not Raven's mother, who could it be?

I watched the two talk animatedly for a moment, then the woman walked into Alex's home and Alex turned away from her, jogging down the porch and climbing into her car.

Where was she going?

Who was the girl she'd just let into her home?

Perhaps the home wasn't Alex's to begin with. Maybe she was borrowing it from a friend in order to trick me even further. I debated back and forth about whether to stay and watch the house or follow to see where she'd lead me, but in the end, as I watched her pull away, there was no real choice.

I pulled out seconds behind her and followed her down the street, then to the next block. Soon, it was evident we were leaving town altogether.

I kept a few cars between us, with an eye on her the entire time. Once, she made two right turns in a row and I was sure I'd been caught, but then she made a left turn and I realized we were heading for the river.

My stomach lurched as she made several turnoffs before I caught sight of the first set of woods and the gravel street that I knew meant we'd reached far enough out of town that my phone no longer had service. I thought of the many days I'd spent enjoying the riverside with my family growing up and with Cam since we'd gotten married.

It was beginning to get dark, a sort of foggy dusk settling around us, and I could see the gravel dust in our headlights. We were the only cars on the road, so I was forced to hang back even further to keep it from being obvious that I was following her. When she stopped her car in a grassy area near the cliffs, I drove past the street, giving her a few seconds before I turned my car around.

I flipped off my headlights and drove down the gravel road quietly, hoping the sounds of the rushing water would drown out the crunch of my tires on the road.

I parked halfway down the road and stepped from my car, walking toward the clearing where I knew she'd be parked with silent, careful footsteps.

As I grew near, I could hear her voice, though I could hardly make out what she was saying.

"Come with Aunt Alex... need to talk to you..."

My stomach tightened at the phrase *Aunt Alex,* knowing it was the phrase Skylar might've called her, had circumstances been different.

"Come over here for a second." Her voice was clearer now, the roar of the water louder, and I knew I was getting close. When she finally came into view, I felt bile rising to the surface, tears stinging my eyes.

She was sitting on a rock near a cliff, too close to the drop-off to the river and the rapids down below. My knees went weak, a lump forming in my chest, expanding so large I was sure I'd lose the ability to breathe.

I couldn't think. I couldn't make myself understand it, but it was true.

She was there.

Skylar.

38 ALEX

I didn't have a choice.

That much was clear.

I'd seen how much Ginny hated her daughter. I'd seen how hurt Cameron was by the marriage, by the lack of love he received from his wife. He deserved better.

Skylar, too.

I could give them better.

When I talked to my sister for the first time as adults, I truly didn't have a plan. I'd watched her grow up; always the golden child. Watched her get adopted straight away, into a family who loved her.

I'd watched her forget about me, move on as if I'd never existed.

That's what everyone had always done, wasn't it?

My sister didn't care about me any more than our mother did. I was sick of watching mothers who didn't deserve their children get to keep them. Sick of watching my sister live a charmed life—all thanks to me—while I scrubbed toilets for a living, with a house that was falling apart and no one to help me keep it up.

I was alone, as alone as I'd ever been, and I was done with that.

Talking to Cameron, I could see how much he needed me,

even if he couldn't admit it. And he never would, not with Ginny around. But with a few extra sleeping pills in the tea I brought over during the last session, I knew he would give in to me. I could see it in his eyes—the longing. The suffering.

He wanted me, but she'd never let him leave.

She latched onto people. Used them.

Like she'd done to me. Like she'd do to him.

I couldn't let it happen, so when Cameron finally gave in to me, when we slept together, the plan began to form. I guess it had been there for a while, honestly—a backup plan, of sorts. But I wasn't sure when, or if, I'd ever get to put it into motion.

I needed Cameron on my side, and until I had him in my bed, I wasn't sure that would happen. But once he'd held me, kissed me, loved me, I knew I had him. I'd never had the same power over people that my sister had, but I knew how to persuade. To manipulate.

To win.

I'd taken the key from the house that night while he was sleeping, made a copy of it, and returned it at the party. They were none the wiser as I snuck back in that night, taking Skylar and leaving behind the toy Ginny had kept as a child.

It was mine first, but she'd wanted it. Like an idiot, I gave it to her and never got it back. That is, until she got a family of her own. She left behind everything—her toys, her clothes, me. We weren't good enough for her new life.

What I hadn't counted on with my plan was having Ginny and Cameron act so quickly with the police. I'd meant to have a few days to get away, to set up a new home for us before I called Cameron to join us.

I knew I could convince him I was scared for Skylar's safety given enough time. He'd see me as the hero, and he'd love me even more. We'd be a family. A real family.

One of my own.

Finally, I'd take back from Ginny what she stole from me.

But the police coming to my house, asking questions and needing alibis had thrown a wrench into the plan.

Having a mother who cared so little for me had done nothing to prepare me for parents who actually gave a shit when their child went missing. I'd cut it close. Ginny had heard Skylar squealing as I forced her up the attic stairs and into the small, hidden room where our mother had kept us when we were particularly bad.

I'd told her it was just me laughing, that I'd been with a friend, the same alibi I'd given to the police, though I'd yet to have said friend give them a call. I thought Ginny believed me, but I wasn't sure.

Now, I had to change the plan. And quickly. I made it up the stairs and walked into the bedroom, then through the door that led to the attic, and finally into the small room inside the attic.

Skylar was there, still munching on the bowl of cherry tomatoes I'd provided her for breakfast. She was tired now. Asking for her parents more.

When she heard me enter the room, she looked my way but didn't smile. She was still angry with me. She'd get over it. This was all for her own good. She'd see.

There was a book in her hands, upside down, and she was clutching onto the small dolly I'd left for her to play with.

"I wanna go home," she whined, stamping a foot. She'd been causing me more issues. All night long, she'd been up, whining and moaning about her parents and how badly she missed them. Couldn't she see how much better I was than her mother? How much I cared?

"I know you do."

"I wanna go now!" she cried, throwing herself backward so she was splayed on the floor, her leg colliding with the bowl of tomatoes and sending them sailing across the floor in every direction.

I rushed over, groaning as I tried to pick them up. "Look what you've done!" I sighed, shoving my hair out of my face. "I know you want to go home, Skylar, but you can't yet. Do you understand that? *You can't!*"

This only made her cry harder, slamming her hands and feet onto the ground. "I want Daddy! I want Mommy!"

She bellowed and whined, her limbs kicking and flailing about, this way and that.

"Now, if you're going to have a fit, I'm going to take your toys away."

She tossed the doll at me without a care, the plastic toy nearly slamming into my head.

"Mommy! Daddy!" she screamed again, her face red and glimmering with tears.

"That wasn't very nice, Skylar." I picked up the doll and placed it on the sole bookshelf in the room—a waist-high one that I'd filled with toys for her.

She rolled over, staring at me with gritted teeth and bulging eyes. *"Mommy! Daddy!"* she screamed again.

I felt my blood pressure rising. Why on earth wasn't she more grateful for what I'd done for her? I'd provided her with a safe space, healthy food, toys to play with.

It wasn't an ideal bedroom or setup, but we'd get there. She had no idea how lucky she was. When I was her age, just to have an adult around who gave me clean clothes or food or water was nice. Toys were a luxury I was never afforded. I remembered playing with plastic silverware I'd found in the back of a drawer and using blankets both as dolls and dressup clothes.

Skylar was spoiled, there was no doubt about it.

I didn't expect her to take to me immediately, but I'd spent so much time building a relationship with her. I'd given her the best birthday gift I could afford. I'd spent months getting to know her, and now I was giving her attention. The promise of a better life. So, why didn't she love me back? Why didn't she care about me?

As a child, I'd loved anyone who paid me any spare bit of attention, anyone who wasn't trying to harm me, so I was really struggling with how she could be so selfish as to not see what I was doing for her.

"You're going to see your daddy again, okay?" I told her, when she'd finally calmed down. She picked up the sippy cup of water on the floor and sucked most of the liquid down. "He's going to come with us. But right now, it's going to be just us for a little while longer."

"I don't wanna—"

"Shhh!" I cut off her scream with a hand over her mouth, my ear cocked toward the door. I hadn't heard it in the soundproofed room, but I'd felt it.

The vibration of the floors. The walls.

Thwomp, thwomp, thwomp.

Someone was at the door. My heart raced as I pictured the police, standing there, armed with a warrant. I removed my hand from her mouth, and she stared at me in shock and fear.

I thought of the handcuffs they'd be holding.

Of the prison they'd throw me into.

What have I done?

I rushed out of the room without a word, leaving her in stunned silence. I shut the door and locked it behind me before darting down the stairs, smoothing my clothes and hair as I rehearsed what to say. They wouldn't hear Skylar from inside the room—my mother had made sure no one ever heard my screams from there—but if they noticed the hidden door somehow, there'd be no way to keep my secret any longer.

As I reached the door, the view blocked by the curtains, I braced myself.

Rap, rap, rap, rap, rap.

The knocking came again, hurried and angry. I put my hand to the doorknob and twisted, just as I heard a familiar voice.

"Oh, thank god," she said, her voice raspy and panicked. "Can you keep her?"

Ella Rae Tate stood in front of me in the smallest shorts imaginable and a shirt that ended just above her navel. Her hair was drenched, eye makeup dark and smudged. I'd given her my name dozens of times, but never heard her use it once. The day before,

Ginny had finally confirmed my suspicions that Ella Rae didn't know it.

Why should she need to know the name of the woman keeping her child, after all?

She reeked of cigarette smoke, body odor, and cat urine as she shoved Raven through the small opening between the door and its frame. The young girl, too, was soaked to the bone.

"This really isn't a good time, Ella Rae. How long will you be gone?"

Raven looked up at me, appearing embarrassed to be there. Her face was so downtrodden it broke my heart.

The woman didn't bother to turn around, smacking the gum in her mouth. She wagged her fingers at me over her shoulder. "Probably tonight. Maybe tomorrow or so... You're the best!" She hurried down the stairs, nearly tripping as she went, and climbed into the passenger's seat of a car driven by a man I didn't recognize.

It wasn't a surprise, honestly. Ella Rae was flaky and wild, always with a new boyfriend for a week or two who'd get her hooked on a new drug. The first time I'd watched Raven, she hadn't been much older than two, and I'd watched out my window as she darted into the road after a ball. A car had slowed to prevent hitting her, and I ran outside, collecting her and her toy and leading her up to her front door. I was prepared to tell her mother what happened, to give her a piece of my mind for leaving a child so young unattended, but after I'd knocked and knocked, I realized she wasn't home at all.

She'd left her toddler at home alone.

Furious, I brought Raven back to my house, fed her, and washed and combed her filthy, matted hair. She was a contented girl, happy to play by herself and keep occupied, which left me plenty of free time to keep an eye on her house and watch for her mother to come home.

It was three days before she did, and I braced myself, prepared for the storm of her wrath, maybe fear, when she realized her daughter was gone.

I watched as she went inside, strung out on God knows what.

I waited.

And waited.

The hours passed.

Then the night.

The next day, she still hadn't come looking for her daughter. Did she even realize she was gone?

That afternoon, another car came and she was gone again. At that point, I called child services and they'd come to collect Raven. To my knowledge, Ella Rae never learned who reported her and, since we didn't know each other at that point, I didn't care if she had found out it was me.

They loaded the little girl up, her few belongings shoved in a trash bag, and they drove away. I wondered if it would be the last time I saw her, and that worry broke my heart.

I'd done the right thing. I knew I had... But that didn't make it hurt any less. I'd just subjected the girl to a childhood like I'd had. Shuffled home to home constantly, no real stability, no lasting love.

Within six months, the girl was back home, looking a bit older and much cleaner. She brought toys with her and clean clothes, and Ella Rae carried her in, hugging her close to her body.

I thought—*I'd hoped*—it would change things for her. I hoped Ella Rae had gotten clean. That she would be there for her daughter in a way my own mother had never been for me.

That hope only lasted for a few days.

After that, I noticed a new car in the driveway for a few days, then another after that. A new boyfriend living with them. Ella Rae was back to her old ways, no longer sober, and Raven was alone and in the middle of it.

It was then that I'd offered to keep her daughter whenever Ella Rae had something going on. Whenever she needed a sitter. And so, without so much as asking my name or what my qualifications to keep her child were—or how I even knew her daughter in the first place—Ella Rae had let me take her.

Now, there were months at a time when I kept her and tried to show her all the love I knew she needed. I tried to drown her in it, give her enough that it would satiate her when her mother came to collect her, as she always eventually did, though for what length of time I could never be sure.

The car backed out of the parking space on the road in the pouring rain, all four windows rolled down, neither passenger buckled in as he sped off, squealing his tires. I bent down, pulling my new guest into a hug.

I really love this one, I could already hear her telling me. She always loved them, and they always broke her heart.

"I've missed you," I told her, brushing her hair from her face. I shut the door and locked it behind us. "We have a visitor for you to play with."

"We do?" Raven smiled up at me, though her smile was muted, the color in her face drained as it often was when she'd been returned to me.

"Yes, but first, let's get you cleaned up, okay?" I led her into the kitchen and got her a glass of milk, which she sucked down in its entirety within seconds.

How long had it been since she'd had anything to drink?

Her hair was filthy, the smell repulsive, so next I led her up the stairs and toward the bathroom, starting the water and helping peel off her wet, stained clothing.

"In we go." I placed her into the bath and helped scrub and rinse her hair, handing her a cloth so she could finish her washing. When she was done, we drained the gray water and I wrapped her up in a towel, pleased to see a bit more color in her cheeks. We walked together toward the bedroom I'd made up for her, the room that had been mine as a child, and I handed her some clean clothes.

Once she was dressed, I brushed her hair, soothing her as she cried while I tugged gently at the matted hair. This was always one of the worst parts. There'd been times when I'd had to cut them out, but today wasn't as bad as it had been. I'd sent her home with hairbrushes countless times, but it hadn't worked.

I wanted so badly to report Ella Rae again, never as much as I did when she returned her daughter to me in a state like this, but what good would it do? No, she was safer with me for as long as I could keep her.

"Almost done," I promised, holding her hair carefully as I worked on the worst spot.

A few hours later, she was clean, dry, and I had her up in the spare bedroom playing with her toys and munching on carrots and cherry tomatoes with Skylar.

Rap, rap, rap, rap.

I froze, my eyes wide. What if she'd come back for her? I couldn't let her leave. I hadn't been able to feed her a proper meal. To give her anything substantial to drink. I needed more time.

I'd have to reason with Ella Rae, to convince her Raven should stay with me for a few hours to give her a break.

I knelt down, eye level with the girl, my hands on her arms. "I'm going to see who that is. You stay here, okay?"

"Okay." She nodded and walked over toward the stack of puzzles on her bookshelf, picking one up and sitting on the floor as she dumped out the pieces.

Skylar moved to join her, but I scooped up the girl and carried her back to the stairs. For being just three years old, she was quite heavy to carry, particularly when she was throwing a fit.

"I don't wanna go!" she screamed, then released a squeal. *"Eeeeee!"*

I moved quicker, opening the door to the hidden room and placing her inside. "I'll be right back."

She launched herself forward, but I was quicker than her. I shut the door and jogged down the stairs just as someone began beating on it again. What was Ella Rae's rush?

But it wasn't Ella Rae. I froze when I saw Cameron and Ginny waiting for me. I wasn't prepared to deal with them again, but I had to. I had to keep up the charade for as long as I could. And I had. I put on a smile and went through the act.

I hadn't planned to tell Ginny the truth about who I was, but when the opportunity presented itself, I realized it was time. She needed to know. Cam needed to know. He needed to know what kind of person he married. The kind who could abandon and forget her own sister.

I'd tell him and let him decide his own fate.

Either way, Skylar was mine.

No one deserved her more than I did.

Once they'd left, I sank to the floor with a long, drawn-out sob. I felt empty, yet full. Broken, yet whole. I was finally free and the truth was out, but I needed to save myself. To save Skylar. We had to leave.

I allowed myself to cry, to release the tears that had been building up most of my life. I rolled into a ball on the floor, suppressing the noise in my chest, trying to keep silent so that Raven wouldn't hear me.

Raven.

I had only hours to carry out my new plan, but I couldn't bring Raven along. As much as I loved her, my obligation was to Skylar. I could come back for her someday. I would. But right now, I could only escape with one child, and that child had to be Skylar.

Snapping out of the sobs, I sat up, drying my eyes and walking toward the kitchen. I unplugged my phone from its charger on the counter, ignoring the dozens of missed calls and texts—from Ginny, from housekeeping clients, from Ella Rae. Instead, I went to my contacts and clicked on the home number for the Jensens next door, one of the few families to still rely solely on a house phone.

"Hello," came the gruff voice at the end of the line. He'd picked up on the second ring with an urgency that said he'd likely been waiting for a call all day.

"Hey, Mr. Jensen. It's Alex from next door."

"Oh, hey, honey. Did Sebastian get out again?" he asked, his voice strained as I guessed he was looking around the room for their small white terrier.

"No, it's nothing like that. Actually, I was wondering if Charlotte was home tonight."

"Charlotte?"

"Mhm." I ran my fingernail over a dark brown stain on the countertop, one I'd bleached too many times to count. "I have Raven over here. Ella Rae's little girl."

"Oh, *yes*," he said in a low, judging tone.

"Anyway, I need to run out. Just for about an hour, but I can't take her with me. I wondered if maybe Charlotte would want to come over and sit with her for a little while? I'd pay her, of course."

"Well, I'd have to ask her..." He paused. "Give me just a second." He put down the phone, leaving it off the hook so I could hear him groaning as he stood, then his heavy footsteps as he padded down the hall and toward his granddaughter's room. They were one of the wealthiest families on my street, and one of my favorite clients. I could picture the layout of the house, see him walking down the hall, past the parlor, and into the bedroom that belonged to Charlotte, with the closet big enough to be a bedroom itself.

I grabbed the sponge from the sink and began scrubbing at a speck of something orange on the counter. After ten minutes had passed, I heard him returning to the phone.

"She can be over in about fifteen minutes, honey. She's just finishing up her homework. Is that okay?"

"Yes, that's great. Thank you, Mr. Jensen. Thank you so much."

"Okay, now, honey." He ended the call, and I opened a can of soup for Raven, pouring it into a bowl and sticking it into the microwave as I thought through my plan.

As the reality of what I was going to do set in, I felt a wave of sadness come over me. I hated that it had come to this. Hated myself for letting it get so bad, but it was what it was and I needed to deal with it.

And fast.

The police were closing in.

Ginny and Cameron were still just as suspicious.

I needed to fix the problem.

I needed to get away. Change our names. Dye our hair. I'd done it before on my own, and I could do it again with Skylar in tow.

I hurried up the stairs, setting the bowl of soup on a bookshelf in Raven's room as the little girl played. I opened the attic door once again and climbed the stairs. Finally, I stepped into the small room where Skylar was now sleeping. When I opened the door, she was curled on the floor, her hair splayed out as she slept. I ran a finger across her cheek gently, once, then twice. "Sk*yyyy*lar."

She stirred, opening an eye. She didn't sleep well here—she wasn't like Raven who can and had slept anywhere she needed to —the heat and unfamiliarity of the room made it nearly impossible for Skylar to relax, but she'd thrown so many fits today, she'd worn herself out.

When she saw where she was, she sat up.

"*Dad? Mom?*" I shook my head when her gaze landed on me.

"It's time to go home, okay?"

Her eyes radiated sudden happiness, and I knew it was the right thing to do. I'd done what I needed to. What I'd set out to. I knew that in my bones.

"I'm going home now?"

"Yep. Right now. Come on." I patted my knee as I stood and scooped her up, grabbing her doll and pressing it to her chest. I hurried out of the attic and back down the stairs, making my way to Raven and placing a kiss atop her head. "I'll be back for you, kiddo. I promise."

She stared at me strangely, but didn't say anything. "Be good for Charlotte, okay?"

"Okay."

"Are we going to my house?" Skylar asked, and I nodded.

"Shhh."

I carried Skylar down the hall, then down the stairs, and wrapped her in a jacket so she couldn't be seen from the street. When I'd brought her there the first time, it had been under the cover of darkness, but now, as evening had just begun to fall, if anyone looked out their window, they'd be able to see what I was up to. I kept her face hidden as I carried her out to the car and placed her inside, starting it up and buckling her into Raven's car seat.

"I'll be right back, okay?"

She nodded, trying to see out the window. "Alex, where do trees come from?"

"From seeds," I told her, sniffling softly as I looked away, trying to hide my tears.

"Big seeds or little seeds?"

"Um, I'm not sure." I shut the car door as I jogged back up the walk. Once I reached the door, I grabbed my purse from inside, regretting instantly that I wouldn't have a chance to take anything else with us. As soon as I saw Charlotte, I waved a hand over my head. "Hey, thanks for doing this on such short notice."

"Oh, sure. No problem."

"She's upstairs coloring a picture. There's a bowl of soup on her bookshelf that she should eat for dinner after she's done coloring. It's fine for her to eat in her room. She knows how to brush her teeth and change into pajamas, so you just need to be there to make sure she's down by eight. I should be back home shortly after that, but if you have any problems... Do you have a cell phone?"

"Uh, yeah." She pulled it out, a small flip phone I wondered if kids teased her about at school. All the money in the world hadn't been able to pay her grandparents' way into 2021.

"Great." I recited my number for her. "Just call your grandpa if you need anything. Tell Rae that I love her and I'll be back soon. She'll be fine."

"Yep, it'll be okay. I'll tell her. What if her mom comes back?"

"She shouldn't," I said, then began to worry. "Well, just lock the door behind me and call your grandpa if anyone shows up, okay? We'll figure it out."

She nodded, looking a little worried, but when I opened the door, she walked inside. "Thanks again, Charlotte. You're a lifesaver."

With that, I walked down the steps again and back to the car. I met Skylar's eyes in the rearview mirror. There was so much I wanted to say to her. Things I wanted to explain. I wanted her to know that things would be better now. That I would take care of her. That I would be the mother she deserved.

But I needed to think first. I needed to get my head on straight. I wanted to take her to my favorite spot, somewhere no one would think to look. It was the place where her mother and I had played so often as kids. The place where, no matter what was going on in the world, I was sure to feel happy. I hoped she would feel happy there, too.

She wouldn't like what I was going to say to her, but I needed her to understand it was for the best. There was no way she could be angry with me if I took her to the magical place—the happiest place on Earth.

Toughen up, Alex. You're a mom now.

Skylar, still dressed in the Peppa Pig pajamas I'd put on her the night before last, was standing in front of Alex.

My heart skipped a beat, my chest tight with silent sobs.

Was it possible? Was she really there? Was I imagining it? It felt like a cruel dream, like I'd soon open my eyes and realize I'd fallen asleep next to Cameron rather than following Alex after all.

I made myself focus, taking in every inch of her appearance. My daughter's hair clung to her forehead and cheeks with sweat, her usually smooth, curly hair was frizzy and tangled.

I wanted to lunge forward and grab my child, but I needed to understand what was happening. Did Alex have a weapon? What was she going to do?

I fought every urge in my body, using physical force to keep my feet planted as I peered out from behind a tree to watch what was unfolding.

"I need you to listen to me, okay?"

"Why?" Skylar asked, picking a flower from the grass and shoving it into Alex's face. "Smell this."

She pretended to sniff the flower, then pushed it away from her face. "Because I said so. I've taken good care of you, haven't I? Auntie's been good to you. But now we have to go, okay?"

"Why?" Skylar prompted again. She bent down to pick a new flower, and I saw both of Alex's hands. She was unarmed as far as I could tell. "Smell this," Skylar said, shoving another flower in her face.

"Sometimes adults have to do things you don't understand. Things that are for the better good."

"What's... what's *the better good*?" Skylar asked, still picking flowers.

I saw my chance as my daughter was now far enough away from Alex, I thought I could jump out without risking her grabbing Skylar.

"Well, it means I wanted to help you—"

"Why, Alex?" I rushed forward, my hands locked into fists at my sides.

Alex looked taken aback. She squinted, trying to make out who I was in the dim light, then her jaw dropped open and she reached for Skylar, but I was there first. I pushed my daughter backward, away from Alex, so I was standing between them.

"Mommy!" Skylar cried, reaching for me. She wrapped her arms around my leg, and I placed a hand on her back, so grateful to be holding her again. I kept my front to Alex, watching her closely.

Skylar squeezed me tighter, her little arms surrounding my thigh, her cheek pressed into my hip. I ran a hand over her hair. "I missed you."

"I missed you too, sweet girl," I told her, still not taking my eyes off of Alex. She watched the interaction with a strange, curious look on her face. "Why? Why do you have her? How do you have her? Why?" The questions tumbled out of me. I wasn't sure which one I needed an answer to first.

"I'm sorry," she said simply, with a puff of air like she was releasing all of her worries.

"Sorry for what? For taking my daughter? For lying to me about it? For making Cam and me sick with worry?"

At the mention of her father's name, Skylar was tugging on my shirt. "Mom? Mom?"

"Just a second, Skylar," I said, gripping her hand.

"Where's Dad?" she asked anyway.

"He's at home." I met Alex's eye. "He will be *so* excited to see you."

She looked away, chin quivering with what appeared to be anger. "You don't deserve her."

"Excuse me?" I demanded.

"You don't deserve her. You don't even want her," she said softly, still not looking at me.

I covered Skylar's ears instinctually, but I knew it was too late. She'd heard the horrible statement. "You have no idea what you're talking about. She is my daughter. I love her!" I shouted, dropping a hand to my side in protest.

"All you do is complain about her," she said as Skylar ducked out from under my other hand and moved away from me, picking new flowers.

"I'll find the prettiest flowers for Dad, Mommy!"

I grimaced, speaking through wild, panicked breaths. Anger spun inside of me with such vengeance, I thought I might pass out. "I was sick! I was sick, but I never stopped loving her. I'm her mother! I would die for that child."

Alex jerked her head to look at me finally, her expression dark and cold. She jutted a hand toward me. "She doesn't want you." Her finger pressed into her chest. "She wants me. They both want me." Her smile grew sinister, and I felt my blood run cold.

"You have no idea what you're talking about," I said, glancing over my shoulder to check on Skylar. "Baby, stay close!" Sky sighed but moved back toward me.

"There are no flowers over here though," she whined.

"Why don't you pick some of these?" I asked, pointing my foot toward a patch of small, yellow buds. "We're getting ready to leave."

"*Did you hear me?*" Alex demanded. "Cam wants me, too. We're going to be a family. He loves me. I'm *better* than you. I bet you he didn't tell you we slept together, did he?" Her smile gleamed with obvious pride.

My body recoiled at the statement. "Actually, he did. He told me what a mistake it was."

"That's not true!" she cried. Her smile fell away in an instant, and she clutched her stomach as if I'd punched her.

"It is, Alex. He doesn't love you. He doesn't want a family with you, and you are never going to be Skylar's mom. I'm taking her home." I took a step back.

"We going home!" Skylar shouted jubilantly.

Alex stepped toward me aggressively, her voice nearly feral when she spoke again. "You never deserved any of it. Everything came so easy for you. Everyone loved you, even as a child. No one ever cared about me," she said, her last sentence broken up by sobs as she wiped tears away with a wild expression.

"If you're hoping to get my sympathy, you won't. *I* cared about *you*. I thought you were my friend. But you betrayed me. In every way possible. I could never forgive you for that."

"I just wanted her to have a good life. I wanted to fix everything for her," she screamed, her voice echoing through the woods. "For all of you. I wanted to fix it."

"Mommy, remember when Daddy fixed the *cabinet*"—she pronounced each syllable slowly—"door? Remember?"

"I do remember," I told her, then turned back to Alex. "Fix everything? By taking my husband? My daughter?" This time, it was me who moved toward her. "How was that going to fix *anything*?"

She retreated, sinking down onto a rock and shaking her head. "I just never wanted Skylar to go through what we went through. You told me she was the most important thing, but you were struggling. She needed someone who could love her always. Not just when it was convenient."

I drew in a breath. "I love her always. Don't you dare use what I told you in confidence against me. You have no idea what it means to be a mother. You're not what's best for her," I said, my upper lip curled in disgust. I could feel my heartbeat in every inch of my body.

She looked up, as if an idea had just come to her. "I know that Cameron thought about leaving you. I know he wanted to, but he felt trapped. He needed a way out, and I gave him one."

"Yeah, he told me you were planning to blame this all on me. Too bad he never believed you," I said, though I still didn't know if that was the truth. "Cameron knows I would never hurt my child. You, on the other hand, Alex, you'll never see any of us again. You claim you wanted a family, but you just threw yours away. You stole my daughter, how could I—"

"Stealing isn't nice, is it, Mommy?" Skylar asked, bouncing next to my feet.

"No, baby. No, it's not." I locked eyes with Alex as I said it. "It's really not."

She shot up from the rock then as I turned to walk away, shouting after me. "You were never my family, Ginny. I thought you were, once. But family doesn't forget. They don't abandon."

I spun around, my body trembling with rage. "I was a *child*!"

She jumped in place, her face red, even in the dim light as she pointed a finger at me. "Yes! You were a child, but I called. I wrote. You moved on and forgot me. You discarded me like an old toy. That's what you'll do with Cameron and Skylar when they're no use for you anymore. That's all you know how to do."

I shook my head, releasing a sarcastic laugh. "You don't know me! You don't know anything about me!"

"That's exactly my point!" Her hands went into the air.

I took another step toward her, finger pointed back in her direction. "No." My lips were tight, forming a small 'o' as I spoke through gritted teeth. "You think you know what you're talking about, but you don't. I didn't know who you were. If you'd come to me and told me about our past, maybe I would've wanted to know you. We could've started fresh. We could've been a family. I can't answer for why my parents didn't tell me about you, but they didn't. I had no idea you even existed. But now, as far as I'm concerned, you don't exist. You will never exist. Not in my life, or my daughter's. And, make no mistake, she is *my* daughter, Alex. I don't take her for granted. I love her. You are nothing to her."

I spun around, reaching for my daughter as we started to walk away. She waited until I'd made it a few feet before speaking again, her voice soft, but carrying so much weight. "Do you think it's fair for her to have a mom who can't connect with her? Who doesn't know how to play with her?"

I stopped in my tracks, placing Skylar down once again. I knew she was hanging on Alex's every word, as they sliced my skin. "I struggled," I admitted with a slow nod. "I do struggle. But that has nothing to do with how much I love her."

"And in the beginning, our mom just struggled, too."

"With drugs!" I cried. "Not depression."

She opened her mouth, then shut it again. "How did you know that?"

"Well, it wasn't hard to piece it together with all you've said. But my mother did tell me the truth about our birth mother once I was old enough. She told me she was an addict."

"She told you about her, but not about me?" she asked, her voice small.

I swallowed, squaring my shoulders to her. "She never mentioned you. And maybe that was something we could've worked through. Maybe we could've been in each other's lives at one point, but not now. Never ever, after what you've done. It's unforgivable."

"You have everything, Ginny. You have a perfect life, and you took it for granted. You took it all for granted, not realizing it could be taken away in the blink of an eye."

"Of course, I realized it could all be taken away. Do you not believe every mother lives with that fear every single day?"

"No," she said, her expression haunted. "No, Ginny. Every mother does not live with that fear every single day."

"I know our mother wasn't good to us—"

"Wasn't good." She scoffed, looking up at the sky. "Our mother used to lock us in the attic until we literally passed out from heat exhaustion. Our mother used to withhold food and water for entire days at a time because we'd spilled something on the floor. Our mother used to take us to the park blocks from our house and make us walk home so she had time to get high in peace. It wasn't just that she *wasn't good* to us, Ginny. She hated us. And do you want to know the one time she didn't hate us?"

I couldn't speak, still processing the horror she'd just laid out, and I knew that only scratched the surface of what she'd—we'd, apparently—gone through.

"Once, she was dating this guy, Ron. Ronnie. He had two kids, too, and they took us to the fair. I mean, they didn't give us any money to do anything, but they took us." She rolled her eyes. "You loved the popcorn. We kept finding random pieces all over the ground, and I kept trying to tell you it was gross, but you were so happy... It was like Christmas. Or, what I imagine Christmas is like in a normal home, anyway."

She wiped a tear from her eyes, going on. "But when the night came, they didn't come back for us. We were in a different town, I don't even remember which one, but we tried to walk home and ended up in the middle of nowhere. The boys were older, and they'd gone off with their friends, so it was just the two of us. We ended up in some stranger's yard, miles from home, and they called the police. When they brought us home, it was the first time I'd ever seen her look genuinely scared over anything. She told us later that they'd come looking for us, but they couldn't find us."

She blinked, shaking her head as if coming out of a trance. "That's the only time in my life that I remember her being genuinely nice to us. I think we ate three meals a day for an entire week, and I remember watching some old, terrible movie on TV with her. She had us curled up on either side of her. It was the only time I remember feeling like a real family. The fear of losing us had changed something in her... At least, for a while."

I was quiet for a moment, waiting to see if she was going to say anything else. When she didn't, I sniffled. My voice was softer when I spoke again. "I'm sorry about that, Alex. I really am. I'm sorry you went through it, and I'm sorry I'm not old enough to remember, but taking my child was not the answer." I shook my head. "What were you expecting? Did you really think you'd get away with it?"

She gritted her teeth, the torment disappearing from her expression, replaced with fury. "I wanted to hurt you. I wanted you to hurt for once in your life. I wanted you to feel that fear that Momma felt because I know, if it hurt her—someone I was sure couldn't feel an ounce of emotion—I knew it would destroy someone like you."

"Well, mission accomplished," I said flatly. My chest was heavy with pain, anger, and fear. I wanted to leave, to walk away from her and never look back. "You hurt me, but I'll be okay. The only person you really hurt in all of this, was yourself."

She sniffled, her upper lip curled bitterly. "Well, that's nothing new. You've been hurting me your entire life. Why stop now?"

"I can't keep apologizing for our childhood. We're adults now. None of that matters anymore."

"It all matters. It matters to me."

"Well, then you need to get help. See a therapist. A real one. And stay far away from my family." I started to turn away again, desperate to leave and end this argument, but her next sentence stopped me.

"Cameron needs a partner. Do you really think you'll be able to keep him happy the way you are? Do you really think he will stay with you?" She had her head tilted to the side when I glanced back at her. "He's cheated on you twice already. It's only a matter of time before he does it again. You don't make him happy, Ginny. You never have." Her words were a blow to my chest, a ripping open of my skin and stabbing straight to the heart of my fears.

"Cameron loves me. We've gone through something terrible, but we'll survive it because we love each other. You lied to him.

You made him trust you. He made a mistake because you tricked him."

She leaned her head back up slowly, a look of pity in her eyes. "I just don't see it that way. I think I gave him an opportunity to go for what he wanted, and he took it."

I shook my head, scoffing. "You know, you called me crazy, but you're the one acting crazy. He didn't want you. He doesn't. He loves me. He loves our family."

She puffed up her chest, refusing to respond.

I'd said it only to be spiteful, but I was right. What she'd done wasn't the act of a stable person. "Cameron loves me, Alex. It will always be me."

"You think you know the truth, but you don't. I know how he feels about me," she said finally, a sense of dread running through my chest.

"You're delusional," I spat. "How did you do it, anyway? How did you take her?"

"I stole your house key the night I slept with him," she said, simple as if she'd been giving me directions. "Made a copy of it and returned it the day of the party. Once you were all asleep, it was easy enough to get inside. And..." She smiled at Skylar. "Sky knew me. She didn't make a fuss when I carried her out."

"How did we sleep through it?" I demanded, suddenly feeling ill. "Did you drug us that day?"

She scowled. "I didn't need to. You'd both had enough to drink by the time I left, I knew you'd sleep well."

"But you had drugged us before then, right? Did you drug Cameron the night he slept with you?" I asked, realizing I'd been right regarding my suspicions around the tea. My jaw was slack as I shook my head in disbelief.

"I did put something in his tea that night, yes. But that wasn't why he slept with me. He was awake. Conscious. He knew what he was doing."

"You... You've been drugging me all along, haven't you?" My

gaze drifted off, the realization hitting me square in the chest. I couldn't catch my breath.

"I've given you something to help you relax, yes. To help you sleep. I needed you to feel like we were actually making progress."

"Rather than *actually* helping me make progress, you mean?"

"Did you hear me before? Cameron *chose* to be with me that night. I didn't give him enough to make him sleep. I didn't force him. I gave him enough to let his guard down, to be honest with himself, and he finally had a chance to see things clearly. Cameron wants to be with me, Ginny. He wants to build a family with me. With me and Skylar..." She gestured toward my daughter, stepping forward as if she thought Sky would come to her.

I moved between them.

"Not a chance in hell," I said, my voice deep and menacing. "You don't get it, Alex. He doesn't want you. Nothing will make him want you. You drugged him. You stole our child! You're a monster. That's the only way he'll ever see you after this. What aren't you getting about that?"

Her eyes went wide, her expression as shocked as if I'd slapped her. "No..." She whimpered. Then, she shook her head, straightening up. When she spoke, her voice was firm. "No. I was protecting her. He'll see that. He'll understand." She was trying to convince herself more than me.

I took a step back, rolling my eyes. I'd heard enough, and I just wanted to get my child home. "I don't have time for this. Skylar?" I called, realizing my daughter had left my side again. "It's time to go."

"Can you honestly tell me you think your family is happy? That you're the best thing for them both?" She hurried forward, trying to cut me off on my way to get my daughter, but I shuffled sideways, keeping my body between them.

"Where are we going, Mommy? I'm not finished with my castle!" Skylar cried, pointing to the small stack of rocks she'd built.

I reached for my daughter's hand, still talking to Alex despite the fact that I wanted nothing more than to leave. "Family is what you make it. That doesn't mean there won't be tough times or mistakes made or hearts broken, but when you try, when you all do your best and you all try, that's all that really matters," I said. "That's what you'll never understand."

"If that's the case, then he'll forgive me." She was still struggling to get around me, to get to Skylar. "Because I was trying. I was trying my best. I was doing what a mother does—a good mother. I was protecting our child."

I pulled Skylar behind me, staring at Alex with disdain. "No, Alex. That's not how it works. You've brought Cameron more pain than you ever brought him joy. Skylar doesn't need your protection. Cameron doesn't need you. We're a family, and because of what you've done, you'll never be a part of that." I scowled as she shook her head, arguing with my every word. "You need to get yourself some help. You're absolutely deranged."

She jerked away from me with a sharp breath, her face ashen. "You're one to talk!"

"Skylar," I called over my shoulder, taking a step back. "We need to leave now, baby."

Alex grabbed hold of my shoulder, nearly shoving me down in her attempt to grab Skylar. With a loud shriek, Skylar darted in the opposite direction, moving away from our exit and too close to the falls. Alex spun on her heel in a hurry to grab her.

"Get away from her," I shouted, holding my breath as I bolted forward.

"Hands and feet to self, Alex," Skylar chanted.

"Skylar, baby, can Auntie have a hug?" Alex asked. Skylar was just inches from the ledge now, and Alex had stopped, staring at her cautiously, her shoulders rising and falling with heavy breaths.

My pulse pounding, heart in my throat, I found myself caught in between the paths going forward. If I moved, I was scared Skylar would step back and tumble down to the falls below. If I didn't, though, Alex was going to grab her. And then what would happen?

Alex's hands outstretched toward her. "Come away from that

ledge, okay?" Skylar looked to me for permission, then back behind her, realizing for the first time how close she was to falling.

"Get back, Alex," I ordered her. "Give her some space."

Alex looked hesitant, but eventually stepped sideways slightly, giving room for Skylar to move toward us. As soon as Skylar had done so, Alex's hands reached for her. I acted on instinct, my body fueled by adrenaline and pure terror as I launched forward, shoving her away from my daughter.

Skylar screamed, and I sucked in a sharp breath as I realized what was going to happen seconds before it did. Alex tumbled backward, her body slipping over the ledge, and disappearing down, down, down.

A sickening feeling washed over me.

What had I done?

With a cautious step forward, I looked over the cliff just as Alex hit the rapids and sank under the water. I watched in horror, holding my breath.

No.

No.

No.

Skylar clung to my leg, crying loudly as I waited for Alex to resurface. My breath caught in my throat, ice settling in my veins as I tried to think. What should I do?

What could I do?

There was nothing. The current was too fast, the rocks below sharp and jagged. She'd hit hard enough from this height that I knew—somewhere deep in my gut—she hadn't made it. I searched the water for a sight of her body, hoping I was wrong, but I wasn't.

I'd killed my own sister.

No. No. No. No. No. No.

I scooped Skylar up in a panic, running away from what I'd done in every sense of the word. How would I ever explain this to her? Would I go to jail? Was I going to lose the family I'd just fought back for?

What do I do? What do I do?

"Where's Aunt Alex, Momma?" she asked, still crying. I shook my head, unable to answer her through my silent sobs. I moved farther from the falls and back toward the road, searching for sight of our car.

As we moved past Alex's car, I stopped, a sudden idea filling me when I saw her phone lighting up in the passenger's seat.

"Hang on just a second," I said as I set Skylar down on the gravel.

My hands were shaking as I opened the car door and picked up her phone. I'd watched her type in her passcode over and over during our meetings at the coffee shop and the park. I typed it in, grateful it hadn't changed, and scrolled to her messages.

I clicked on my name, typing out a final message.

From her, to me.

I thought this was what I wanted, that it was a way to get closer to you, but I can't handle what I've done. I took Skylar the night after her party. I stole a key and made a copy. It was a mistake and I realize that now. I'm sending you the location where I'll leave her and I'm going to disappear. You'll never hear from me again. Please hurry. I'll miss you, I'm sorry.

I pressed send without allowing myself time to second guess and sent a ping of the location. Then, I reached in the car and grabbed her purse.

"Mommy?"

"Wait here." I held out a hand to keep Sky back as I moved toward the ledge and tossed the items over into the water. I looked down below to make sure they'd made it, then turned back to my daughter.

I bent down, gathering her into a hug with shaking hands as I kissed her head over and over again. "I love you so much. Oh my god, I love you. I missed you. I love you. I missed you." I repeated it over and over, wanting that to be what stuck out in her head about this night rather than the lies from her aunt. Then, I hugged her so tight I was sure she would break, before standing up, taking her hand, and leading her back to the gravel.

"Let's go home."

40 CAMERON

I was awoken by the sound of my wife crying. She shook my shoulders with force.

"Cam! Wake up. She's home. Cam... she's home."

I tried to understand what she was saying, pulling myself from sleep with such force it was almost painful.

"Hm?" I asked.

"Daddy! I'm home! I'm home!"

My eyes shot open, and I felt hope fill me before consciousness had a chance to. I searched the dark room, lit only by the lamp on my bedside table. I made out a small, blurry form, bouncing in front of my face.

I rubbed sleep from my eyes, half convinced I was dreaming.

"Skylar?" I blinked faster, sitting up and throwing the covers off of me. She was there. It was real. She stood in front of me, a wild, gleeful grin on her face.

I scooped her up, holding her close and breathing in her scent. Ginny was sitting on the edge of the bed, near my legs, and she smiled at me, her eyes full of tears the same as mine. Confusion filled me, but it was overwhelmed and surpassed by outright joyful relief.

"How?" I asked, when I put her down, looking her over. She was dressed in the new pajamas we'd put her in on the night of her birthday. "How is she... How are you... Where were you?" I asked Skylar, but it was Ginny who answered.

"Alex," she said bitterly.

"Alex?" She held out her phone, letting me read over a text message with blurry vision. "I don't understand."

She drew in a long, steady breath before speaking. "She... took her. I don't know why or... or how." She stopped, her words choked up by tears. "She said she stole the key, I'm assuming one of the nights she was over, or maybe at the birthday party, but she took it and she took her."

"Wait... When did you talk to her? Skylar was at her house?" I felt guilt rising like bile in my throat as I struggled to piece it all together.

"I was with Aunt Alex. Momma bringed me home!" Skylar cheered, clapping her hands together.

"Oh, sweetheart." I scooped her up again, feeling sure I was going to be sick. We'd been at her house. We'd walked out the door and left her. "I never want to let her go."

Ginny nodded, rubbing Skylar's back as she batted away her own tears.

"Are you hurt? Did she hurt you? Why didn't you wake me?" I asked, and Ginny pulled her hand back.

Skylar glanced at the floor, as if worried she'd be in trouble, but Ginny answered for her. "She's okay. We need to call the police and take her to the hospital to be sure. I tried to wake you when I got the text message, but you were out. I think Alex drugged your tea. Same as she did the night you slept together. Same as she's been doing to me after my sessions."

I ran a hand over my face, trying to make sense of it all. "She what? I don't... She *drugged* us? What text message? When did you talk to Alex? Where is she now?"

Ginny spoke slowly, not meeting my gaze as she swiped away

her tears. "I didn't talk to her. She texted me and told me where to find Skylar." She sniffled, shaking her head. "She wasn't there when I arrived."

"She just left her?" I asked, my lips curling with disbelief. How could she? How could she take her in the first place? And why?

"I guess," Ginny said simply.

"She went bye-bye!" Skylar said, shrugging one shoulder.

I had so many questions, but all I wanted to do was hold my little girl. "I'm so glad you're home. And you're safe." I looked her over, still not sure I wasn't dreaming. It felt too good to be true and too terrible to be true all at once. How had Alex managed to trick us in such a way? And why? Why did she take her? In the end, it didn't matter. What mattered was that we had our daughter home with us again. Finally. She was safe and she was back.

"We need to take her to the hospital to get her checked out," Ginny said again. "We'll call the detective on the way and let the police know she's with us and she's okay. You should get dressed."

I sat up further, sliding out of bed. "Your parents' flight will be landing soon."

"Yeah, I'll call them when they land. You should call your parents, too. And Margie," she said, a small, sad smile on her face. There was an apology in her eyes that I'd needed to see. She'd been wrong about Margie, but I'd been wrong about so much.

We didn't need to discuss any of that now.

I hugged Skylar again. "Oh my god, I can't believe this is real. I can't believe she's home. Daddy missed you so much, baby."

She threw her arms around my neck, giggling with delight. "I missed you, Daddy."

"Not more than I missed you," I told her, meeting my wife's eye. I squeezed her hand, my heart so full I was sure it would burst.

Thank you, I said silently to my wife. To our daughter. To the universe.

Losing Skylar had put so much into perspective for me. I now understood where my priorities lay, and it seemed Ginny did too.

No matter what happened, Skylar was okay. We were okay. Our family was okay.

Everything was going to be okay.

"Hey, birthday girl," my mother called, walking into the room and scooping Skylar up, planting rapid-fire kisses on her cheek.

Skylar giggled. "Hey, Gramma."

She set Skylar on her feet and pulled me into a hug, placing a single kiss on my cheek. I hugged her back. "Hey, Mom. How was the flight?"

"Oh, not too bad. Your father slept the whole way," she said, elbowing my dad's side. "I had my audiobook."

Dad hugged me next, gentle and brief. "Hey, kiddo."

"Where are you putting gifts?" Mom asked.

"Wherever you can find a spot. No particular place this year."

"Artie, can you go get the present from the car?" she asked.

He turned around and walked back out of the room just as Cameron reappeared, his arms outstretched for my mother.

"Joselyn, looking beautiful as ever."

She slapped his chest playfully. "Oh, you big ole flirt."

"I can't help it when you look that good," he teased, kissing my cheek. "Hey, beautiful."

"Hey." I smiled, meeting his eyes as warmth flooded through me. "Is the table set?"

"Yep, just about ready." He grabbed the tray of burgers and disappeared out the door again.

"So, how is work going?" Mom asked, making her way to the sink and washing her hands.

"Really well. I'm glad to be back."

"I'm glad to hear it, honey." She joined me at the counter, grabbing a knife and helping to chop the vegetables.

My mother and I had endured a rough year. After the revelation about Alex, I'd confronted her and she'd admitted the truth straight away. Everything Alex had told me was factual. But, what Alex hadn't told me—what she either hadn't remembered or cared to admit—was how in the beginning, they *had* let me visit with and talk to her on the phone.

But each conversation, each visit would end with me dealing with so much trauma. I'd relive the loss of my sister and my birth mother all over again. Though I was young, I still understood what I had lost when I'd been taken from them.

While it had been hard on my parents, they were willing to put themselves through it if it was what seemed better for me. But that wasn't the case.

Eventually, my caseworker had suggested keeping us separated. She thought it would be easier on Alex and on me, for us to learn to live apart. My parents wanted to adopt the both of us, but they just didn't make enough money or have the space in our home for two children.

When she'd told me that, she'd been crying. She apologized for any role she'd played in causing me pain.

I knew my mother loved me. I knew she'd done what she could to take care of me and provide me with a good life, one far away from the pain I'd suffered at the hands of the one person who was supposed to protect me.

There were good mothers and bad mothers in this world, and maybe, like Alex had said, they all damage their children somehow. But the good mothers care. My mother—the only mother who counted—had always, always cared.

While things were still strained at times, I did understand the sacrifices that my mother had gone through for me. And I appreciated them more.

In the past year, I'd found a psychologist who'd been able to put me on a treatment schedule of medication and therapy that actually worked for me. I hadn't had a truly bad day or the brain fog that had once plagued me in months.

Skylar and I were growing closer, too. I'd returned to work part-time, and on the days when I was home, I'd filled our schedule with Mommy and Me dance classes, art classes, and other adventures. My therapist had helped me to realize that most of my anxiety regarding Skylar had to do with not feeling adequate in creating plans for us. I never knew how to play with her, so she suggested we participate in classes instead.

"Take the work off of your shoulders. Let someone else schedule and plan; you just enjoy."

And it worked. Simple as that.

And because Skylar and I were no longer stressed over each other, my marriage had improved drastically. Cam and I had gone to hell and back together, and we'd come through the other side better than ever.

Though I'd never admit it to anyone else, there was a part of me that was grateful for what had happened. Alex had been right, in a way. Losing Skylar had forced me to deal with what wasn't working in my life. Cam too, I think.

It had made me take a long, hard look at what had gone wrong and deal with it head on. I was still dealing with it all, Cam's betrayal, the truth about my past being revealed, and the fact that we'd almost lost our child, but we were getting through it. I knew we would because I'd seen the strength of our love.

We'd told the police the same story I'd told Cam. That Alex had texted me, and when I'd arrived, she was gone. No one really understood why she'd taken Skylar, but all that mattered was that she was home.

On the way home from the river that day, I'd explained to

Skylar that she shouldn't talk about that day because it would make everyone sad. And that if she talked too much about it, Mommy might end up in trouble. Besides, she didn't really understand what had happened to Alex, and the more I talked to her about it, the more I was able to shape the memory of that night for her.

I knew it was wrong. It felt disgusting. On top of that, I wasn't sure it would even work. Honestly, I expected it not to, but I knew that if she told them I'd seen Alex that night, that I'd been there, the rest of the story would quickly unravel. It was better this way.

I lived with the guilt of knowing I was a murderer every single day. It had been an accident, sure, but it didn't change the fact that it had happened. I'd killed someone and not just *any*one. I'd killed my own sister, and I had to live with that for the rest of my life.

I hated that no one had gotten Alex the help she needed when she was young, but I had to protect my daughter. Alex's name had become a bit of a swear word in our house, with us rarely speaking of her at all, though when we did, we'd whisper it or call her *you-know-who*.

The first time she came up was when Cameron asked me if I noticed her house had gone up for sale.

I told him I was sure she was leaving town.

He'd asked a few other times if she'd reached out to me, but the answer had been a simple no, and we'd left it at that.

Six months after she disappeared, the police found her cell phone near the falls. This had resulted in a thorough search of the river, and though they'd never found her body, they found her purse and a shoe. Enough to confirm that she'd gone over, enough that they could officially declare her dead.

She must've been wracked with guilt, they decided. It was a theory I was fine with. Though the Alex I saw in those last moments didn't seem to have an ounce of guilt in her, I liked to think her memory would live on as remorseful, despite being evil.

A kidnapper with a conscience.

All that really mattered to me was that I didn't have to worry about her ever again. My family was safe.

As the months passed, she'd been brought up less and less, and I found myself rarely thinking of her at all. It wasn't easy. I had to work at it, but it was necessary for my survival.

Once dinner was prepared, Mom and I carried the food out to the long table on the covered porch, where our friends and family were gathered round. Old friends and co-workers, and new friends from our various Mommy and Me classes made their way to their seats, everyone marveling at how good the food looked. Skylar talked animatedly to her new friends and, when she spilled her drink, I refilled it without complaint.

After finding out the trauma of our childhood and growing up in near squalor had caused both Alex and me to develop an obsession with keeping our houses tidy, I no longer cared a thing about keeping a spotless house. I'd been actively working against anything that stemmed from my past, and it could start with something as simple as that. Keeping the house perfect had taken too much of my focus last year, which was why the vast majority of this party would be held outside.

"Alright, big girl, cake or presents first?"

"Presents!" she cried, giggling wickedly as her father handed her the first gift. Everyone *ooh*-ed and *aah*-ed at the gifts as she opened them, everything from new books and clothes to new dolls and an art set.

When the presents were done, we sang "Happy Birthday" to her before she blew out the candles—four bright, shining reminders that we'd been lucky to get another year with her. Reminders of what we'd almost lost.

As we cut the cake, Margie asked, "So, when are you all planning to have another? It's time to make Miss Skylar a big sister, don't you think?"

I forced a smile through the grimace. "I don't know about that. One is plenty for me."

To that, everyone laughed.

"I don't know, another wouldn't be too bad," Cameron joked, nuzzling his head onto my shoulder.

I rolled my eyes. "You can carry this one, then. This momma is done. Miss Skylar"—I wrinkled my nose playfully at her as she shoveled another spoonful of cake into her mouth, grinning at me with purple-and-blue-stained teeth—"is a handful. I don't think either of us could handle another. Could we, girl? You're enough, aren't you?" I teased her.

"Hmm... I want a sister," she said thoughtfully, and the table roared with laughter.

I was outnumbered, but it was all in fun. Cam squeezed my hand, kissing my shoulder. "Someone at this table might have some news though..." He turned his head toward Margie, whose eyes widened.

She looked at David, her smile bright as her hands cradled her flat stomach. "I wasn't going to say anything today. It's Skylar's big day!" She scowled playfully.

"Wait, what?" I asked excitedly.

Their smiles grew as the anticipation did, and finally, Margie nodded. "Do y'all have any plans for February twenty-first?"

"What?" I cried out again. "You're pregnant? Really?"

She grinned and nodded as Rita stood from the table, bumping it and scooting everyone's plates as she ran to her daughter, hugging her as they squealed together. She placed her face next to her daughter's stomach, speaking sweet nothings to it, then groaned, swatting at Cam with a napkin. "I can't believe you knew before I did."

"She likes me better than you. I've told you this."

Margie laughed, joined quickly by Rita and Cameron, and eventually the whole table.

The party was filled with love and laughter and warmth. Nothing had changed from the previous year really, and yet, everything had changed. It seemed we were all so incredibly grateful for everything we had.

———

After dinner had been cleaned up, the kids scattered to go and play in the yard, and I grabbed a bottle of wine, gathering around the table with the women.

"I guess you can't have this anymore," I told Margie, who puckered her bottom lip.

"Unfortunately, no."

"I'm so happy for you," I said seriously.

"I can't believe I'm going to have another grandbaby," her mom said.

"Kids are such a blessing," Zola, the leader of our Mommy and Me art class, said. "If you're ever in the area, you'll have to join us for a class."

"How many kids do you have, Zola?" Margie asked, leaning into the table with genuine interest.

"Four," she said, her smile wide. "All girls."

"My god, you're a saint," Jasmine quipped.

We all laughed, but eventually, the table grew quiet. I felt I needed to say something, to address what I knew most of us had spent the day trying to avoid thinking about.

"I hate to bring down the mood, but I just want to say thank you all for sticking by us this past year. I know it hasn't been forgotten what today is the anniversary of. Almost losing Skylar was the hardest thing Cam and I have ever gone through—will ever go through—and I just want you to know how much we appreciate and love all of you."

Mom had tears in her eyes as she reached across the table and squeezed my hand. "I love you, babe."

"Me too, sis," Margie said, adding her hand to the stack.

"You've really come a long way," Zola said. "I know I didn't know you back then, but I've seen your relationship with Skylar flourish so much just in the time I have known you."

"Well, you're partly to thank for that," I told her. "We love your class."

Suddenly, Jen, another mother from class who was seated at the head of the table, gasped.

"What's wrong?"

She stood, shaking her head and holding her phone out. "Sorry, I just, um... Sorry. Zola, do you recognize this girl?"

Zola took the phone in her hand and stared at the picture on the screen. I felt my heart begin to race as it so often did whenever there was any sort of breaking news. If they ever found Alex's body, I worried about my future. It was still a miracle to me that they hadn't.

"She looks familiar, yeah."

"She's the one who came to our class a few times with her foster mom. Nicole or something..." She tapped the screen, reading.

"What's going on?" my mother asked.

"She's missing," Jen said. "Raven, that's her name. Raven Tate." My heart skipped a beat. My throat suddenly became dry. It couldn't be the same Raven, could it? "Apparently her neighbor reported that he hadn't seen the little girl around in a while. Charles Jensen. They don't know how long she's been missing. Her mother's been arrested."

Zola clutched her chest, looking as if she were going to be sick. "That's awful."

Jasmine took the phone as it was passed around, reading through the article. "Sounds like this mother was a real piece of work. Drugs, in and out of jail, DUIs... That poor baby... I'd say she's been dead for months."

"Don't say that," Jen scolded, taking the phone back.

Just then, a sickly feeling washed over me and I looked around. "Where are the kids?"

I hadn't heard their laughter in a while. Everyone stood up practically at once, the harsh reality of our world setting in on us.

"Skylar?"

"James, Erica?"

"Tierra? Taya? Tristan? Trina?"

"Nolan?"

"*Skylar?*"

We scrambled from our seats and down the porch steps, our cries getting louder. *No. God, no. Please, no.* I couldn't lose her again. I rushed around the side of the house where Cameron and the husbands and boyfriends were.

"What's wrong?" he asked, seeing the worry on my face.

"Have you seen Skylar? The kids?" I whipped around, searching in every direction.

He shot up from his chair, dropping the beer he'd been holding. It crashed to the ground, yellow foam spewing onto the grass. "Skylar?" he bellowed, his voice carrying.

Suddenly, panic set in and parents scattered in every direction, everyone shouting their children's names. My vision began to tunnel as a sickly sense of déjà vu overwhelmed me. *Not again. Please not again.*

"Skylar?" I cried again. I was going to be sick.

"Momma?" I heard her voice and spun around on my heel. The children were standing near the edge of the woods, their heads poking out between the trees.

I puffed out a breath. "God, get over here," I said with another quick, heavy breath. She darted toward me as everyone noticed and began to gather up their children.

"You're not supposed to play in the woods, Skylar. You know the rules," Cameron told her, but there was no anger in his voice, only relief.

"I'm sorry," she said, hugging us back.

"What do you have there?" I kissed her head, spying the white envelope in her hand. "What is that?"

"It's my birthday present."

"Your birthday present from who?"

She stared at me strangely. "Am I allowed to say?"

"What are you talking about?" I tore the envelope from her grasp, just as she whispered her response.

"It's from *you-know-who.*"

I tugged the card from the open envelope and stared down at it, a yellow background with a Boston Terrier wearing glasses on the front. *Happy Birthday*, it read.

I opened it with shaking hands.

No.

No.

No.

I looked up, around the woods, spinning in a circle. Where was she? Why had she come back? How was she alive?

Then, I glanced down at the card, reading the words carefully as Cameron leaned his head over my shoulder to see them too.

"What does that mean?" he asked, his voice low.

I shook my head, unable to tell him. To explain it would mean I'd have to tell him the truth. The whole truth. I clutched my daughter close to me as I read the words a final time.

There was no question what the warning meant. The scratchy, handwritten message said simply:

You took her back the first time.

I gave her back this time.

Don't let there be a third.

Prove to me you deserve her or else. She isn't a handful. No more negative talk in front of her. I warned you.

No more chances. Don't fuck this up.

I'll be watching. We'll be around.

Love,

Aunt Alex and Rae

A LETTER FROM KIERSTEN

Dear Reader,

Thank you so much for choosing to read *Missing Daughter*. If you enjoyed this twisted, emotional story, and want to keep up to date with all my latest releases, just sign up at the following link. Your email will never be shared, and you can unsubscribe at any time.

www.bookouture.com/kiersten-modglin

When the idea for this story came to me, I initially shied away from it. As a mother myself, the idea of writing about a missing child was terrifying. But, the more I thought about it, some of my favorite books I've written have stemmed from something I feared. As I began to consider the idea more seriously, I heard Ginny's voice in my head. She had a story that needed to be told, and I knew I could explore so many things I'd wanted to say for so long with it: things about mental health, women's health, motherhood, societal expectations, marriages, families, mistakes, trusting your gut, and, maybe most of all... finding hope in the darkest places.

There were so many things I wanted to touch on in this story, but as you can always expect from one of my novels, I had to make sure it was placed inside a twisted, unputdownable package.

I hope you loved the story than unfolded in *Missing Daughter,* and if you did, I would be so grateful if you could write a review. Reviews mean the absolute world to me as I love learning what my readers thought about my novels, and each review makes such a difference in helping new readers to discover one of my books for the first time.

If you'd like to get in touch, please don't hesitate to do so. I adore hearing from my readers! You can always find me on Instagram, Facebook, Twitter, Goodreads, TikTok, or my website. You can also send me an email here: contact@kierstenmodglinauthor.com

I can't wait to hear from you!

Thanks again for reading!

XO,

Kiersten

www.kierstenmodglinauthor.com
www.tiktok.com/@kierstenmodglinauthor

 facebook.com/kierstenmodglinauthor

 twitter.com/kmodglinauthor

 instagram.com/kierstenmodglinauthor

ACKNOWLEDGMENTS

First and foremost, to my wonderful husband and amazing little girl, I'm so lucky to be able to do life with you. Thank you for being my biggest cheerleaders and for never losing enthusiasm for my career. Thank you for celebrating every success with me, for going on adventures that inspire wild stories with me, and for not complaining (too much) when I'm on a deadline. I absolutely adore you both.

To my incredible Mom, thank you for being my first friend. Thank you for always telling me I could and I would. Thank you for reading my first stories and sharing them with your friends long before they were good. Thank you for believing in me before I believed in myself. You are my inner voice. I love you.

To my closest friend, Emerald O'Brien, thank you for everything you do for me. Thank you for our late-night calls, for always being my sounding board when I have a new idea, for being there for the highs and lows and everything in between. I couldn't do this without you.

To my immensely talented editor, Sonny Marr, thank you for your fantastic insight and advice, for asking the hard questions, and digging deep to understand the story I was trying to tell. This book is a thousand times better thanks to you and I'm so honored to have had the chance to work together on it.

To the wonderful team at Bookouture, thank you for all you do! I'm so grateful for your belief in me and your tireless efforts to help my stories reach new readers. I'm forever humbled to be among your roster of ridiculously talent writers.

To my insanely talented cover designer, Lisa Horton, thank you for putting such a gorgeous bow on this twisted package.

To my loyal readers, my KMod Squad—thank you for believing in me, for cheering me on, for celebrating each new story, for your excitement with each and every release, for the reviews, the recommendations, the emails, the social media shares, the book club invitations, and the absolute love you have for my characters and their stories. Without you, I'd just be a girl with a head full of twists and no one to surprise. Every single one of you are my dream come true.

Last but certainly not least, to you—thank you for reading this story. For a very long time, I dreamed of the day someone would pick up a book with my name on the cover and dig into a world that once existed only in my mind. You've made that dream a reality. Thank you for supporting my art and my dream. I hope that you enjoyed every minute of this twisted journey as much as I enjoyed crafting it for you.

Whether this is your first of my books or just one of many, I hope it was everything you hoped for and nothing like you expected.

Made in the USA
Coppell, TX
19 January 2022

71931545R00194